The Coracle Boy and the Pagan Gold

By
Edwin T. Sayers

The Coracle Boy and the Pagan Gold
First Edition
Published by DreamStar Books, December 2016
ISBN: 978-1-904166-47-4
EAN: 9781904166474

Set in 'Garamond'

Enquiries: etsayers@btinternet.com

Printed and bound in Great Britain by Imprint Digital, Devon, England

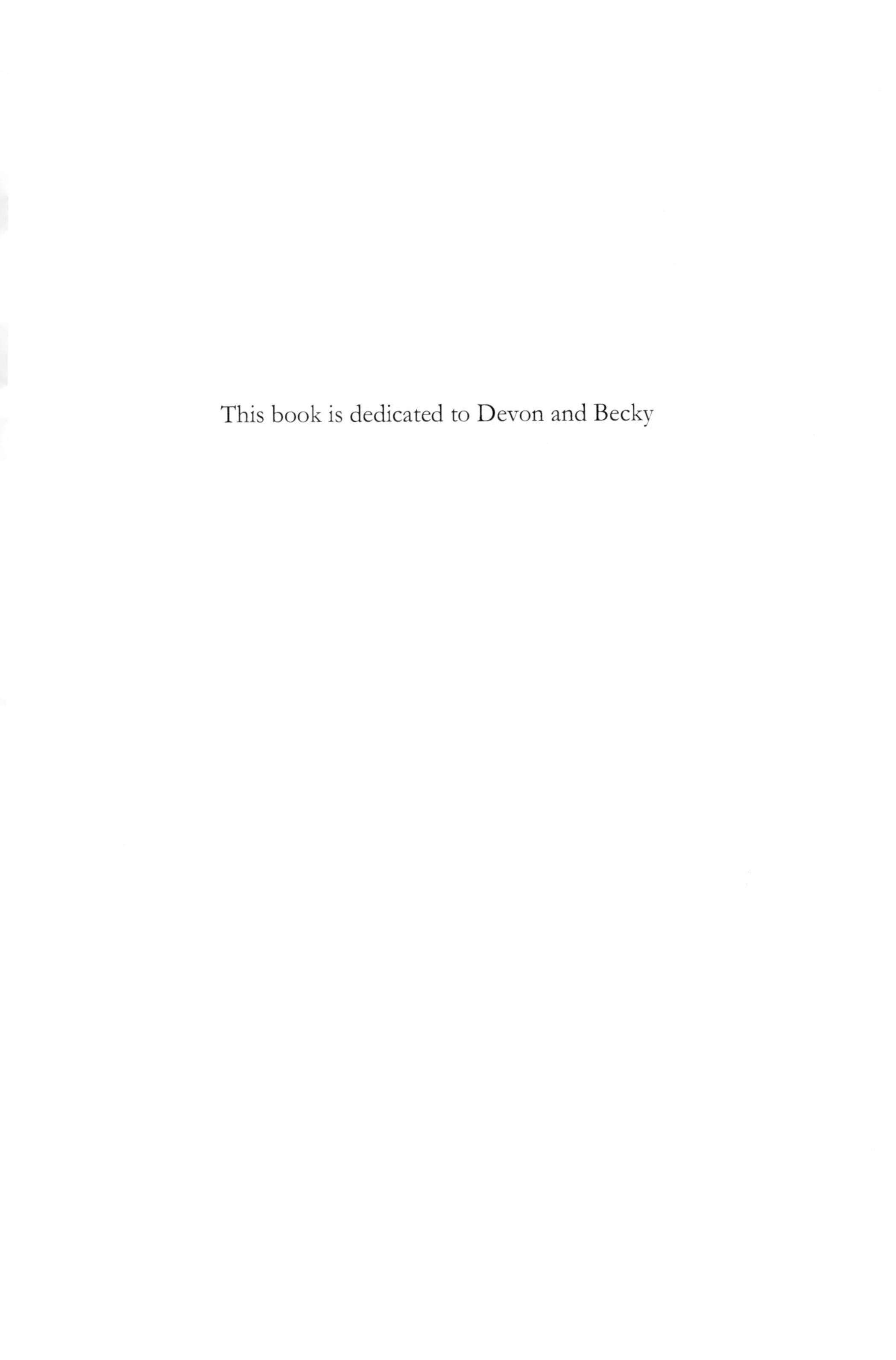

This book is dedicated to Devon and Becky

About the author

Edwin T. Sayers was born in the Corvedale, Shropshire and spent much of his young life in the county. After a lifetime in construction throughout the Midlands, Wales and the North, he settled back in Shropshire and took up writing on retirement.

His first published book, about a young boy, known as 'Harry the Coracle Boy', was published in 2011 by DreamStar Books. This is the second book in the trilogy.

Acknowledgements

With special thanks to my son Martin, for his sensitive interpretation in creating the illustrations and cover
And again, special thanks to Miss Beryl Bedford for her help and encouragement.

Prologue

Two days march to the north of Westown, on a low point in the precipice, there stands an abbey where the monks operate a ferry to the east bank of the Great River. A mornings walk from the river and set on the only high ground to be found in this endless, eastern forest, stands the village of Abe Tull the blacksmith. Abe Tull's village is protected by a high, timber palisade. But there are slave traders about and these are the dark ages.

It is a wild, untamed land where forests and swamps are home to bands of robbers and slavers, known as the Raiders. It lies to the east of the Great River that flows at the foot of a limestone escarpment which is the height of ten men or more and almost vertical for most of its length said to be greater than twenty leagues. To the west the land is good farmland and is ruled by a King who maintains an army to defend the people who have settled on this high plateau.

An attempt by the Raiders to invade the western Kingdom failed, but not before they destroyed the only bridge crossing the Great River. With the Raiders driven back into the wilderness and the prisoners, taken during the conflict, rebuilding the bridge, life is getting back to normal in the few villages on the east bank. But there are still outlaws out there, one has to be wary. These are the Dark Ages.

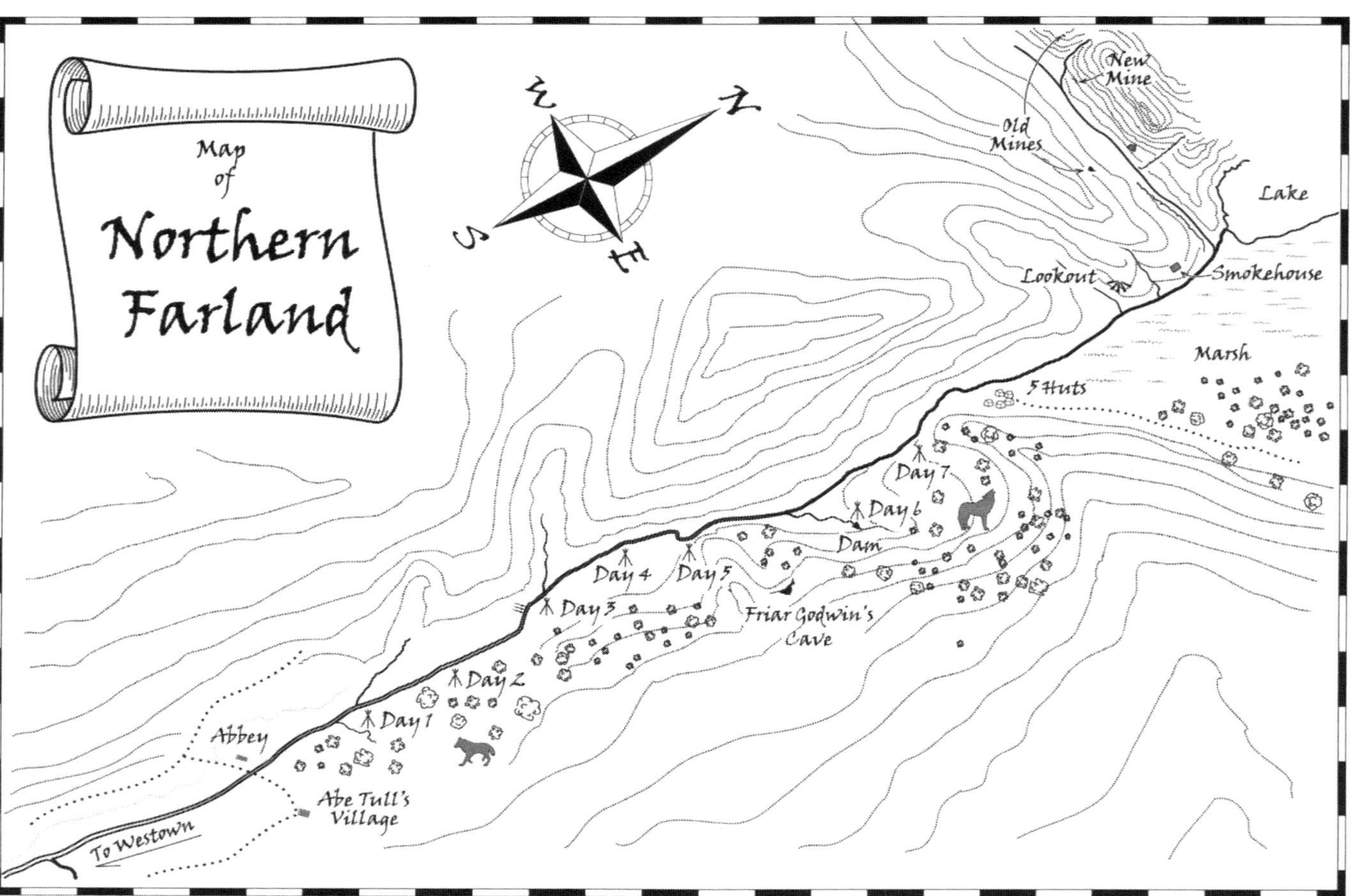
Map of
Northern Farland
N
E
S
W
New Mine
Old Mines
Lake
Lookout
Smokehouse
Marsh
5 Huts
Day 7
Day 6
Dam
Day 5
Day 4
Day 3
Friar Godwin's Cave
Day 2
Day 1
Abbey
Abe Tull's Village
To Westown

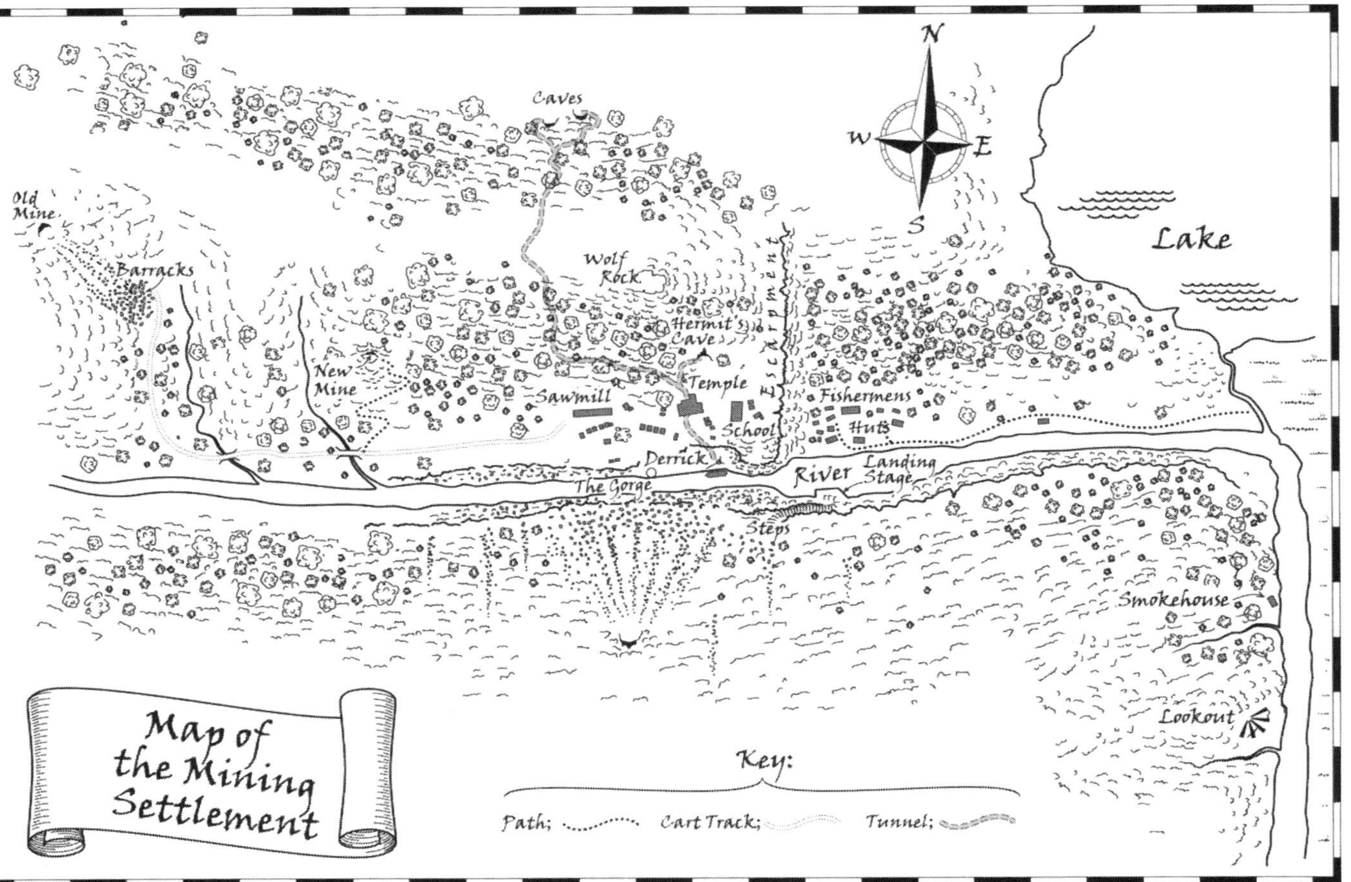
Map of
the Mining
Settlement
Caves
Old
Mine
Barracks
New
Mine
Wolf
Rock
Hermit's
Cave
Temple
Sawmill
School
Escarpment
Fishermens
Huts
Derrick
The Gorge
River
Landing
Stage
Steps
Smokehouse
Lookout
Lake
N
S
E
W
Key:
Path;
Cart Track;
Tunnel;

Chapter One

Harry sat down on the riverbank; he could not believe his eyes. He had been told what to expect, but nothing could have prepared him for this. Abe Tull had described the scene accurately, as had Allen the huntsman. Now as he sat on the damp earth, he experienced a devastating shock. It was almost as if he had been told nothing, but he must not show weakness in front of the others. He hid his hurt by sliding down the bank into the water. In spite of the heat of that mid July afternoon, the knee deep water was still very cold. The boulder strewn river bed made for difficult progress. He reached the far bank and hauled himself up onto the trampled garden. Harry moved towards what had been his home for all of his thirteen years. Now all that remained was a blackened pile of rocks that had been the chimney breast, the focal point of the dwelling. It was all that was left of a cottage that Tom the forester and his fisherman friend, John, had built, where a year later he had brought his wife, Winifred. She made it a home, a very happy home until she died more than two years ago. As Harry remembered all of this, he was consumed with anger and hatred for those who had done this to his family. They had killed his father and destroyed the one thing that he could have used to hold the family together, a home. Now they were beholden to others for food and shelter. Yes he had a little money, but what did he know of commerce and the acquisition of property?

The Coracle Boy moved slowly towards the ruins; nothing remained of the timber frame or the wattle and daub infill. The reed thatch of the roof would have burned with a searing heat. Nothing was recognisable, nothing could be salvaged. Even the stone was shattered and split by the white-hot inferno.

Allen the huntsman held the party back and let Harry wander around the pile of rubble. 'Let the boy have time to come to terms with what he has lost,' he had advised those eager to go to the boy. There were eight in the party. This was considered nccessary because there were still groups of Raiders robbing and killing in the eastern forests, although none of these renegades had been seen this far north now that the army had set up a barracks in Eastown.

Harry wandered up towards the burnt-out remains of his father's workshop, the back of which was hewn into the sandstone now blackened by the fire that had consumed the stock of prepared timber. This would have provided some small income. The boy took up a piece of charred timber and dug into the debris where he guessed his father's bench would have stood and began to clear away the rubbish. Allen appeared at his side.

"What is it Harry? What are you looking for? Everything will be burned, lad."

"My father hid some of his tools in a hole cut into the rock floor and covered them with a stout oak lid. The iron tools should be alright."

Allen found a piece of wood and worked alongside the boy, digging away at the charred wood and half-burned logs. They pulled at the larger off-cuts and found them only partially scorched and lower down unaffected by the heat.

"Look, Allen, not even the wood shavings are burned down here. How can that be with such a fire above?" Harry asked excitedly.

"I don't understand it, but now that I come to think about it, I have seen it before. Two summers ago a grain store caught fire and although some of the grain was spoiled the biggest part was unharmed."

It took a while to clear away enough debris to free the thick slab of oak covering the chamber, but eventually the lid was lifted and the forester's tools were found in near perfect condition. The implements were recovered and carried across the river and loaded on the packhorse. Harry took one last walk past the place of his birth and then crossed the river. He stood and looked at the small white cross that marked his mother's grave and said a silent prayer.

The party moved off. It was a while before the mood lightened; the cause of the change was someone else's discomfort, as is often the case.

One of the younger riders was so busy arguing with the man behind him that he failed to see a low branch in his path and was swept clean off his horse. It was this relaxing interval that shook Harry out of the black mood that threatened to consume him as he trailed along at the rear of the column. He realised that he was not the only one whose home had been burned to the ground by the Raiders. Allen and his brother, Hugh had lost everything too, as had the Miller who had travelled with them on that first journey.

Meg had refused to come on this expedition to their old home. Abe and Allen had told her of the devastation. She said she could not bear to have her heart broken again. It had seemed perverse to Harry, but he could understand her reluctance now. But he was glad he had made the journey, it helped him come to terms with what he had found on his return to Abe Tull's village. It had been difficult for him to understand why Meg, Simon and even little Ruth had become part of this new way of life, village life.... the noisy, boisterous crowding in that the Coracle Boy found so suffocating. But now he was beginning to understand that both his sisters, Meg and Ruth, enjoyed the company. Meg, who was fourteen and a year older than Harry, had made friends with the medicine woman and had asked if she could become her assistant, a request that was granted by Eliza Pegg who was renowned for her skills as a herbalist and midwife. She was a tall, strong woman near to middle age and had long wanted an assistant and Meg was an eager pupil. She quickly learned the names of many of the plants she gathered for Eliza's salves and potions. Harry smiled to himself as he remembered a remedy that Eliza had taught Meg to make to relieve muscular pain. She tried some on Harry's aching shoulder two days ago. She was delighted when Harry sang its praises, perhaps a little over enthusiastically, but he was pleased for Meg.

Harry's brother, Simon, was ten and had a natural gift with horses and worked under the supervision of Grandfather Josh, who was in charge of the ten horses that belonged to Abe Tull. If Harry wanted to find Simon he had to look no further than the stables. The boy would be there, talking softly to the horses while he groomed them. Harry was mounted on one of Abe Tull's horses for this journey because his own sturdy chestnut mare, whom he had named Star because of the white blaze on her forelock, had given birth to a fine healthy son during the night. The Coracle Boy had given the foal to Simon who was overjoyed.

They stopped at a clearing to rest the horses and take some refreshment; Allen sat on a fallen tree beside the boy.

"Harry, we need to talk. There is a rule in the village that requires every man to take part in training for the defence of the village."

"Yes I have heard of this, but I have no wish to be a soldier. I couldn't kill anyone."

"Not even a Raider who might be attacking your family?"

"Well, yes, I suppose, but I don't think I could actually kill a man."

"None of us want to kill anyone Harry, but we must be able to defend our families and our land. Surely you saw that when the Raiders came to attack the village. Abe Tull is a wise and courageous man and it was his leadership that kept us all safe from that attack. It is his wish that every man over the age of twelve trains for three reasons; to keep fit, to learn the value of discipline and to defend our village."

"If that is what Master Tull wants, then I will join your army, Allen."

"Good lad, you'll find it a lot of fun. Now there is another subject that Abe Tull will be asking you about and that is how you intend to earn your living. We have fishermen enough for our needs and your old market in Westown is too far away."

"I have been thinking about that too. I could go to Westown and work with John the fisherman, but I don't want to leave Meg and the young 'uns."

"I'm sure your family would hate that."

"What else could I do Allen? I only know coracle work and fishing."

"Surely you helped your father in the forest or the workshop?"

"Oh yes, I can shape handles for most tools and I can make and use a pole lathe. I made a chair last winter."

"How would you like to help my brother and me to fell that stand of trees over there? Abe Tull wants to extend the stockade during the winter so we need to get the timber felled and hauled back to the village."

"That's great, Allen, I have the two axe heads. I can make handles for them and with father's tools there might be other jobs I can do to pay my way."

"I'm sure there will be Harry, but first of all we have to establish a camp close to the trees and then move our men out here to get the timber felled."

"When will you start cutting down the trees, Allen?"

"That will be decided by Abe Tull, but I expect he will want to start right away. We have no proper forester in the village so my brother Hugh and me said we would give it a go and as we are now so close I think we should consider where our camp should be sited. There is water in that stream and a nice level patch over there and plenty of game in the woods. We should live well here."

The shadows were very long as the party returned to the village, tired and hungry. They had cleared the site for the camp close to where the trees were to be felled. They had cut a rough track through the brush and scrubland so that the trees could be dragged to the road for loading onto carts. And now, having stabled the horses, they walked towards the meeting house to report progress to Abe Tull. Harry the Coracle Boy was met by his youngest sister, Ruth. She was eight years old. She couldn't wait to tell him her exciting news.

"I am going to learn numbers and letters Harry. Sister Mary has come to live in the village, she's kin to Master Tull and she is ever so nice and she said she will teach me to read and write. I have to do my work in the morning but in the afternoon I go to school." Ruth ran out of breath and after gulping in air started on another cascade of words like a stream racing down a mountainside. Harry held his little sister's hand as she walked beside him telling him all about her big adventure into the world of learning.

Meg and Ruth lived with Abe Tull, his wife and his youngest daughter who was sixteen and his young son who was only five years old. Simon lived with Grandfather Josh and his wife where he had a room to himself above the stables, which he was now glad to share with his brother.

Abe Tull was busy and said he would listen to their report in the morning and insisted that they all go to their beds. It had been a long and eventful day, especially for Harry.

Chapter Two

Almost a week earlier Harry had ridden into Abe Tull's village on the chestnut mare given to him by Colonel Breck. News of Harry's exploits had preceded him. Everyone seemed to know something of his adventures. Even strangers wanted to shake his hand and the boy found it all a bit overwhelming. The archers, who had arrived at the village with Sergeant Defoe, had gone back to Westown as had the mercenary soldiers, except for Dan who had stayed behind and was going to marry Susan, one of the village girls. Dan was a tracker and understood the stars. He was also a pagan.

Soon the pagans would hold a ceremony to celebrate the height of summer and they said it was the longest day of the year. For the pagans it was a holy day. There were only a handful of devout pagans in the village and Dan the tracker was one of them and would be travelling to a ceremonial stone circle out on the heathland. They would set out the day before the ceremony. It was important to them that they saw the sun rise and the sunset at their place of worship on the longest day. Dan and Susan would be married at the great altar there.

The Coracle Boy's reception at the village had been a very happy occasion. It was early evening when Harry had arrived and after the initial boisterous welcome, when the whole village had turned out, a feast was put on in the square. Meg had cried and so had Ruth. Simon was much more mature, he was more interested in Star. He saw that the mare was pregnant and with not long to wait for the event. Over the next two days the story of Harry's adventures was told and retold.

Harry gave his fullest report to Abe Tull on that first evening. His sons by an earlier marriage, Ben and Luke, were present and also Allen and Hugh, the two huntsmen. Harry ended his report by placing the money that

Sir John, Lord John of the High Plains had given him, on the table. Harry asked Abe Tull to take it for looking after his family.

"There's enough here to keep your family for a whole year son. I'll keep it safe until such times as you have need of it."

"Thank you sir," the boy said respectfully, "Tomorrow sir, I shall go to our cottage and see if the Raiders found it. I need to..."

"I'm sorry Harry, I can't allow you to do that. It is not safe to travel any distance into the forest alone. Besides son, there is nothing left of your old home, the Raiders burnt it to the ground." The boy reeled back at this, his face ashen, his eyes wide and wild. He turned and rushed from the room.

"Shall I go after him Abe?" offered Allen.

"No, let the lad be. I shouldn't have blurted it out in that fashion. Give him a moment and I will go and try to make amends."

The big blacksmith was obviously angry with himself for his blunder. When he opened the door he saw Harry talking to Dan the pagan. Dan had his hand on the boy's shoulder. Abe closed the door and turned and spoke quietly.

"That boy will have to see what he has inherited and the sooner the better. When will we be sending out a hunting party, Allen?"

"We have plenty in the store, Abe, but we do need to find the timber for the new stockade you want to build. Shall I organise a trip over the next two or three days? I know of a good stand of ash that would probably provide all we need."

"I will leave it to you Allen."

In his blind dash from the presence of his four friends, Harry had collided with Dan, the tall blonde young man who had come to the village as a mercenary soldier. A young man with strange beliefs who could read signs and tracks that were invisible to others, who could read the stars or find his way on the darkest night. Harry had only met Dan briefly several weeks ago but liked him instantly and now he was spilling out his sorrows for the loss of his home and his hatred for the Raiders.

"I agree with you Harry. You need to see your home. I have been there just before you came back. Every dwelling within a day's march of here has been burnt to the ground, but my word is not good enough. You must see what has been done. You must learn to cope with such terrible things and face up to reality. It is part of growing up, of becoming a man. I would take you there but I leave for the stone circle at first light and my marriage ceremony the next day. Speak to Abe again tomorrow, I am sure he will arrange something."

Four days after his return to the village Harry and eight other men went to the place of his birth and there Coracle Boy came to terms with his loss and saw the futility of trying to rebuild the old cottage.

But two days after his visit to his old home, Harry was away at the river. He and Rob the weaver had gone to Otter Brook to collect Harry's coracle from where Gareth had hidden it after his escape from Eastown. It transpired that Rob was a skilled coracle man having used a similar small craft to move between the withy beds, and to guide floating bundles of cut withies downriver to the weaving sheds. Rob and his wife Sadie and their two children were building a hut and weaving platform outside the stockade at Abe Tull's village. He was also planting his own withy beds on the marshy land to the west of the village. Rob was not one to sit around and wait for others. He intended to build up a business making baskets of every kind, fish traps and hurdles for sheep pens. There seemed to be no end to the things he and his wife could make from willow, hazel and reed.

On their return to the village they were met by an anxious Gareth. He was relieved to know that they had found the coracle undamaged. He also had news from the River Master; he was to take young John Turnbull back to his aunt in Westown. There was also hope that the boy's mother and her maid were among a large group of women and children freed from a forest camp. Young John had not been told of this possibility for obvious reasons.

The next day Harry and Hugh and two other village men escorted Gareth and young John Turnbull down to the ferry. After crossing the river, a cart would take them to Westown and a new life and, hopefully, a happy reunion for the young John.

Chapter Three

Work at the timber camp began a week after Harry's visit to his old home. Temporary shelters were formed mainly of animal skins draped over hoops of hazel or willow. There were fourteen men including Harry. Harry's job was to trim the branches off the trees as they were felled and pile up all his offcuts to be used as fuel for cooking fires and to dry their clothes. Unfortunately it began to rain on the first day and rained every day for a whole week. The weather improved in the second week and the horses were brought in to haul the logs to the road. The third week saw the arrival of the wagons to transport the timber back to the village. There were four of them, each drawn by three heavy horses pulling in line.

Abe Tull had marked out the area to the east of the village he wished to extend into. He estimated that he required eight hundred pieces of timber, each twice the height of a man and as thick as a milk pail. Each of the six men felling the trees had two gauges so that they only felled trees that satisfied these requirements. To find sufficient trees to fill the order the camp moved at the end of the second week and again in the middle of the fourth week. They had assembled the full quantity of timber needed to complete the enlargement of the stockade by the end of the fifth week. By the end of the sixth week all the timber was at the village, stacked ready for the work on the stockade to begin, but that would not start until all the crops had been harvested.

With all the men back in the village, everyone, men, women and children from the age of ten, were all expected to assist in the gathering of crops. The grain was cut and dried and, when ready, was taken to the meeting hall that now became the threshing floor. Some of the grain was ground into flour in a stone hand mill called a quern, the rest was stored for use later. Abe Tull had plans for a water mill, but that would have to wait for a while.

Other crops such as onion, shallots and leeks were tied into bundles and hung up to dry. Peas and beans were picked and shelled and then dried. Root crops such as parsnips, carrots, beetroot and turnips were stored in a shallow pit and covered with straw and then earth. Some root crops were left in the ground and covered with straw or bracken to be dug up when required.

Apples and pears were picked and stored in frost-free rooms or some were peeled and sliced and sun dried. Wild berries were picked and dried or made into cordial or even wine. Honey was gathered from the hives and stored in earthenware pots or used to make mead, a type of wine. Beer was brewed, plus cider and perry as well as a variety of wines and all were added to the winter store. Animals were slaughtered and the meat cured for use later in the year. And then of course there was the fuel for the fires. Most of the wood was stored outside the stockade and brought in as required. Peat, cut and dried through the summer, was brought down from the moors.

The animals were not forgotten; several small hay ricks were made out in the fields and set well apart in case of fire. The straw from the threshing floor was stored for bedding for the horses, cattle and pigs. There were no sheep kept in the village. They attracted the attention of wolves. Wool and mutton were bought, or bartered for with farmers on the other side of the great river. There were six goats kept by an old widow who lived in a hut outside the stockade, but they were hardy animals and almost looked after themselves and six were easy to tend.

During all this activity Eliza Pegg and her assistant, Meg, broke off from time to time to attend to various injuries and also the delivery of babies. Meg had assisted Eliza at three births while the men were away at the timber camp.

However, even with all this work, there was still time for some fun. There was folk dancing and occasionally minstrels or a troubadour would entertain the villagers.

There was also the regular training for the defence of the village. Archery and swordsmanship were the principal skills. There was wrestling and obstacle races and exercises to tone the muscles. Tests of strength and endurance were undertaken. This would determine the most suitable role for each person on the battlefield. Fire was feared almost as much as attack from an enemy; every villager had to know what to do. They all had tasks allotted to them.

Harry enjoyed the training. He became an accurate archer with the hunting bow. The long bow would come later if he wished. His swordsmanship needed more aggression he was told. The Coracle Boy enjoyed the wrestling and the endurance sports, especially the long distance running and there was no one to equal him in the water. But what he liked most was the time he spent with Dan the pagan. Harry learned about the stars and how to track and read the signs left by humans and animals and how to live off the land. He made shelters and slept out in the forest, even through a thunderstorm. He could make a fire using a fire stick. He learned to cook what he hunted or gathered, but most important he learned to move about the forest or moorland quickly and quietly. Dan said that he was the best pupil he had ever had, the Coracle Boy was a natural tracker

Gradually autumn gave way to winter. The snow came very early in the middle of October. It was fortunate for those who lived in Abe Tull's village. His wisdom and forethought made sure that there was plenty in the stores.

Harry had set up a small workshop next to Rob the weaver's hut and began to make handles for all sorts of tools that Abe Tull fabricated at his forge. He had also set up a pole lathe and was turning pegs for securing the horizontal beams to the vertical timbers of the extension to the stockade. Working together, Harry and Rob manufactured two large sledges for use over the snow covered land, designed to be drawn by horses. Of course they had to make several smaller ones for the children. The Coracle Boy was glad to be kept busy but he still missed the river. Setting and emptying fish traps at this time of year was not an enviable job. However it was what he would rather do. Harry also built another coracle, a larger one with two seats. He had not forgotten his promise to his friend Peter, who was now apprenticed to the stone masons working at Westown church. He would teach him to swim and use a coracle, but that would be next summer.

The Christians were now talking about their festival, still almost three moons away, the biggest in their calendar. It celebrated the birth of Jesus Christ, the son of their God. They called it Christmas. Sister Mary, a cousin to Abe Tull and a devout Christian, had been a nun in a convent just outside Westown. She had left the cloisters to come out into the community to teach Christianity, but she also gave a basic education to any child who wanted to learn. Meg and Ruth were among Sister Mary's first pupils and each received a small wooden cross. Simon had expressed an interest, Harry said he was too busy right now, 'perhaps later'.

At Christmas time there was to be a great feast in the meeting hall, which had been reclaimed from the threshers. Extra tables and benches had to be made to accommodate the growing population of the village. A moon and ten days before Christmas, Harry and Simon joined a hunting party led by Allen and Hugh. They would be away for three days and they were taking one of the horse drawn sledges. As they left the village it was a bright sunny morning, the snow was about a hand's span deep. They met a troupe of mummers just outside the stockade whose performing dog did a dance for them as they passed. They were hoping to bring home deer and wild boar from the forest, goose, duck and bustard from the heath and carp from the lake.

Their first kill was a large wild boar followed by a smaller wild pig and a roe deer all before noon. After a meal they saw their first red deer, a small herd that scattered before they could get close enough to be sure of bringing one down. They had not added to their bounty by the time it was necessary to stop to make camp. They found a clearing where the snow was little more than a dusting and soon had a fire blazing and a lean-to shelter erected. There were ten in the party and Harry was left in no doubt that he was expected to do a man's share of the work. It was the Coracle Boy's job to clean and cut up the roe deer for their evening meal. He also had to dig a deep hole and bury the entrails of the animal. The huntsmen had dealt with the wild boar where they were killed. Simon, the youngest in the party, was expected to look after the horse and keep the fire supplied with wood. Brushwood was gathered and covered with dead bracken to make a sleeping platform under the simple lean-to. Animal skins would be their blankets.

Allen allotted the sentry duties, which included making sure that the fire was always kept burning; there must be two men alert at all times. There were still many outlaws wandering in the forest. Harry had been selected for the first watch and was to partner Brian, a huge giant of a man whose dog was called Scrap, a long, lanky, walleyed dog, who looked frighteningly fearsome. In fact Scrap was a very friendly dog and was as good as ten men as a sentry, Brian insisted. Harry got along famously with Scrap, something that Brian found surprising. The dog usually ignored everyone except his master.

The snow was almost knee deep when Harry was woken. They ate a hasty breakfast, broke camp and prepared to resume the hunt for meat for the Christmas banquet. They stayed in the forest and caught two more wild boar, younger ones this time, and also two roe deer. Allen and Hugh left the party at midday to go in search of red deer up on the high moors, where they were sure they would be successful. Harry asked if he could go with the brothers but he was told that deer stalking was something he would learn when the conditions were more favourable.

Brian was left in charge, they were to hunt small game such as duck, geese and bustard to be found on or around the many small lakes on the heathland at the edge of the forest. Their orders were to camp in the forest and move towards the largest lake next morning and meet up with Allen and Hugh, where the stream left the lake. The two huntsmen would be spending a cold night in a shelter they had built last year for just such an eventuality. The snow had stopped falling as Allen and Hugh left, but it was bitterly cold. Nonetheless, the afternoon's hunting produced a substantial haul of geese and duck, but they didn't see a single bustard.

After another cold night they rose early. There had been no more snow but the frost persisted. When they left the forest and moved out onto the heath where the sledge proved to be great success, they no longer had to thread their way through the trees. Harry and Simon were glad to be going home to Abe Tull's village, they had heard wolves in the forest last night!

The party met up with Allen about midmorning and had to make a detour to pick up Hugh, who had been left to guard the large red deer stag they had killed. They too had heard the wolves. The lake was frozen over but the ice was not thick enough to bear a man's weight. There would be no carp on the menu this Christmas.

The route back to the village followed the stream and was gently sloping down all the way. They made good progress but it was almost dark when they saw the beacon lit to guide them home. Allen lit a torch to announce their imminent arrival. Against the white background they saw three horsemen leave the village and come at full gallop towards them. Allen looked across at Hugh. Harry saw the look and knew that all was not well.

Chapter Four

Harry watched the three horsemen coming from the village at full gallop. Something was wrong. The anxiety quickly engulfed the whole of the hunting party as they watched the approaching riders apprehensively. The first rider arrived well ahead of the other two; it was Luke, Abe Tull's second son.

Luke dismounted in a flurry of snow to stand in front of Allen. "I have some grave news for you. Those mummers who arrived as you left have made off with six of our children." There was immediate uproar as men asked after their families. Luke shouted above the hubbub and demanded quiet and then he said that only three members of the hunting party were affected. An ominous silence fell on the group as men looked from one to the other, fearful of what they would hear. The other two riders arrived and dismounted.

"Brian, your boy Sami is one of them and Harry and Simon, I'm sorry but they have taken little Ruth as well."

Simon, who was up on the sledge, threw the reins aside and jumped down and ran to Harry screaming, "No, no, no…."

Brian let out an agonised roar.

"Brian, take one of the horses. Harry, you and Simon take the other and follow me."

Harry hadn't uttered a word as he held his brother and then moved to where he took the reins from a man he had not seen before. When they were mounted, Luke led off at a canter. The other riders, Bart and Felix, stayed to help the hunters with their heavily laden sledge. Scrap raced after his master.

Brian broke into a gallop. Luke and the two boys followed suit and were soon riding through the open gates and up to the meeting house. It seemed to the Coracle Boy that the whole village was there. Meg came running across to the door to throw her arms around the two boys. Harry spoke for the first time since hearing the dreadful news.

"What happened? How could this happen? Has anyone gone after them?" The words tumbled out as people crowded round the small family, all offering advice and help, but no one answering Harry's questions.

"Luke." The booming voice of Abe Tull drew immediate silence and continued, "Bring Brian and the youngsters to my house. They need food and rest and some questions answered."

The small party hurried after the big blacksmith and into the kitchen of his house a meal was prepared for them on the table and a fire blazed on the hearth.

"Sit down and get some warm food in your bellies and I will tell of the dreadful events that have come to plague our village."

No one touched the food as they waited for Abe Tull to tell them what had happened to their loved ones and what was being done to find them.

"You saw the mummers arrive as you left. They said that they had been directed here by the monks at the abbey. They would perform a play about the birth of Jesus the next day in the meeting room. They appeared to be a friendly lot so I gave them a hut outside the stockade. That first day they entertained the children with the antics of their dogs and clowns and tumblers. But somehow they persuaded some of the children to slip away after they were put to bed. They were promised a special treat. We know this because one of the children went to sleep and so was left behind."

"Never mind all this, Abe. What's happening? What are you doing to get them back? Have you sent out a search party? Have you…."

"Steady Brian, yes. I sent Ben and eight men after them as soon as we discovered the children had been taken. One of the fishermen has gone to the abbey to enlist their help. There are six children missing. Two girls, Ruth and Jennie, they are eight and eleven and four boys, all aged ten."

"Is Dan the tracker with Ben?" Brian asked.

"No, Dan has the fever. Eliza Pegg is with him now…."

"Dan should be out there, he's the only man who can track in this weather. Can't you put him on…." Abe Tull cut in angrily.

"Dan is close to death's door Brian. Why do you think Eliza is with him? If the fever doesn't break soon she fears he will die."

"Well, we can't just sit here. Where's my wife?"

"All five mothers and one of the fathers. That's Jed, he can't ride with a broken leg. They are at Sister Mary's house but Mal, Bram and Bernard, the other fathers, are in the search party."

"I'll just speak to my wife and then I'll go and get my horse and catch up with the search party." Brian rose to go but Abe Tull caught his arm.

"No, Brian. They have a day and a half start on you and there is more snow on the way according to Old Josh. Go to your wife, Brian, she needs your support and get some rest, we will need you in the morning." Abe couldn't think what for but it might slow the angry man down.

Harry, Meg and Simon had sat silent throughout the exchange between Abe Tull and Brian. Harry broke the silence.

"Do we know which way they have gone sir?"

"They will have gone downstream, the fisherman has just reported back. One of the ferry boats was stolen from the abbey. He was also told that the monks know nothing of a group of travelling mummers. Brother Michael has sent young Ned on their best horse to Westown. If the lad can get through the snow in time, they may be able to intercept the villains at the new bridge works."

"Is there nothing we can do sir?" Meg asked.

"You can pray. Brother Michael says that the Abbot is holding a special mass for the children, whatever that is. Sister Mary can explain it."

"We will say the prayers that our mother taught us," Meg said firmly.

Abe Tull's eldest daughter, Jessie, came in and expressed concern that nobody had touched their food. Abe Tull said he had to check the guards and left Jessie to see that Harry, Meg and Simon ate some of the food.

It was agreed that the three young people would stay together in the kitchen. Jessie gave them blankets and they huddled together, fully dressed, on a pile of animal skins. They talked about their parents and what they ought to do. Harry said he must go after Ruth, he couldn't just sit around waiting. Meg said that she would go with him and so did Simon. The

Coracle Boy resisted such a plan saying that he would travel quicker on his own. They argued for a while and then agreed to wait until morning. There might be good news. The exhausted trio were soon sound asleep. Outside the wind howled and a blizzard raged.

Harry was awakened by a commotion outside. Dogs were barking and men's voices could be heard. He left the makeshift bed and went to the door and pulled the heavy bar from its housing and looked out. He saw torches bobbing about in the blackest of nights. Men were just animated smudges moving through the blinding snow. Had the search party returned?

"Close that door Harry and help me get a good fire going," Jessie said quietly as she entered the kitchen.

"Is that the search party returning Jessie? Have they found Ruth and the other children?" the boy demanded in a hoarse whisper.

"No Harry, they……"

"Then why have they come back?" Harry demanded angrily as he carried a basket of wood chips across to Jessie.

"Don't make so much noise Harry, you'll wake Meg and Simon."

The warning came too late. Meg was sitting up, the light from the blazing wood chips illuminating the room now. Harry moved to her side and told her that the riders had returned without the children. Meg scrambled to her feet and announced that she would go and ask the searchers what they had found, but Abe Tull entered at that moment and said that he wanted to talk to them. Simon woke up and asked what was happening. Jessie lit more candles.

Abe told them to sit on their temporary bed and pull the blanket around them. He pulled up a chair so that he sat in front of the young people. "I'm sorry; I have no good news for you," Abe Tull said bluntly.

"We believe that the mummers stole the ferry boat and took it downstream." He paused. "Ben thinks they may have transferred to a barge somewhere near the heronry. They found the wreckage of the ferry among the rocks in the shallows below Eagle Rock."

"Oh no! They could be drowned." Meg almost screamed the words.

"No Meg, Ben is sure that they transferred to another boat." But it was little comfort to the girl as she sobbed bitterly on Harry's shoulder.

Simon too was crying and hid his face beneath the blanket. Harry just stared into the fire, his face grim. He looked so much older than his thirteen years.

"Harry, Harry, are you alright son?" Abe Tull asked, concerned.

The Coracle Boy slowly turned his gaze to meet Abe's sympathetic countenance and asked quietly,

"How would they get a barge that far upriver at this time of year, sir?"

The question surprised the big blacksmith. He thought for a few moments and suggested that perhaps the mummers had brought the barge up when the conditions were more favourable.

The boy shook his head but he knew that he must not argue with Abe Tull and so he kept his thoughts to himself.

"I think that you should try and sleep now Harry. I must go and see how the men are, two of them are in a bad way. Exhaustion, I fear."

Abe Tull's wife came in and said that they would not need the kitchen fire until morning and that they should leave the young people to get some rest. Jessie extinguished the candles and wished them 'goodnight'.

Meg and Simon eventually cried themselves to sleep, but Harry lay awake for a long time. Something was not right.

Chapter Five

Harry woke to the sound of a busy kitchen where breakfast was being prepared. Meg and Simon were already up and Meg was helping with the preparations. Simon had gone to look after his beloved horses.

The Coracle Boy suddenly remembered the dreadful news that Ruth had been abducted by the mummers. He wanted to scream out his anger and frustration but he must not show weakness. After all, he was head of his household now. He looked about him and saw that, although the shutter at the window was open, there was very little light getting through the opaque animal membrane that kept out some of the cold draughts. He realised that there was a snow drift burying that side of the house. After completing his ablutions he discovered that the blizzard had blown itself out and there was a clear blue sky and bright sunlight outside. The small village square was almost clear of snow; it had been blown up against the huts and houses almost burying some of the buildings.

Every man in the village was expected to help clear the snow so that all the animals could be properly looked after, fuel could be collected and water drawn from the well. But Harry found it difficult to concentrate on anything. All he could think of was Ruth, out there in the cold or worse. 'No!' he would not contemplate not seeing her again. She was alive. He was sure of it and he would find her.

By evening Abe Tull was satisfied that all had been done that could be done to preserve their way of life. Eliza Pegg reported that Dan's fever had broken and that she was sure he was over the worst. She was also able to tell the village that there was another new arrival, a bouncing baby boy. Meg had assisted Eliza throughout the confinement, it had helped to keep her mind off Ruth's abduction, but it all came flooding back when she saw Harry and Simon in Abe Tull's kitchen. Harry was able to tell Meg and

Simon that he, Ben and Brian were going across to the abbey in the morning to find out if there was any news from Westown.

It was fine but bitterly cold when they set out for the abbey. Amos, one of the hunting party, accompanied them to take care of the horses while the boy and the two men crossed to the abbey. Harry was riding Star. He was used to the saddle now and he or Simon rode the horse most days. The snow had blown into drifts, but the majority of the track was clear and they were able to make good time. The ferry was signalled and the rowing boat was seen coming across, crewed by two oarsmen. As they drew near and pulled alongside the rock where Ben and Brian had broken the ice, the Coracle Boy saw that it was Brother Michael and Ned. Ned was not grinning broadly this morning. Brother Michael stepped ashore and addressed the small party.

"Good morning to you all. Master Ben and young Harry I know. Now, how many of you wish to cross?"

"Brother Michael, we would like to go to the abbey and enquire after the children who were abducted by those scoundrels."

"Then I can save you a journey, my young companion here is called Ned. He came back from Westown last evening. No barge has been above the new bridge works since work started in the summer and no other craft has passed downstream. They have soldiers at St Mary's Rock, keeping watch for possible saboteurs or large floating objects that could do damage to the scaffolding at the bridge. They have seen nothing. We are sure that the miscreants did not go south. They could have gone into the swamp. It's much safer in this cold weather and the sickness has been eradicated."

"Could they have gone north following the river?" Brian asked anxiously.

"To what end? There is nothing but mountain and impenetrable forest up there. I know, my friend, I travelled for five days looking for signs of habitation and found none. They couldn't use a boat, the current is far too strong where the river narrows, and there are rapids. There is not a living soul in those mountains, your mummers must have gone east."

"Then who stole your ferryboat Brother Michael and why?"

"Perhaps we accused them wrongly master Ben. We are inclined towards the opinion that it was some passing vagabonds who took our ferry.

Unfortunately they came to grief in the shallows below Eagle Rock. As you know Ben, I was able to identify it as our craft. My mark is on the piece of the stern you and your search party brought back."

"Was anything else taken? Were there tools in the boat? Did they steal food or break into any of your storehouses?" Ben asked.

"Nothing else was taken and there was nothing in the boat."

Ben was silent for a thoughtful moment and then he asked how many men would be required to row the ferry across the river.

"That depends on the cargo, but two men at least especially at night. We do not use the ferry after sunset except in extreme emergencies."

"It couldn't be done by one man then?"

"It could be done but he would have ended up way downstream.

"Can we see the piece of the boat Brother Michael, sir?" Harry asked.

"It's over there under those trees. Show him, Ned."

The young novice bounded across the snow, his grin slowly returning, and made for a mound of snow that turned out to be part of the stern board of the flat bottomed ferry.

"There's Brother Michael's mark, Harry." Ned indicated the shape of a fish burned into the wood with a branding iron. The Coracle Boy examined the piece of wreckage carefully and asked why there were axe marks on most of the boards.

"Probably because your men had to cut this bit free so that they could drag it back here behind one of the horses," Ned suggested and then added, "I am sorry about your little sister, Harry. I have prayed so hard and asked God to keep her safe and return her to you." The young novice had lost his infectious grin momentarily.

Harry had met Ned briefly last summer and they had struck up a friendship immediately. Ned was older than Harry by about a year. He was stockily built, not much taller than the Coracle Boy. He had a round, freckled face, blue eyes and hair the colour of ripe corn that sat on top of his head like a curly mop.

"Thanks Ned, but Brother Anselm once said that it was no use waiting for God to do everything. You have to try and sort things out for yourself and he will help you. So that's what I am going to do." Ned saw the determination on Harry's face and said that he would like to go with the boy but he was sworn to the abbey until after Easter.

"I must leave as soon as I can Ned, but thanks anyway."

The boys returned to the men who were still questioning the monk, but soon they had exhausted their enquiries. The party took its leave and headed back for the village.

Abe Tull was surprised to see them back so soon and was disappointed with their report. It was midday and the village gathered in the meeting room to discuss the lack of information and to decide on a way forward. It was agreed that a party would go the village in the swamp. Any mention of going up the river was met with derision. Old Josh predicted that another blizzard was imminent; a decision on when the search party would leave would be made in the morning.

It was a full day's travel to the village in the swamp in good weather. In these conditions it would be necessary to load a sledge with provisions for a week. Harry the Coracle Boy was not included in the search party, everyone was surprised when the boy accepted the decision without question. As the meeting broke up Harry sought out a man who had been in the first search party, he was called Lem. The boy asked him about the finding of the ferryboat at the shallows below Eagle Rock.

"I'll tell thee all I seed that day if ye'll help me get my firewood in, for I ain't in too good a fettle since I got back from that awful journey."

"Thank you sir." Harry found it difficult to follow the man's accent and he spoke very quietly. By the time Harry and Lem had carried in the fuel for the fire the boy had discovered much and he was convinced that the kidnappers had not gone south or east, but that they had gone north.

Harry caught up with Meg in the cowshed where she was milking the cows with two other girls. They arranged to meet later at old Josh's house and talk over the abduction of Ruth with Simon.

Meg told Jessie Tull that she was going to spend the evening with her brothers at old Josh's house and hurried through the gathering storm to a tiny wattle and daub cottage adjacent to the stables. The boys were waiting and let the girl in quickly. Old Josh was fast asleep in a chair beside the fire. Up in the boy's room, by the light of a single candle, Harry began.

"I have spoken to one of the men on the search party. He told me that there were signs that someone had been at the heronry and evidence of a large fire. The snow covered any tracks but a lot of branches had been broken off the trees and yet there was plenty of dead wood lying about. They wanted their smoke to be seen. The part of the ferry they brought back had axe marks on some of the boards, Lem said that they weren't made by them. There was also a rope holding that piece of the ferry to a tree. They were meant to find the wreckage and assume that all were lost or that they had been transported downriver. I'm sure that they went north, upriver."

"But Harry, Brother Michael said there was nothing up there."

"I am sure he is mistaken. I intend to take a coracle and portage at the rapids. Brother Michael was hacking his way through thick undergrowth, the coracle will be so much quicker. I hope to travel as far in two days as he did in five."

"There are still wild animals, bears and wolves in the forest."

"I shall have to be very careful then. I'll take my bow, sword and a spear. I shall have my slingshot and I will make a fire every time I land. Dan has taught me how to live off the forest and how to track men and animals."

"Why don't you put your idea to Abe Tull?" Simon asked.

"You heard the reception the idea of going north got at the meeting, Simon."

"So when do you intend to go?" Meg asked.

"As soon as possible. I suppose that I ought to let this blizzard pass but I shall start right away and get prepared. I'll use the bigger coracle, the one I have just finished. I'll let Rob the weaver know what I plan but nobody else."

"Why Rob and nobody else Harry?" Simon asked.

"We get on very well, I can trust him and he will help me. If Abe Tull finds out he will try to stop me."

"There is just one other thing that will help your plan succeed Harry."

"What is that, Meg?"

"I'm coming with you."

"No Meg, it's far too dangerous and besides you're a girl.

"And what difference does being a girl make?" Meg replied angrily. "I can use a coracle almost as well as you, I can swim almost as well as you and I could look after your health and when we find Ruth she will need my care and attention."

"Can I come too?" Simon asked. Harry knew that this question was coming and had prepared for it.

"We need you to stay here Simon. Ruth may come back with the other party and she will need you." Harry knew that his brother had little affinity with water and was always nervous in a coracle. He detected the slightest hint of relief when Simon agreed to stay behind.

"Meg, I really think that you should stay here as well."

"I am going with you Harry, and if you try to go without me I shall follow."

The Coracle Boy could see that further argument was useless. Meg was so determined and oddly, he was warming to the idea.

Chapter Six

The blizzard was not severe but the carpet of snow still had to be cleared. The search party did not leave that day and Harry and Meg busied themselves, collecting anything that would be useful on their journey. Harry visited Dan, the pagan tracker, hoping to gather some last minute tips on survival in the wilderness. But Dan was still very weak, he decided not to mention the forthcoming trip.

Rob the weaver was against Harry and Meg's decision to go after the kidnappers, but he agreed to help all he could and he would not betray them. Harry asked for some coins from the money that Abe Tull held for him and purchased flour and oatmeal, some smoked meat and left the provisions with Rob, and also the weaponry he would need for their defence. Meg too had been busy collecting supplies for her medical bag. After securing a solemn promise from Eliza Pegg, Meg told her of her forthcoming trip to find the children. At first Eliza was horrified but when she saw the determination in Meg she agreed to advise on a suitable medicine pouch for Meg to take on the journey.

The next day the search party, led by Ben, set off for the village in the marshes as soon as it was light. When they had gone, Harry said that he was taking his new, larger coracle down to the river to try it out. He was also taking his smaller coracle for Meg to use. He carried the provisions in the craft, which Star towed on a small sledge. Meg went with him to collect herbs that Eliza didn't really need and would be hard to find under the snow. There was little conversation during the journey, both were preoccupied with what they were about to undertake.

They arrived at the river some distance upstream of the ferry landing place, at a point that was densely wooded right down to the water's edge. Harry emptied the coracles and launched them. He took the paddle and pulled upstream for a short distance. He carried out a series of manoeuvres and was well satisfied with his new boat. Meg was used to using Harry's coracle but she also did a short practice run upstream. Together they carried the coracles into the forest, placed all the provisions in the slender boats and hoisted them up into a large, ivy covered oak tree to keep them clear of wild animals, and hopefully, human interference.

They were much more loquacious on the journey back as both rode Star and discussed the plans for their departure, but as they came in sight of the village they realised that the sky had darkened. The snow started to fall again and as they reached the stockade the wind increased.

"We'll not get away tonight, Meg. We would never find our way to the river in the dark with snow falling like this."

"But Harry, the kidnappers are getting farther away all the time."

"No Meg, the weather will hold them up too. Now you take those herbs to Eliza and I'll go and find Simon. He needs to be kept in the picture for as long as possible." The Coracle Boy found his brother with his horses, he explained why they would have to wait another day.

The storm raged all night and most of the next day. There were snow drifts up to the top of the stockade on the north wall. The pens that held the geese were completely buried and had to be dug out. The pigs too had to be rescued and fed. Every man, woman and child seemed to have been given a task to work on. By sunset everyone was exhausted.

At old Josh's cottage Harry met up with Meg and Simon and they all agreed there was little point in attempting their journey until they rested and the weather had cleared. Old Josh snored contentedly. Suddenly Meg burst into tears, sobbing that yet another day was lost.

"Sister Mary says that the children have been lost for seven days now," Simon said holding up seven fingers. That didn't help.

"We must go tomorrow night Meg," Harry said firmly.

"Go where, young Harry?" The deep voice of Abe Tull was unmistakeable. Harry swung round. Meg and Simon too looked up, alarmed.

"Well Harry, are you going to run out on us without a word? Come along Harry, tell me about your plan to go up the great river in search of your sister."

"Who told you, sir?" Harry asked, desperately trying to hide his anger.

"Why you did Harry, when you asked for some of your money. I got to thinking, 'What's the lad up to now?' So I kept an eye on you. I asked the fishermen to find your new coracle, but they couldn't track it down so you must have hidden it well."

Abe stepped out of the shadows. Harry couldn't decide if the big blacksmith was angry or not. His face was unreadable in the dim light and behind that black beard.

"Sir," Harry said hesitantly. "Sir, I have to do this. I have…."

"I am going with Harry, sir. We are going to find Ruth. I know Harry can do it but he will need me to help him and he has agreed."

"Steady on you two, have you thought this through? How can you possibly survive in weather like this? And taking a girl on a trip like that is…."

Meg was on her feet glaring angrily at Abe Tull. She told him that she was as good as any boy of her age in the village. She could handle a coracle, she could swim and she had survived the long walk to the village better than any other woman. She was going to look for Ruth. She had to, nothing would stop her and she would go alone if she had to. There were no tears, only grim determination.

"Why didn't either of you talk this over with me?" the big man asked.

"We knew that you would stop us sir."

"Oh, so Harry the Coracle Boy can read my mind, can he?"

The boy was stung by the jibe but he remained silent. Abe Tull leaned on the table around which the small, broken family sat. He spoke quietly.

"We will talk about this in the morning and hear your plans for the trip. I will try to dissuade you from this undertaking, but you will be allowed to put your case. Now come along Meg, we have had a very busy day and need our rest. We will talk in the morning."

Harry was angry as he climbed the ladder up to the room above the stable. He had so wanted to slip away without all this argument. Now there would be endless discussion and more time would be wasted and the abductors of Ruth and the other children were getting further away. The boy could see his mistake and was very angry with himself. He should not have asked for his money.

The boys were up early. Harry went to help Simon feed and water the horses. Tilda, old Josh's married daughter, who lived a few doors away and looked after the old man and the boys, called them in for their breakfast.

"Master Tull wants you and Simon up at his house as soon as you have had your meal," Tilda informed them. Harry was dreading the meeting. Abe Tull had said that he would try to persuade him to abandon the trip and he was dead set against Meg going with him. The boys didn't hurry over their breakfast and wrapped up well against the cold. It was just getting light when they left for the blacksmith's house. They found Abe Tull and his second son, Luke, Allen the huntsman and Rob the weaver sitting at the large kitchen table.

Harry immediately felt betrayed and even more so when he saw Eliza Pegg standing by the fire with Lyn, Abe's wife and Jessie, his daughter. Meg came from the storeroom and stood by her brothers.

"Sit down all of you. Harry, take the seat at the other end of the table opposite me with Meg and Simon beside you. Before you jump to any wrong conclusion, Harry and Meg, I have ordered both Rob and Eliza to be here. They have not admitted to helping you with this hare-brained scheme, but it was obvious to me that you would have to confide in somebody. I think that you should release them from any undertaking they gave and then tell us all of your plan." Abe Tull had spoken quietly but firmly. Meg replied first.

"I'm sorry Eliza, I didn't mean to get you into any trouble."

"I am sorry too Rob," Harry said, and addressing Abe Tull he continued," Rob and Eliza tried to talk us out of our plan. Please don't punish them sir."

"There is no talk of punishment for loyalty to your friends. We are fortunate to have such people as Rob and Eliza in our community. Now tell us about this grand scheme of yours Harry."

He didn't know why but Harry stood up and addressed the small group. He told them that they planned to use coracles up to the rapids and then portage up to the calmer water and continue this procedure until they caught up with the kidnappers.

"And then what will you do?" Abe asked.

"Rescue the young 'uns if we can sir. If not we will follow until they reach the end of their journey. If we still can't rescue the young 'uns we'll come back and lead the soldiers to their village sir."

"You make it sound so simple lad, what about the weather?"

"The weather is just as bad for the kidnappers sir and we will wrap up warmly. We have got two of most things sir."

"But they have eight days' start on you. How can you possibly catch up with them? And you can't be sure that they have gone upriver."

"They made a great show of stealing the ferry and left some of the wreckage tied to a tree for us to find sir. But the axe marks on the planks tell me that the ferry was deliberately sunk so that we would think that the young 'uns were all drowned sir." The Coracle Boy looked at the faces of his friends. They all looked serious, but nobody spoke so Harry continued, "As for their getting far in front of us sir, they have six youngsters who will slow them down and I think they will make a camp and sit out the bad weather sir."

"What is this about axe marks on the ferry wreckage? Why has nobody mentioned this before and why didn't you bring this to my attention, Harry?"

"I thought you already knew sir."

"I know nothing of any axe marks, but continue with your plan Harry."

"There is no plan sir. We will take as much food as we can safely carry in the coracles, weapons, fire making equipment and a blanket each, Meg will have her medicine bag. We plan to use the upturned coracles for shelter."

"You said coracles. How many boats do you intend to use?"

"Two sir, Meg can handle a coracle. We used to have races in the summer on the river that ran past our cottage and she can swim sir."

Abe Tull's face gave nothing away as he considered the boy's words. He sat back in his chair and looked directly at Harry and then Meg, He spoke. His rich, sonorous voice was not angry or censorious, as Harry expected, but it had a relaxing quality. He spoke quietly.

"Harry my son, listen to me." The boy could not remember Abe Tull ever addressing him in this way. He looked up at the big man and saw the friendly smile he knew so well. He too smiled and nodded, afraid to speak.

"Harry, and you too Meg, I want to persuade you both to abandon this perilous journey, at least until Dan is well enough to travel and Ben's search party has returned."

"Sir, the kidnappers are getting farther away every day we wait. Even Dan will not be able to track them sir, if we don't leave very soon."

"Please sir, let us go after our sister." Meg was on the verge of tears, her anguish about to overwhelm her. She turned her head away from the table and hid her face behind her brother's shoulder.

"I think that the three of you should return to old Josh's house," the big blacksmith said. "The rest of us need to talk this through. I will send for you when a decision has been made. Now leave us, please." The order was given with the calm authority that left no room for argument. Harry would have liked more time to plead his case.

As they walked back to old Josh's house, Meg said that there was one small comfort. Jennie was a really nice girl and she was the oldest of the group, she would look after Ruth.

Chapter Seven

The three, Harry, Meg and Simon arms round each other, trudged miserably through the snow to the old man's cottage. Simon went through to the stable and began grooming Star. Harry and Meg watched him as he talked to the horse in almost a whisper and patted her foal. The animals were getting restless because they could not go out into the fields, so it was necessary to keep the mare and her foal fenced off from the other horses.

Old Josh came to stand in the doorway beside Harry. He chuckled and said, "He be a fine lad with the animals. Never seed' a better with hosses, 'minds me of when I was a lad. I was allus' good with hosses."

It seemed an eternity before there came a message from Abe Tull's house requesting their return to the meeting. As Harry, Meg and Simon entered the kitchen, they could read nothing in the faces that greeted them. Abe Tull asked them to sit down. He looked very grave.

"We are all against allowing this trip to go ahead, however we cannot hold you prisoner. If we asked you to give us your word that you will accept our decision and not attempt to go upriver, would you be able to do that?"

Harry glanced at Meg and saw the slightest shake of her head. He turned to the man he had come to respect and wished that he didn't have to say these words, words that he knew would disappoint the man who had opened his home to Harry, Meg, Simon and Ruth.

"Sir, we have to go and find our sister. She will be expecting us to follow and rescue her sir. Please let us go sir."

"Your reply is what we expected Harry. If we are to allow you to go, we have to make sure that you are making this decision on reliable information. I need to see these axe marks on the stern board of the ferry. I need to see if a coracle journey is possible at this time of year. I need to be sure that you are equipped properly for such a journey. To that end, Harry, I propose that you come with me to the river this afternoon and show me this evidence. Show me your new coracle and then we will talk again." The big man stood up, "We eat now and then Harry and Meg will accompany me to the river. Allen and Rob will come with us. Luke, you will be in charge during my absence and you will arrange horses for our journey."

"Yes father, will you be riding Star Harry?"

"No Luke, Meg will ride Star."

"I will lend you my horse Harry. He's a bit frisky but he has a nice nature."

The meal was on the table in minutes and the five travellers all ate well, knowing that they had a cold, hard ride in front of them. Meg went with Lyn, Abe's wife, to get into some warm clothes. When she returned she was dressed like a boy, not an uncommon practice for girls during the winter.

There was a holdup and Meg found the opportunity to whisper to Harry. She asked him why she had to go to the river.

"I think Abe is testing you Meg. He wants to see how you hold up against the cold and the hard ride to the river. That's why I want you to ride Star. She's a tough, sturdy horse and easy to handle."

The delay was explained by Luke when the horses were led up to the blacksmith's shop. One of the horses was found to be lame and had to be changed for a fit animal. Abe Tull was to lead. Harry and Meg were to follow. Allen and Rob would bring up the rear.

The party mounted up and walked the horses down to the track that led to the river. Where the wind had blown the snow into drifts clear of the track, they broke into a trot. Progress was slow and their trek was often impeded by deep drifts. At one point they had to dismount and walk the horses into the trees to get round the deep snow. Harry kept a close watch on Meg but he need not have worried. The girl was keeping up with the Coracle Boy easily. It was almost noon when they arrived at the river, the wreckage of the ferryboat had to be dug out of a snowdrift for Abe Tull to examine the axe marks. Some of the planks were held in the frozen earth, the big blacksmith insisted that they be carefully uncovered. A fire was lit and the ice and frozen mud was cleaned off the wood. The cut timbers were closely examined and placed where they had been torn from the stern board.

While Allen and Rob worked on defrosting and reassembling the timbers, Abe asked to see where Harry and Meg had hidden the coracle. They led him to the ivy covered oak tree. He watched as Harry climbed, almost hidden in the ivy leaves, to one of the spreading limbs. Now he could just make out the shape of the small craft hanging high above him. Harry threw the rope down to Meg and told her to take the strain, there was a sudden jerk on the rope and then Meg slowly lowered the coracle to within a hand's-breadth of the forest floor. She tied the rope off at a nearby sapling as Harry came across from the oak tree. Abe Tull looked on but said nothing. He walked across and saw the smaller coracle lay inside the larger and the bundle that contained the flour and oatmeal, the two hunting bows, short swords and the spear. A coil of rope lay in the bottom of the smaller coracle. He nodded approvingly. The big blacksmith told them to put the coracles back in their hiding place. He stood back and watched as the two young people hoisted the boats back up into the ivy clad limb of the oak tree. Harry went back up the tree and made the coracles secure and hauled up the hoisting rope before descending to the snow covered ground. It was difficult to hide all their tracks, but with the aid of a branch Harry did the best he could to obliterate their footprints. They made their way back to where Allen and Rob were by the fire, their reconstruction of the stern board complete.

Allen and Rob showed Abe Tull how they had assembled the cleaned boards loosely against the stern board. Harry and Meg looked on in silence. The big man spoke slowly and thoughtfully as he stroked his black beard.

"These cuts were made with a sharp axe and they were made from the outside of the boat. We were meant to find this wreckage and assume that the children were drowned. Allen, you were in the search party. Did you say that the stern board was tied to a tree?"

"Yes sir. The rope was about ten paces long. It was old but in fair condition. We used it to drag the wreckage here."

"Where is the rope now?"

"Under the snow, I reckon. I'm sure I saw it when we pulled that last bit of timber out." Allen, Rob and Harry began to scrape with mitten covered hands at the snowdrift, but it was Meg who saw the end of the rope showing through the melted snow near the fire. She pulled about an arm's length clear of the snow. Allen joined her and together they freed the full length of rope. Abe Tull took the rope and examined it carefully but said nothing. Allen suggested that they should eat something before they started back for the village but Abe Tull insisted that they eat in the saddle if they were hungry. He was keen to be back at the village well before nightfall.

They were within sight of the village when they heard it, the long drawn-out call of the wolf. It was some distance off and the answering calls were even fainter but the sound carried that sinister warning on the night air.

"Did you hear that Meg?" Abe said as he half turned in his saddle.

"I heard it sir, somewhere towards Otter Brook, I would guess sir. They must be hungry to venture this close to the village so early in the winter sir," Meg replied nonchalantly. Abe Tull returned his gaze to the way ahead, a big smile concealed in his black beard.

He saw the torches at the palisade and on the incline up to the south gate he knew that Luke would be supervising setting of the night-watchmen, and there was no warning beacon to alert them to danger.

The great gates closed behind them and men came running to take their horses. Simon was there to take Star's bridle from Meg. They slid tiredly from their saddles. They went to their respective dwellings with Abe Tull's order to meet at his hearth at first light.

Chapter Eight

The Coracle Boy was up early in spite of a poor night's sleep. He had spent a long time trying to anticipate Abe Tull's arguments that would prevent Meg and him leaving. They had to go regardless of how reasonable or persuasive the village leader's opinions were. They had to go, no matter how slender the chances were of finding the children. But Harry would be defying a man he had come to respect, and that hurt. However, he had promised his dying father that he would look after Meg and the young 'uns, Simon and Ruth, and he couldn't do that sitting about waiting for the weather to improve. Yes, that would be his counterargument. They had to go and they had to go now. There was no time to waste.

Harry and Simon went despondently across to Abe Tull's house where Meg met them at the door, they were not looking forward to the meeting. The big kitchen was warm and the smell of newly baked bread pervaded the room. There was nobody else in the kitchen and Meg suggested that they all sit at the table. Master Tull was inspecting the guard and getting their reports. The boy hoped that they would not be kept waiting, he was eager to get the meeting over and to get away now that it was getting light. His anxiety was quelled when the big blacksmith came in from his workshop that adjoined the kitchen.

"Good morning Harry, Simon. Have you changed your mind about the trip up the great river, Harry?"

"No sir, we have to go. I promised father that I would look after the young 'uns sir. I can't do that if I don't go after Ruth and try to bring her back sir."

"Then that is the end of the argument. You and your sister will go with our blessing and all the help we can give you." Abe Tull's statement had taken Harry by surprise, so much so that the boy was speechless.

"Well Harry, tell us what you need. The quicker you tell us your plans the sooner you will be on the way to getting the children back."

Harry was still not sure that he had heard the village leader correctly. He stammered out something about not knowing how to thank the village leader, but he was sure that they had got most of what they would need already.

"We have put a few things together that you may find useful. They are on a packhorse. We can sort them out at the river. Simon, will you go and help Luke to get the horses ready. Harry, you and Meg go and get dressed for the journey." Abe Tull suddenly seemed as eager as Harry to see the adventure start now that the decision had been made.

Harry hurried across to Josh's house and found that Tilda had laid out two warm, woollen shirts for him to wear. They were made of finer wool than Harry would normally have worn. They were a gift from Lyn Tull. There was also a pair of strong moccasins with leggings that extended up to the knee. They had been provided by Jed, the tanner, whose daughter, Jennie, was the other girl in the kidnapped group.

Fully dressed in this winter clothing, Harry returned to Abe Tull's kitchen where Meg was dressed similarly. Her hair was cut short making her look more like a boy than a girl. Harry and Meg were taken through to where the horses were being prepared for the journey, it was fully light now and promised to be a fine, sunny morning. There was a small crowd, mainly of people close to the missing children. Simon was there holding Star for Meg. People came forward wanting the couple to take gifts, others pressing them to take warm winter clothing for their children. There seemed to be no doubt that Harry the Coracle Boy and Meg would find them.

Abe Tull stood on a mounting block above the crowd and demanded silence. "Harry and Meg are undertaking this hazardous journey to rescue their sister and your children, if that is possible. They will be travelling light so they will have to decline your gifts. Save them until their return. Now, my friends, we must leave for the river. I expect that Harry and Meg want to be well upriver before nightfall, so mount up everyone. Luke, you are in charge. Make sure that the lookouts are wide awake."

The party moved down onto the track that would take them to the river. Some of the snowdrifts had been breached and it was possible to travel at a canter for almost all the journey. Abe led the way followed by Harry and Meg. Rob came next with the packhorse behind him. Allen was the last in line.

The river looked as smooth as a millpond with little sign of debris or floating ice. They turned upstream to the point where the forest halted their progress. While Harry and Meg fetched their coracle out of the ivy covered oak tree, the packhorse was unloaded. The goods were spread out for the young travellers to select what they needed. Harry had a clear idea of what was essential for each coracle to carry: a blanket and a change of clothing, food for two days and the tools to make a fire and a small cooking pot each. They would each carry a knife, a short sword, a hunting bow and an axe. Harry would have his spear. If they were separated, they had some chance of survival. Meg carried a shoulder bag that contained her fire lighting equipment and medicine bag made of beaver skin, prepared for her by Eliza Pegg. With her coracle fully loaded, Meg launched her tiny craft and struck out into the river. She performed a couple of manoeuvres and returned to the bank. She was delighted with her coracle and said that she could take another blanket, a small coil of rope and one of the water carriers. Harry too carried a shoulder bag with flint and striker, a spare knife, snares, slingshot and fishing tackle, twine, bodkin and beeswax for coracle repairs.

Harry's coracle was larger and had a slightly deeper draught and held a roll of animal skins, four extra blankets, a water carrier, the flour and oat meal and two coils of rope. There was also a basket of food provided by Lyn Tull. They were ready to leave and it was not yet noon. Abe Tull called them together.

"Harry and Meg, are you sure about making this journey?"

"Yes sir," they answered together.

"Then you have our blessing. There is something I have not mentioned because I didn't want to influence your decision, but I am inclined to agree the kidnappers have gone north. The rope that held the stern of the ferry for us to find, belonged to our fishermen and they have also lost a coracle from their hide near the heronry."

"Thank you for telling us sir. It sounds as if they sent one man down the west bank to steal the ferry and lay a false trail sir."

"I agree Harry and as soon as Ben gets back I'll organise another party to come after you to tell you if he has been successful or not. You will need to lay a trail for them to follow."

"I can do that sir. Dan has shown me the signs and how to tie a branch, mark a tree or pile the stones for a change of direction."

"Then you had best be on your way and may our God be with you both and those children out there. May He bring you all back safely."

Chapter Nine

Harry and Meg launched their coracles together with Harry who was slightly in front and further out from the riverbank, which was on their right. Their farewells were brief as they were soon lost behind the overhanging, snow laden trees. The Coracle Boy was back on the water at last. Here he was in his element. He glanced across at Meg, she smiled, happy to be on the way to find her sister at last. The current was not fierce here where the river was very wide and the swirling eddies worked in favour of the shallow draught coracles. The willow on the banks gave way to a mixture of alder and poplar with a lot of tangled undergrowth. They could see that progress through the forest would have been extremely slow. From time to time Harry would stop at an overhanging tree and tie some of the lower branches together, thus leaving a marker for Dan to follow. Every time they made camp he would mark the spot close to the river bank with a tripod of sticks the height of a man.

It was about mid-afternoon when they became aware of an incoming river from the east, not a big river but it was flowing in fast and appeared to be carrying some debris. Harry pulled hard on his paddle and got in front of Meg. Getting across this fast flowing crosscurrent was going to be difficult enough, then there were the floating hazards to be considered. Would Meg be strong enough? The boy could see lumps of ice in the water that would hole a coracle easily. He indicated to Meg that they should move to the shore. There was no ice under the trees and they were able to step ashore onto a narrow ledge of rock. They were glad of the chance to stand up and ease their aching muscles.

"That incoming current is very strong Meg, we are going to have to use the ropes. I would like to get past this obstacle and find a place to camp before it gets dark."

"How do you mean Harry? 'Use the ropes'."

"We fix a rope to my coracle and then I try to cross the fast water. You pay out the rope as I go. If I can't make it, let the current take me but you keep the rope tight. We will pass the rope round that small tree so that you don't get pulled into the water. But I am fairly sure that I can get across. You keep paying out that rope. If I raise my paddle, you stop and let the rope tighten. The current will take me out but I can handle that. I'll just swing round on the end of the rope and come back to you, but you will need to take up the slack as I come back upstream."

"What happens when you get across?"

"I land and tie the rope off at a suitable tree, then you tie your end of the rope to the thwart of your coracle and I pull you across. You don't have to paddle, use it to fend off the debris, particularly the ice."

"I can do that Harry." The Coracle Boy could see that Meg was nervous.

"There is one other thing, you need to tie yourself to the thwart. That way I can pull you and the coracle in if you have an accident."

"I'll be alright Harry. I'll pass the carrying strap around my waist. When do we go for it?"

"Now, while the light is good," Harry said as he tied the end of the rope to the thwart of his craft. He joined a second rope to the first to be sure of enough to cover the distance. "I'm ready, are you sure you know what to do?"

"Yes. Keep paying out the rope, but if you raise your paddle, I stop and let the rope tighten on the tree."

"That sounds fine to me Meg. Well, here goes."

The Coracle Boy paddled forward and Meg let the rope slide through her hands. She watched nervously as the coracle approached the turbulent water. Harry seemed to almost stop at the edge of the incoming flow and then he struck out and the light craft was snatched sideways towards the great river. But the boy fought the strong current and was holding his own against the sudden onslaught and gradually cleared the savage flow before pulling across into the main river water. It took several strong paddle strokes to get back to the riverbank and a few more to find a suitable landing place where he could fasten the rope to a tree.

With the coracle fastened off at a sturdy young ash tree, Harry untied the rope from his coracle and stepped ashore to find a sound place to stand. He discovered the ideal place, a jutting out rock the height of a man, above the water and a convenient tree to pass the rope round. He moved downstream and called to Meg, instructing her to tie the rope to the thwart of her coracle and tell him when this was done. Moments later she replied that the rope was attached and she was strapped to the seat.

"I am going to pull you closer to the incoming river. Keep close to the bank. Are you ready?"

"I'm ready Harry, pull away." Harry drew the coracle forward until it was only a couple of paces from the racing water.

Harry stopped pulling. "Change of plan Meg. I want you to kneel in the bottom of the coracle and put the paddle inboard too. I'll watch for a time when there are no big pieces of driftwood coming down. When I shout 'Now', I want you to get as low as you can. Lie across the thwart and hold the rim of the boat. Expect to be thrown out towards the big river. Just keep calm and stay low. Tell me when you are ready."

"I'll be alright Harry." A pause and then, "I'm kneeling down and ready when you are."

"Now!" The shout came and the rope tightened and the coracle moved rapidly into the swiftly flowing water. Immediately Meg felt the small craft swing out towards the great river. It dipped and tilted in the turbulence but shipped no water. Harry appeared not to be pulling and Meg felt the panic begin to rise. Then she looked up and saw Harry pulling hand over hand, slowly teasing the coracle into the smoother water of the great river. Soon they were clear of the confused, competing currents and moving forward. Harry was grinning as he pulled Meg's coracle to the bank and then climbed down before helping her step ashore.

"Are we going to camp here Harry?" Meg asked, looking around.

"No, we made better time with the crossing than I expected so I think we should try to find a better place."

They paddled on for a while, but when it began to snow they agreed to make the best of a small clearing just above water level. They pulled both craft up onto dry land and found that the clearing was protected by a huge cedar tree and almost free of snow beneath its evergreen branches. Harry cut four forked sticks and pushed then into the ground and then turned his coracle upside down on them. This was their roof for the night. Meg's coracle was stood at the back to give further protection. There was plenty of firewood and they soon had a blazing fire.

Meg made a meal of toasted oatcakes and a meat pie that Lyn Tull had made for them. There was an apple each to follow.

It was quite dark when they finished their meal. The snow had stopped and so they decided to improve their shelter by cutting some cedar branches and leaning them against the coracles. They also collected a good stock of firewood. They spread out the blanket of animal skins and found that it was big enough to act as a groundsheet and a cover over the blankets.

With the darkness of the night came the snow. This time it was quite heavy. Harry and Meg decided not to set a watch. Who would be about on a night like this, they thought. They climbed into their blankets fully clothed, pulled the animal skins over them and sat together watching the dancing flames.

"Harry," Meg said pensively as she stared into the flames. "Harry, have you seen any sign of the kidnappers or the children yet?"

"No and I don't expect to, not yet. We have to get closer. They have such a big head start on us Meg, and the snow is covering their tracks. We need to have travelled several days before I start going ashore to look for signs."

"But Harry, how can you be sure that they went up this side of the river?"

"I can only follow my instinct Meg. I don't know how I know but I am convinced that they went this way. Perhaps father and mother are guiding us. I really don't know why I feel so sure, but I am Meg, so very sure."

"Then I am sure too Harry. But look at the snow Harry, it's falling really heavily now." The flame of the fire illuminated the flakes in a kaleidoscope of dancing colours. As the snowflakes hit the hot embers, they set up a splutter and sent up tiny clouds of steam. There was very little wind and the eerie silence was broken only by the crackling and hissing of the fire. But both Harry and Meg found a strange contentment in their situation. They had begun the search for Ruth. They were entering a land that was a mystery, a land no one had explored and yet such astonishing tales were told of strange beasts and fierce tribes. Harry dismissed the stories and asked how could anyone know what was in the forest if no one had ventured into this land.

Chapter Ten

The Coracle Boy slept fitfully and each time he woke he would put more wood on the fire. Eventually he fell into a deep sleep and was awakened by Meg shaking his shoulder. He sat up and realised that the fire was almost out and Meg was trying to revive it. She turned a frightened face towards him.

"Harry, there are wolves. They are close." As if to confirm Meg's statement, they heard the mournful howl of an animal not more than a hundred paces away, the boy guessed. There were several replies but from a greater distance. Harry threw aside the skins and blankets and scrambled for his spear and stood facing the direction from which the loudest call had come. The fire began to flare up in response to Meg's vigorous blowing on the embers, gradually she coaxed the wood into a fearsome blaze and they crept back into their shelter.

"Sorry, Meg, did the wolf wake you?"

"I woke and saw the fire was almost out and I was trying to revive it when I first heard him call. I almost died of fright and shook you."

Another howl, this time closer, Harry thought. Spear in hand, he went back to the fire and took out a firebrand and threw it in the direction of the wolf call. It travelled only a short distance to the edge of the clearing where it came to rest in some dry bracken sheltered by the cedar. The dead vegetation caught alight and flared for a few moments, long enough for Harry to see the glowing eyes of an animal. A wolf! There would be more of them very soon he feared.

Harry was not able to see the sky without leaving the safety of the fire but he was sure that dawn could not be far away. The snow had stopped falling but it was bitterly cold. The weight of snow on some of the branches was making them dangerous. Such weight could bring them down.

Neither of them slept and Harry was right. Dawn soon came to illuminate the river and soon the far bank was visible. Meg started to prepare their breakfast while Harry folded the blankets and the animal skin. After their meal they dismantled the camp and launched the coracles. Both were safely tethered to a tree on the bank. A good blaze was kept going until everything was loaded on the coracles. They hadn't heard the wolves since it became fully daylight but they were taking no chances. They were soon under way.

Meg remarked that the river was a little higher than yesterday. The Coracle Boy agreed but said it was nothing to worry about so long as there was frost, but a quick thaw could slow them down. They had to move from under the trees because snow was falling off the branches in large dollops, many of which could sink or capsize a coracle. This meant that they were often adversely affected by the current of the main river, it made hard work all morning. At midday the boy could see that Meg was near exhaustion.

They moved for the shore when they found a break in the trees near an incoming stream and a rocky outcrop. After a cold meal they set off again, but Harry was looking for a safe place to land. He was worried about Meg. She was not used to such long periods of strenuous paddling.

It was early afternoon when Harry saw a possible landing place and signalled to Meg to head for the shore. They made camp and erected the shelter again. It proved to be a more suitable campsite with a rock face at their backs and no overhanging trees. There was also a small natural spring coming from a under the rock. There was plenty of wood and the snow was quickly cleared. Meg soon had a fire ready for the two small cooking pots. Tonight she intended that they would have a hot meal. Harry pulled a huge quantity of dead wood from the forest to form a wall to give them some protection from the wind but also to provide firewood. He topped the wall with branches of the blackthorn to deter any hungry wolf. The boy also set a night line to catch fish.

Meg had made beef stew in one cooking pot and a herbal hot drink in the other, an infusion of dried leaves and berries provided by Eliza Pegg. They ate their food as soon as it was ready.

Harry had made a dam at the spring and formed a reservoir in which to wash themselves and their cooking utensils. It was getting dark as they settled down for the night. There had been no snow all day but the frost had persisted. It had been bitterly cold and now as darkness came it grew colder. The boy piled wood on the fire and told Meg to get some sleep, he would wake her later when she would take over the watch.

With so much wood gathered it was not difficult to keep a good fire going. Harry guessed that it must be about halfway through the night. His constant feeding of the fire had produced a mountain of red hot ash, enough to keep the fire fiercely hot until dawn. He would not wake Meg, she needed the rest. He would pile the wood on the fire one more time and then get some sleep.

If there were wolves about that night the couple didn't hear them. It was fully daylight when Meg shook Harry. She had wakened much earlier just as it was getting light and had taken the fish from Harry's night line that he had set under the overhanging trees where the water was clear of ice. By the time Harry awoke, the trout were cooking in the embers of the fire. Meg scolded Harry for not waking her to do her share of the night watch but had to admit that she felt so much better for having had a good night's sleep.

They were getting into a routine now and breaking camp and loading the coracles was done without the need for discussion. Harry erected the tripod of poles he had prepared yesterday to mark their camp but there was an added chore this morning. The frost in the night had been so severe that the river was frozen from the bank two full paces out at their treeless landing place.

Harry broke the ice and pushed it downstream clear of their path out to the river. They filled their water carriers from the spring and set off on their journey.

Chapter Eleven

It was three days since Harry and Meg set out on their quest for the missing children and each day they had seen rivers on the west bank spilling torrents of water from the mountain valleys into the great river. The incoming streams from the east were much smaller and the great river itself was also getting smaller.

Harry and Meg had to make two small portages where they encountered rapids. They were not significant obstacles, but it was obvious that they had reached the point where a water craft, of any description, would have to be dragged overland to progress further upriver. At both these diversions Harry saw no sign of boats being hauled past the obstacle, but there had been several days of snowfall, enough to obliterate any tracks.

They spent two more bitterly cold nights in the forest, but the topography of the flat, forested area to the east had suddenly changed. The forest had given way to barren, treeless hills. These hills were not grey limestone like the cliffs of the west bank escarpment, but red sandstone. There were steep cliffs on both sides of the river, not very high yet on the east bank, and the river had become much narrower and dangerously faster flowing.

At about midmorning Harry signalled that they should land at once. Meg pulled up alongside her brother and asked in a whisper what he had seen.

"Smoke coming from the other side of that hill. I think we should land and secure the coracles and go and see who they are."

"Do you think it's the children Harry?"

"Don't get your hopes up Meg, I expected them to be much farther ahead than this. Trouble is there's nowhere to hide the coracles."

"What about that stream we passed a while back? That had some overhanging bushes and reeds."

"I don't want to go back that far Meg. I think we should see what is round the next bend. I'll go first, wait for my signal and keep a sharp lookout. They may have seen us before I saw their smoke."

The Coracle Boy guided his craft slowly upstream, keeping close to the eastern bank that was now the height of a man. As he drew near to the bend he took advantage of the cover offered by a bramble bush. It hung down until its thorny tendrils floated on the water.

Harry studied the scene for a long time before he ventured round the bend. Now he could see that there was a good landing place, well concealed and completely clear of snow. He drifted back until he could signal Meg to join him.

"What have you found Harry?" Meg whispered as she drew alongside his coracle and peered past him.

"The current is very strong right on the bend Meg, so be prepared for some hard paddling. Keep tight to the cliff without actually touching it, if you can."

The boy struck hard for the bend where the flow hit the rock face and then turned downstream. The strong current caught the little boat and tried to wrench it out from the bank, but Harry fought hard and pulled into the calmer water beyond the bend. Getting Meg into the small bay was going to be dangerous. He swung the coracle round to warn Meg. To his horror she had started round the bend and he dared not call out to her. She needed all her concentration focussed on her battle with the maelstrom. Whether it was the smaller, lighter craft or Meg's skill with the paddle, whichever it was, she seemed to skip across the turbulence.

"That was great Meg. I think we should move over to where the cliff is lowest. Mind the rubbish, it collects in this small bay."

They were in a narrow gorge that opened out into a broad valley up ahead. The cliffs gave way to a wide sandy beach, sloping up to where low, stunted trees grew. Higher up willow and birch were bowed down with the weight of snow. The opposite bank still appeared to be covered in an impenetrable forest. Closer to them there was a break in the shallow cliff where they would be able to step ashore onto a narrow strip of rock.

Beyond this ledge the ground sloped up steeply and was covered in small birch saplings. A stunted yew tree clung to the rock and hung down and provided sturdy moorings.

Harry scrambled ashore and tied his coracle to the yew tree and then took a line from Meg and made her boat secure.

"We need to know who these people are Meg. We have to be sure they have the children. If not we will have to bypass them."

"This would be a good place to camp Harry. It's sheltered from the wind and snow here."

"But we wouldn't be able to have a fire. They would see the smoke and we must have a fire Meg. We need at least one hot meal each day."

"So what do we do Harry?"

"We can't pull the coracles up onto this rocky surface. They will have to stay in the water. The trouble is they can be seen from the other bank."

"Shall I stay here while you go and see if it is the children?"

"No Meg, we mustn't split up unless we have to. No, we will have to take a chance and leave them. We will just take our weapons and some food.

They took their hunting bows and swords. Harry didn't take the spear, it would be awkward to carry up the steep slope. They also took a blanket each. Meg wrapped some bread and cheese in a cloth and put it in her shoulder bag and they were ready. Harry slung the water carrier across his shoulder.

The climb up the steep slope was exhausting, it had been their arms, shoulders and backs that had had the greater part of their exercise until this point. Now their legs had to get them up this precipitous climb. When they left the cover of the trees they were in snow covered heather, it slowed their progress considerably. Beyond the heather deep snow covered loose scree and the going was even slower. Suddenly the slope changed and became gentler. They stopped to rest a while. Harry looked back across the windswept hillside and then on to the snow-capped forest beyond. How far had they travelled he wondered. Meg turned and set off again. Harry quickly caught up with his sister and warned her to proceed cautiously. As they approached the crest, they lay in the snow and crawled forward.

Gradually they saw the horizon appear like a jagged saw. Its teeth were snow clad mountains, and then they saw tree covered foothills. Crawling slowly forward they were able to look down into the valley below. Immediately they saw the smoke rising from a cleft in the rock face of a small hill.

"It looks as if somebody is living in a cave down there Meg."

"I can't see any sign of the children," Meg replied.

"It can't be a proper home, there is no garden and I don't see any animals. There is a pile of firewood stacked against the rock face. You can see where the snow has been cleared to get at it. Perhaps it's a hunter's resting place, Allen and Hugh have one by the lake."

"Dare we go down there? Do you think they have the young 'uns in that cave? What shall we do Harry?" Meg asked anxiously.

"We stay here and watch. We'll dig a snow hole in that deep drift over there to get out of this wind. We can wrap the blankets around us. If we have seen nothing by noon we go back to the coracles and try to sneak by. We have to find a safe place to camp further upstream before nightfall."

Meg kept watch while Harry dug the snow hole. They moved into their temporary accommodation and wrapped the blankets around them before beginning their surveillance.

They had hardly got comfortable in their shelter when they both exclaimed in a hoarse whisper, "Look!" There was movement down near the woodpile.

"What is it Harry? Is it a man?"

"I think so, yes. He seems to be crawling towards the pile of firewood."

"He's stopped, Harry. He's throwing pieces of wood. What is he doing?"

"He must be alone. Look, he's trying to stand up. We need to get closer Meg. If we can get down to that clump of bushes we will have cover for a good distance. Come on."

Harry folded his blanket and crept out of their hideout. There was much more vegetation on this side of the hill and the snow looked deeper. The wind was stronger and directly in their faces now. Keeping a watch on the dark figure at the woodpile, they moved cautiously forward and reached the shelter of the bushes without being seen. The bushes were leafless hawthorn and the snow lay thick under them.

Their route was tortuous under snow laden bushes and there was no opportunity to see what was happening at the woodpile. At last they reached a patch of bare rock and were able to see that they were still well above the dwelling, if that was what it was. The hooded figure was now sitting with his back to the stack of wood. He appeared to be hacking at a log with a small axe.

"It is a cave Meg, and look, there is the Christian cross at the entrance. Perhaps he is like Brother Anselm. He lived alone in a hut in the forest."

"What shall we do? Do you think it is safe to approach him? He may not be alone, there could be others."

"Then why doesn't somebody come and help him? Look, he's crawling back to the cave," Harry said and then looked up at the sky. "It's past noon Meg, we have to start back for the coracles now or take a chance with the man at the cave. I think we should take a chance."

"I agree Harry. Sister Mary said that wherever you see that cross you can be sure of a welcome."

Chapter Twelve

The young adventurers moved cautiously down until the bushes became sparse and young birch trees grew profusely. Now they could see the cave. The entrance was covered with tattered animal skins fixed to poles leaning against the rock face. Below them they saw a fenced off area that was probably a garden, but there was no sign of animal enclosures. Nor was there evidence of fishing, such as a boat or coracle. There were no tracks from the cave in any direction and there hadn't been a heavy snowfall for a couple of days.

"This is it Meg. Shall I go on alone or…."

"No! We stick together," the girl replied sharply.

"Then we should string our bows, just in case we are not welcome."

Harry and Meg stepped out of the birch grove near the fenced area. A few bedraggled, snowcapped cabbages confirmed that it was a garden. They moved to within hailing distance. Harry cupped his hands to his mouth.

"Hullo, the cave. Can we come forward sir?"

There was no reply. The silence was almost frightening and then an animal skin moved at the entrance. They saw the head and shoulders of a man. It was obvious that he was crawling along the floor of the cave. Meg caught her breath and moved forward. The boy seized her arm and told her to wait. Again he cupped his hands.

"Sir, we mean you no harm. Can we speak with you?"

They saw the figure push himself up on one arm and beckoned with the other but he made no sound. Harry and Meg went forward, each with an arrow on the bowstring. The path from the garden sloped gently down to the cave and now they could see the man clearly. His hood was pushed back to reveal a mass of tangled white hair and a deeply lined, weather-beaten face. He pushed himself up and supported himself on his forearms. He spoke breathlessly and as if in pain.

"Who are you? Have you come to torment me again? Ah! You carry bows, are you here to kill me this time? Then may God forgive you as I must."

"Sir, we are not here to kill you. We seek your help and will help you in return if we can. My name is Harry sir, and this is my sister Meg." Harry took the arrow from the bowstring and laid the bow on the ground.

The old man looked puzzled and shook his head slowly and then he looked from one to the other and whispered, "The good Lord has sent you and I have neither food nor drink to offer."

"Sir, we have no need of your food. Perhaps we could share some of ours with you. We were about to eat when we saw you at the woodpile," Meg said as she took the parcel of bread and cheese from her shoulder bag.

"Come into my humble dwelling. At least I have a fire, Thank the good Lord they didn't put that out. They smashed almost everything I have and they threw my book of prayers on the fire, may God forgive them."

"Sir, are you not able to walk?" Harry asked as he went to his assistance. The offer was declined as the old man turned and crawled back into the cave.

It was not a huge cave, just about high enough for a man to stand upright. It was too dark to see how far back it went. There was broken pottery on the floor. The crude furniture was smashed. The old man had made a bed of animal skins close to the fire. He pulled himself onto his bed. He looked exhausted.

"One of them threw hot ashes onto my feet." He paused and screwed up his face as if remembering the pain, before adding, "He thought it was funny and fell to the floor laughing." The old man sighed and went on, "I managed to get my sandals off but he picked them up and threw them on the fire."

"Who are these men who did this to you sir?"

"They are heathens," was all the old man said.

"Harry I have some salve in my medicine pouch. Eliza said it is very soothing. Perhaps it would ease the pain."

"Sir, my sister is learning the art of healing. She has her medicines with her. Will you allow her to treat your feet?"

"Could I have a drink of water first please?"

Harry took the water carrier from his shoulder. He found a horn beaker on the floor, rinsed it out and gave the old man a drink of water.

Meg treated the blistered feet with the salve. She was gentle but aware that she had not yet acquired the skills of Eliza Pegg.

Harry brought in wood and built up the fire. He tied down some of the loose skins that protected the mouth of the cave and proceeded to examine the table and chair. If he had brought some tools with him he could have repaired them. He smiled at the thought.

Suddenly he remembered the coracles and knelt down beside Meg and spoke to the old man. "Sir, we have our coracles moored in the little bay downstream, we need to collect them. Will you be alright? We will be back as quickly as we can."

"Of course my son."

"We will leave the food and water with you," Meg said as she packed the medicine pouch and put the meagre victuals within easy reach of her patient.

"Sir, is there a quicker way of getting to the bay without going over the hill?" Harry enquired.

"Yes, if you go to the river's edge and turn downstream, you will come to a path leading up into the trees. Follow the track up until you come to the cliff that shelters the bay. Go up into the trees until you can climb down where the cliff is shallower."

"Thank you sir, we will be as quick as we can."

Harry picked up his bow and strung an arrow and indicated that Meg should do the same. They followed a slight depression in the snow that suggested the line of the path to the river's edge. They turned left and headed downstream. It became difficult to find the path at first and then Harry noticed the wider spacing of the trees, it was the path. They did as the old man had directed and were soon reunited with their coracles. The Coracle Boy left clear signs for Dan to follow. A sign that would tell him that there was a Christian dwelling further upstream.

They piloted their craft up to the snow covered beach and stepped ashore. Harry pulled the coracles up onto the snow to be clear of the water.

"We will ask the old man if he will allow us to camp under those trees by the cliff. We will just take the food up first."

They found the old man dozing by the fire. He was startled by their arrival but soon regained his composure and Harry asked about setting up camp nearby.

"You cannot camp out in this weather, you must come and share my humble abode. There is straw and dry bracken down there." He indicated further down the cave, "You must share my hearth."

"Thank you sir, we will bring our few possessions up from the coracles."

"I would suggest that you bring your little craft up and put them just inside the entrance." The food and water had revived the old man, he was smiling broadly now and talking much more coherently.

As soon as the cargo was stowed in the cave, Harry and Meg brought up the coracles and set them down in the lean-to that protected the cave entrance. Meg set about cleaning up the cave whilst Harry was planning their breakfast.

It was early evening when Harry returned to the cave. He had speared two large trout and had set night lines for tomorrow's supplies. The old man was delighted. Meg was making oat cakes and a brew of Eliza's refreshing drink.

The old man sat up and leaned back against the wall of the cave. He took a drink of Eliza's brew, smacked his lips approvingly and said, "It is time I introduced myself to you young people. I am Friar Godwin, sent into exile many years before you were born, but I found God here and have spent a life of prayer.

"Recently the solitude I have come to love has been disturbed by heathen pagans who mine for gold in the mountains. Five times in the past two years they have tormented me, but this is the first time they have attacked and injured me. Usually they are content with just taking all my food and this is the first time they have come in the winter. They usually ply their dreadful trade in the summer." The old monk gazed pensively into the flames.

Harry looked anxiously at Meg. He turned to the old man. "Sir, what is this dreadful trade you speak of?"

"Why the slave trade, my son. Worse, child slaves to work in their mines."

"Oh no!" Meg cried, burying her face in her hands.

"We are trying to catch up with these villains sir. They have taken our sister and five other children from our village."

"And what will you do if you catch up with them? There are a dozen of them and they have two rowing boats. What happens if you are captured?"

"Meg will become my brother who is not able to speak. I will tell them as little as I can but keep as close to the truth as possible."

"A wise plan, but they have two days' start. You will never catch up with them."

"They were about ten days in front of us when we started out sir. We have no idea what we will do when we catch up, but we will think of something. We have to sir."

"Our mother and father are looking after us. Sister Mary says so sir," Meg added fervently.

"And what is the name of this village you have travelled from?"

"It is Abe Tull's village sir. It is…."

"Abe Tull?" the old Friar cut in. "He was just a boy when I saw him last. His father is Zach Tull, but no, he must be dead now and Abe was his only son. Fine man was Zach."

"You know him sir, you know Abe Tull?"

"I knew him son. It is so long ago. He was about sixteen when last I saw him and swinging a blacksmith's hammer like a full grown man."

"Sir, did your attackers have any children with them?" Meg asked.

"Yes, I counted sixteen, but there could have been more."

"Sixteen!" Meg almost screamed the word. Her brother looked at her enquiringly. She held up her left hand three times and then one finger. Harry gasped and shook his head. Meg asked the question he was considering.

"Where did they get the other children from sir?"

"The villages in the marshes, and there are wanderers in the land to the east. Some people even sell their children to these evil men."

"Sir, Abe Tull sent a search party to the village in the marshes. When they discover that their village has suffered the same fate they will return to our village and then follow us sir. I have left a trail for Dan the pagan to follow. He's the best tracker there is and Ben Tull is leading the party sir."

"Then your best plan is to stay here and wait for Ben and his men to arrive."

"No, sir. We intend to move on tomorrow and find out all we can so that Ben is warned of the dangers ahead."

"Then may God go with you both. I shall be sorry to see you go."

"We will get a good supply of wood into the cave for you and there should be some fish on the line in the morning, enough to last until Ben gets here."

"Don't worry about me. If Meg can wrap my feet in some strips off this old blanket I have a secret pantry down yonder." He nodded in the direction of the inner reaches of the cave.

What was left of the daylight was spent cutting up firewood and stacking it as near to the fire as was safe. Harry also repaired the damage to the cover that protected the entrance, so that practically no light was visible from the outside. He entered the cave pulling the wind and snow proof covering tight closed. The smell of Meg's cooking made him realise that he was ravenously hungry. He was also very tired and after the meal they bedded down for the night. Friar Godwin said he would stand the first watch, not that he expected any visitors, but recent events advised caution. But he didn't wake the young people. He remained awake all night, thus ensuring a good night's sleep for them both.

A small chink of daylight told him that it was dawn. He roused Harry. After a quick wash the Coracle Boy went to check his night lines and came back with six fish. Meg cooked some for breakfast, leaving the remainder for Friar Godwin.

Sure that the Friar was able to get about and had plenty of food and water, Harry and Meg took the coracles to the water and loaded their supplies and possessions. They went to take their leave of the old Friar, who was clearly distressed at their departure and begged them to call to see him on their return. He would pass on their messages to Ben Tull when he arrived. He insisted that they prayed together and then he gave them his blessing.

"Do you think he will be alright Harry?" Meg was clearly concerned as she stepped into her coracle.

"Yes, he's lived alone for a long time Meg, and the salve you used and the wrappings you made for his feet enable him to get about. He'll be alright."

They turned and waved. The old Friar was sitting by the entrance to his cave waving to them as they drove their paddles into the ice-cold water.

A good night's sleep, the warmth of the cave and a hearty breakfast had put them both in good spirits. As they set off it began to snow, the headwind was getting stronger, making their journey much more tiring. By noon they were almost exhausted and Harry said that they should look for a place to camp. He led the way into a small river. The willows on either side arched over making a dark tunnel that sheltered them from the biting wind.

"This is a good shelter but there is nowhere to build camp. We'll rest a while and as soon as the storm passes we will move on."

But the storm didn't pass.

Chapter Thirteen

Sitting in their coracles they were getting cold and Harry saw that they had to either face the storm on the main river or continue up this tributary. They agreed to follow the smaller meandering river. It was narrow but deep and free of weed. The flow was quite gentle and the sheltering willows protected them from the wind. They quickly warmed up. Harry and Meg both became aware of the sound of a waterfall up ahead and as they rounded a bend they saw a stand of tall pines growing up the steep hillside on their left. Deciduous trees grew on the flatter land to their right, but in front of them they saw the waterfall, which had been created by a beaver dam. Harry had only seen one once before. His father had taken him to see a similar structure in the forest near to Brother Anselm's hut. This one was smaller, it was less than the height of man above the river.

"We will have to make camp here Meg. Goodness knows how far we will have to carry our coracles to get above the level of the beaver's lake."

"Can we find a place in those pine trees?"

"It looks very steep. We need to find a place very soon, this storm is getting worse and we are getting cold sitting here," Harry said as he pulled into the bank and tied up at the roots of an alder. Meg followed suit. They clambered up the riverbank and went up into the trees where it was calmer, although the wind roared in the branches above them.

"Look Harry, there is a flat area over here." Meg pointed to her right. They were well above the lake.

"It looks wide enough to get my coracle in. Yes, we will have to make it do. Come on, we must hurry Meg."

They ran back to the river and Harry climbed down to his coracle and emptied the contents of both craft onto the bank. Meg carried the food and blankets into the shelter of the trees. Harry hauled both coracles up onto the bank and then took the larger boat up to their chosen campsite. He returned for Meg's coracle and the remainder of their possessions.

They had perfected the method of forming a warm lodge out of their coracles and the animal skins, they quickly had a shelter erected and a fire blazing. The light was fading and Harry hurried down to the river to set his night line for a good breakfast tomorrow. It was almost dark when Harry cut branches from the evergreen pines to give added protection to the weather side of their camp. With the fire on the leeward side they felt safe. There had been little time to gather a large store of firewood. A smaller blaze would have to suffice. However, it would mean that someone would need to keep it fed with wood, a strict watch would have to be kept. Harry and Meg talked well into the night and then the wolves were heard in the distance, their howl carried on the wind to strike fear into their prey.

It was a dreadful night. The wind lashed the trees and threatened to uproot them, snow piled high at the back of their shelter and they were getting low on fuel for the fire. They were glad to see the dawn and with it came a drop in the strength of the wind and the wolves fell silent.

Harry's first task was to gather dry wood from under the fir trees. He went cautiously, carrying both axe and spear to be ready if a wolf had decided to try its luck. There were no wolves but plenty of firewood. Harry brought a huge stock and soon they had a good blaze and Meg started to cook breakfast.

The snow from the trees to the river was up to Harry's waist. He used his paddle as a shovel to dig a path down to the river. He found his night lines held four fish. A pair of ducks flew up from the water and the Coracle Boy decided that he would come back later and try for a change of diet.

After breakfast they agreed that to attempt to move camp today would be pointless. First, they both needed sleep since neither had slept last night. Second, it would take until midday to get the coracles to the water and loaded. Third, by the time they reached the main river they would have to start looking for another campsite.

Meg would smoke the fish and bake bread and oat cakes. Harry decided to improve the path to the river, try to shoot a duck and gather more firewood.

They had completed their tasks by noon and Harry, having shot a duck, prepared it for the spit. It was the only way to cook it with their limited resources but it would be a welcome change from fish.

Harry suggested that Meg should try and sleep during the afternoon and then she could take the first watch when night came. The boy would keep the fire going and turn the spit from time to time, he would also fill the water carriers.

The sun came out in the afternoon and Harry was tempted to allow himself to doze in the dappled shade. Instead he walked a little way into the wood and saw a young roe deer, but it caught his scent and fled.

Harry's thoughts turned to their mission. It depressed him that their progress was so slow. He thought of Ruth and wondered how she would cope with this extreme cold and what was to become of her. Friar Godwin spoke of children working in the gold mines in the mountains. The thought chilled the Coracle Boy and he returned to the camp in very low spirits.

Meg was fast asleep in the shelter. The sun had gone below the high ground to the west and Harry could feel the air getting colder. He expected another hard frost tonight but there was no wind to keep them awake.

It was getting dark when Meg woke up and joined her brother beside the fire. They ate the duck with bread and followed it with some dried fruit. It was Harry's turn to sleep and he quickly fell into a dreamless slumber.

He was awakened by Meg shaking him. She didn't have to tell him the reason for the intrusion, he could hear it and it was too close for comfort. Meg already had an arrow on the bowstring and a good blaze going. Wolves do not like fire.

"I tried to leave you as long as I could Harry, but they are closer than I have ever heard them and when I actually saw one, I'm sorry if I panicked, Harry."

"You did the right thing Meg." Harry was busy stringing his bow. Placing his bow against a tree root, he bent the yew and slid the loop of the bowstring into the upper nock and reached for an arrow. There was a scraping sound coming from the back of the shelter. Harry swung round, the bowstring at full stretch, but he held fire. The sound was coming from behind Meg's coracle. He dared not hole his sister's coracle. He waited and then he saw the evergreen branches move. He fired at the movement. There was the faintest yelp. Harry strung another arrow and waited. This time there was no movement. He turned his attention to the animals beyond the fire and sent a fire arrow into their midst. It ignited the dry, dead brash that littered the ground under the pine trees. It flared up until it reached the snow and there it died. But there had been enough light for them to see several wolves run back into the darkness.

Harry and Meg agreed that they would prepare everything ready for a quick move to the small river as soon as it was daylight and the wolves had left for their daytime lair. As the dawn pushed back the shadows, Harry saw that the wolves were not retreating. Some were lying down, others padding back and forth as if waiting. Waiting for what?

"We have to move soon Meg. We can't lose another day."

"Can we pack everything in the coracles and drag them across the snow?"

"We can't risk tearing a hole in one or even both coracles Meg."

"Look at them Harry, sitting there just waiting for us to move away from the fire. I'm frightened."

"So am I, but we have to keep calm. Why don't we start by folding the blankets and gathering all our possessions together by the fire and then start to strip the branches from around the sides?"

Meg answered by collecting the bedding and the animal skin groundsheet and began folding them. Harry began to pull the pine branches away from Meg's coracle. He gave a sudden cry of alarm, sprang back and grabbed his spear.

"What is it Harry?"

"Stay where you are. Don't move," Harry said, his voice tremulous and hoarse. He stepped forward slowly, the spear held two-handed and aimed at a point a hand's width from the side of Meg's coracle. With the point of the spear he pushed aside one of the branches. As it fell away it revealed the head of a wolf. Meg screamed. Harry stepped back and then drove the spear into the animal. There was no sound. The creature was dead. Just to the left of the spear an arrow protruded from the wolf's skull. It was Harry's arrow.

It was a long time before either of them spoke. Meg sobbed and Harry put a trembling arm around her as gradually they came out of the shock.

Eventually the Coracle Boy suggested that he would go to the back of the shelter and drag the carcass back into the woods. Meg begged him to be careful. Harry dragged the beast a few paces away and broke the head of his arrow off the shaft. Good iron arrow heads were precious.

They set about clearing the branches from the coracles and righting them.

"Harry, why don't we take your coracle down and tie it safe and then take the cargo down in my coracle, which we can carry between us, even if it takes several small loads."

"That's a good idea, we can have a firebrand in one hand and carry the coracle with the other. Come on, let's give it a go."

With Harry's coracle safely moored, each carrying a firebrand, they started back. They saw that the wolves were moving a little closer. They hurried for the safety of the fire and Harry loosed a couple of fire arrows at the animals, which sent them scurrying away. They loaded Meg's coracle, including the boy's bow and some arrows and hurried down to the river. Harry kept watch while Meg loaded the craft, it took two more journeys to complete the task.

The fire was left to burn itself out. There was little chance of causing a forest fire in this weather and so Harry and Meg rode the gentle current back to the great river.

Chapter Fourteen

The great river appeared to be flowing deeper than when they left it. Perhaps there was a thaw on the way, which could mean flooding and they might have to travel overland. They would surmount that problem when, or if, it arrived. By midday they saw that the water was rougher, suggesting large submerged rocks. Harry indicated that they should land at a point where an ash tree had fallen into the water. There was calmer water downstream of the tree and it looked like an ideal landing place. They scrambled ashore along the trunk of the fallen tree and stepped onto firm ground.

Suddenly there was a cracking sound. They turned to see the large ash being torn from the bank, its roots breaking as the force of the river pressed the tree against the collected rubbish held in the floating branches. Harry ran back across the tree, Meg made to follow him. He shouted to her to go back and climb down the bank and be ready to catch the mooring lines.

Meg's coracle was nearest to the bank, so Harry stepped down into the craft and loosed the line and threw it to Meg. She caught it and scrambled back up the bank, tying the line to an undisturbed tree. She turned and saw that her brother had reached his own coracle and was stepping down into it. And then she saw that the tree was beginning to roll and was taking the mooring line down under the water. Harry would not be able to untie it. She saw the glint of the sun on the metal as the boy drew his knife and cut the line. A moment later and the slender craft would have been dragged under.

But now another danger faced Harry. The tree started to roll in the opposite direction and the limbs were coming up out of the water. He paddled furiously as the leafless branches threatened to tear his craft to shreds, and then he was clear only to realise that the tree was swinging back towards the bank. Both coracles would be crushed and all their possessions would sink to the bottom of the river. Harry could only watch. His only hope was to jump for the shore just before the coracle was crushed. The thought of being plunged into the ice-cold water caused him to reconsider. He paddled downstream as fast as he could to get clear of the tree before it hit the bank. He made it with only moments to spare.

Meg had watched helplessly at first and then she too saw the danger. She scrambled down to her coracle and began to throw everything she could get hold of up onto the bank. Suddenly the tree stopped its advance, but Meg continued her frenzied work until it was empty, before climbing back up the bank. She saw that Harry was doing the same further down the river and turned her attention to her little craft, hauling it up onto the snow covered ground. Meg ran down to help her brother carry his coracle up onto safer ground.

They were both exhausted, however, they could not rest until they had gathered all their property and decided on the next course of action. They brought Meg's coracle and its cargo to where Harry had come ashore. It was not ideal but a little higher above the river.

"I think we should follow the river upstream and see if the flow improves farther on and we need to look for a more suitable campsite," Harry said.

"We can't leave our things Harry. Animals might tear them to pieces. You go ahead and scout and I'll stay here and get a fire going."

Harry insisted on making sure Meg had a good fire burning and a plentiful stock of firewood. He also strung his bow, just in case.

"Are you sure Meg? I'll go as far as that high ground and climb that tall fir tree and see what's up ahead. I'll not be long."

Harry set off at a steady pace through the snow until he was met with a wall of blackthorn that covered the steep slope ahead. He moved to his right to skirt the obstacle. He came to a stand of birch trees and turned up the slope again. It was steeper here and he was glad of the trees to hold onto. And then he remembered Dan the pagan, who had taught him some of his tracking skills. 'Don't shake the tree you hold onto. Others can follow your progress by the movement of the treetops'. He soon left the birch wood and entered an area of tall firs. At the top he could see nothing through the trees. He would have to climb higher. He selected a tall pine that didn't look too difficult to climb and began his ascent. At a gap in the foliage he looked back and saw the smoke from Meg's fire and smiled as he contemplated a hot meal when he got back.

Finding a gap that would allow him to look forward was proving difficult and the snow that fell on him from the branches above was not pleasant. But there was a break just a little farther up. Harry realised that his tree was at the top of a ridge that fell steeply down to the river to his left and continued to rise for some distance to his right. In the far distance a range of snow covered hills curled round to the east in a great arc to join the ridge on which his tree grew. There was a lake to the west of the hills and rapids spilling from the lake. Here and there he could see the river racing towards him as it cut its way through the green canopy. He saw a wide valley protected by the hills that cradled the forest like a defending arm. But it was what lay in front of him that set the Coracle Boy's heart racing.

There was smoke from a fire! He saw five huts thatched with reed and men, four of them walking towards the river, but he could see no women or children. There appeared to be no animals down there, not even a dog.

Pulled up way above the water there were three boats, long rowing boats. Harry had never seen craft like these, they were almost as long as a river barge. He saw a track leading from the village. Well, it looked like a village, he thought, except that it had no stockade. The track followed the river and then was lost amongst the snow covered trees that were thickly packed over the whole of the valley and up over the lower hills.

Harry turned his attention to the men. They had arrived at the boats but were too far away for him to see what they were doing. He guessed they were clearing the snow off them. Suddenly he realised that if they launched a boat and went downstream they would see the fire and Meg. Harry was about to hurry down the tree when he took one last look and stopped. The men had turned one of the boats upside down to reveal the keel of the boat, now black against the snow covered ground. The boy waited. The second boat was turned over as was the third and then the men turned and followed the track upriver, each man appeared to be carrying a bundle. Were they leaving?

Harry wanted to stay and see how far he would be able to follow the men's progress but he knew that they would soon be lost in the trees. He left his precarious perch and realised that he had become very cold, but the exercise soon warmed him as he hurried down through the trees.

Returning to his sister, Harry found Meg waiting anxiously. She said she was worried. He seemed to have been away such a long time. He told her what he had seen.

"I think we will have to stay here tonight Meg. If we make camp where those trees are on that higher ground, we can keep a small fire going and be able to defend ourselves."

"Have we got time to move before it gets dark, Harry?"

"We are too close to the river, Meg. We have to move but we should eat first. I'm starving."

The hot meal was just what they needed. As soon as they finished, they started the move to higher ground. The clump of fir trees proved to be ideal. They were becoming experts in converting the coracles into a rainproof shelter and were installed in the new location well before the darkness came. With the fire in a depression in the ground and kept to the minimum size they felt quite safe here. They spent an uneventful night. There were no howling wolves and there was no snowstorm, but they still kept watch to maintain the fire.

The next morning they ate a breakfast of smoked fish and oatcakes. They discussed their situation and agreed that they would have to take a better look at the village and it would have to be done on foot, the river at this point was far too dangerous to risk using the coracles. Their supplies would have to be protected during their absence and so they hoisted the coracles up into the trees, high enough to be out of the reach of animals. Their little craft were not very well camouflaged but Harry was sure that they could not be seen from the river. They set off to observe the encampment on the other side of the hill. They had no firm plan. They would play it by ear, travelling light with only their swords for defence and a blanket each. The Coracle Boy remembered how cold it had been on that chilly perch.

Their first observations told them that the village was deserted and they debated whether to go down there.

"There is no sign of smoke or people. I think we should go down there and see if there are traces of the young 'uns," Meg said purposefully.

"I agree. We can't wait for much longer if we are to go down there and still be back here before nightfall. If we keep to the pine trees Meg, where there is not much snow, we will leave less of a trail."

But there was little chance of hiding their tracks. The slope was so steep they skidded through the pine needles. Their route was clearly defined. When the way ahead finally levelled out, the pine trees gave way to leafless, deciduous trees and the ground was covered with a generous layer of pristine snow.

Harry told Meg to step in his footprints to give the impression of only one traveller. And then they came to the first signs of human habitation, a confusion of footprints and indications of wood cutting and gathering by many. They followed the well trodden path, all the time seeing evidence of fuel harvesting. And then through the thinning trees they saw the first hut. It appeared to be in a poor state of repair. As they crept closer this was borne out by the gaping holes in the wattle walls and a collapsed roof at one corner. They peered through the gaps and it became evident that this building had not been used recently. They moved on to the corner of the hut. From there they could see the other four identical, rectangular huts. They were assembled in a 'U' shape with the open end towards the river. None of these dwellings, if that is what they were, looked habitable. There was very little snow in the area in front of the buildings. An abandoned besom and piles of snow between the huts suggested that some effort had been made to clear the snow. There had been a large fire in that open space. Now only a pile of smouldering wood ash remained.

The two young adventurers crept right round the camp and looked into every room. They saw no one. Satisfied that there were no inhabitants, Harry stepped out into the open. He waved his sister forward and together they examined the only hut that looked just about habitable. At least the roof was intact. The door opening was low and covered with an animal hide. Inside it was almost totally dark. As their eyes became accustomed to the gloom they could see that straw and bracken covered the floor as deep as a man's knee. It was evident that many people had been accommodated in here.

Suddenly Meg fell to her knees and scrabbled in the bracken near the door. "Harry, look!" She held up a small wooden crucifix. She was weeping.

"Harry. Look Harry," she said through her sobbing. "Sister Mary gave it to Ruth." She reached into her shoulder bag and took out her medicine pouch and from it she produced a similar cross. "Sister Mary gave me one too."

"Are you sure it's Ruth's cross, Meg?" the boy asked.

"I am sure Harry. Look they are almost the same. Oh Harry, this means Ruth is alive and we are on the right trail. This is the first sign we have had, I had almost given up hope." The words poured out as Meg laughed and cried and kissed the tiny cross.

"Steady on Meg." Harry reached down and helped the excited girl to her feet. He gazed at the emblems of Christianity in the palm of Meg's hand. They were just bits of wood but if it was really Ruth's cross, then he was proved right.

He went down on one knee and examined the snow at the side of the hut. After a few moments the boy stood up. The cleared area was frozen mud and littered with bracken and ash, but at the edges there was a margin of undisturbed snow and in that snow Harry saw footprints.

"Meg, look at this, these are the footprints of a child," Harry said as he knelt again. Meg joined him as they studied the small imprint of a child's right foot.

"That proves it Harry, we have proof that the children came this way."

"Look around, see if you can find other traces the children were here."

After a while they had found four more sets of footprints of varying sizes, but definitely children and one of them was barefoot. This upset Meg when she found it. Harry said that they had found evidence enough.

Suddenly Harry tensed and looked about.

"What is it Harry?" Meg asked apprehensively.

"I think we should get back. I am getting an uneasy feeling. Come on!"

Chapter Fifteen

Harry grabbed Meg's hand and hurried across the open space and into the sparse woodland. He quickly found their tracks in the snow that would take them back to their camp. Harry told Meg to step in their old tracks. He turned round and walked backwards for a short distance to suggest that the impressions were made by someone going to the village, not away from it. They followed their earlier route back to where they had emerged from the fir trees and started their climb up the steep slope. After a short while the boy looked back and was horrified by the clarity of their tracks. It was no use trying to hide them, they would have to hope that no one came in their direction.

Eventually they reached the top of the ridge and sat down to rest.

"I'm going to climb the look-out tree Meg, I'll not be long."

True to his word Harry was back in quick time. He looked anxious as he ran to where Meg was resting.

"What is it Harry?" Meg asked the breathless boy.

"They're back, there are men down there. I counted a handful and they have made a fire. Come on Meg, we must get back."

There was no attempt to hide their tracks now as they scrambled down the slope, shaking showers of snow down as they crashed into trees and bushes. They skirted the thicket of blackthorn and turned back towards the river. Suddenly Harry stopped and signalled Meg to keep low.

"What is it Harry?" she whispered.

Harry was searching the sky. She looked up and saw nothing.

"Did you hear that?" the boy asked.

"It sounded like a buzzard making that mewling call but I can't see it."

"That's no buzzard, Meg. That is Dan the pagan letting us know he is here. I have to answer his call." Harry cupped his hands around his mouth and mimicked the laughter-like call of the green woodpecker.

"We need to go carefully Meg."

"But why, Harry? If Dan is here he must be with the main search party."

"Some other tracker could have found our camp and he might use that same signal, but he didn't acknowledge my return call and that tells me that it was Dan. It's an arrangement we set up together in the autumn, when Dan was teaching me how to leave a trail. He also taught me to take nothing for granted, so we go in carefully."

Moving quickly but stealthily along the route that they had used that morning, they soon came to a point where Harry indicated to his sister that they were to leave the track. He moved to his left, away from the river, and gained the cover of a clump of hazel bushes. A little farther on they discovered that they could look down on a group of men. They were standing where Harry had lit the first fire.

"Look Harry, the tall man, it's Luke Tull and I can see Mal and Bram too."

"Yes, I see them, but where is Dan? Come on, let's get down there." The boy called out, "Hullo, the camp. It's Harry and Meg. We're coming in."

The three men turned as one and then Luke Tull stepped forward and strode to meet the young people, his arms held out to them.

"Harry, Meg, how are you both? We were about to come looking for you. We saw your tracks going up the hill and Dan said that they had been made this morning. Have you discovered anything?"

"Have you found any sign of our children?" Bram, one of the fathers asked. There were tears in his eyes. Before either of them could answer, Harry and Meg heard their names called in a mighty roar. They turned and saw the huge form of Brian running down from their hidden camp. Scrap, the dog, was bounding ahead of his master.

"My son, Sami, have you found him Harry? The big man came down the slope at such a speed that he collided with Mal.

"We are sorry sir, but we have not found any of the children. But we are sure that they came this way. We have found a village over the hill behind us. Meg found a small wooden cross that belonged to our sister, Ruth."

The three distraught fathers rained questions down on the young couple. It was almost impossible for them to reply.

"Hold it right there," roared Luke, "How can Harry or Meg answer your questions with so many talking at once? We will go up to the camp and allow them to tell their story to everyone and in their own time."

Harry and Meg led the way up to their camp. They were surprised to see so many men waiting for them, some of them strangers. And then they saw Dan. The pagan was reclining on a kind of litter and kneeling beside him a young woman. Meg instantly recognised her as Susan, Dan's young wife. Dan pushed himself up into a sitting position and held his hand out to Harry.

"Harry, my boy, so good to see you. You have made very good progress and left me a trail I could have followed in the dark."

"Dan, what are you doing here? You look so ill. Is there anything we can do for you? Meg has her medicine bag with her."

"I'm fine Harry. I'm getting stronger every day, but come and sit by me and tell us what you have found."

"Aye, what have you found?" a ragged chorus asked.

Harry and Meg gave a detailed account of their adventures from the time they arrived at this camp. They told of the village in the next valley and of their visit, once the men had departed, and their discovery of the small wooden cross left by Ruth. Harry described the huts and their condition and how they had found children's footprints in the snow. Meg told them of Harry's premonition and how he had been proven right by the return of five men.

"The hermit, Friar Godwin, told us of your visit. He says you probably saved his life. He told us that there are at least sixteen children in the group."

Luke Tull interjected, "Could you tell if that many children had been in the village?"

"No sir. I saw about a handful of different footprints but the ground in the open area in front of the huts is trodden smooth and is frozen hard."

"Are there any defences to this village?" Luke asked.

"None sir, not even a wall of thorn bushes."

"Will they know of your presence there? Did you leave any tracks?"

"Only if they look at the backs of the huts sir."

"We must assume that they have seen your tracks. I know it's getting dark but I would like to take a look at this village. Will you come with Allen and me and show us your vantage point?"

"Of course sir, but we had better hurry."

Luke Tull gave orders for a meal to be prepared and then called Allen the hunter to bring some weapons and then they set off into the twilight.

When they reached the top of the ridge they could not help but see the village. There was a great blaze coming from a fire in the centre clearing.

"They can't have seen your tracks Harry," Luke said quietly.

"Or they could be trying to draw us down there," Allen suggested.

"Good point Allen. What do you suggest?"

"We keep watch right through the night, two men spaced twenty paces apart with a signal line between them. A thin cord buried in the snow will do."

"That sounds like a good idea. Allen, can I leave you to set up the night watch? I would not use either of the two strangers if I were you."

"No Luke, I don't trust either of them. There is one other thing, you ought to put Harry fully in the picture with what has happened since he and Meg left on their trip. I'll go back to camp and organise the first two sentries."

"Yes of course Allen. We will keep watch until you return with them."

As soon as Allen was on his way, Luke began his narrative.

"Well Harry, Ben's trip to the village in the marshes was both fortuitous and disastrous. They discovered that another party of players had taken six boys and three girls and emptied one of their storehouses in the village. The marsh people had sent men after them, but the storm drove them back and they were only able to guess that they had gone to the great river and then turned north. Ben and his men arrived just after the village party had returned. Both groups of searchers were exhausted. It had been a terrible storm. Ben rested while the storm lasted and then started back with six men of the village who wanted to join our searchers. It was Ben's intention to follow your trail, Harry. They made camp on the night of the first day and were attacked by a gang of robbers. Fortunately the extra six men gave them the advantage. They killed two of the robbers and the rest ran. One of the villagers was killed and another injured. Ben took an arrow in his shoulder and Bernard was stabbed in his thigh. Bernard and the injured villager went back to the village in the marshes, taking the dead man with them. Ben returned home but he was in a bad way. Eliza is doing the best she can. My father sent me with as many men as could be spared, including two strangers who claim to have lost children to the mummers, to follow you into this awful wilderness."

It was almost dark now but the boy could tell from Luke's voice that he was upset by his brother's injury. He decided to change the subject.

"Why did you bring Dan with you? He looks very poorly."

"None of us can track well enough to follow a river laid trail, but Dan had no trouble following you. He must have taught you well, Harry."

The Coracle Boy grinned and said that Dan was a great teacher. And then he asked about all the strangers in the camp, particularly the ones Luke and Allen distrusted.

"There are six people you will not have met." Luke held up his hands and indicated that number. "Four are from the village in the marshes and two walked into our village, claiming that they had lost children too and begged to be allowed to come with us. But their story differs with each telling. They wouldn't go and talk to Friar Godwin, they said they were afraid of the sign of the cross and yet they seemed not to notice the crucifix on the door of our meeting room."

"What are you going to do Luke?"

"Watch them like a hawk, but we have another advantage. They speak our language well enough, but on their own they use a tongue none of us have ever heard before, except for Susan, Dan's wife. She is a pagan like Dan but from different clan. She can understand most of what they say, but so far they have said nothing incriminating. We will have to be vigilant."

"We have sent a messenger to Colonel Richmond at the Westown castle with a detailed account of what has happened. We have requested that soldiers be sent to follow us and help us get our children back. Our fear is that he may not be able to spare any soldiers with all those prisoners rebuilding the bridge. They have to be guarded. We can only hope and pray Harry."

"How did you travel up the river?" Harry asked, "I saw no boats or coracles."

"The Abbot gave us two rowboats. One uses four oarsmen, the other two. Dan insists that we haul them ashore each night and conceal them near the camp."

The soft owl hoot warned them of Allen's return with the first watch. He had brought Mal and a man from the village in the marshes. They quickly set up the shelters for both men and rigged the communication cord between them. They were apprised of their duties and the actions they were to take in a variety of situations.

With the sentries in place, Harry led the way back to camp where a hot meal awaited them. Harry saw that several crude shelters had been erected, mainly pointed branches pushed into the snow and bent over, their tops tied together and covered with animal skins, and each with its own fire. Meg had lowered their coracle and set up the coracle roofed shelter she and Harry had perfected, much to the amusement of some of the men, until they realised just how efficient it would be in a rain storm.

It was totally dark now, heavy cloud obscuring the moon and stars. The wind had risen and warned them of a very cold night ahead. Luke and Allen had set up their shelter so that they would be able to watch the two strangers. They were sure that the pair would act tonight if they were spies.

"I will do a tour of the camp and select the two men to relieve the sentries up on the ridge," Luke said, when everyone had eaten and was settling down for the night.

He first went to speak to Dan and his wife who were sharing their campfire with Harry and Meg. Susan had heard the strangers mention a path along the edge of the river. This suggested that they knew the area, but nothing else that indicated what their intentions might be. He moved down to the next shelter where Mal, Bram and Brian with the dog, Scrap, had set up camp. He discussed the strangers with them.

"We need to split them," Luke said thoughtfully.

"Send one of them with me and Scrap to do the midnight relief. I'll keep a sharp eye on him. Allen can do the next watch with the other stranger," Brian suggested.

"Good idea Brian, but I won't tell them until it's time to change the watch. That way they won't have time to modify any plans they may have made."

Luke wandered over to the next fire where he found the three men from the village in the marshes, he asked them if they were alright. They replied that they were fine and was there anything they could do. They were willing to keep watch if required.

Next, Luke walked across to the two strangers who had built a very strange looking shelter. It was obvious that they were not woodsmen and used to camping out in all weathers. Their fire had burnt low and inside the crude bivouac both men were snoring loudly. Luke smiled and piled more wood on their fire to better illuminate the entrance to their abode. He returned to Harry and Meg's glowing fire and told them what had been planned.

"What do you want me to do, Luke?" Harry asked.

"Get a good night's rest Harry. I have a feeling that we are going to be busy tomorrow."

Chapter Sixteen

Dan, with Susan's help, had set up a timing device using a candle set in a cylinder made of leather. It measured about a hand's span in diameter and about four high. There were two holes in the bottom of the cylinder to allow a free flow of air. The top of the device was left open and a candle was placed in the centre of the tube and lit. The candle was marked in five equal places and when the flame reached a mark it was time to change the sentries. Midnight was the second mark.

Allen was watching the strangers' lodge when Susan came to say that it was time to change the second watch. Allen roused Brian and together they went down to the strangers' hut where Allen shook the man on the right. There was an instant commotion as both men sprang to their feet, each holding a knife. Allen sprang back and narrowly avoided a slash that would have disembowelled him, but he collided with Brian and fell to the ground. The second man lunged at Brian who sidestepped and kicked his assailant in the groin. Allen's attacker was falling on him, the knife raised to strike, but the man hadn't bargained for Scrap who clamped his slavering jaws on the wrist of the knife hand. Allen grabbed the other arm, a sharp twist and a hefty kick and his attacker had a dislocated shoulder. Brian called off the dog and hauled the second man to his feet. By now the whole camp was alerted. Several people came running to the scene. The man with the dislocated shoulder had somehow managed to get to his feet. He turned and ran down the riverbank followed by one of the men from the village in the marshes, but the injured man had no intention of being captured. He jumped off the bank into the deep, swirling water. In moments he was lost in the darkness as the current pulled him to the centre of the river. If he didn't drown he would quickly succumb to the cold.

The sentries up on the ridge would have heard the noisy disturbance. Luke dispatched Brian and one of the marsh men to relieve Bram and his partner.

The remaining stranger was bound hand and foot, made to sit against a tree trunk and was secured to it. Bram and his partner came into the camp to find almost everyone standing by their fires and talking excitedly about the fracas with the two strangers. He was quickly brought up to date with developments. Speculation as to who the strangers were and their purpose in joining the search party was rife, but the general opinion was that they were associates of the men in the next valley. Bram reported that the big fire was still being fed and was still quite a big blaze and he wondered if it was a signal fire to guide night travellers to a rendezvous.

"But who would be travelling on a night such as this?" Luke queried.

"A gang bringing in another group of children," Allen replied, bitterly.

"You mean that those huts down there could be some sort of staging post."

"Yes Luke, the army call them transit camps. If we are going to find our children we have to bide our time and see what happens. If we go charging in we could lose any chance of finding out where they have taken those youngsters."

Eventually everyone went back to their shelters but few slept. Mal and one of the marsh men took the last stint of lookout duty. Then, just as dawn was breaking, Mal's partner came down from the lookout on the ridge. There appeared to be a large party of people moving towards the camp where the fire was still blazing. Luke, Allen, Harry and the sentry went as fast as they could up to the ridge. Mal met them and took them to the best vantage point.

"I've counted ten young 'uns Luke."

"I see no children Mal."

"They herded them into that hut, the end one on the far side. They appear to be preparing food on this side of the fire, but I can't see for the roof of the nearest building. I wish I could get closer."

"How many men are down there?"

"I reckon there be about ten who came with the young 'uns. Then there's the handful that Harry see'd. That'll be fifteen by my reckoning Luke."

"Is that a cart I can see just at the edge of the trees?"

"They got a cart and two sledges pulled by hosses and they got dogs too. I only see'd two but there could be more."

"Where did they come from Mal?" Allen asked, "I can't see a track."

"From the east I reckon Allen," Mal replied shading his eyes against the morning sun. "But darned if I can see any sign of a track. There must be a pass through the mountains."

"Mal, will you and your partner stay here for the time being? I will get food sent up to you." Mal agreed and Luke continued, "We need to call a meeting Allen. There are some difficult decisions to be made."

Back at the camp the meeting was called, the prisoner was secured to a tree well out of earshot and Luke told the gathering what they had seen from the ridge and asked for suggestions. Some wanted to attack the village and rescue the children, but there was little hope of them being among the new arrivals. It appeared that the children from Abe Tull's village and those from the village in the marshes had already passed through this transit camp.

"If we attack now," Allen argued, "We will lose the advantage of surprise. We need to know what lies further up the river. How do they get the children up to the lake? Those rapids look impossible to me."

"The rapids could be two days' march away and it's not possible to see if there is a path up to the lake," someone commented.

"Sir, perhaps they don't go up to the lake," Harry suggested.

"What are you saying Harry?" asked Luke.

"I think the flow in the river is far greater than the amount of water coming down the rapids. The river must turn northwest and go further into the mountains. Why else would they need three large rowing boats? They could walk the children up to the rapids."

"This is all speculation. What are we going to do?" Brian asked angrily.

"I think I should go and see how close to this transit camp I can get," Allen said. "We need a better measure of their strength."

"Sir," Harry addressed Luke. "I would like to go up the river tonight in the coracle and scout the area beyond their camp."

"I don't think I could allow that Harry. Suppose you were caught, you would have to tell your captors about us."

"I would tell them nothing sir," Harry replied hotly.

"I'm sorry Harry, you are just a boy. You are lucky that you weren't caught when you entered that village down there."

"And where would you be now Luke? That boy had the guts to take on the great river and follow the ancient voices."

Everyone turned and saw Dan sitting up on the crude litter. He looked angry.

"The boy is a Christian Dan, not a pagan," Luke replied sharply.

"Now calm down you two," Allen said dispassionately. "You have to admit Harry led us to this place and we have found a group of men with many children with them. Now we don't know who they are or what their business is. We can be fairly sure that they are the kidnappers. Harry has a point. We need to know what we are up against and the more information we have the better chance we have of finding our young 'uns.

"But Allen, I am responsible for everyone in our party."

"Harry and Meg have led the way so far. I think they could be recognised as a separate group, Luke and you should let them scout ahead."

"I don't like it Allen, but if you can gather some information before nightfall, I will make a decision then. Who will you take with you?"

"I go alone and I go now. If I am captured I will say that I am a hunter and I saw the light of their fire last night from the top of that hill to the northeast."

Without further discussion Allen gathered his hunting bow and arrows and his shoulder bag with some food and a few essentials in it. He carried a short sword and a dagger. With a wave of his hand he set off through the crisp snow and was soon out of sight amongst the bushes and scrub that grew on the lower slopes of the ridge.

Luke set up a rota of sentries to keep watch at the top of the ridge. Everyone else was employed gathering firewood, but fires had to be kept as small as possible. Their smoke might be seen by the people in the next valley. Harry was detailed to catch fish. With the lines and traps set, he returned to camp to prepare his coracle in the hope of being able to set off on his reconnaissance trip tonight.

"I am coming with you Harry," Meg stated as if it were a fact.

"Thanks Meg, it is a job for two really," Harry replied, much to Meg's surprise. She had expected an argument.

"We will take my coracle. It will carry two easily," Harry continued. "If you sit on the floor you can watch out for floating debris."

Harry and Meg explained to Dan and Susan the need to replace Harry's coracle with a roof of animal skins. When this was done, Dan imparted some of the pagan lore of gathering intelligence secretly. He stressed that risks were not taken unless it became essential. "There is no point in gathering information if you are captured before you have been able to pass on what you have discovered," Dan said. "There is something else, Harry. What will you tell them if the pagans capture you?"

"The truth. We are looking for our sister and that we are alone."

"Meg is dressed like a boy but she has the voice of a girl. The pagans will separate you if they discover you are brother and sister."

"I shall pretend to be dumb and leave all the talking to Harry," Meg replied.

With the coracle down on the ground they set about selecting what they would need. They would take enough food and water for two days, plus fishing line, two blankets each and a fire making stick. They would take their hunting bows and knives and Meg's medicine pouch, of course.

By late afternoon they were ready. Harry collected a good harvest of fish from the lines and traps he had set and brought his bounty into the camp just as it was getting dark. He and Meg sat down to an excellent meal cooked by Susan.

The meal over, the group sat waiting for Allen's return, Harry and Meg somewhat impatiently at first and then apprehensively. Suddenly they heard the yelping call of a vixen.

"It's a bit early for a vixen to be calling," Dan said, adding, "That'll be Allen and not too far away if I'm not mistaken."

Sure enough Allen came into the camp a short time after. He was tired and breathless. Everyone wanted to know what he had discovered.

"Let the man get his breath back and some hot food in his belly. Can't you see he's near to exhaustion." Luke berated the questioners, but he too looked impatient to hear what Allen had discovered. Susan gave him a beaker of hot blackberry cordial. Allen soon recovered and began his story.

He had travelled east until about midmorning when he came upon the trail of a herd of deer coming from the north. They had been pursued by wolves, the tracks were at least a day old. By noon he had found the road he was sure was used by the cart and sledges, and followed it down until he could see the smoke from the large camp fire.

"I left the road and went into to the trees," Allen continued, "and got to within sight of the group of huts. I could see some of the children standing by the fire. They were all wrapped up so it was difficult to make out if they were boys or girls. I counted eight but they went into the hut. I waited but no other children came out. I tried to get closer but the wood had been coppiced and there was little cover. Their dogs must have got my scent and one of them came after me. He was a big, evil looking hound, half wolf I'd guess. I came to a small river where the water was about waist deep. I waded across and waited in the bushes, but he found me and began to swim across. I had to put an arrow into him and then pull him out and bury him in the snow. We have to hope that they don't look too hard for him." Allen took a drink of the cordial.

"It was late afternoon by now so I started back. I found the road again and because it was easier going I stayed on it. I realised that I was not far from the point where I joined the road this morning. I found the deer herd crossing and then I heard voices. There was little cover close to the point where I had come to the road this morning, but there was a stand of young pine trees on the opposite side and so I followed the deer track through the bracken and small trees. I found a hiding place under a snow covered fir tree, well back from the spoor left by the deer. The travellers were moving quite slowly and I had time to make a small hole through the snow so that I could see who they were." Allen paused and took another drink and emptied the beaker.

"The first thing I saw was a horse's head and then I froze. There were dogs, three of them. They stopped at the deer tracks and began sniffing. Suddenly there was the crack of a whip. A dog howled and all three fled on down the road. The man holding the reins and coiling the whip was standing in the cart. He was tall and well built. In the cart I could make out the heads of at least four children. There could have been more. Another horse came into sight, it was ridden by a youth who also carried a whip. Both horses were in very poor condition. "

"Could they have been our children?" one of men from the village in the marsh asked.

"I don't think so," Allen replied. "The road is heading well north of east."

"What happened next?" another voice enquired.

"I thought that perhaps the owner of the dog I had shot might come looking for his animal, so I decided to plant the idea in his mind that the dog had gone in search of a mate, a female wolf. I followed the deer tracks up the hill and came to a bare, treeless area and a pinnacle of rock. I could see the smoke from their fire but no sign of the cart. I made the call of the wolf a couple of times and then I hightailed it out of there. It was almost dark by this time. I had to make my way back here cautiously. I had concealed my footprints where I had stepped from the virgin snow onto the churned up ground left by the deer. If I missed that point I could have been walking all night."

"Thank God you are back safe and sound Allen," Luke said.

"But it was all a waste of time Luke. I have discovered nothing useful. I have killed a dog needlessly and if they have a good tracker dog they may be able to find us here."

"That's if they suspect that there is anyone this side of the ridge," Brian remarked. "I have been up there with the sentries most of the day. I saw nothing suspicious in their behaviour. One man gathered wood for the fire without an escort. There was a man fishing all alone and out of sight of his colleagues. These are not the actions of men who suspect that they are about to be attacked."

"I have to agree with you Brian," Allen said. "There was no sign of sentries and no defence work at the huts and I did discover one other thing." Allen paused and looked at Harry. "You were right Harry, the river does turn west. The rapids are wide and make a lot of white water but the river that flows from them is nothing like the size of the river beside us. I saw all this from the pinnacle of rock."

"What else did you see Allen?" Luke asked.

"I saw an escarpment the height of ten men that continues on upstream to where the river pours through a narrow gorge with high cliffs on both sides. I could see smoke and several fires from what looked like dwellings at the foot of the escarpment. I would guess that the larger settlement and the mines are beyond that river gorge, probably some way up the river. But it was almost dark and I was eager to get away from there." There was silence for a while and then Harry spoke.

"Meg and I will go upstream and scout the river as far as we can. We may even hide in the forest for a day and come back tomorrow night."

"Now hold on young Harry," Luke said indignantly. "I say who does what and who said anything about taking a girl on such a dangerous foray?"

"Sir, we came alone on this journey to find our sister and the other young 'uns. We will go on alone if we have to." Harry paused, "If we scout ahead and report back you will have a better idea of what to expect."

"The lad's got a point Luke," Brian said and there were mutterings of agreement. "We have no idea what lies ahead of us. Allen speaks of a large village. There could be a hundred men up there.

"Brian is right Luke, and I should have paid more attention to what lay way up the river. There could be a small town up there. If they are mining for gold they would have some sort of armed guard. We need all the information we can get and Harry and Meg are the ones to get it," Allen concluded.

"Perhaps we should wait for the soldiers to get here," Luke replied.

"We don't even know if the soldiers are coming," Dan said.

"Harry and Meg can do this Luke," Allen urged.

Luke was obviously rattled by what he saw as his authority being undermined, and yet he could see the sense of gaining better intelligence before deciding on a course of action. If he was honest with himself, he hadn't the faintest idea what action to take. He thought back to the day when his father had put him in charge of this party. He had said that Allen, Dan and Bram were the best woodsmen and Brian and Mal his two toughest fighters. He should listen to their counsel if he was not sure of a particular course of action. Luke looked at the expectant faces.

"My father told me to listen to the voices of the men he sent with me. You have persuaded me that we need every bit of information that Harry and Meg can pick up. Harry, Meg, you go with our blessings."

"Thank you sir," the Coracle Boy replied.

Chapter Seventeen

It was as dark as it gets when Harry and Meg cast off. Luke, Allen and Brian were there to see them leave. The current was very strong and there were high cliffs on either bank. They kept tight to the eastern bank, which soon became free of vegetation, leaving a smooth rock wall towering up into a cloudy sky. They were thankful for a dark night. There were very few eddying currents, making it very hard work for Harry. Meg used her paddle to fend off floating debris and keep them from hitting the cliff face. The river turned slowly to their right and they lost sight of the torches held by Luke and the rest of the party. Harry sensed that the river was widening and the current was less swift. Their progress improved, trees began to appear and they knew that they were now on the other side of the ridge. Soon they saw the reflection of the flames from the fire at the village in the smooth water up ahead.

Harry made the decision to cross to the other side of the river. He told Meg of his plan and asked her to watch out for ice where the river had frozen because the current was slower. His caution was rewarded. The river was frozen several paces out from the west bank. There were no trees overhanging to give them even a small amount of cover. As they came opposite the village where Meg had found Ruth's tiny crucifix they felt that they would be seen for sure, but no shouts of alarm came across the dark waters. Harry guided the small craft away from the trees and progress improved markedly. It was a bitterly cold night but driving the coracle safely through the water kept them both warm.

Harry decided to explore the west bank. They would have to go ashore at a point where there was plenty of cover. They had agreed with Luke that they would land before the river changed direction and travel northwest to meet up with the river a good distance past the sharp bend. They would scout the forest and the riverbank during the day and return the following night. It all sounded so simple. Never before had the Coracle Boy travelled this far on the river in the dark and he found the experience daunting. Without known landmarks it was difficult to gauge how far they had travelled. Allen had told him that the terrain at the point where they thought the river changed direction rose steeply up from the river and was bare, almost treeless. They would have to land a good distance short of that point and walk through the forest. They passed a point where a stream flowed into the river. Some distance upstream of this confluence they almost ran into what appeared to be an ideal landing place, a flat slab of rock that jutted out into the river. Meg stepped ashore warily in the darkness and took the painter with her. She was about to tie it off when she froze and in a hoarse whisper called "Harry."

Harry silently left the coracle and joined Meg. She took his hand and guided it to where she held the painter. Harry felt the smooth surface of an iron ring and then the roughness of another, thicker rope. His eye followed the line of the thicker rope into the gloom and he faintly saw the stern of another boat. He was sure that it was a dugout canoe. Meg tugged his sleeve and guided his hand to an object by her foot. Harry recognised the woven willow to be a fish trap. They retreated to the coracle and Harry took the craft back downriver to the incoming stream and followed its course. After a short distance their progress was hindered by a huge fallen tree festooned with ivy. They could only just get under it. Beyond the tree they were halted by a waterfall the height of a man. It was so dark here that it took an age to find a safe place to land. Harry was fearful of pulling the coracle clear of the water.

"We can't risk tearing a hole in the coracle Meg. I think that we should wait for some daylight. That bend in the stream should conceal us from the main river."

"We are not far from where we saw that boat Harry. I don't think we can risk a fire."

"I agree. This seems like a good place to hide out until it gets light. We will leave the coracle in the water."

They emptied the small craft of their few possessions and made it secure and camouflaged it with some fronds of ivy. They wrapped their blankets around them and curled up under the fallen tree. Meg soon fell asleep but Harry could only catnap. It was a very cold night. He awoke from one such snooze and wondered what had roused him and then he realised that it was getting light. Dare he leave Meg asleep and go and scout around? No. If she woke, she would be upset by his absence. He would have to wake her. As soon as he touched her shoulder, she was awake and sat up and whispered 'good morning' to her brother. Harry suggested that he should reconnoitre the area. Meg agreed and said she would prepare a cold breakfast for when he got back.

Harry climbed up into the thick ivy and crossed the stream by the big tree. He moved, keeping to the high ground, toward the point where they had seen the boat. His progress was hampered by the tangle of undergrowth. To move without leaving an obvious trail was near impossible. Presently he came to a stand of ash trees and the bramble undergrowth gave way to gentler bracken and to his right he could now see the main river. Cautiously Harry picked his way down through snow covered boulders and leafless trees to reach the cover of an ancient yew tree whose evergreen foliage afforded him good cover. From here the Coracle Boy was looking down onto the flat rock and the moored boat they had seen last night. It was an old dugout canoe and appeared not to have an outrigger. Suddenly Harry smelt wood smoke. He assumed that people would not be far away. He must return to Meg, it had been further than he had expected, his sister would be worried.

Meg was becoming anxious but she had a breakfast of oatcakes and cheese ready. They drank water from the supply they had brought with them. Now that it was light they saw that it was possible to pull the coracle out of the water and carefully manoeuvre it into the space they had slept in. What they couldn't do was hide their tracks.

Harry could do nothing to hide his exploration route. "I just have to hope no one stumbles on my trail," Harry said optimistically.

"What do we do now Harry?"

"I think that we should follow the stream, it should take us to higher ground. We need to be able to look down into the valley."

First they had to climb high enough to get past the waterfall. The fallen tree came to their aid here, its branches forming an irregular ladder that took them well above the stream. From here they looked down on the waterfall and saw stepping stones crossing the stream several paces above the cascade. A snow covered path wound its way through the willow and birch trees. They had to cross over this path without leaving any signs of their presence. Harry reached up and caught hold of an overhanging branch and went hand over hand to drop well clear of the path. Meg followed him.

The climb became almost precipitous, but the rock of the escarpment had many handholds and was not too difficult. At last they crested the cliff face and they were in a beech wood, but still on a steep slope that fortunately had very little undergrowth. The snow under the trees was about a hand's span deep. They agreed to strike up the hill to higher ground. It seemed a long time before the steep climb levelled out. and they were now in a forest of fir trees. Very little snow covered the ground under the evergreen trees and so they decided to follow the contour they were on. Harry estimated that it was midmorning and suggested a rest. They took a drink of water and chewed some dried beef.

"We need to start to find out what is going on down in the valley. I think I ought to climb a tree and take a look."

"Do you think we should move down the hill to where there are no leaves on the trees Harry?"

"I would rather keep out of the snow for a while longer Meg."

They emerged onto a steep, treeless, boulder strewn mountainside and they could see right down to what looked like a high cliff dropping down to the river. They had travelled to a point where they were looking down on the narrowest part of the gorge. There appeared to be no habitation on their side of the river, the south side, but on the north bank there was quite a large village with smoke rising from almost every chimney. A few people moved between the thatched buildings and there were two rowing boats on the river below the gorge, they appeared to be fishing. Only one boat was moored at a quay above the narrow gap in the escarpment, close to a loading derrick. The black lines in the snow indicated wheel ruts, the telltale sign of a road leading west from the quay. This was confirmed moments later when a cart was seen travelling west, drawn by a large draught horse.

The village was built on a wide strip of land, high above the quay, accessed by a zigzag staircase cut into the rock. Behind the village the mountain rose almost vertically. Most of the buildings appeared to be constructed of stone with thatched roofs. The forest gave them only a limited view and Harry decided to move down the slope to be able to see further up the valley. Keeping to the edge of the fir trees, they went down until they could see more buildings and more activity, and then high up the opposite mountain and almost on a level with them they saw a great scar in the side of the hill. As they watched they saw something like a small cart emerge from a cave, pushed by a man. It travelled a short distance before it discharged its contents down the scar.

"That must be the gold mine we have heard about Meg. That is where they tip the rubble, but how do they get up there? I can't see a road."

"More important Harry, where are the children?"

"We have to get closer."

"But Harry, it must be midday and we should think about getting back while we can still see. We'll never find our way in the dark, especially down that cliff."

Harry was torn between the longing to know more about this mysterious place and the need to get back to report what they had found. Common sense prevailed. "You are right Meg, we will have a short rest and some food and then start back. Let's move back to where we came out of the pine trees."

As they turned and looked up they saw the gaping mouth of a cave.

"How did we miss that?" whispered Meg and they both ducked behind a large boulder.

"I think it's a disused mine and this rubble is the waste. There can't be anyone up there, they would have seen us. Come on, let's make for those trees and get closer."

"Is that wise, Harry? I think we should get back," Meg said nervously.

Suddenly something happened that changed everything. As Harry took one last look at the yawning hole in the mountain, he saw a slight movement. He looked away and without a word to Meg they moved across to the cover of the trees. From here they could not see the mine entrance, if it was a mine. Harry told Meg what he thought he had seen. "I am sure that it was a child Meg. If he has been watching us, he could tell others. I would like to know who he is, but dare we risk it?"

"But we can't just leave him Harry."

"You are right Meg, let's move up to where we came out of the pine forest and stop for some food."

They followed their trail and Harry selected a place to sit so that Meg was visible from the cave, but Harry would be out of sight. He would be able to slip away unseen and go up to see who their observer was. Meg made a light meal of bread and cheese and sat with her back to the cave and, from time to time, made gestures to suggest that she was talking to Harry. Meanwhile Harry had crept back into the trees and up until he was just higher than the mouth of the cave. He was looking down on a flat area like a wide road that led back into the trees, but it was overgrown. It hadn't been used for ages.

At first Harry saw nothing and was about to step out into the open when there was a slight movement. He saw a small head rise up and then a hand reached out and pushed the small head down and then he saw a foot move as the body of a small boy emerged. He was pushing himself back on his stomach. A moment later a slightly larger boy moved back in a similar fashion. They then both rolled to the entrance to the cave and stood up. The bigger boy appeared to be about ten years old, the other boy a year or so younger. They were both pale and malnourished. Their clothes were in tatters and they were very grubby.

Harry was in a quandary. If he stepped out, would the children run? They didn't look as if they could run far. Or he could speak to them from the darkness of the trees. He decided to speak to them from where he stood.

"Hullo there. My name is Harry and that is my sister, Meg, down there. Can we help you?" Both boys swung round and stared in the direction of the voice. The younger boy clung to his friend who looked this way and that and then took a step towards the darkness of the cave.

"We are friends. We're looking for our little sister. She was taken away by bad men. Have you seen a little girl with fair hair?" Still the two boys stood transfixed.

"Can I step out so that you can see? I mean you no harm. Perhaps I can help."

Harry got no reply and so decided to move a little closer, but only a couple of paces brought him just visible to the boys.

"My sister has some food, we would like to share it with you." Harry saw the younger boy look up at his companion and say something, Harry took another pace forward.

"It's only bread and cheese but you are welcome."

"We ain't goin' back," the older boy said defiantly.

"We won't take you back. Can I come closer? I don't want anyone to hear us." The older boy nodded. Harry went warily down the slope and stopped at the level roadway.

"My name is Harry and my sister is Meg. What's your name?"

"I am Hal, he's Ted. We are runaways. You ain't goin' to take us back down there. Are you runaways? Have you really got somethin' to eat? We ain't had a bite of food for days."

"Hullo Hal. Hello Ted. If you follow me we will go and see what Meg has got for dinner." The younger boy, Ted, stepped forward but was held back by Hal who went back into the cave. A few seconds later he came out again carrying a bundle of what looked like sailcloth, but it was too dirty to be sure what it was.

Harry went back into the cover of the trees and waited for the two young 'uns to join him. He looked back, a whispered conversation was taking place. Harry waited patiently and then the boys advanced warily. Harry turned and went slowly down the slope. He saw Meg through the branches, she had left her seat in the open and as he met her he saw that she had an anxious frown.

"I was just about to come looking for you Harry. Was there anyone up there? I couldn't make out what was happening."

"We have two new friends Meg. They are a little way behind and they are frightened and very hungry." The boys came into view and Meg gasped.

"Have you got some food? He said you would give us some food," Hal said.

"Of course you shall have something to eat boys." Meg took off her shoulder bag and soon had bread and cheese and an oat cake, each spread with the last of the butter. The boys attacked the meal like ravening dogs and Meg had to tell them to take their time. When they had eaten, a decision had to be made. They had to move soon if they were to beat the darkness. They must have light if they were to launch the coracle safely.

"We have to think this through Meg," Harry said. "Can we risk travelling at night with two passengers?"

"What else can we do?" Meg asked, "Unless you take the boys down and come back for me."

"No Meg, never. I will not do that, we stick together."

"But will the coracle carry all four of us?"

"The young un's are nothing but skin and bone Meg. No, it's not their weight, it's how will they react to travelling in a coracle. If one of them panics they could drown all of us. We had better talk to them and we should start back now and talk as we move along."

"Hal, we have to talk. What do you want to do? We are going back to our friends who are also looking for their children. We will be going down the river in a coracle at night. Do you know what a coracle is?" Hal nodded. Harry went on thoughtfully, "Is Ted your brother?" Hal shook his head. "Do you think he would travel in a coracle?"

"My dad's got a coracle an' he lets me ride in it," Ted piped up. He was smiling now, but Hal was still very cautious.

"Well, what's your answer Hal? Do you want to stop here or come with us? We have to know now and we have to be back at the coracle before dark."

Hal looked down at Ted and then at Meg and finally at Harry.

"We'll come with you," he said firmly.

"Then let's get started." Harry set a steady pace. He would have preferred to go faster but the two boys looked so weak. Despite this they kept up remarkably well and they arrived at the coracle well before it was dark. They made a cautious approach but none of the warning traps that Coracle Boy had set had been sprung. All communication was conducted in whispers now, something that appeared to be second nature to the boys.

The boys were given a blanket each. They were to lie under the thwarts in the bottom of the coracle with their feet pointing to the front. Meg would sit on the front thwart, keeping their path through the water clear. Harry would sit on the rear thwart to use his paddle as a rudder. Propulsion would not be a problem as the river would carry then down at the speed of the current. It was dark now but they waited and rested a while longer and ate the last of their food, much to the boy's delight. It was as dark as it gets when they squeezed under the fallen tree and ventured out towards the main river. Harry guessed that it was well before midnight. A light wind was coming from the north and would be behind them. He felt a few flakes of snow and hoped that it would not get worse.

Chapter Eighteen

Silently they let the current of the small stream carry them down to its confluence with the main river. Harry held the coracle back and approached the merging with the faster flowing river with extreme caution. He had no wish to bump into some late returning fisherman, or collide with a floating obstacle. Although travelling downstream was less dangerous and much quicker than the hard work of paddling the coracle upstream, nonetheless, Harry had to concentrate very hard to keep them safe. The Coracle Boy was in his element as he kept the flimsy vessel in the middle of the river. Meg decided to kneel in the bow with her paddle, ready to fend off anything that threatened their safety. The two young fugitives behaved like seasoned coracle travellers. They spoke in whispers to each other but neither addressed Harry or Meg.

Harry began to worry about their speed. They would be at the village where the big fire would illuminate their passing before the men had retired for the night. Harry guided the small craft into the west bank and found a stretch of calmer water with an overhanging willow tree. Meg looked back at her brother.

"We need to talk," he said, reaching up to hold a branch that brought them to a halt.

"What is it Harry?" There was concern in Meg's voice. Hal too looked up. Ted was fast asleep.

"We shall be at the village soon and their fire will give us away. We can either land here and wait or camouflage the coracle."

"We can't sit about in this cold Harry and we can't light a fire," Meg replied.

"Then keep the boat steady while I break off some of these branches."

Harry gathered an armful of willow and alder and some dead bracken from the riverbank and fashioned a crude screen down the left hand side and across the stern. Satisfied that the coracle was as disguised as he could make it, Harry moved off but kept closer to the west bank now.

It began to snow more heavily now and the wind increased a little. Soon Harry could see a thick coat of snow covering Meg's head and shoulders and the visibility was down to a few paces. He felt both boys move and told them to keep as still as possible. Ted said that the snow was falling on him and it woke him up. He was pulling the blanket to cover his face.

Harry realised that the snow was collecting on the camouflage screen and was beginning to affect the balance and handling of the coracle. He told Meg of the problem and asked them all to keep very still as he removed the branches. It was a risky operation. He had to rely on Meg to keep the coracle in the centre of the flow and also prevent the flimsy craft from spinning. With the foliage and bracken removed, Harry took control again. He realised that the visibility had reduced to less than a single pace. They were travelling blind and very fast. Could he risk going close to the riverbank to take advantage of the eddying to slow him down?

At that moment Meg turned to look over her shoulder. He read her concern and said that he was heading for the east bank. Gently he eased the coracle away from the middle of the river and felt the small craft twitch as it was caught by the first backing current. The tendency was for the coracle to spin in these conditions and it took some determined paddle work to avoid the many small whirlpools. It took time for the effect of the backing currents to slow their mad rush downriver and there was the added danger of driftwood being drawn into their path by the same swirling surge of water. Eventually the speed reduced to a more manageable level, but Harry was discovering that going downstream in these conditions was almost as strenuous as paddling upstream.

The Coracle Boy became aware of a glow ahead. He fought to reduce their speed. Meg had seen it too and looked back at her brother. He saw the alarm in her eyes. They were at the village and they still had a big fire burning. They were too close to the east bank and it was too late to try to get across to the west bank. Harry swung the coracle towards the middle of the river and then turned into the flow, he was still too close to the east bank. He had to hope that no one would be out in a snow fall this heavy. He was also aware that they were nearing their destination and he felt the thrill of returning home. But first they would encounter the fast flowing current where the river narrowed. They would have to stay tight to the east bank. Even so, Harry was sure that they would be swept way past the marker torch that Luke said he would keep burning by the landing place, but first he had to get past the village.

'They must have a huge fire burning tonight,' Harry thought as he drew close. By now he was opposite the glow and could make out the riverbank, but there was no sign of anyone. As soon as he could, Harry brought the coracle close to the wooded east bank and began to look out for the vertical rock cliffs. He saw the cliff face and felt their speed increase at the same time.

He didn't have to tell Meg what to do. She already had her paddle aimed at the rock face as they were swept along with the racing current at an alarming speed. They rounded the left hand bend but the current pulled them towards the centre of the river and the danger of submerged boulders. Harry had to fight hard to keep clear of that fearsome middle current that seemed to be racing past them. Meg shouted something and pointed ahead. Harry saw the glow of the torch but they were going too fast. The Coracle Boy decided to overshoot and paddle back upstream. As they passed, they saw a lone figure jump to his feet and shout something. Gradually Harry got the coracle under control and realised that he was just below the fallen tree. The excitement of being almost there gave him a new surge of energy. Meg turned and smiled and then looked back upstream into the blinding snow. She used her paddle to fend off the branches of the fallen tree. Soon the glow of the torch came into view. Two hooded figures stood waving. Now they could hear their voices. As they drew near, Meg held out her paddle which was gripped by one of the figures. Another grabbed hold of the edge of the coracle. Meg stood up and stepped onto the riverbank and let go of the paddle. The hooded man pushed back his headgear to reveal a grinning Allen. The two children sat up in the bottom of the coracle. Harry stepped ashore and then turned to help first Ted, and then Hal, out of the boat.

"The children, Harry, are they ours?" Allen enquired as he pulled his hood up against the driving snow. Harry and Meg were wrapping a blanket around each child.

"No Allen. Perhaps someone could go up and warn the others. We don't want to raise anyone's hopes," the Coracle Boy replied.

"I'll go." The other figure had been holding the coracle and as he stood up they saw that it was Mal. "I was hoping the little lad was my son. Have you seen any of our children Harry."

"No. I'm sorry Mal."

"Aye, well, we'll just have to keep lookin'. I'll go and tell the others and send a couple of men down to carry the coracle."

"Can we pull the coracle up clear of the water?" Allen helped Harry lift the small craft up onto the deepening snow. Hal and Ted clung to Meg as she waited for Harry and Allen. Harry picked up young Ted but Hal declined Allen's offer to carry him. He strode manfully forward.

The camp had changed considerably during their absence. A tall screen of branches had been erected to form a lean-to in a semicircle and now there was only one big fire. Mal had warned everyone of the Coracle Boy's return and that the two children they had with them were not theirs. By the time they reached the group, everyone was out of their shelter to greet them. Luke shook Harry's hand and kissed Meg's cheek, and then turned his attention to the children who were doing their best to hide behind Meg, away from these inquisitive people.

"Now, who are these two young gentlemen?" Luke asked in a kindly voice, but both boys clung tightly to Meg.

"Hal is the big boy and this is Ted. They are very tired and hungry. They have been on the run for over a week now. Perhaps the questions could wait until tomorrow morning Luke?" Meg suggested.

"Of course, and you and Harry must be exhausted too. Alright, everyone back to your beds, we will get the full story in the morning."

The four travellers enjoyed a meal of hot broth and bread before they settled down for the night. The two boys curled up in clean blankets between Harry and Meg. They slept long and late.

Chapter Nineteen

Meg was up first, quickly followed by Harry. They roused the boys and after their ablutions sat down to a freshly cooked breakfast. The huntsmen had been busy, judging by the carcasses that hung from the branches; two deer and one small wild pig, out of the reach of wild animals.

Dan was taking some exercise with the aid of a stick and leaning on Susan's shoulder, but it was only a few paces. He still looked very ill as he sat down on his bed, he spoke to Harry.

"Have you noticed that we are a man short Harry?"

The Coracle Boy looked about and then turned to Dan and asked what had happened to the prisoner.

"He escaped the night you left." Dan wore a wry grin as he went on, "One of the men from the village in the marshes saw that his shelter was empty and raised the alarm. Allen and Brian ran down to the boats just as the man pushed the smaller boat into the water. He saw Brian and the dog and panicked. He jumped into the boat without taking a pair of oars with him. He reached up and caught hold of an overhanging branch, but the current was too strong and took the boat from under him. The branch broke and we lost both boat and prisoner."

"How did he get free?" Harry asked.

"I reckon he had a blade hidden in his footwear or his leggings," Dan replied.

Luke and Allen came back after inspecting the guards up on the ridge. They said that the snow was much deeper down at the village.

"We are protected by the ridge," Luke explained. "But down there it appears to be waist deep on the men. What must it be like for the children?"

"Did you see any of the children?" Meg asked.

"No, but the men are dismantling the hut nearest to us and using the wood and thatch on their fire. Bram thinks that the weight of snow may have brought the roof down."

"I think Bram may be right Luke," Harry said. "That first hut was in a very poor condition, the roof was damaged on the front corner and there were holes in the walls."

"Well, it gives us a better view of the entrance to the hut where the children are held. Talking of children Harry, when can I question the two boys?"

"They are very timid Luke. What Meg and I suggest is that we tell our story first. The boys can listen and perhaps they will join in if we get it wrong."

"Can we all listen?" Allen asked.

"Yes of course, and if the two boys sit between Meg and me they may feel less self-conscious." Harry went on to propose that they all sat in a circle round the fire.

Harry and Meg gave a detailed account of their trip up the river in the dark and of their night under the fallen tree. They described their walk up to a higher level to be able to look down into the valley. They described the buildings they had seen and the boats on the river and the road from the quay and the vertical cliff that formed both banks of the river. They told of the rubbish tip outside what they took to be the entrance to a mine. Harry described how they had found the two boys spying on them from the mouth of an abandoned mine and how little conversation they had had with the boys. Meg told of Hal and Ted's bravery during the trip downriver in a dreadful snowstorm. She added that they too were eager to hear Hal and Ted's story.

Coaxing the story of their abduction and their subsequent incarceration at the mine took time and patience, something that Luke seemed to lack as he fired questions at the boys until Ted started to cry. Allen suggested that they take a break, during which he advised Luke to let the children tell the story in their own time.

It transpired that Hal and his older brother were sold to the gold miners when their parents died two years ago. These people called themselves 'Cordlanders' and operated two mines in the mountains. One of the mines Harry and Meg had seen. The other was some distance upriver and was much bigger. Hal didn't know how many children worked in the mines, but he had heard that it was over fifty. Gradually they pieced together Hal's story. Only boys worked in the mines. The girls were taken to the coast to be sold as slaves. This revelation brought a cry of pain from Meg. Harry turned and put his arm around his sobbing sister.

Hal had heard that most of the girls went to work in the houses of the rich people. Normally the boys were bought at the slave markets, but there had been a massive rock fall in the small mine and a lot of the men and children had been killed. Replacements could not be brought in from the coastal towns in the north because the pass over the mountains was blocked for most of the winter. It was decided to get young miners from the south and east and so the kidnapping scheme was adopted.

It was during their transfer to the small mine that Hal, Ted and another older boy called Fin had escaped and found their way down to the river. When they heard the baying of the hounds, they knew that the dogs were after them. They stole a dugout canoe but Fin was hit by an arrow and fell into the water taking the paddle with him. The two youngsters were carried by the current towards the opposite bank of the river and then it started to snow and that probably saved their lives. They drifted for a while until the canoe became part of a raft of river flotsam that was caught behind a logjam close to the south bank. Before it became dark, they were able to climb over the floating mass and reach the riverbank. They brought a length of sail cloth and a fishing line from the canoe and the ragged clothes they stood up in and that is all they had. Jon, Hal's brother, was still working in the large mine. Ted had been enslaved for almost a year. He was taken away with several other boys. He quickly teamed up with Fin and Hal because they came from the same village.

Ted had been sold by his stepmother when his father was sent to prison, he didn't know why his father was in gaol. Both Hal and Ted knew how to count and Ted could read and write. His father had been a shopkeeper and had taught the boy from an early age.

Hal and his brother had been planning their escape for a long time. They had accidentally broken into an old, earlier tunnel, which Jon explored and found a way out into dense forest. They planned to wait for the spring. In the meantime they would collect all the tools, rope and extra clothing. Food was going to be difficult. There was so little of it, they would have to steal what they could nearer their departure date. They stored their booty in the old mine workings. They had accumulated probably more than they could carry. They had decided to tell nobody, because down there, anyone would betray you for an extra crust of bread to go with the watery soup they called a meal. The boys concealed the access to the old mine workings by making it look as if a collapse had taken place and they had shored up the side of their tunnel. Two of the horizontal poling boards could be slid out to give them access to their escape route and could be slid back into place once they had passed through.

The splitting up of the two brothers was done without prior notice. They barely had time to say goodbye, but it had always been agreed that if either of them saw an opportunity to escape they would take it. What they would do with this freedom they weren't sure. Jon had said that they would live in the forest, wild and free, and never go underground again. Hal's experience of freedom so far had been near disastrous, until Harry and Meg met up with them.

"You ain't going to take us back are you?" Hal asked anxiously.

"No Hal, we'll not take you back to the mine, but what we need to know is what has happened to our children. Did you see any new arrivals?"

"No, but we heard that some new kids were coming. They are still down at the sawmill. They have to cut timber into lengths in the saw pit for props to hold the roof up and poling boards for the sides and roof. Jon and me had to clean out the stables one day. There were six horses, the biggest horses I have ever seen. We were there for about a week before they took us down the mine."

"Do the girls have to work in the sawmill too?"

"No. They stay in the village and live in the long house, a big, long hut, until the pass through the mountains opens in the spring. They will go out when the soldiers come to collect the gold."

There were sighs of relief that the children were not yet in the mine, but freeing them was another matter.

"We are trying to think of a way to free all the boys at the mine Hal, and rescue the girls before they are transported to the coast. Do you know how long it takes to reach the coast?"

"I think it is a whole moon's journey. I heard one of the soldiers say that is how long it took him to get home. I supposed that he lived at the coast."

"We need to know more about the numbers of men employed up there. Can you help us?" Allen asked the boy.

"I'll try sir. I know that there are more than twenty soldiers at the big mine and there are four overseers. I don't know how many miners or how many people live in the village by the river. A few of the miners have families living in huts in the woods near the big mine, about ten I think."

"I think that we should give the boys a rest Luke," Meg suggested.

"Yes, of course Meg and it's time to change the sentries. But if the boys think of anything else let me know." Luke made it plain that he thought Meg was the best custodian of the boys.

It was shortly after Luke and Allen had left that Harry and the boys were making a snow wall at the end on the lean-to. Harry laughed and said that the pile of snow looked like the mountain they had climbed yesterday.

"Look, here's the old mine entrance and down there, where that stick of wood is, that's the riverbank." Harry put another stick to indicate the north bank of the river. Ted found some bits of tree bark and used them to represent buildings on the north side of the river.

Harry became aware of Dan standing unsteadily behind him.

"What are you doing Harry?" the pagan asked.

"I'm showing the boys the mountain where we found them."

Susan and Meg joined them. Meg recognised the scene almost immediately. "Harry, that's our mountain. Pile some more snow down here to show where the stream and the fallen tree are."

"Hold on," Dan said thoughtfully. "You need more room. Start again over there. Susan, get me something to sit on and a blanket. I saw Richard, our leader, do this with sand to show the officers what our patrol had discovered."

Harry had caught on to the idea and started to shape the snowdrift with his coracle paddle. Meg and the boys gathered sticks to represent the banks of the river. They packed the snow round to the south and marked their route with bits of bark. They used duck feathers to show the stream and a twig to represent the fallen tree. They stood back to admire their work and Dan asked the boys if they could remember what the land looked like further upstream.

"The river goes up there and there is a branch off." Hal pointed deeper into the snowdrift. "The bridge over the stream leads to the pass. The track before the bridge follows the stream up to the big mine and the soldiers camp.

"I'm not sure I follow you Hal. Perhaps we should dig further into the drift Harry," Dan said.

Harry was already cutting into the packed snow by this point and attracting quite an audience, some wanting to help. But Dan insisted that they let Harry get on with it, Hal and Ted directing Harry where to dig and where to pile up more snow. After all, they had looked down on the scene for the best part of a week. The snow was piled up waist high and the model looked very impressive. Dan wanted to know what lay downstream of the village.

"Don't know sir. There ain't no road 'cos the river goes between cliffs."

Hal didn't know how the children from the south got into the village, he guessed that they came in by boat.

"That explains the three rowing boats just over the hill," Harry exclaimed.

Moments later Luke and Allen returned. They were astounded at the sculpture that greeted them. "This is excellent," was all Luke could say.

"We need more detail," added Allen. "Particularly on the sharp bend in the river, and the flow of the river between those cliffs, it could be dangerously swift through there."

"What do you suggest Allen?"

"I need to do a proper reconnaissance. Will you take me up there Harry?"

"Yes, when would you want to go?"

"Tonight, if you are recovered enough from your first trip."

"Hold on Allen, I think we should discuss this," Luke said irritably.

"Of course Luke, the decision has to be yours, but you have to agree we need to know if there is any point in us attacking them. If we are outnumbered we could only make things worse. And that current between the cliffs could make it impossible to row through."

"If it's not possible to row though the gorge, how else do they get the children up there?"

"They could land downstream of the gorge and walk them over the hill."

"You are determined to do this Allen, whatever I say."

"No Luke, I take my orders from you. All I ask is that you give the plan serious consideration."

"I think you and Harry should get some rest. We'll talk later."

Allen took that to be a tentative 'yes' to his plan. He told Harry to get some sleep and be ready to leave soon after dark.

Meg was not happy that Harry and Allen were going back upriver. The coracle would not carry three safely. She would have to stay behind, but she saw the value of the mission and reluctantly agreed.

It was quite dark when the changeover of the sentries took place. They reported very little activity down in the village. They had seen several children at various times. It was still difficult to know just how many there were down there. The only other operation appeared to be wood gathering for the fire. No attempt had been made to dig a path to the riverbank, they seemed content to wait for the thaw.

Chapter Twenty

As soon as the evening meal was over, Harry and Allen took to the water waved off by Meg, Luke and Brian. Meg shed a few tears, she would dearly have liked to have joined her brother on the journey. Harry felt the difference in the handling of the coracle with the heavier passenger. Allen chose to sit in the bottom of the coracle, facing Harry, whilst holding onto the sides. It was obvious that he was a reluctant passenger, unlike Meg, who contributed much to the progress.

As they reached the smooth water and saw the reflection of the village fire on the water, the Coracle Boy dared not risk crossing to the west bank with this heavier passenger. He would have to risk setting a course that would take them within sight of anyone looking from the village towards the river. Keeping tight under the riverbank Harry flexed his paddle and took them past the path down to the river, past the rowing boats hauled up on the bank that now gave them cover from prying eyes. They made it past the village without challenge. Even though there was no headwind they made very slow progress. It was almost dawn and Harry was near exhaustion when he found the stream and took them up to the fallen tree. Landing their supplies they bedded down for a very short sleep.

They woke to a sunny morning and after a cold breakfast pulled the coracle up into its hiding place. Allen suggested that they stay with the river and walk towards the sharp bend in the river. They had hardly crossed the fallen tree when they smelt wood smoke. The huntsman indicated that they should move up the hill and circumvent the source of the telltale odour. They found a not too difficult climb up the escarpment and emerged into an area of scrubland, mainly gorse in full bloom.

A clearing of bare rock and scree barred their way. They would be ill-advised to step out into the open here, there was no cover and they could see the river. Anyone down there would see them and so, keeping to the cover, they climbed up further until bushes of gorse and broom covered the bare slope. From the bushes at the top of the clearing they could see the source of the smoke that carried a strong, pungent odour. A round, stone built hut with a conical planked roof, with a hole at the apex that allowed smoke to escape. A smaller hut was close by.

"That looks like a smokehouse Allen. They must be smoking fish."

"I'm sure they are, I can't see anyone down there," the huntsman replied.

"They are usually run by a family, a man and his wife and children. Look, the dugout canoe is still moored at the flat rock," the Coracle Boy said.

"That is worth remembering," Allen replied. "We may need to borrow it if things turn awkward."

They reached the other side of the scree slope and went back into the trees, but the wooded area was getting thinner and the whole of the mountainside below them was bare again. But now they could see the sharp bend of the river. They saw several rowing boats on the far bank upstream of the river coming down from the lake, which they could now see clearly was much smaller than they had expected. They continued along the same contour that took then round the bend until they could see the vertical cliffs where the river cut through the mountain. They couldn't actually see into the gorge, but Allen was sure that to get to the village by this route would be impossible for children. There was a collection of several huts just downstream of the gorge.

To get far enough down the mountain to be able to see upriver to the village beyond would mean venturing out into the open. They agreed to continue their climb up the mountain and hope to find the trail that Harry and Meg made. The trees were very sparse here, which caused them to follow an erratic course until they saw the wide band of boulders.

"This must be where Meg and I were able to look down on the village. We ought to move up higher for better cover Allen." The huntsman agreed.

They found the spot where Meg and Harry had stopped for their meal and noted the smaller mine and memorised all they could. Further up they inspected the abandoned mine. They stopped and ate a meal. From here they could see how far the village extended downstream. The last building, which had its stone gable end facing them, was at the foot of the mountain through which the gorge flowed. At this distance it was not possible to gauge the rate of flow between the cliffs, but it looked impressive. Outside another building they saw piles of logs, this was probably the saw pit. A large building built of stone stood against the vertical cliff. It was a rather sinister building. They saw the zigzag steps down to the quay and the pole derrick with a barge tied up nearby.

"We should follow this track through those pine trees Harry. We might be able to see the second gold mine."

It was obviously a man-made track. It descended at an even gradient for quite a distance and then it turned back in a hairpin bend. Allen decided that it would be wise to leave the track and continue forward into the forest.

After a while Harry reminded Allen that they must be back at the coracle before it became dark. Allen looked at the sky through the trees and said they had a little while yet. Soon they came to a rocky bluff and had to climb higher. At the top they saw a narrow ridge of mountain with a valley on either side and they saw the river that joined the main river coming out of the first valley and the small stream coming out of the second valley. It was in this second valley they saw what they were sure was the big mine where the boys had worked. They could also see the roof of a long building. A flagpole held a motionless flag and uniformed men were lined up as if at drill. Allen counted ten men. There was very little activity elsewhere. The small mine was now clearly visible on their right. Two men could be seen moving about.

"It's time to get out of here Harry; we need to report back to Luke."

The journey back to the coracle was done at a trot. Allen was concerned that the regular use of the route through the pines was creating quite a path and the short section through the snow could be seen from quite a distance. As they drew nearer to the place where the coracle was hidden beneath the fallen tree they exercised extreme caution. They both drew their swords, Allen whispered that he would go first. The Coracle Boy followed keeping Allen just in sight, difficult now that it was getting dark. Their hiding place had not been disturbed and so they launched the coracle in the fading light before settling down to another cold meal and a rest.

There was no wind blowing that night and the frost was not so severe. Allen suggested that a thaw might be on the way. They set off cautiously down the small stream and out into the great river. There were moments of pale moonlight from a waxing moon that appeared through the breaks in the cloud. The improved illumination meant that they made excellent time and arrived quite unexpectedly at the village where the children were being held. Harry had to pull hard for the west bank to keep away from the big fire that was blazing even brighter on this night. He saw that a path had been dug right down to the river's edge. They passed the village without being challenged and headed for the swiftest part of their journey. Harry wished that Meg was with him to use her paddle to fend off the debris and keep them away from the cliff face. It was wiser to head for midstream.

The ferocious current hurled them downriver at the most alarming speed. They swept through the narrow gorge and past the torch that marked their landing place. Allen was clearly shaken by the impetus of their headlong dash past the landing place. Harry saw the alarm in Allen's face, he told his frightened companion that he would have to go further downstream to find calmer water. Getting out of the grip of the strong current in the centre of the river was proving difficult for the Coracle Boy, but gradually he coaxed the small craft away from the powerful hold of the swirling water. By now they had been driven way downriver and it was quite a long haul back up to the landing place. Brian and his dog, Scrap, were waiting anxiously at the torch. They had seen something go by way out in the middle of the river, which Brian had dismissed it as floating debris. Scrap's reaction however, made Brian sure that it was a coracle and his wagging tail suggested he knew the occupants.

"I was about to alert the camp when I saw you coming up alongside the riverbank. Here let me help," Brian said as he grabbed the side of the coracle.

Allen seemed to be frozen to the bottom of the tiny boat, his gloved hands gripping the sides as if afraid to let go. Harry stepped ashore with the painter. Allen, helped by Brian, stood on the bank and gradually forced a smile.

"I have never been so frightened in all my life, I thought we were going to drown Brian, I really did. And yet when I looked at Harry I saw that he was enjoying the ride. The way he handles that coracle, he must be the best on this or any other river."

Harry looked embarrassed and asked Brian to help him lift the coracle from the water. "You and Allen get up to the camp and a hot meal. I'll deal with the boat."

Brian shouldered the coracle and followed the adventurers up to the camp. Meg ran to meet them, relief and happiness her dominant emotions. Others soon joined them as the commotion roused them from their sleep.

It was not far off dawn. Luke came from his shelter to greet them, eager to know what they had discovered. "Just one question," Luke said loudly, "And then we must let our wandering friends get warm and a hot meal in their bellies and then they must rest. Allen, have you seen any of our children?"

"No, I am sorry. We saw no children, but we can add considerably to the model of the mountain that Harry and Dan made."

"Then get some rest, we will talk in the morning." Luke turned and told the onlookers to return to their beds. They would hear the full story later.

Chapter Twenty One

At about midday, Harry, Allen and Dan went back to the model of the gold miners' village and extended it to show all that they knew of the area. Luke was really impressed. "I wish we could take this back to my father. He would know what to do." Luke said wistfully.

"I have been thinking," Harry said, "I think I know how they get the children into the village."

"I have been pondering that one too Harry," Luke replied. "I think they walk them from the flat rock where you saw the dugout canoe, over the hill and lower them down the cliff here and into boats upstream of the gorge," he indicated the various points on the model with a stick.

"We saw no sign of a track over the mountain or any device for lowering them into boats Luke, but of course we haven't examined the area thoroughly and we could easily have missed a lot of important information."

"Could they have dug a tunnel through the mountain on the north bank? After all, they are miners," Mal suggested.

"We saw no sign of a track leading to or from a tunnel Mal, but it is possible. As I have already said we could have missed a lot of things. What was your idea Harry?"

"Well, I think they float a cable down from the village, fix the cable to a boat and then use the draught horses in the village to tow the boat through the gorge. Why else would they need six heavy horses? Hal says that they are not used in the mines, there is not enough headroom."

There was total silence for a moment and then Brian clapped Harry on the back and roared with laughter.

"The lad's a brainbox and no mistake, of course that is how they do it," he said, laughing and ruffling the Coracle Boy's hair.

"The lad's got a point, Luke," said Allen thoughtfully. "We saw timber outside the last hut in the village. They probably harvest the trees from the forest in the flat area between the river and the mountains. They must pull them through the gorge in the same way and I'll wager the last hut houses the sawpit. If we could get that far, I'm sure we would find our boys in there and the girls in the village above the gorge."

"Hold on Allen," Luke said authoritatively. "I have been taking stock of our situation. We have enough meat to see us supplied for months, but we have little or no flour, enough oatmeal for about two days and precious little else. With only nine fit, fighting men what chance do we have against what might turn out to be an army of a hundred men?"

"He's right Allen." Dan was standing without having to lean heavily on Susan. "You would need some highly trained men to sneak in and rescue our children. And think of the consequences for those left in the mines. What would happen to them? No Allen, this needs to be taken to Colonel Richmond. We need skilled soldiers and the blessing of the King."

"There's no time for all that," Allen argued.

"Yes, there is Allen," Dan replied firmly. "And you are the man to put our case. You have seen the mines and the village."

"How can I persuade our King to free slaves when he allows slavery to exist in his own country? Go into any merchant's house in Westown and you will see all the menial tasks done by slaves. You will see the mark of the whip on their backs. Some even brand their slaves with the family cipher. It sickens me. Abe Tull will not allow residents in his village to own slaves."

"The plight of slaves in our country is regrettable Allen," Luke said, "but the rescue of kidnapped children is another matter. These children are not slaves, they are the flesh and blood of men here. I commend you for your loyalty to the less fortunate, but we are here to rescue our kith and kin. The wider problem is for others to solve."

"So what is your plan Luke?" Allen asked testily.

"We return to our village," Luke said with authority. "We gather as many men as can be spared. We need provisions for at least a moon, and there may be news from Westown. Oh I don't know Allen, but what I do know is that our small band can do nothing against a foe protected by the river and the mountains. We need soldiers."

"Luke is right Allen. We can't sit here and wait for something to happen. We need to get help quickly," Dan said as he sat down by the fire.

"It will break my heart to leave my little Sami," Brian said. "But we stand no chance against that lot of villains. They must have defences to protect their gold mines. The boys said there are twenty soldiers at the big mine, but surely there must be others. Luke is right, we need more men, a lot more men."

There were nods and grunts of approval.

"Now for the problem of how we get back," Luke said thoughtfully. "We have lost one boat, fortunately the smaller of the two. There are thirteen of us and the two children, but Harry and Meg have the coracles. I think we can squeeze thirteen in the larger boat."

"That won't be necessary Luke, Susan and I are staying here." Dan stood up and continued, "We have talked this over and we can't face another journey on the river, not until I am fully fit."

"And I have decided to stay here too." It was Brian who spoke as he moved to stand by Dan and Susan.

"And so have we," Harry said as he put his arm on Meg's shoulder.

"That means that only ten people will be travelling," Luke said. "The boat should cope with that easily, especially going downstream, but that does not solve the problem of provisions.

"I have lived off the land all my life, there are roots and leaves we can gather." Dan went on, "They will see us through until you return with fresh supplies."

"Well, if you are all sure, I think that we should prepare to move off at first light tomorrow."

The meeting broke up and immediately the camp became two separate units, those staying and those returning. Nonetheless, everyone helped to get the rowing boat prepared for the morrow's journey. It had to be dug out of a deep snowdrift first and by nightfall the travellers were ready for an early start. They expected to be down as far as Friar Godwin's cave by the end of the first day and at the abbey two days later. Brian volunteered to guard the rowing boat through the night with his dog, Scrap.

When they were alone, Harry and Meg discussed what they would do once Luke and the returning party had left.

"I want to return to the old abandoned mine and keep a watch on the village and also find a place for the soldiers to land when they get here."

"Are you sure that the soldiers will get here Harry?"

"Yes, I'm sure."

Chapter Twenty Two

The next morning Luke marshalled his party with authority so that they were ready to set off at first light as he had planned. It was done without ceremony and almost in silence, except for a handshake. There were no tears from Meg or Susan, but everyone was quiet for a while after the departure.

At midday Susan had prepared a meal and it was then that Harry announced that he and Meg would be returning to the abandoned mine to watch the miners' village. Dan said that he had expected this announcement and asked when they would leave.

"Tomorrow night. We will be living off the land apart from some smoked fish and dried meat, which we will take with us, and you taught me about the leaves and roots we can eat Dan."

"That's all very well in the summer Harry, but at this time of year the snow covers the leaves and the earth is frozen too hard to dig."

"We will be fine Dan. We will be back in a handful of days."

"I wish me and Scrap could come with you Harry," Brian said.

"You'd sink the coracle as soon as you stepped in." Susan laughed and teased the big man.

Harry spent the rest of the day catching fish to replace that which he and Meg would be taking from the stock of smoked fish. Meg packed an extra couple of blankets and another sheet of animal skins. Dan and Brian made up a bundle of torches, while Susan made some oatcakes with half of the remaining oatmeal.

When darkness came, they sat around the fire and speculated on how long it would be before the soldiers reached them. No one was in any doubt that the soldiers would come. They discussed how they would celebrate when they got the children back to Abe Tull's village. Again they were sure that they would rescue the young 'uns. Their certainty was palpable.

The next morning, after another very cold night, they woke to a blue sky and bright sunshine. By noon the young adventurers were ready to start their journey upriver, but they had to wait for darkness and so they slept most of the afternoon. Brian had been up to the top of the ridge and said the fire was not as big as usual and there was some activity at the rowing boats, but nothing alarming he thought. By late afternoon the sky had clouded over.

At nightfall, after a good meal, Harry and Meg said their farewells and set off on their journey. Keeping tight to the river's east bank they battled with the fierce current. Harry was glad he had a lighter and more helpful, passenger this trip. The river began to bend to the right and the smoother water greeted them. At the same time he saw the reflection of the village fire on the water up ahead. Time to swing across the strong current and aim for the west bank. As they drew closer to the villagers' path down to the river, they saw something that alarmed them both. Meg looked over her shoulder at her brother and pointed. He acknowledged her signal with a nod and then said quietly, "We daren't go into the trees, there is too much ice. I'll make a dash for the shadow upstream."

Harry drove the little craft forward and reached the shadow and then pulled hard for the east bank and the darkness of a low cliff. Here they stopped to consider their options. Just below them, where the path came to the water's edge, they saw two of the large rowing boats in the water and tethered to the bank.

"What do we do Harry?" Meg asked, anxiously.

"I don't know, Meg, if we turn the boats loose, they will head off downstream looking for them and then they'll see Brian, Dan and Susan. If we put a hole in them, they will know that there are strangers about. I don't see what we can do."

"Shall we stick to our plan then?"

"Yes. We may even see how they get the children into their village."

Harry swung the coracle round to face the current and headed north, making good progress, and in a short time the cloud had broken and soon they had a bright moonlit night. They were getting close to their destination when the moon went behind heavy cloud. Harry was becoming uneasy. He couldn't explain why and so he crossed to the west bank where the shadow was deeper. He expressed his disquiet to Meg.

"There's a big overhanging tree behind you Harry. That will give us cover while we decide what to do."

Harry moved back the few paddle strokes and found the near total darkness comforting. The tree was an alder that was festooned with ivy that reached to the water and would give them good cover, even in daylight, Harry guessed.

"What is worrying you Harry?" Meg whispered anxiously.

"I don't know, something is not right. If they have found our hideout under the fallen tree, they could be waiting for us."

"How far are we from the hideout?"

"Not far. I could see the stream up ahead and that's when I got the feeling that something was not right and so I swung across to this darker side."

"Perhaps we should stay here until daylight Harry."

"I agree. Let's tie the coracle to these roots and get some rest."

"You get some rest Harry, you've done all the work. I'll keep watch."

Wrapped in their blankets the young adventurers settled down to wait for dawn. Harry slept whilst Meg kept watch.

Across the river Meg saw the first hint of dawn. The cloud was still low and heavy and there might be snow later, Meg thought. It was bitterly cold.

Suddenly, Meg heard voices. They were some distance off but getting closer. She shook Harry's shoulder. He roused and heard her whisper to keep silent, then he too heard the voices. They were speaking their language but with an unusual dialect, but Harry and Meg understood most of what was said. There seemed to be two of them, maybe three, and they were moving slowly downriver. Now they were right above them. Their movement sent small rivulets of fine snow through the thick vegetation to trickle down the riverbank. The talkative walkers couldn't have been much more than a man's height above them. Harry assumed that they were trudging through deep snow. Gradually their voices faded and Harry and Meg were able to have a whispered conversation about what they had heard.

It was certain now that their hideout under the fallen tree had been discovered and that there were people watching for the return of the visitors.

"I have no intention of falling into their trap Meg."

"What are we going to do? We have people above and below us and if they come upriver with the rowing boats loaded with children they will see us unless we can camouflage the coracle somehow."

"I think the people who just passed by turned inland Meg. It might be safe to move back downstream to the last river we saw coming in from the west. We can go up that river and wait for the rowing boats to pass and then return to Brian, Dan and Susan."

"Should we stop here for a while Harry? Those people might come back."

"We can't wait for long, we don't know when the rowing boats set off."

"We'll have a couple of Susan's oatcakes and then move off, Harry."

After the food and a drink of water, Harry ventured out onto the river. Keeping close to the west bank they crept downstream, all the time expecting an angry shout from a fast moving canoe or rowing boat. It seemed an age before they saw the confluence of the incoming river with the main river. It was a very fast flowing river and Harry could see that they would be swept right across to the east bank. They would be at the mercy of the turbulent currents that would force them a considerable distance downstream before they would be able to cross to the west bank and return. Harry decided that the current of the incoming river would be too strong for the coracle. He felt trapped. The Coracle Boy kept his small boat still as if he was treading water while he considered what to do. They would try to land upstream of the meeting of the two rivers.

He moved slowly down towards the confluence and as he drew near he saw a jumble of fallen rock and a huge overhang. Harry kept tight to the west bank to take advantage of the cover this projection would afford him. They decided to land several paces upstream of the junction where they saw huge blocks of red sandstone littered with debris from earlier floods. Meg used her paddle to clear a way through the floating rubbish to enable them to disembark. She stepped ashore taking the painter with her. She scrambled up onto a flat ledge and secured the rope to a tree branch lodged tightly in a crevice. Harry joined her and surveyed their surroundings. They were looking down on the smaller river that was flowing fast and turbulent. It was evident that there were submerged rocks. A coracle would not travel upstream in those waters. The valley through which the smaller river flowed had steep, wooded sides, mainly willow and birch along the riverbank and then some stunted oak before the conifers covered the mountain way up into the late morning mist.

Where they stood was free of snow because they were under an overhanging cliff, but it was very exposed to the cold wind that was coming from the north.

"Let's get the coracle up here Meg, it will be out of sight behind these rocks," Harry said in a little more than a whisper. Meg understood the need for caution.

Harry went down to the little boat and handed their possessions up to Meg and then he shouldered the craft and, with Meg's help, brought it up to its hiding place.

"We need to get out of this biting wind Harry," Meg whispered as she pulled her blanket around her shoulders. The boy nodded and pointed to the pine trees further up the valley. They would head in that direction.

Suddenly there was an almighty shout from above them. Meg clapped her hand to her mouth and almost fell into Harry's arms as they pressed back under the overhanging rock. Both of them were looking up at the sandstone roof above them. Someone way up above them was haranguing others for not doing as they were told. It was difficult to follow the diatribe but someone was getting a harsh telling off.

"They could be lookouts for the rowing boats bringing the children," Harry whispered and then went on, "I reckon the lookouts were asleep, which is a good thing for us. They might have seen or heard us otherwise."

The young adventurers were now in a very difficult position. They could not go up the valley of the small river or downstream on the main river, they would be seen. And if they tried to go upstream, they couldn't be sure of not being seen and where could they go? They were trapped!

As quietly as they could they gathered their belongings together and pulled the blankets and animal skins around them and waited. It was bitterly cold as they huddled together in the lowest place they could find. The time dragged by so slowly. They would hear an occasional rumble of conversation from the people above them but nothing they could make sense of. They chewed on some dried fish and drank a little water at about midday and as the afternoon wore on Harry became anxious. He whispered to Meg, "If they stay up there all night, we will have to call off our hunt for information and try to slip away in the dark and go back to Dan." Meg nodded in agreement.

Suddenly! "Look, look the boats are here," a voice shouted.

"About time! They should have been here two days ago." The reply seemed to come from further away.

Harry came out of the shock first and took his arm from around Meg's shoulder. He crept forward and eased himself up to peer through a gap between the rocks. He saw the first boat, three oars up each side, still some distance away. The second boat of similar size was close behind. There was a noisy exchange above them. It sounded like two men sharing a joke, but only the odd word could be understood until one man said that he would be glad to sleep in his own bed tonight. Did that mean that they would be moving soon? Harry hoped so, but what would they do once the coast was clear?

There were only two options; return to Dan's camp or continue with the intelligence gathering. If soldiers were on the way they would need the information, however sketchy. But until the men on the rock above had gone they would have to sit tight and let events unfold. Another glimpse through the gap told the Coracle Boy that the first boat had moved over to the east bank and the second was following. Soon he would not be able to see them, he would have to find another spy hole. He moved back to sit beside Meg.

The men on the rock above them hailed the boat and after several exchanges they asked if there was any sign of strangers on the river. The reply was that there was no-one. They said that they had been down as far as the hermit's cave and there were no strangers. Harry was sure that was a lie.

Harry was desperate to see if there were children in the boats, but he dared not stand up. The sun was shining right into their shelter. And then he had an idea. He pulled up a handful of dead bracken and held it to his face. He pressed back against the sandstone cliff and pushed himself up until he could see over the rocks. The first boat had almost passed them but he was able to catch a glimpse of two youngsters sitting beside the man at the tiller, but the second boat was filled with children. Meg had copied Harry's method of camouflage and slid up the rock wall beside him.

"I counted fifteen young 'uns Harry," Meg whispered. The Coracle Boy replied by holding up his right hand and opened and closed it three times. Meg smiled and nodded.

There were noisy exchanges between the people above them and the men on the boats, mostly garbled ribaldry. An authoritative voice told the discordant jokers to put out their fire and get back to their boats before he took a whip to them. The receding voices told Harry and Meg that they could now move up the valley and into the pine trees.

There was no way up to where the strangers had been standing from the south side. It was a sheer cliff, but round to the east facing side that followed the river it looked possible to haul oneself up through the undergrowth.

"Why do we need to climb up there?" Meg asked.

"I need to know where that path leads. You stay there, I'll not be long."

Meg watched anxiously as Harry scrambled up through the bushes. He had to climb the height of six or seven men and traverse a similar distance to get round the overhang to reach the path. As he reached a flat area he could see a crude thatched hut backing onto the cliff face that went on up and was too sheer to climb. There was a heap of steaming snow where there had been a fire. The platform ended in a sheer drop to where Harry could see the jumble of fallen slabs of rock. He could not see Meg, she was hidden by the overhang. From this vantage point it was possible to see the junction of the two rivers and quite a way down the main river, but the flat area extended only far enough to see a very short distance up the valley of the smaller river. The path up to this lookout point went north and sloped down and turned back into the trees and was soon lost in the tangled undergrowth. Harry climbed back down to where Meg was waiting.

Meg was eager to know if Harry had discovered anything of importance. He described what he had seen and suggested that now the path had been well trodden they might be able to use it without leaving fresh tracks. But their hopes of that were quickly dashed as it began to snow as they spoke.

"Come on Meg, let's get our stuff across to those fir trees."

They both gathered as much as they could carry and with Harry leading they set off. The going was difficult, a mixture of broom and gorse bushes at first and then the stunted willow and birch all weighed down with snow.

They were leaving a track through the snow that would be seen by the lookout from his post above the overhang. It was only a short distance but enough to arouse suspicion, but there was nothing they could do about it. Perhaps the light snow that was falling now would obliterate their tracks by morning.

It took three journeys to get all their property up into a snow free area under a large, spreading cedar tree and it was getting dark. They quickly established their camp and debated whether to have a fire or not. The distant calls of a wolf and several replies made up their minds. As the snow appeared to be getting heavier and the tree canopy was quite dense, they agreed that no human traffic would be about to see the fire. Harry set a night line in the river while Meg prepared some hot food. With the darkness came the wind, howling down from the north. They were reasonably well protected in this valley.

After their meal they wrapped their blankets and the animal skins around them and huddled by the fire. There was no shortage of firewood here, even so they kept only a small fire burning. Neither of them wanted to sleep. The noise of the wind discouraged slumber, as did the occasional howl of a distant wolf.

Suddenly there was a shaking of the ground, a loud rumble and crashing sound that was very close. The ground under them still shook. There was the noise of trees crashing down and the snow laden cedar shed its load down from the upper branches and piled it up on the lower limbs so that Harry and Meg were buried under the weighed down branches. A massive pile of snow forced one branch down onto the fire and acrid smoke quickly began to fill their living space. It stung their eyes and choked them. The heat was becoming unbearable.

Harry grabbed his paddle and dug frantically to excavate a chimney through the snow to get rid of the smoke from the burning wood. They were both coughing and their eyes were smarting and then Harry's paddle went right through the snow and a fair sized hole appeared and the smoke began to disperse, but this caused another problem. The draught merely fuelled the fire and it began to blaze alarmingly.

"Get behind the trunk of the tree Meg," Harry shouted. Again there was another tremor, but they tried to ignore it as they pulled their bedding, food and everything else they possessed round to the back of the tree.

Here they began to dig their way out. The heat from the burning timber was becoming intolerable, but together they finally had a hole they could crawl through. Meg went first and Harry passed their belongings through to her. The coracle was going to be their biggest problem. Harry dug frantically to widen and deepen the hole. There was another loud crash and Harry was buried under an avalanche from the branches of the cedar. He fought wildly to get his hands free to claw the snow from his face. He could move his feet so he struggled to move backwards, but that was taking him closer to the fire! He was able to get his knees bent. That gave him some leverage, but there was a lot of snow on his back and shoulders. His frenzied thrashing with his legs dislodged some of the weight. With his arms free he attacked the snow in front of him with his bare hands and then, in the total darkness, he found the handle of his paddle, but it was stuck tight in the compacted snow. And where was Meg? Was she buried under the avalanche? Harry shouted her name and increased his efforts. He called out to his father to help him. He begged his mother to keep Meg safe as he made space to fight his way through the needle foliage and branches of the tree and the tight packed snow. If only he could get his paddle free, he would be able to dig properly, and then he remembered his knife, the one his father gave him. He drew it from its sheath and attacked the avalanche, it seemed so puny against the obstacle in front of him. Harry realised that there was no heat coming from the other side of the tree. Perhaps the last inundation had smothered the fire. He was now able to push himself up onto his knees and extend his attack on the snow, but his efforts were so often frustrated by limbs and branches. Something hit his hand. He drew it back, but the object struck again and then he realised that it was Meg's paddle. When it came a third time, he was able to grab hold of it and hold it for a few moments and shake it to let Meg know that he was alive. The paddle was withdrawn and Meg almost screamed through the small hole, asking if Harry was alright. They both doubled their efforts and eventually Harry crawled out and fell back on the snow, close to exhaustion. Meg fell on him, crying and hugging him and repeating her question over and over, "Are you alright? Do you have pain anywhere?" Gradually they regained their composure and stood up to evaluate the situation. The wind had dropped and the snow was no longer falling but it was still a very dark night.

"We must get a fire going,Meg. Where are our things?"

"Under that pile of snow, I'm sorry Harry I was trying to keep things together and then the earth shook and brought all the snow down from the tree, it just missed me but buried all our stuff."

"Don't worry about it Meg, I think it would be best to leave everything where it is until daylight. I've got my flint, we can start another fire if we can find a dry place under the fallen trees."

Almost entirely by feel they found a virtually snow free area beneath a crisscross of fallen trees. The space was barely high enough to stand up in but it was adequate and once the fire got going it was quite cosy. All they could do now was wait for dawn. Their blankets and most of their property were buried under a huge pile of snow.

"Was that an earthquake Harry?" Meg asked as she stared into the flames.

"I suppose it must have been, I have heard about them. The pagans say they happen when the gods are angry. Brother Anselm said that was nonsense, but he didn't say what made it happen."

Harry and Meg were almost afraid to go to sleep. Not only were they afraid of another earth tremor, they couldn't allow the fire to go out, not with haunting call of the wolf still ringing in their ears.

Chapter Twenty Three

A very weary Harry watched as the darkness of the night slowly gave way to a dull, grey day. The cloud was low and promised more snow. The boy stood up and stretched and then put more wood on the fire. He looked down at his sleeping sister. He would not disturb her.

Harry looked about at the devastation that surrounded him. He had never seen anything like this. A great swathe of pine trees had been flattened either by the earth tremor or by the avalanche the quake had caused. The tall cedar was the biggest of a clump of evergreen trees that remained standing.

It was as if the destruction had tailed off just before it reached their temporary camp. Harry climbed onto the piled up trees they had taken shelter under. From here he could see up the valley. It appeared that the mountainside had had all its vegetation stripped and piled high in the bottom of the valley. The Coracle Boy turned to look towards the great river but the view was blocked by the trees that had sheltered them. He would see what the damage was later, but first he had to dig out their possessions and his coracle.

Meg sat up as Harry entered their shelter. She looked tired and was not her usual cheerful self as he wished her a 'good morning', but she managed a wan smile as she huddled close to the fire, saying that she felt chilled to the bone. Harry added more wood to the fire.

"I'll go and dig our supplies out of that pile of snow. Meg, you get warm. I'll have to use your paddle, mine's still under the cedar tree."

Harry attacked the huge pile of snow beside the hole he had crawled out of last night. He soon found the sheet of animal skins that Meg had had the presence of mind to use to cover the small heap that was their survival kit. As he exposed each item, he took them across to Meg to melt the snow off them and check for damage. Remarkably, there was nothing missing except the coracle and Harry's paddle and gloves. They would dig them out later, first they needed a good meal. The boy said he would check his night line. There were four fish on the line, but what alarmed Harry was the flow in the river. This was not the raging torrent of yesterday. The water was now waist deep and he could see fish floundering in shallow rock pools. No need for a line. As he pondered on the reason for the low flow, Harry became alarmed and hurried back to the campfire, not sure what he should say to Meg. He decided to eat first and gauge Meg's mood after breakfast. She was delighted with the catch and cooked all four moderately sized trout. She had made a brew of one of Eliza Pegg's beverages, which warmed them both and raised Meg's spirits. Harry decided to tell his sister of his fears.

"Meg, the river is really low, so low that there are fish stranded in some of the shallows. I could pick them out with my bare hands."

"That's great Harry, I'll come with you. We could smoke some…."

"That's not the point," Harry cut in. "Why is the river so low? I think that all these trees and snow have dammed the river somewhere up the valley."

"What are you saying Harry? Are we in danger?"

"I don't really know, but if that dam bursts we could be swept away. I think that we should move higher up the mountainside. Perhaps we should try and get up onto that flat area above the overhang."

"Harry, I think that we should reconsider the whole situation. Can we gather any really valuable information in these conditions? If we have to move camp now, it will be too late to go to the disused mine today."

"And we don't know what damage the earthquake, if it was an earthquake, has caused at the gold mines and the village where the children are kept."

"Oh no! Poor Ruth. Oh, what am I thinking? Of course we have to find out all we can before we go back."

"The first thing we have to do is dig the coracle out. Can you unwrap one of the torches Dan and Brian made? It's dark under all that snow and I lost my gloves in the rush to get away from the fire."

Harry enlarged the hole and dug out his paddle and then crawled into the snow cave. The torch illuminated a tangle of branches and tight packed snow. It also revealed the crushed remains of his beloved coracle, squashed beyond repair. Broken branches had pierced the canvas. It was not worth recovering. Harry was devastated. He drove his fist into the snow to give vent to his anger. How would they travel back now? They had discovered nothing. They had few provisions and they were threatened by a flood that could descend upon them at any moment. And what could he tell Meg?

There was no need, Meg had followed him into the snow cave and saw the splintered willow and the torn canvas. She knew that it was hopeless but had to ask, "Can we do anything with it, Harry?"

"No, it's completely ruined," the Coracle Boy replied disconsolately.

"How shall we get back? Can you make another one?"

"I haven't the tools or the covering to make another. We will have to steal a boat. There is no other way."

"Let's get out of here. Have you found your gloves Harry?"

"No. They are on the other side of the tree. You go out, I'll catch up with you." Harry wanted a moment alone to compose himself. The loss of his beloved coracle had been a bitter blow. It had been the best he had ever built. He found his gloves and paddle, a little singed by the fire but still serviceable.

Meanwhile Meg was gathering their blankets and provisions ready for the move to higher ground. He suggested that they find a suitable location to move to first. Meg agreed. They climbed over the fallen trees onto the piles of snow that had gathered rocks and broken branches to become the avalanche that had careered down the mountain. They cleared the obstacles to stand on ground that looked as if it had been swept clean with a broom. Harry looked to his left and saw the mountainside bare, except for a few trees still standing, drunkenly leaning down towards the valley bottom.

"Harry, look at the cliff. The overhang has gone."

Harry swung round and looked to his right and saw a massive pile of red sandstone stretching down to the main river and almost blocking the smaller tributary. The overhang and a huge part of the cliff above had gone.

There was no way up to the path that had led to the overhang. A smooth vertical rock face prevented any progress in that direction.

"I think we have to consider our options Meg, and at the moment I can see only one," Harry said thoughtfully, as he looked up into the morning mist that hid the top of the ridge.

"Go on Harry, what are you thinking?"

"We should spend the day discovering what we can and then 'borrow' one of their boats and go back downriver. What do you think?"

"I can see no other way Harry. I suggest that we take just our food and one blanket each and leave the rest and travel as light as we can. I also think that we should change into our second set of clothes."

"Then that is what we will do. We will need our weapons of course, but we can drink from the streams so the water carriers and the cooking pots can stay here to be collected later. We will need one of the torches, we may have to go into the mine." The goods to be left behind were placed in the hole left by an uprooted tree and covered with the animal skins, branches and snow.

The adventurers set off up the steep slope using their coracle paddles as walking sticks, although there was not much walking. It was mostly scrambling. As the morning mist lifted, they saw at last the crest of the ridge and there were trees still standing up there. Eventually they were at the top. Their exertions had caused them to perspire and they felt the bite of the cold north wind as it cut over the mountain. They saw below, similar devastation to that behind them, but they hurried down amongst the trees that still stood on the higher slopes. They moved diagonally across the hill to keep within what little cover was afforded by these windswept woods.

"Harry," Meg whispered, "I think that the village is down there. Surely those are the rocks we saw below the abandoned mine where we found the boys."

"You could be right Meg. If this low cloud would lift we would know for sure, but it could work in our favour. We could move out into the open and we might even get down to the abandoned mine unseen."

"Let's give it a try." Meg was eager to be off.

"Steady Meg, we don't know who else might be on this mountain."

They moved stealthily down between the fallen trees. They were just about able to see the blurred shapes of the buildings down in the valley.

"Look Meg." Harry stopped and pointed down and to the west. "That is the track from the old mine. Allen and I followed it." They went on cautiously until they were down on the track and only a few paces from the mine. Two large fir trees hung down over the entrance which was almost blocked with snow. Harry dug a way in and lit the torch and they rested out of the cold, biting wind. They ate smoked fish and an oatcake and talked about their next move. They quenched their thirst with water caught in their cupped hands as it trickled from the roof of the mine a short distance down the sloping tunnel. Meg asked Harry if he had decided on a plan. It was past midday and it would be getting dark soon.

"We need to locate a boat while it is still light, that means going down to the river. I suggest that we go back towards the fallen tree where we first landed."

"What about the men who were up on the overhang?" Meg asked.

"We have to hope that they and the fish smokers moved away when the pagan gods shook the ground, but we can be sure that the canoe will not be there, that is why we need to locate another one in the daylight."

The couple left the old mine very cautiously. They studied the village down below. There were a lot more people about than there had been on the two previous occasions and there seemed to be quite a crowd around one particular building. There were no signs of an avalanche down the mountain behind the village. As they looked further west, they could see the first mine. Now that some of the forest in the foreground had been flattened, it looked undamaged, but they were too far away to be sure. There was also a pall of smoke rising above the hills to the west.

Taking advantage of whatever cover they could find they moved down and across. They could see the beech wood now, most of the trees were still standing. The avalanche had not reached the beech trees by some distance. They were leaving quite a trail in the pristine snow, but Harry was not too worried, they would be gone by the time anyone found their tracks. The beech wood was on a very steep slope and there was very little undergrowth, it made their descent extremely difficult. They left clearly defined tracks as they skidded and churned up a mixture of dead leaves and snow.

Eventually the ground levelled out and they came upon a distinct path, not used since last night's snowfall and which probably led to the flat area that had existed above the overhang. Harry would have liked to have checked this theory, but there was no time or need.

They moved back into the beech wood and, keeping the footpath in sight, followed the path which now led them through a stand of young birch trees. The path turned away from the fallen tree and crossed the stream above the waterfall by a series of stepping stones, which they were obliged to use if they were to keep their feet dry. And so Harry and Meg joined the footpath. The next thing they saw was the roof of the hut used for fish preserving. They had expected this and planned to go back into the trees to avoid the obstacle.

Suddenly Meg grabbed her brother's arm and held her finger to her lips and then her hand to her ear. Harry listened. At first he heard nothing and then there came a mournful keening that carried a dreadful sorrow, faint at first and then a wail rose on the gentle afternoon breeze. Meg gripped Harry's arm harder and looked at him, her anguish evident.

"What do you think it is?" Harry asked.

"It is a woman. She sounds in great pain. I think I know what it is Harry. I must go to her and see if I can help."

"No Meg, it could be a trap."

"That was real pain. That woman needs our help Harry. I must go to her."

Meg turned to go towards the hut but Harry held her arm.

"No, you can't do this Meg. It could ruin our chances of rescuing Ruth."

Meg hesitated. She looked at her brother and tears started down her cheeks and then there was a terrible scream from the hut. Meg turned and snatched her arm free and ran down the path closely followed by Harry. Crude steps had been cut into the steeper slope as they raced down to the levelled area where the two huts stood. The cries were coming from the smaller of the two structures. Meg brushed Harry's restraining hand from her shoulder and went into the hut. Harry, sword drawn, looked anxiously about and then he looked inside the smoke house and saw a smouldering fire and collapsed drying racks. Someone had wrecked the place. Back outside the Coracle Boy looked around for possible opponents and saw none. He began to wonder what was going on in the other hut. Just then Meg appeared at the door of the hut and beckoned him across.

"There is a young woman in there Harry and she is having a baby. They took her husband away at first light. We have to help her."

"But Meg, what can we do?"

"I have helped Eliza Pegg deliver three babies, I know what to do. What I need is plenty of hot water. They have no cooking pots and they heat the water by dropping hot stones in this leather bucket filled with water from the spring at the end of the path."

Harry returned his sword to its scabbard, took the bucket and ran down the path. The spring bubbled up into a still pool about two paces across and about one pace deep. Back at the smoke house Harry used a branch of hazel to scrape among the embers to find a deep layer of red hot ash. Some round stones by the door had obviously been used for this purpose many times. While the stones heated, Harry looked around for something to handle the hot stones and found a wooden, spade-like tool that was probably for just that purpose. Sounds of the woman's agony alarmed the Coracle Boy. He was sure there would be people rushing to her aid. He went up the steps so that he would be able to see further afield.

Meg, calling his name, brought Harry to the smaller hut. She was at the door holding a wooden bowl and she needed some warm water to wash her hands as soon as possible. Harry took a stone out of the red hot embers and dropped it into the leather bucket. It barely took the chill off the water. A second stone raised the temperature sufficient for Meg's needs and she returned to her patient. The bucket was topped up and more stones were added to the fire. He wondered if they had another bucket.

While he waited for the stones to get hot, Harry looked around their surroundings. Beyond the spring he saw a roughly cultivated area and a crude building that had housed pigs recently. Now the door hung open. The huts were about the height of two men above the river, above flood water level Harry guessed.

The ground rose steeply behind the north facing huts and timber was stacked all round ready to feed the smoke house and provided some protection from the wind-driven snow. Harry noted that the smoke house was round and built of stone, the roof was conical and very steep and made of oak planks, as was the door. The dwelling, however, was square and the walls were wattle and daub with a thatched roof. The door was animal skin laced to a hazel frame. There were no windows.

Chapter Twenty Four

The shadows were lengthening and Harry began to wonder how long they would be here. He had heard the woman cry out and scream from time to time and he had heard Meg's calm, reassuring voice, but she had not left the woman all afternoon and it was getting dark. He found a wooden pail which he filled with water and then he heated more stones.

Harry heard Meg call and went to the entrance to the hut where he saw her holding a baby wrapped up in one of Meg's blankets.

"Look Harry, a beautiful baby girl. Isn't she lovely? Here, you hold her while I look after Lisa, her mother." Harry found himself holding the baby. He vaguely remembered holding Ruth when he was very small and his father had told him not to drop her. Soon Meg was back and took the baby from him and took it to its mother. She asked Harry to bring the hot water down and could he make a fire in the tiny dwelling. There was a crude hearth in the centre of the hut. It was now quite dark and Harry was sure that there would be a hard frost. There was little protection in the small hut and the fire could not be very big because of the fire risk.

With mother and child as comfortable as Meg could make them, she turned her attention to preparing a meal for them all. How she wished she had one of their cooking pots. The meal was ready and some of Eliza Pegg's hot fruit and herb beverage refreshed them all and Harry was introduced to Lisa and the baby again and they listened to Lisa's story.

Lisa and her husband Peter were slaves. There was also Peter's young brother, called Cal, who was about 16 and also a slave. They were all bought by the miners two summers ago, after their village had been razed by slavers. Many of their people had died. Peter and his father had owned a large smoke house in their village and Peter had just married Lisa. They were brought to this valley from the north through the mountains. The couple were to be separated but when the owner of this small smoke house suddenly died, Peter and Lisa were told that they would have to take on the job, his brother would work in the mines. If Peter had any ideas of absconding, his brother would be killed.

"We were not too unhappy with the arrangement," Lisa told them, "Because we were together and away from the slave masters and overseers and their savage whips, but we had to work very hard to keep up with their demands.

"Why have they taken your husband away Lisa?"

"The shaking of the earth caused the mine to collapse. It killed many in the big mine and some of the soldiers too were killed. At first light this morning a slave master and a messenger came down and said that every able-bodied man must return to the village at once. Peter said he wouldn't go and leave me because the baby was coming. The slave master hit Peter on the head and they tied him up and threw him into their rowing boat. They also killed our chickens and the pig and took all the fish in the smoke house. The messenger said that the food store at the village had been destroyed."

At this point Lisa gave out an awful wail and cried bitterly. It was a long time before Lisa could compose herself sufficiently to continue. Eventually she told them that there had been four soldiers, six slaves and a slave master to meet two boats bringing the children up to the mines. They always stayed behind for an extra day to make sure that no one followed the rowing boats, but for some reason no one was left to keep watch this time. Harry thought that it was fortunate for them.

Later that evening, when Lisa and her baby were sleeping, Harry and Meg went up to the smoke house to see if they could salvage some of the dried fish dropped by the slaves. They found a good supply at the rear of the building. They also found a ham that Peter had concealed amongst the framework of the drying racks. The slave master and the messenger had obviously not known how to empty the racks judging by the broken hanging rails thrown aside.

"That's what caused the drying racks to collapse and quite a lot of fish to spoil," Meg observed. Harry agreed and suggested that they leave any further attempt to recover more food from the smoke house until daylight. They put more wood chips on the fire to keep it alight until the morning and closed the door.

"We have to discuss what we are to do Meg, now that our situation has altered again," Harry said as they stood in the darkness.

"I can't leave Lisa, not for a day or two."

"I knew you would say that and I agree. But when will it be alright to leave her, Meg? We could be trapped here at any time, it means that one of us will have to be on watch constantly."

"Lisa is a strong young woman and the baby is healthy. I'm sure she would be able to manage in a couple of days under normal conditions. But out here with her baby, without her husband and not knowing whether he is dead or alive, it would be a terrible ordeal for any woman. And Lisa is only eighteen."

"In the morning we will have to talk to Lisa, explain our situation without mentioning the others. We will say we are on our own. We are looking for our sister."

"I agree Harry, I hate telling lies. Come, it's getting cold and I don't want Lisa waking and thinking we have left her." Meg hurried down to the smaller hut clearly concerned for her patient. Harry followed, collecting an armful of wood for the fire to keep a warm glow in the hearth. Harry guessed that it must be close to midnight. He was feeling very tired and he was sure that Meg must be exhausted after bringing Lisa's baby into the world.

Lisa woke first and fed her baby. She wanted to get up and make a meal for them, but Meg insisted that she must rest.

"But I would like to make some oatcakes for you and some bread to take with you when you leave." Lisa spoke as if she had been talking to neighbours who had just popped in to see the baby.

"We were going to talk to you about our reason for being here later Lisa, but since you have mentioned our leaving perhaps we could talk now," Meg suggested and Harry agreed.

"Someone you love was taken by the slavers and you want to rescue them, am I right?" Lisa made the statement calmly and with wisdom beyond her years. "You are not the first we have met and the pagans know that you are here. The hunt for you will continue when the disaster at the mine has been dealt with."

"How do you know this Lisa?" Meg asked.

"Three days ago soldiers came down off the mountain. They were searching for two runaway boys who had been seen up at the old mine and they came across the tracks of two people and the boys. They traced them to a fallen tree, downriver from here, where they think they had a boat hidden. The man in charge of the soldiers questioned us for ages but we hadn't seen anyone."

"You said that we are not the first you have met Lisa," Harry said.

"We have seen three other groups all on a mission to rescue their children and all of them were killed or taken into slavery. The first group was a party of six or seven. Peter saw them on the east bank and warned them of the sentries, but they walked right into an ambush and were killed. And then there was a man on his own. He was here for many days, but they caught him trying to steal a boat and took him into slavery. And then, last spring, two men came up the river in a boat they had stolen from the slavers' camp. They too were captured and taken as slaves."

"We are here to rescue our sister and several other children from our village and another village out in the marshes," Meg explained.

"It is not possible Meg," Lisa stated firmly. "There are only two ways into the mining village, one from the north, which is closed during the winter and heavily guarded in the summer, and one from the south, which is the river." Lisa paused to look at her sleeping child and then went on, "The river flows for some distance through a narrow gorge. The pagans call it the Devil's Gorge. The miners' village is at the upstream end of the gorge and to get there horses tow a barge up through the raging torrent. In the summer it takes three horses to pull the barge through. At this time of year they sometimes use six horses. There is no other way in or out of that village."

"Are you saying that we give up and abandon our sister to a life of slavery?"

"You will become slaves yourselves Meg, if you attempt to get into the village. They have spies everywhere, except at night."

"What do you mean, except at night?" Harry asked.

"These pagans are very superstitious and rarely go out at night, unless they are carrying a flaming torch. All the sentries have a fire because they believe that there are goblins and all sorts of evil spirits about at night."

"That is the time to gather all the information we can Meg," Harry said excitedly. "I know you are going to ask what we can discover in the dark..."

"The sentries have dogs, vicious, horrible animals," Lisa said dejectedly.

"I will travel on the water. Can I borrow Peter's canoe Lisa?"

"No Harry, I can't let you take the canoe. He could be back at any time and Peter will be expected to produce even more fish, fresh fish if they have lost their stores. There are only three of them who fish the river and the other two are both free men and will probably come down with Peter and trawl with nets. They have done it twice before."

"When do you think they will release Peter?" Harry asked.

"If they are really short of food they might send him back soon. They could send the other fishermen with him."

Harry spent the afternoon and evening fishing and he shot two ducks to replenish their meagre pantry. They roasted the ducks and put the fish in the smoke house. It had been a difficult day.

"It's getting late and you two need to sleep. I'll keep watch until dawn. I will wake you only in an emergency," Harry said as he settled down opposite the door into the hut, his sword out of its scabbard and laid on the floor at his side.

Chapter Twenty Five

Harry woke with a start, it took a moment for him to remember where he was and why a baby should be crying. The fire had burnt low and he quickly brought it back to life. It was very cold in the hut and Harry was angry with himself for falling asleep. Lisa sat up and lifted the baby from the blanket and prepared to feed her. The disturbance had wakened Meg who shivered and pulled the blanket tightly around her. Harry looked out and in the east he could see the hint of dawn in the dark sky. There had been no snow, but it was very cold out there and he quickly tied the door back in place and turned his attention to the fire. Meanwhile, Meg had decided to get up and prepare some food, but Lisa insisted that she would prepare a proper meal for them all and produced flour and oatmeal from a lined basket suspended from the roof.

There was some discussion about what they should do if someone came down to check on Lisa or if Peter returned.

It was agreed that a sharp lookout would be kept on the river at all times and as soon as anyone was seen Harry and Meg would retreat into the wilderness to the south, as far as the disused mine if necessary. Meg agreed to do the first watch, Harry had slept very little in the night.

It was about noon when Harry awoke, annoyed that Meg and Lisa had let him sleep so long, saying that he should have been out scouting for a boat to take them out of this dangerous situation.

"But what about Lisa and the baby?" Meg asked. "We can't just leave them to fend for themselves."

"Don't worry about me Meg, I have learned to survive here. Anyway Peter will be back soon, I just know he will," Lisa said confidently.

Harry busied himself collecting a store of firewood in for the night. He also kept the smoke house fire alight. He noticed that it was much warmer today and towards mid afternoon he was aware of a fine drizzle and moisture dripping from the trees. Meg joined him as he stood at the top of the steps leading to the path that went south to where the lookout hut had been only two days ago.

"What are we going to do about Lisa and the baby, Harry?"

"Until we have a boat, we can make no plans."

"But you have a plan Harry, that is what you are doing now, planning?"

The Coracle Boy said nothing for a while and then announced, "I am going on a scouting trip tonight Meg. I would rather go alone but if you insist on coming with me, I won't mind."

"I know that I should go with you, but I also know that Lisa should not be left alone at a time like this. If you want to go alone then I won't argue. I know that you are the only one who can get us out of this dreadful wilderness."

"Thanks Meg, I'll go as soon as the light begins to fade. I'll take the path along the top of the escarpment, but I'll talk to Lisa. She may know of reasons not to take that route, in which case I'll have to go along the riverbank."

"Come inside and have some food and you must keep warm and dry, until it's time to go. Talk to Lisa about the route you plan, she may be able to help."

Lisa told Harry to follow the path at the foot of the escarpment until he came to a landing stage. He should approach with caution, there might be a sentry there but his fire should warn him. He could follow the river for a short distance but then the precipice became the riverbank and the only way forward was to climb the cliff, a dangerous feat in daylight, but at night, impossible.

"I'll have to go and see if some kind pagan has left a boat at the landing stage for us," Harry joked.

All too soon it was time for Harry to leave. Meg wanted to beg him not to go, but she knew that her brother had to make this journey. Armed with just a hunting bow, his short sword and his knife, he set off into the darkest of nights. Thankfully the rain had stopped.

The path along the bottom of the cliff was not difficult to follow and Harry almost walked straight onto the landing stage. He could make out the hut and the stone hearth in front of the shelter. He felt the stones and they were as cold as ice. There had been no fire in the hearth that day. There was no boat tied up at the small jetty waiting to be 'borrowed' by Harry.

Stealthily he continued along the foot of the cliff. The going was uneven and there was a tangle of undergrowth waiting to trip him at every step. Suddenly he was aware of the sound of the river close to him now, he tested each step.

With his left shoulder tight against the cliff face he moved cautiously forward, trying to see what lay ahead, listening for any sound that might warn him of danger, any smell that might tell of a nearby fire. But it was touch that made him freeze and remain motionless. He recognised what he could feel. It was a rope. Why was it hanging down the cliff face? Was it used by someone to help them climb the precipice or was it a mooring for a boat?

'I can't stand here all night. I have to climb up to find out, but it may be a very old rope and too rotten to take my weight, or there could be someone waiting up there, or maybe they will cut the rope when I am near the top'. All these arguments and many more went through the Coracle Boy's mind. He smelt the tar in the fibres and concluded that it was not an old rope and would have resisted the decaying effects of the weather. It was thick and would easily carry his weight. With a steely determination he gripped the stout cord and very slowly transferred his weight to the rope. He hung there for a few moments, his feet clear of the ground, and then jerked hard, but the rope did not break.

Harry reached further up and pulled himself up clear of the ground and hung there for a few moments and then, throwing caution to the wind, he placed both feet on the cliff face, leaned back and began to walk up the sheer wall. He came to a flat ledge and took a rest. He could hear the gurgling swirl of the river waters below, but there was no sound from above. There was no wind and it was not so cold. Harry just had to carry on to the top. Another short rest at a convenient shelf and he could sense that he was near the top. The first sign he met was a tree root, followed by a flattening out of the cliff and the bole of a tree and the knot that held the rope to the tree trunk. There was hardly any snow here under the pine trees and Harry just lay there, getting his breath back and listening for sounds of people. There were no alarms being raised. He tried to stand up but the branches of the pines made this difficult. His only way to progress further was to crawl on his belly and so he turned right and continued upstream, following to the top of the escarpment on his hands and knees. It was some considerable distance before the trees gave way to tussocks of grass or heather and Harry was able to stand up. He was loathed to leave the trees for the open snow where his tracks would be all too visible and so he kept to the cover and veered to his left. The ground was beginning to slope down slightly and suddenly Harry saw the glint of a fire through the trees directly in front of him, still some distance away. He guessed that it was the sentry on the pinnacle at the point where the river turned sharply west. He decided to aim for a point well to the left of the fire. The trees were sparse here and the rain earlier had dispersed the snow.

Harry's guess was right because he arrived at the edge of the cliff slightly lower than the sentry's fire way off to his right. He was looking at several fires along the opposite riverbank and the sheer rock wall through which, he assumed, the river poured. He could hear a dull roar below in the darkness, but he was some distance downstream of the gorge and it could be the noise of the water tumbling down from the lake. Harry sat down beside a lone blackthorn bush near the edge of the cliff and realised that he could see nothing to add to the intelligence gathering and as for 'borrowing' a boat of any kind, well, that was hopeless this far above the water. He had to get down there somehow.

Suddenly Harry became aware of a moving light some distance off to his left and coming his way, following the cliff top he guessed. He could make out that there was only one man, but he might have a dog. Harry tested the wind direction and was relieved to discover that it was in his favour. The dog, if there was one, would not pick up his scent for a while yet and not at all if he moved back up the hill. Harry turned to take one last look at the moving light and realised that it was no longer moving. He saw that the light was going down! Was there a path down to the river after all?

Chapter Twenty Six

The Coracle Boy ran in the direction of the disappearing light and then realised the folly of such haste along a dangerous cliff top and slowed down to a brisk walk. The glow of the torch had almost gone now and Harry was sure that he would never find the point where the light had disappeared, but he had to remain cautious. Finding that access down to the river level was all that mattered and so he strode on trying to keep his eyes on where he saw the light disappear and also on where he was going.

Luck was with him. Harry arrived at the top of a flight of irregular steps and, even better, a man carrying a torch was nearing the bottom of the steps. Gradually a wooden landing stage came into view and a small rowing boat was tied alongside. Harry started down the steps to get below the skyline. He crept down slowly, watching the torch carrier as he went. He saw the torch fitted into a sconce on the bow of the small craft. He saw the man climb aboard, fit the oars and pull for the north bank. Harry had to go cautiously, the steps were uneven and wet, although there was no snow or ice on them. At the bottom the landing stage was very crude and there was no boat tied up and waiting to be 'borrowed', but this was all good information. There was a way to get men across, but it was on the wrong side of the Devil's Force. Harry reasoned that if they could make a flight of steps here, why not further upstream on the other side of the gorge? Perhaps he could test that theory the next night. And then he remembered Lisa's words, "The pagans know that you are here." To risk another visit would be foolhardy.

Harry turned his attention to the landing stage, which was no more than a raft tethered to the cliff. It was similar to the one he had seen downstream of Westown, a number of floating logs lashed together and held to the bank by two ropes secured to the rock face, a man's height above the water. This allowed the floating platform to rise and fall with the water level.

An idea came to Harry. Could this be their mode of transport out of here? He examined the raft and realised that it was not well made and whilst it might be adequate in calm water, it would soon fall apart in the rough water downstream. Nonetheless, it would serve to take him to where he might find a better form of transport. The ropes that held the landing stage were thick and looked strong, but on examination Harry found them to be very old. In fact the upstream rope was badly worn where it passed through the iron ring in the cliff face. Harry stood on the raft and considered the risk he was taking. Rafts are difficult to handle, he would need a good rudder. He found a length of timber floating amongst the debris caught against the upstream side of the raft. It was the right length and would make a good rudder. Harry's spirits soared as he slotted the make-shift rudder between the two centre logs. He was now concerned to make the loss of the landing stage look like an accident. It must be assumed that the ropes had parted due to their age. The upstream rope would part easily at the ring in the cliff, but downstream the rope was newer. Harry drew his knife and began to scrape along the length of the rope near to where it was fastened to the landing stage. He knew he must not make a clean cut. Suddenly the rope parted and all the weight of the raft was now on the upstream mooring as the current began to draw the raft.

Harry was taken by surprise and had to make a grab for his make-shift rudder before it was carried away with the flotsam. He thrashed it about to try and get some control of this cumbersome vessel. The clumsy craft swung on the remaining rope allowing the rubbish to surge past and then the rope at the ring gave way and Harry was on the river. The current was fast but he was expecting that. He manoeuvred the raft as close as he dared to the cliff face. When he was clear of the lights on the opposite shore, Harry used the rudder to steer for the north shore, where he knew there had been several boats moored when he and Allen had made their reconnoitre. The current was really fast now and there was a danger of hitting the bank. At this speed it would smash the raft and probably throw the boy into the water, something he must avoid.

Suddenly Harry heard the lapping of the water against the north bank. By now he was travelling much too fast and with no means of slowing down, and then the raft hit something. The outrigger of a canoe came up onto the raft and almost hit Harry who was thrown to the floor. He scrambled to a crouch, just avoiding a wash of water over the raft, only wetting his feet. The craft had slowed a little and Harry was able to make out the river bank, steep at this point, and the raft was turning and in danger of being pulled out into the river. Harry jumped across to grab the rudder before it floated away. Wedged between two logs, he worked the rudder like an oar and stopped the gyrations as he felt the clumsy craft scrape the muddy bank. Then another collision, this time the logs rose up as if they had mounted an obstacle. Harry worked the oar furiously and then he realised that the logs were parting. He turned and ran to the higher end and saw the bow of a boat. He heard the scrape as the raft slid across a gravel surface, pushing and crushing the boat in front of it. Willow branches struck his face as Harry strained to see if it was safe to land here and then the raft stopped. He looked back and realised that half the raft had gone and the outrigger of the canoe was wedged between two of the remaining logs and the whole conglomeration was grounded.

Harry stepped into ankle deep water but quickly found dry land and breathed a sigh of relief. He was across the river and only had wet feet. Gradually he was able to make out what had happened. He had collided first with a canoe and then a crude rowing boat that was a rough frame covered with some sort of fabric or animal skin. The whole pile of wreckage had been pushed up onto the shallows by the current.

Harry became aware of a light on the river, a moving light and then he heard the sound of oars splashing. Soon the boat was only a dozen paces away and in the light of the torch in the bow he saw five men, four on the oars and one at the tiller. One of the oarsmen shouted something about the amount of rubbish there was in the water and couldn't the steersman guide them clear of these obstacles. There were further angry exchanges but Harry was not interested in their problems. It must be well past midnight and he must be clear of this north bank soon if he was to be back at the smoke house before daybreak.

The urgency to find a suitable craft and get away from this shore became Harry's priority now. Under his feet he felt shingle. He would not be leaving footprints in the mud, but the water was very cold and it had started to rain, but that was the least of his worries. Then he stepped on something. He stopped and felt for the object with his hand. It was a rope and proved to be the painter fixed to a small dinghy complete with two oars. Harry had to think of a method of removing the small boat that would leave the owner sure that it had fallen victim to the other half of the raft. He followed the rope back to the bank and found that it was secured to a wooden peg. A few sharp tugs and the peg was pulled out and dragged away.

Harry scrambled into the 'borrowed' boat and set the oars into the rowlocks and pulled for the middle of the river. He was excited, it had been easier than he had expected and then he realised that finding the smoke house in the dark was not going to be easy, the rain was falling steadily now. Perhaps it would obliterate any tracks he had left up on the cliff top. He could only hope.

Once in midstream, Harry shipped the oars and stood up, he would have to face the direction in which he was travelling if he was going to find the place where Peter moored his canoe. He took up one of the oars and put it into the water at the stern of the boat and used it like the rudder on the raft. The current was fierce here and carrying him downstream much too fast. He knew he must try something else. Harry put the oars back in the rowlocks and sat on the thwart and attempted to turn the boat, almost capsizing as he did. It would have to be accomplished slowly. Using only one oar, the Coracle Boy succeeded in turning the dinghy until the bow was pointing upstream. By rowing against the current he was able to slow down and coax the boat to the west bank, where he could take advantage of the eddying currents. Overhanging boughs were a problem, twice Harry was struck hard by low branches and he was forced to move further out into the river. His speed was increasing and he was beginning to wonder if he had missed the landing place. It seemed an age since he started his journey down the river. Harry guided the boat back to the west bank and the calmer water.

Suddenly Harry heard a scream. He pulled hard to slow down but the wailing had stopped. He was filled with fear and uncertainty. He disregarded the willow branches that brushed his face as he strained to listen. Moving slowly downriver, he heard it, a long, high pitched keening that filled the boy with anxiety for Meg and Lisa and the baby.

Throwing aside all thought of caution, Harry let the boat go with the flow. He saw it almost too late. It was the flat rock. He narrowly missed Peter's canoe as he steered his small craft between the canoe and the river bank and mounted the flat rock, transom first, with a speed that threw him into the stern of the boat. Harry was quickly on his feet and out of the boat, dragging it up onto the rock all in one movement. He rushed, sword in hand, up the steps that led to the smoke house. Now the anguished lamentation was joined by a baby crying and Harry ran towards the small dwelling hut. The door was hanging open and the fire was very low. Discretion forgotten, Harry burst into the hut sword in hand. He saw Lisa sitting in the corner, crying and holding the protesting infant in her arms.

She saw him but did not recognise him in the gloom and screamed at him and from the folds of the blanket that wrapped her child. She produced a hunting knife and pointed at him. Harry stopped and dropped to one knee and shouted, "Where is Meg?"

"Go away, I will kill you if you come near," Lisa screamed.

"Lisa, it's Harry. Where is Meg?"

"I don't know anything. Go away, leave me alone. My Peter is dead. Go away, leave me alone.

"Lisa, listen to me. It's Harry. Where is my sister? Where is Meg? What has happened here?" Harry looked around the hut and saw that there was nothing left that had belonged to them or Lisa.

Lisa stopped the awful wailing and nursed her daughter. She crooned quietly as she rocked back and forth. She looked across at Harry as he fed the fire and got a small blaze.

"Harry? You are Harry?" Lisa stared at him. "Oh Harry, it was so awful."

Harry thought she was going to start crying again but she managed to control herself and continued in a series of short sentences, broken by sobs as tears filled her eyes. "They have taken Meg.... They told me that Peter is drowned.... An archer shot him and he fell into the water at the Devil's Force and was swept away.... His hands were tied, Harry. He must be drowned." Again she broke down and it took time to get the whole story.

"When did this happen? How long ago?" Harry almost whispered.

"Not long after you left, I don't really know. Meg and I were talking."

Gradually Harry was able to piece together the story of the attack. Five men had arrived to tell Lisa of Peter's death and collect everything that had belonged to Peter, especially food. They said that there was no room in the boat for Lisa. She and the baby would be collected tomorrow. They thought Meg was a boy because she was dressed like a boy. They said he was probably Peter's brother who had disappeared with several other boys, after the earthquake. They tied Meg's hands behind her back. She struggled, but didn't say a word as they took her away."

Harry went outside to get some more wood for the fire. Lisa had finally drifted off to sleep and the baby was in its improvised cot. He saw the first hint of the dawn away to the east. He could hardly believe it. Where had the night gone? They would be back soon to fetch Lisa and her baby and he had to be clear of this place before that happened. He had to get back upriver before it was light if he was going to stand any chance of finding Meg.

With an armful of firewood Harry went back towards the hut. Suddenly he was grabbed from behind and shoved through the open door. He dropped the firewood. He felt a kick behind the knees and he fell to the floor, dangerously close to the fire. Lisa started screaming and then she stopped and began laughing hysterically. Harry was thrown aside and turned onto his back. He was staring up at his own sword pointing at his throat. It was held by a dishevelled figure with long blonde hair.

"Peter, oh Peter, they said you were drowned."

"Who is this? What's he doing here?"

"Oh Peter, look at you. You are soaking wet and you are bleeding. Oh look Peter, you have a lovely daughter."

"Stay where you are boy, or I'll kill you. Daughter? Let me see her."

Peter thrust the sword into his waist band and cradled the crying child in his strong, muscular arms. He was a tall, broad shouldered young man, not more than twenty years old, Harry guessed. He had long blonde hair, a wispy blonde beard and a moustache.

"Meg brought her into the world. That's Harry, her brother. They have been so kind to me, love. Look at the beautiful blanket Meg gave our daughter. They have taken Meg and will come back for me and the baby in the morning, Oh God in Heaven, Peter, they must not find you." The words just tumbled out as Lisa tried to tell her husband everything at once.

"They won't be back for days," The young man said. "Every able-bodied man is being taken up to the big mine in the morning, I reckon we have a couple of days to come up with a plan, but first I need to dry my clothes. Is there any fire in the smoke house? I think there might be an old coat in there."

"I kept the smoke house fire alight." This was Harry's first contribution to the conversation. Peter looked down at him, uncertainly at first, and then he grinned and held out his hand.

"Sorry about the rough introduction Harry. I owe you an apology and your sister my gratitude."

"I must be going now that you are back sir, I have to find Meg…."

"You must not call me sir, Harry. I am Peter and a slave, and so is Lisa."

"Abe Tull does not allow people to own slaves in our village," Harry replied.

"Then this Abe Tull is a very wise man. But about your sister, she will be held in the old storeroom until there is time to transport her through the Devil's Force and that could be several days away. But tell me what you are doing here in this dreadful wilderness. Are you alone or are there others?"

"Just me and my sister, Meg. We are looking for our little sister, Ruth. She was taken from our village with five other children," Harry replied. He was not yet prepared to mention Dan, Susan and Brian or Luke and his party, or the possibility that soldiers might be on their way there until he was sure of where Peter's loyalties lay.

Chapter Twenty Seven

It was getting light and Lisa stood up and said she would make breakfast and then realised that there was no food to make a breakfast of. Peter said that he would see if there was anything edible in the smoke house.

"Come with me Harry and you can tell me more about yourself and this wonderful village you live in."

"There are four of us. We are orphans and Master Tull took us in after the Raiders killed our father and burnt our house down."

"And what do you do for a living, Harry?"

"I fish from a coracle, they call me the Coracle Boy." But Harry was eager to hear more about Peter's escape.

"How did you escape from those men? Lisa said that your hands were tied behind your back."

"I didn't escape from the rowing boat. They took me to the old storeroom just below the Devil's Gorge and locked me in a cell with two other slaves who had tried to escape in the confusion. One of them told me my brother was killed in a landslide that took the side of the mountain away and some of the tunnels with it." Peter paused, "Over the next two nights we worked on one of the bars in our cell window and then last evening we removed the bar and the three of us escaped. The other two went into the forest and up to the lake. I tried to steal a canoe but one of the guards saw me and shot an arrow at me, thankfully he missed. I screamed that I had been hit and dived into the river. I swam underwater for as long as I could and when I surfaced I found I had been carried further downstream than I expected. It was a hard swim across the river. I wanted to reach the steps on the south bank, but as I got within sight I saw someone on the landing stage."

By this point they had arrived at the smoke house and Peter began to work his way to the back of the building. The first thing he handed to Harry was the ham he and Meg had found on their first visit. There were other pieces of dried meat and fish, they would not starve. Peter found an old woollen robe rather like those worn by the monks at the abbey. He stripped off his damp clothes and hung them to dry and then pulled on the strange garment. Harry was eager to hear the rest of Peter's story and prompted him by asking who he saw on the landing stage.

"That had me puzzled. This man was not carrying a torch and I couldn't see a dog. Pagans never go out at night unless they carry a torch. I was no more than ten paces away, but it was so dark I couldn't see what the man was doing. And then the landing stage suddenly broke free and the man must have seen me because he struck at me with a piece of timber as the whole platform floated away. But that now meant that I could reach the steps, I think I made it just in time. I ran up those steps to try and get warm. I saw the sentry up at the point and thought I should go and get rid of him and dry my clothes by his fire, but there might be two guards and possibly dogs. I decided that I was in no condition to take on two armed men and vicious dogs."

Harry and Peter arrived back at the hut where Lisa took some of the fish and placed it on the hot stones that surrounded the fire. It was their only method of cooking.

"I decided to make for a place on the cliff where I have a rope fixed, but I couldn't find it and it began to rain. My clothes had begun to dry on me but the rain soon soaked me again. I was about to give up on the rope and go further up the escarpment. I hoped to find a way down the cliff, but then I found the rope, abseiled down the cliff and ran like the wind to get here. You can imagine my fears when I heard Lisa talking to someone. I could only hear two voices so I waited and then you came out and I saw the sword in your belt. Well, the rest you know."

The smell of the fish cooking reminded Harry that he was very hungry and he gladly accepted his share of the fish, served on a piece of firewood. The wooden platters had gone with everything else. They ate with their fingers and hunting knives. By now it was daylight and Harry went out into the fresh morning air. The rain had stopped and there had been no frost in the night and he saw melt water running off the escarpment, which would mean a rise in the water level of the river. The river! Rising water levels! The boat, it would be washed away. Was he too late? Had it been swept downriver?

Harry raced down the path and the steps to the flat rock. The small rowing boat was still there, safe on the rock. The Coracle Boy secured the painter to the mooring ring that held Peter's canoe. He turned to examine his prize and found it to be a sound little craft that would easily take the five of them downriver. The five of them! He had to rescue Meg first. And then the dreadful truth hit him and he wanted to scream his hatred of these awful people. What was he doing messing about here? He should be out there looking for her.

Harry turned and ran up the steps and collided with Peter at the top.

"What's going on Harry? I saw you run for the river and wondered what you had seen or heard."

"I forgot to tell you Peter, I stole a boat last night and I suddenly remembered that I had only dragged it up onto the rock by your canoe…."

"You did what? You stole a boat? Where is it? Show me."

Peter followed Harry down to his mooring place and saw the boy's prize and he began to laugh.

"You have stolen the sturdiest rowing boat on the river, Harry; it belongs to one of the overseers. But how did you manage that? It was moored on the north bank with the fishermen's boats. How did you get across the river?"

"That was me you saw on the floating landing stage. I didn't mean…."

"That was you? You cut it free and used it as a raft. Well I'll be blessed."

"I didn't see you in the water Peter. I didn't try to hit you with the plank. It was what I used for a rudder. I was trying to bring the raft under control."

"That's a story I shall be telling for many years to come," Peter laughed.

He then became very serious and said that the overseer was called Trisk and he was an evil man, renowned for his cruelty and that they ought to hide the boat as quickly as possible. The boat was quite small and it could be easily concealed. They returned to the hut and told Lisa about the boat and of their plan to hide it.

"I think we should hide it on the other side of the river," Peter said. "There's a stream entering the river some distance downstream that would be ideal. I'll lead the way in the canoe."

Harry followed Peter down past the stream where the fallen tree had concealed them on their first trip, and then on past the pile of sandstone that once hung out over the river and now stuck out into the water. The side river was choked with a jumble of torn up trees and water gushed from any aperture it could find through the tangled fir tree dam. There must be quite a lake in the valley now.

Just round a slight bend in the river they came upon a shallow stream coming from a swampy, reed covered area to the east. Peter tied the canoe to a willow and stepped ashore and told Harry to head into the stream. The boy was soon pushing his way through tall, concealing reeds. Peter said that would be far enough and instructed Harry to tie the painter as high as he could reach to an alder tree to allow for rising water levels. With the boat safely moored, Harry joined Peter and they returned to the canoe. Harry told his companion about the things they had buried in the hole left by the uprooted tree and suggested that they collect them. Peter agreed and they landed at the fallen rocks and quickly found the stash, just clear of the flood. They loaded everything onto the canoe and set off again. With two of them paddling they made good progress and were soon tied up at the flat rock. It was now almost midday.

Lisa was amazed to see a cooking pot again. She hadn't seen one since they had left their village and the two blankets were sheer luxury to her. Her gratitude was shown by the hugs and kisses she forced on Harry who turned bright red. He quickly excused himself saying that he would go and try to shoot something to cook.

Harry followed the escarpment south, to the point where it was an easy climb up into the woods. He stopped to rest and sat with his back against a huge beech tree. From here he could see the devastation left by the avalanche and it depressed him. He thought of Meg and he was filled with despair. He wanted to weep, but that he must not do. He must talk to his father and ask his advice.

Harry stood up and looked up through the leafless branches at a cloudless, late afternoon sky. He brushed aside a tear that threatened to escape.

"Father, I know that you can hear me." The Coracle Boy spoke clearly and confidently. "You know that Meg has been taken by the pagans. I need your help father. I must rescue Meg and Ruth. Tell me what to do." He lowered his head and slid, gradually, down the trunk of the beech, before closing his eyes and drifting into a dreamless sleep.

It was the cold that woke Harry the next morning. He was huddled at the base of the large tree and found movement difficult and painful, and it took time to get his limbs to obey. He had slept since well before noon and now it was getting dark but there was a cloudless sky above so that he would be able to find his way back to the smoke house. Soon he was able to set off down the slope to the escarpment. There was just enough light to allow him to descend safely and follow the path back to Peter and Lisa's home. As he approached, he detected the odour of cooking. He was feeling very hungry, but he was feeling something else. He wasn't sure what it was. He felt calm, determined and unafraid and he knew what he had to do.

Chapter Twenty Eight

Lisa had made good use of the cooking pots, one contained boiled ham, the other stew with turnips, which Peter had buried in a clamp beside the pigsty, and cabbage that had survived the winter under the snow and the attention of the pagan thieves.

"We were beginning to worry, Harry and it would appear that the game was hiding from you," Peter said, laughing.

"Come and sit by the fire." Lisa indicated a seat covered with the skins they had rescued earlier. "Peter has made platters for us with one of your axes and some spoons to eat our food with."

The hot food soon lifted Harry's spirits and warmed him through and he was ready to reveal his plan to Peter and Lisa.

"I am going to find Meg in the morning. I plan to get myself captured so that we can be together. I would like you and Lisa to take the boat down to where I have friends waiting…."

"Hold on Harry. What are you saying? I will help you rescue your sister and then we can all go down the river," Peter suggested.

"No, Peter. We are not going back without Ruth and the only way to rescue Ruth is for Meg and me to be in the miners' village."

"This is a stupid idea. What are you going to do? Walk up to the nearest pagan and say, 'I have come to be a slave'? You'll be lucky if they don't kill you on the spot," Peter said scathingly.

"They won't kill me because they need boys like me to work in their mines. And if Meg and I can be together, we will work something out. I know we will."

"I didn't take you for a fool Harry," Peter said angrily, "If you were able to rescue your little sister, how would you get out of the village?"

"I don't know but we would find a way."

"And who are these friends you have waiting? This is the first we have heard of them. What is going on Harry?"

"Meg and I set out to find and rescue the six children taken from Abe Tull's village. Our little sister, Ruth, was one of them. No one believed that they had been taken up the river. A search party was sent east to the village in the marshes. It was led by Ben, Abe Tull's eldest son. We left three days later and after eight days we found the camp where the pagans hold the children before they put them into the rowing boats. It was deserted so we went down to look around, Meg found a small cross that belonged to Ruth. When we got back to our camp a party from Abe Tull's village, led by his younger son, Luke, had arrived. They had followed the trail we left. From there we made two scouting trips up here and camped under the fallen tree and on our return Luke said we would all go back to the village and send for soldiers, but Meg and I said we would stay and make another attempt to gather more information. Dan, the pagan tracker, and his wife wished to stay as did Brian, a giant of a man and a good friend. We should have returned to them yesterday, they will worry. That is why you must go downstream and take Lisa and the baby to safety. You can tell them more about this place than all our scouting trips."

"You say this man Luke will have sent for soldiers. Is it likely that they will come?" Peter said sceptically.

"I am sure they will come," Harry replied confidently.

"I have been to the camp where you found your sister's cross. There is a narrow gorge downstream with fierce currents. I wouldn't risk the lives of my wife and daughter through that gorge. The pagans have a great fear of it."

"And you would have to go through at night because the pagans would see you from the camp."

"Hold on, there are no men at the camp. They have been brought back to help with the emergency. We could land there and walk over the mountain. What am I saying? We are not going without you and your sister."

"If you don't go, Peter, you will be caught, you, Lisa and the baby, and me too probably, and it would be too late to surrender and my friends would be none the wiser. They would lose the valuable information you could provide."

"But Harry, I can't run away and leave you…."

"You have to. You must tell Brian and Dan what this place is like and they will tell the soldiers who will know how to deal with these people. Please Peter, it's our only chance," Harry pleaded. "Tell Brian to speak to Captain Redman, he will know what to do."

"And you would be a free man again Peter." Lisa spoke for the first time.

"And your daughter would be free," Harry added.

"It goes against all I believe in to let you walk into that hell hole," Peter said as he stood up and walked to the door and opened it. He looked up at a starry sky for what seemed an age to the Coracle Boy. Peter closed and fastened the door. He looked at Harry and then at his wife and child and back to Harry.

"Alright Harry, when do we do this? What are your plans?" he asked.

"We go as soon as possible," Harry replied. "Can we collect the boat tonight and be ready for you to leave at first light?"

"Yes, but why the hurry?"

"Do they know that you are a strong swimmer?"

"Yes. I have pulled a couple of men out of the river when their boats capsized and there was a young boy who got into difficulties last summer."

"Suppose they realize that you weren't injured and swam across the river, they might even accuse you of cutting the landing stage free. They could be down here any time and they would be very angry."

"To find me alive at all would mean a trip to their torture chamber and certain death. But what are your plans Harry?"

"I leave here as soon as possible. If you could take me across to the east bank, I'll walk up to the village."

"That is almost a day's walk and dangerous in the dark. There is no track along the east bank and there are treacherous bogs and deep rivers coming into the main river. No, I will take you to a safe place to land," Peter insisted. And then he went into deep thought and was silent for a while. Slowly he returned to his place by the fire and sat down.

"Here's what we do Harry." Peter's manner suggested that he would not tolerate an argument. "We load my canoe with our few possessions, some food and water and our weapons. Lisa and the baby will come too and with three of us paddling we should have you on the east bank by midnight."

"But why take Lisa and the baby?" Harry asked.

"Because I am not losing sight of my family again," Peter replied.

The discussion continued as they gathered the few things that Harry and Peter had collected from their stash buried under the tree root.

Lisa had woven a rush basket to be a cradle for the baby and lined it with one of the blankets. With the aid of Harry's torches they loaded the canoe. The cargo looked very small for a young couple to start a home with. It took up very little space. Peter would take the leading paddle in the bow and Harry would be in the middle. Lisa would be at the stern with the baby at her feet. It was a task she often undertook and appeared to be as skilled as Peter.

"When you surrender to the pagans, how will you explain your sister being at the smoke house and where you were when they took her away."

"I shall not tell them that we are looking for our sister. I shall say that we fled from the Raiders and are looking for a place to settle. Our coracle was stolen by the two boys we took down to our camp. I shall tell them that they capsized the coracle and drowned. A few days later we stumbled on the smoke house. The woman had a little baby. She was terribly upset. She feared that her husband was dead and robbers had stolen all her food. I said we would go hunting. She wanted Meg to stay with her. She was afraid to be alone. When I returned, Lisa said the pagans had taken Meg."

"They separate the boys from the girls. How do you hope to meet up with Meg? She will be taken to the village."

"They think that Meg is a boy and she will keep up that appearance. She will also pretend to be dumb. It's something we agreed on when we set out."

"How will you explain being on that side of the river?" Peter asked.

"I stole your boat and got as far as I could, when I hit a rock and put a hole in the canoe. I had to get out in a hurry and the canoe sank."

"You seem to have thought it all out Harry, I hope your plan works. There is something else I have been thinking about. I would rather continue the journey down to your friends in the canoe. We are used to it, you see. The boat can stay where it is. You may find it useful at some point."

And so with a following wind they set off upstream. It was a starry night and they were able to see both banks of the river. They pulled across to the east bank and found the eddying currents much more helpful. They encountered two incoming rivers, but Peter knew the river well and they were not adversely affected by the turbulence.

Peter turned and told Harry that they were approaching the point where he would land, there would be no talking from now on. They moved tight to the riverbank under the overhanging trees. It was dark here and Harry could see no landing place. Peter was standing up now and indicated that the Coracle Boy should stop paddling. Harry saw him step out of the canoe onto something solid. He disappeared into the darkness. Lisa tapped Harry on the shoulder with the tip of her paddle. He turned and she was holding out her hand. He took it and they shook hands warmly.

"Good luck Harry, and give my love to Meg. Tell her my baby will have her name," she whispered.

"Good luck Lisa, safe journey." That was the best Harry could manage for there was a lump in his throat and a tear in his eye, He was glad that it was so dark under the trees. He felt the boat rock as Peter climbed back on board.

"The track to the village ends at a landing stage. I will take you that far. So gather your things and say goodbye to Lisa and the baby."

Harry was only taking his hunting bow and the clothes he stood up in. He could vaguely see Lisa and the baby was asleep.

"Goodbye Lisa, goodbye little Meg, see you soon," he called in a hoarse whisper. He heard a faint, 'Goodbye, Harry' and saw the wave of Lisa's hand.

Harry felt Peter's hand on his shoulder. "The step is level with the gunnel and there is a rope on your right."

Harry left the canoe and mounted the steps using the rope to guide him. As he ascended, the light improved and he saw that he was now on top of the riverbank where Peter joined him.

"Follow me, just keep me in sight, it's not far." They were pushing their way through a tangle of scrub willow and then they were out of the willow and walking through dead bracken. There was snow but it appeared to be melting quite quickly. Peter stopped and held up his hand and called Harry forward.

"This is as far as I can take you Harry, can you make out the landing stage down there?"

"Yes, I can see it fine," Harry replied.

"Go down to the landing stage and you will see steps leading up to a boardwalk that takes you onto a cart track that leads to the river that comes down from the lake. There are stepping-stones alongside the ford. Once you are across you are more than halfway to the Devil's Gorge. You should be at the landing stage below the Gorge well before first light. Your sister Meg will be held in the old storeroom, it's the longest hut there. The first hut you come to is the best place for you to wait for daylight, it's a store for ropes and boat tackle. I think that is all I can tell you Harry. All I can say is that I think you are very brave to do this for your sister."

"She would do the same for me Peter."

"Yes I'm sure she would," Peter said as he held out his hand.

Harry felt the sincere, firm grip. As he started down the slope he turned to wave and heard Peter say quietly, "May the gods go with you, my friend." Peter was lost in the night as he made his way back to his family and a journey to freedom.

Chapter Twenty Nine

The landing stage appeared to be rigid and not a floating construction. The well made steps up to the boardwalk led Harry to the rough and poorly maintained cart track. Soon after he came to a junction with a road coming from the east that turned to follow the river. This road was wider and in better condition. Harry began to jog, he wanted to be at the first hut well before dawn. The sound of rushing water warned him that he was getting close to the tributary that tumbled down from the lake. The Coracle Boy slowed to a brisk walk and soon saw the road disappear into the water of the ford. He found a path leading upstream and discovered the stepping-stones and crossed them without mishap. He found the road again and returned to his jog trot.

Harry sensed that he was nearing the small settlement and slowed down to a steady walk. He smelt the wood smoke first and then, as he came round a bend in the road, he saw lights of fires or torches still some distance away. It set his heart pounding and so he stopped to consider his next move. There were three fires. He would approach with care, there might be dogs.

As he got closer Harry could make out the shapes of huts illuminated by two fires some distance apart. A third source of light was nearer to him. It was a flaming torch fixed to a post and as he got closer Harry could see the first hut that Peter had described as a store for ropes and boat tackle. The hut was a distance from the torch. He would be able to get close to it without being seen.

Harry noticed that the fires and the torch were between the river and the huts. He reasoned that if he climbed to the higher ground at the back of the huts he would have a silhouette of the whole settlement. And so it proved to be. Harry was able to identify the longest hut where Meg would be held. There was good cover from this position. He could get down to within a few paces of the long hut without being seen, but it was a very risky strategy. He could be walking into a trap. But wasn't that the idea? Didn't he intend to be captured? If he could forewarn Meg there would be less chance of her true gender being discovered in the excitement of their reunion, Harry thought to himself.

It was only a moment's consideration and then Harry began moving down through the gorse and broom bushes that populated the lower slopes of the mountain. There was no snow on this south facing slope, but the bushes were wet with melt water and Harry had to pick his way carefully. He had no wish to get a soaking. The undergrowth had been allowed to creep right up the wattle and daub walls of the hut. The holes that could be regarded as windows were lit from within the hut and appeared as a brownish yellow rectangle about four hands square with three vertical bars. The window on the extreme right was boarded up and Harry wondered if this had been Peter's escape route. Harry could not see through the openings, he was not tall enough. He searched with his hands in the darkness and found a large stone, but even this wasn't high enough for him to see through the window. It started to rain, a fine drizzle, but here under the wide overhanging eaves of the thatched roof it was dry and comparatively warm. The sky had clouded over, the stars no longer visible and the darkness under the eaves was complete. Harry was very tired. His sleep under the beech tree yesterday afternoon had not been really restful, but he must not sleep now. He had to be ready to meet whatever challenge was put in front of him. He felt about in the darkness and found a piece of wood and some dry straw, which he used to make a seat. He sat with his back to the wall of the hut and began chewing a piece of dried meat to ease his hunger, but soon his eyelids drooped and Harry fell asleep.

Loud voices barking orders and others shouting as if in panic brought the Coracle Boy out of his dreamless sleep. It was broad daylight. The rain had stopped and there was a stiff breeze blowing. He looked up and saw a clear blue sky. He stood up cautiously and looked around at his surroundings. The back of the hut was almost buried in brambles all dead at this time of year but no less capable of drawing blood with their sharp thorns. Harry found the best way to reach the end of the hut was to crawl on his belly under the bushes. He decided to leave his hunting bow, he would have little use for it from now on. The noise continued unabated as he reached the end of the hut and stood up. There seemed to be some sort of commotion down at the river. Suddenly a short elderly man approached from the next hut about ten paces from Harry.

"Don't just stand there boy, get down there and help. Here take this rope, you'll be quicker than me."

"Yes sir." Harry grabbed the rope and ran in the general direction of the noise. He ran down a slope and across the road. From here he could see a capsized rowing boat and several men in the water between the boat and the river bank. One of the men was on the other side of the boat and the ropes that were being thrown were falling short of him. Harry saw the man's plight. He also saw a coracle, upside down, on the bank some twenty paces away and ran to the small craft. In one practised move he had the coracle on his shoulder and the paddle in his left hand. He ran to the water's edge and launched the coracle and himself with it.

The man lost his grip at this point and Harry saw him being pulled out into the middle of the river. He struck out after him, it was apparent to the Coracle Boy that the man could swim but in this current he was fighting a losing battle. Harry got within a few paces of the man. He called out that he would throw the rope and tow the man to the shore. The man seemed calm and understood and caught the rope on the first casting. He also knew what Harry meant when he was asked to try and lie on top of the water. With the paddle in his left hand and the rope in his right, Harry took up the slack and pulled for the shore. Despite his efforts they were being drawn downstream at an alarming speed. The thaw was raising the river levels and debris could be seen out in the middle of the river. Gradually the Coracle Boy coaxed the craft into the eddying currents, but the man in the water was obviously tiring and the water was very cold. It was doubtful if the man could hold on for much longer, but hold on he did and very slowly Harry guided the man close to the river bank. Helpers who had been running along the road following them now rushed into the water and dragged the man to safety. Harry turned and paddled back up to where he had launched the coracle.

Perhaps he had a bargaining chip now. No, these people did not make bargains. He would stick to the plan and hope to find Meg.

As he approached the small crowd they began to cheer. Obviously someone had run back to tell the gathering that the man was safe. A boy of about sixteen stepped into the water and grabbed the rim of the coracle and took the paddle from Harry.

"You know how to handle a coracle, boy, who are you?"

"I am Harry. They call me the Coracle Boy and I am looking for my brother. His name is Greg. He doesn't speak. I believe that he was brought here."

"You believe right, young feller. He might be dumb but he'll make a good miner and so will you. Come here, let me get a good look at you."

The cheering stopped and the well-wishers fell silent.

Harry was looking at a big man almost as big as Abe Tull. He had a black beard similar to that worn by the big blacksmith, but this man's beard was dirty and matted. He was dressed in animal skins and wore a wide leather belt from which hung a coiled whip, a vicious looking weapon. Harry moved forward.

"Sir, after rescuing your man I thought you would give me my brother and let us go on our way."

The big man laughed and said that he was short of a couple of good strong lads and told two of his men to bring Harry up to the old storeroom. Harry knew he would have to be careful here and hope that Meg would not let the cat out of the bag and reveal that she could speak.

Harry was shoved roughly through the door of the old storeroom and told to sit on a bench. The big man went into another room and spoke to someone and returned almost at once. He told Harry to stand up straight and be respectful. Presently a man dressed like a gentleman appeared and stood in the doorway to the room. He looked hard at Harry who returned his gaze for a moment and then looked down, respectfully.

"So who are you?" the gentleman asked. He spoke like Sir John and Captain Redman and so he must be a gentleman and could be trusted, Harry thought. He raised his head and answered confidently.

"Sir, I am Harry and my brother is Greg." If captured, tell them as little as possible but anything you do have to say should be as close to the truth as you can risk. That had been their agreement since speaking to Friar Godwin.

"So the dummy has a name. So what are you doing in our land and where are you from?" the gentleman said. This told Harry that Meg was playing her part well, but he must not forget she was now believed to be a boy.

"Sir, we lived half a day's ride north of Westown. Our father was killed and our house burned down by the Raiders sir. We are looking for a place to settle." Harry maintained the respectful but confident manner, the mark of a free man his father had taught him.

"That was last summer. Where have you been since then?"

This was a question the Coracle Boy had not expected and he hesitated and was prompted by a sharp "Well?" from the gentleman.

"Sir, we stayed at the village of Master Abe Tull sir."

"So why are you trespassing on our land?"

"Mummers stole our sister sir. We followed them."

"How many know you are here?"

"Many people know of our plan sir. They sent search parties east and south. The south searchers found the wreckage of a stolen ferry and it was agreed that the children were all drowned and we abandoned the search."

"So what are you doing here?"

"I had a dream sir. I dreamed of a land to the north. In my dream I was told to follow the river and I would find a valley where there was good hunting and no Raiders sir." This was Harry's first deliberate invention. But was it invention? Why was he so certain that Ruth had been taken north? Was this his father guiding him? Harry was aware that he was being spoken to.

"Do you hear me boy?"

"I'm sorry sir?" Harry replied questioningly.

"I said how did you get this far from Abe Tull's village?" the gentleman demanded irritably.

"Greg and me travelled by coracle sir."

"Don't lie to me boy, it is not possible."

"We are fishermen sir. We make our living on the river and your people have just seen me handle a coracle. Gregg is even better than me sir."

"How long have you been here?"

"I don't have the numbers sir, but I think it is about this many days." Harry held up both hands with his fingers spread.

"Ten days and you were not caught? Why was that do you think?" Harry saw the gentleman look angrily at the big man who stood beside the boy, the coiled whip now held in his hand menacingly. Harry just looked blank.

"Did you see any other boys on the mountain?"

"Yes sir, a pair of them. They stole our coracle and food but they didn't get very far. They lost the paddle and they capsized. They must have drowned sir."

"Are you sure? Couldn't they swim to the banks?"

"No sir. They were right in the middle when we saw the coracle capsize. No one could have got clear of those currents." Harry realised that the lies were coming too easily. He must be careful.

"Can you explain why your brother was with the woman at the smoke house and where you were when we caught him, what did you call him? Ah yes, Greg."

"The woman had no food so I went hunting. When I got back the woman had gone mad and threatened to kill me. She screamed at me and said that her man was dead and soldiers had taken Greg and she would kill herself and the baby. I went up to the smoke house and cooked the duck I had shot and took some down to the woman's hut but she had gone."

"Do you normally hunt in the dark?" the gentleman asked, casually.

"No sir."

"Well it was dark when your brother was taken."

"I didn't get back to the smoke house until first light. There was a bear and her cub between me and the way down the escarpment. I circled round and got below her but I couldn't find the way down, and then as it was getting light. I found a rope just above where the cliff meets the river, a short way upstream of a landing stage."

"You saw a bear and cub at this time of the year?" the gentleman asked suspiciously.

"She was limping sir. I think she was woken up by the earthquake sir."

At that moment the boy, who had taken charge of the coracle Harry had used to rescue the man in the water, came into the hut and announced that the second barge was ready to go.

"Get the other boy and take them up to the schoolhouse and put them in the secure room, I need to talk to them. And no rough stuff Trisk, do you hear? You don't lay a finger on them until I have finished with them."

So that was Trisk. Peter had said that he was an evil man, renowned for his cruelty. Well, forewarned is forearmed.

Moments later Trisk emerged from a room on the other side of the storeroom, pushing Meg in front of him. She was wearing her shoulder bag that held the pouch filled with medicines and salves and many items needed for their journey.

"Greg! Are you alright? How have they been treating you?"

Meg waved her hands about and made signs with her fingers as if it was some kind of sign language. The two shook hands and walked side by side out of the storeroom.

Chapter Thirty

Trisk hurried the 'boys' in front of him across the road and down the riverbank to the waiting barge, a most unusual but sturdy boat that was pointed at both ends. There was iron strapping extending from the bows to almost halfway down the side of the boat. A hawser, the thickness of a man's arm, was attached to a huge ring in the ironwork. There was no similar ironwork at the rear of the boat, this puzzled Harry. The 'boys' were herded aboard and to their relief Trisk was not travelling with them, but his two henchmen were and they looked more unpleasant than Trisk.

Soon the tension was put on the hawser and the barge swung out into midstream, Harry noticed that almost every face on the barge bore the imprint of fear. Even the two brutes sent to escort the boys were ashen and gripped the gunnels with knuckle whitening force. The boat was now moving forward slowly and then the speed increased a little and they were making a bow wave that caused them to ship a little water, much to the consternation of some of the passengers. The water was truly a terrifying spectacle. It was smooth, almost like molten glass sliding beneath them at speed. Occasionally the boat would buck like a horse and there would be a chorus of gasps from the petrified voyagers. Harry gave Meg a slight nudge and leaned forward with his forearms resting on his knees nonchalantly. Meg followed suit and they grinned at each other. Their minders would have liked to haul the pair back, but were afraid to let go of whatever they were holding.

Once they were into the gorge the bucking stopped and the speed increased slightly. Harry sat up and looked about. He saw the towering cliffs of the gorge, looking black and ominous. Ahead, he saw the thick hawser slapping the river from time to time and he saw the four horses a long way in front.

Suddenly Harry realised that there was another boat of similar size coming towards them. Two boatmen stood up and each picked up a sturdy pole from the floor of the boat. One man went to the front, the other to the rear. Their task was to make sure that the oncoming boat did not collide with them. Harry quickly saw the reason. The other boat was unmanned. It was merely a counterweight, filled with ballast to help the horses draw the passenger boat through the narrow gorge. Once the fierce current gripped the ballast boat, the horses were no longer needed. Harry stood up and saw that there were two hawsers fixed to the bows of the boat. The first was tied to the passenger boat and passed around a wheel on the quay and fixed to the ballast boat. The second lighter rope went to the horses' harness. Harry admired the ingenuity of the system. He watched with interest as the boatmen poled the ballast boat clear of the passenger craft. He felt the increase in speed as the counterbalance met the stronger current. The two boatmen shipped their poles and took up ropes and prepared to cast the lines to men on the wharf. With the boat secured, they stepped ashore beside a small derrick. This simple crane was used to offload heavy cargo.

Harry, Meg and their guard had to wait while a group of men left the boat and climbed onto a horse drawn cart together with a quantity of tools and equipment. Harry took the opportunity to look around at his new surroundings. He saw the near vertical cliffs that appeared to be much higher than they looked from the abandoned mine. There were two rough lean-to buildings on the wharf. Further upstream he saw the almost horizontal wheel that balanced the two boats. It was like a huge wagon wheel with a deep groove in its rim, and tilted to the gradient of the rope. Upstream Harry saw that the wharf became a road rising steadily into the distance. He saw the horses being led back to the wharf. Near to the view was more sinister. The dark rock of the cliff face broken only by the zigzagging steps cut into the cliff. Two men were carrying loads up this precarious stairway. He wondered if that was the route they would be taking. He so wanted to discuss their situation with his sister. So far there had been no opportunity for Harry to communicate with Meg, but they were together again and that was all that mattered for now.

Harry, Meg and their escort ascended the zigzagging steps that took them up to a level area way above the river. It was rather like a market square. The snow had almost gone except where it had been shovelled into heaps, but higher up the mountain there was little evidence of the thaw. In front of them they saw a large stone building built against the cliff. Harry was reminded of a church.

"This way! Move yourself Dummy." Meg was given a hefty shove that almost knocked her to the floor. They were taken across to another large building. It stood at right angles to all the other structures in the village and faced upriver. It was long and low and had stone walls up to the eaves and then reed thatch on the roof. A stone gable with a large chimney breast filled one end of the building. A second chimney pierced the roof further to their left. There were several barred windows but only one door in the front wall, it had embrasures on either side.

The sound of children chanting something came to them as they neared the building. It sounded like multiplication tables being learned by rote. They exchanged looks each knowing what they both were dreading. Their little sister might be inside the building. If she recognised them the true purpose of their arrival here would be discovered and the consequences of that would not be good.

One of the guards went forward and opened the door and the chanting became louder. Harry was shoved forward first and then Meg followed. They were in a wide, dark hallway with a door on either side of them and another in front. There were store cupboards on both side walls, but they could see no children. Fortunately the door was closed to the room from where the chanting was coming. One of the guards pushed open the door in front of them, the other shoved them through. The door was closed and locked. They were in a room the width of the hallway, it was dimly lit by an iron barred window high up on the rear wall. There was a bench along the rear wall, a heavy table on their left and a cupboard to the right. They both hurried forward to sit on the bench.

Harry put his finger to his lips and pointed to the moving shadow showing at the bottom of the door. Someone was listening.

"I wish you could speak, Greg. I can't read your signs in this gloom."

His sister leaned across and whispered in his ear asking him why he had come. They would never escape from here.

"I had to come Greg, what else could I do with no coracle and no food? And the mad woman at the smoke house has probably walked into the river with her baby, I couldn't stay there. I decided to come and join you, so I borrowed the canoe that was moored by the smoke house." Harry paused to give the listener the impression that he was reading his sister's sign language.

"No, the canoe sank. I was lucky to escape. I was keeping tight to the east bank when I hit something and tore a hole in the canoe. Fortunately I was under some overhanging trees and was able to climb out, but I lost the blankets and some smoked fish I found at the smoke house and my hunting bow and the last of my arrows. It all went down with the canoe or floated away. But tell me about your capture. Have they treated you well? Have you been fed?"

Meg leaned across and whispered that she was so glad that Harry had come, but she had little hope of ever getting out of this place. Harry felt a hot tear as he touched her face reassuringly.

"Don't worry Greg, I'm sure these people will see that we are free men. Perhaps they will employ us to fish for them. But you haven't answered my question. How have they treated you?"

Meg whispered that she had been treated well. She asked about Lisa and the baby. Harry whispered that Peter, Lisa and the baby had gone downriver to safety and then out loud he said that he was glad that Greg had been treated well and no, he had no idea what was going to happen.

"But the man I spoke to where I met you seemed a reasonable sort of chap. He spoke like Captain Redman, I reckon he's a gentleman." All of the time Harry spoke he watched the bottom of the door. He saw the shadow move slightly from time to time and then they heard a door open and close and a woman's voice. Their prison was unlocked and a guard pushed the door open and entered the cell. He saw the young prisoners seated at the back of the room and then stepped aside to reveal a tall white-haired woman carrying a tray that held two bowls of steaming hot soup and two chunks of coarse bread. She smiled at the pair and told them to enjoy their food. The soup was very hot and there wasn't much of it and the bread was stale, but it was a meal of sorts. Harry was desperately hungry and he was also very tired. After they had eaten he whispered to Meg that he needed to sleep, but she must wake him at the first hint of anyone coming to see them. Harry lay down on the bench and was soon sound asleep.

Meg roused Harry. It was late afternoon and he found the room almost in darkness. He could barely see his sister. Suddenly he remembered where he was and that Meg was Greg now. He must be careful.

"Greg, what's wrong? Why did you wake me?"

Meg cupped her hand over his ear and whispered that it was getting dark and she thought it best to wake him while he could still see her. She also said that she was sure that there had been someone outside the window for quite some time.

"You have been asleep too," Harry laughed ironically. "So you don't know if we had visitors or not. Perhaps they have forgotten us." He kept up his one- sided conversation for a while and then they heard voices, several people talking and then there was a sort of chanting.

Meg whispered that she had heard this when they locked her in the storeroom. She thought it was some kind of pagan worship or prayer meeting. It lasted a long time. However, this ceremony was soon over and there was the noise of people moving. They could see light coming under the door, the flickering light of a torch, and then the door was pushed open and they saw the silhouette of a man. Someone handed the visitor a burning torch. Harry and Greg rose quickly to stand by the bench at the back of the room. They saw that it was a man dressed from head to toe in a white, hooded garment that was belted at the waist with a thick cord. He carried a long staff that was topped with a ram's horn. He strode into the room and shouted angrily in a language that they could not understand and then he spoke in their own language and ordered them to stand in the middle of the room. He walked around them chanting the strange words and striking the stone floor with the staff. He stopped in front of Meg and seized hold of her ear and twisted it. Meg reached up and tried to scratch the hand and made a deep, throaty sound. The priest, for that is what he was, let go of her ear and slapped Meg hard across her face. Harry made to attack the priest but the guard punched the Coracle Boy and sent him sprawling across the floor.

"You two need to be taught a lesson in good manners," the priest shouted before addressing the man who had struck Harry. "Give them to the slave master at the landslide, we need to get that section back in production."

"I'll see to it at first light, Nargor."

"You will do it now," the priest shouted. "Tonight!" He almost screamed the word and struck the floor hard with his staff and stormed out of the room.

"Get up! There's nothing wrong with you, or do you want a proper beating?"

Harry had remained sitting on the floor when he was knocked down but now decided that it was wise to obey and stood up and moved close to Meg. At that moment the tall white-haired woman told the man to get out of her way as she entered with a tray that held two hunks of bread and a lump of cheese. A jug of goat's milk was brought in by a young girl.

"I have to get these two up to the mine now," the man complained. "The priest, Nargor, is not in a good mood," he added.

"I take my orders from the High Priest, not that bad tempered brute Nargor. Now go and get the cart ready, the boys are to be fed before they go to the mine." She turned to Harry and Greg. "This is the best we can do, we are very short of food since the earthquake destroyed our food store."

"It looks fine to us mistress, thank you," Harry replied politely.

"I will leave the door open so that you can see to eat your meal. The outside door is locked and there are people in the two rooms either side of the hall so don't go exploring. Come along Jennie, let the boys eat their meal." The woman put her arm round the girl's shoulder and guided her out of the room.

Harry and Meg stared at each other, both afraid to believe what they had seen. Harry thought quickly and said that they ought to eat their modest meal before the guard came back and then whispered in Meg's ear. Meg nodded in agreement and there were tears in her eyes and the question, 'What do we do now'? was in both their minds.

The girl carrying the jug was Jennie, Jed's daughter and Ruth's companion at this dreadful place.

"Thank goodness she didn't recognise us Meg," Harry whispered.

"I wanted to speak to her and ask about Ruth. Harry, what are we to do?"

"It's not fair to burden her with such a secret or raise her hopes of rescue when we might be held captive at the mine for goodness knows how long."

Both fell silent for a while and then Harry remembered that he ought to carry on a conversation with his 'dumb brother'. He waffled on about the bread being stale but the cheese was good and the goat's milk was a pleasant surprise.

Meg whispered that they ought to stay in the shadows, just in case Jennie accompanied the white-haired woman when she collected the tray. Her brother agreed. With the food consumed, they both returned to the bench at the back of the room to wait.

"I don't fancy working in a mine Greg," Harry said, continuing another one-sided conversation. The door to their cell being open allowed them to see that the hallway was lit by several candles. There was a heavy iron bar across the main entrance and the embrasures were shuttered. They could hear muffled voices coming from the rooms either side of the hall.

Suddenly the door on their right opened and the voices were louder for a moment until the door was closed again. And then Jennie ran right up to them. She was crying.

"Harry, Meg, I saw you from the hall when they brought you here. Are you here to rescue us? Is my father with you?" she said in a low, hushed voice as she wiped away the tears.

"No Jennie, we are here alone but we have sent messages back. Meg is pretending to be a boy. She is also pretending to be dumb, but you must tell no one. Where is Ruth? Is she alright?" Harry whispered.

"She is getting better. She was very ill on the journey. I won't tell her you are here. She would not be able to keep it secret. I must go. I know you will get us out of this terrible place Meg and you too Harry. I have to go."

Jennie picked up the tray and hurried back through the door on the right and it all seemed like a dream. Meg was crying and Harry tried to comfort his sister, but he felt pretty miserable himself. Gradually they regained their composure and Meg asked for the umpteenth time what they were going to do. Harry had no answer, he saw only the bleakest of horizons. They could be held prisoner here for years. He thought of working underground for all that time and it filled him with dread. How would Meg survive such conditions? She was tough but to keep up the charade of being a dumb boy would be very difficult. And then he had a thought.

"Meg, can I suggest something?" he whispered. "Would it be a good idea for you to reveal that you are a girl? That way you would be with Ruth and Jennie. Think about it for a while and if you want to go through with it we could ask to speak to the white-haired woman."

"I had the same idea Harry, but no, I want to stay with you. I know we will find a way out of this mess. Anyway the soldiers will be here soon and we will all be free again."

"Are you absolutely sure Meg? It will be awful working in a mine."

"I'm sure Harry. We have made a good team up until now and suddenly I feel so sure that there is a way out for us all. You will get us out."

"No Meg. We will do it together. We will get us out."

Outside it was totally dark now and they could hear rain falling. It sounded like a very heavy storm that would wash away the snow. Presently the white-haired woman came in. She was carrying a lantern. She told them that they were not going to the mine tonight, they would be taken there in the morning. Tonight they would sleep in the loft, but first she told them to follow her. She led them through the door on the left of the hallway. It was the room from which the chanting had been heard earlier. A fire blazed in an iron basket on the other side of the room. Harry and Meg were taken through a door in the rear wall that led outside. They were in a sort of courtyard about three paces wide and extending almost the whole length of the building. The back wall was the sheer wall of the cliff and the two ends were sealed with a man-made stone wall against which a thatched lean-to had been erected. A candle in a lantern illuminated each lean-to.

"There is water to wash in and a cloth to dry yourself and the privy is at the other end of the yard. When you have finished come back into this room and stay by the fire to warm yourselves. I will fetch you shortly."

With their ablutions over, they hurried back to the warmth of the fire, but it was not a pleasant room. Pagan symbols were painted on the walls. A ram's horn adorned the wall above the fireplace. A coiled whip hung above the door.

Chapter Thirty One

The fire was the only illumination in the sinister room and made the ram's horn icon even more frightening. Harry and Meg kept their gaze on the dancing flames of the burning log and said nothing, not even daring to whisper in case they were being watched from the shadows.

Presently the white-haired woman called them into the hall and opened one of the cupboards to reveal a vertical ladder going up into the roof space.

"Up you go," the woman said. "There are blankets up there but you can't have a candle. You might set the thatch alight. I will leave this door open while you get settled. Now get some sleep, you will have a busy day tomorrow."

Harry led the way in almost total darkness. As he went through the hatchway, his body blocked all the light out. It wasn't until Meg joined him and sat on the straw, clear of the opening, that they were able to look at their surroundings. The light was so weak they could only just make out the blankets placed beside the hatchway and the thick layer of straw they were sitting on. They gathered a blanket each to wrap around themselves and lay down on the straw. Their whispered conversation was soon overtaken by sleep. It had been a very long day especially for Harry.

They were awakened by a man's voice shouting for them to get down or they would feel the lash of his whip. A woman's voice could be heard remonstrating with the man.

Harry and Meg folded their blankets and placed them where they had found them and descended the ladder. There was no sign of a woman. Instead they were confronted by a short, red haired man who was wearing a large coat, much too big for him and made of animal skins. It was filthy. In his grimy left hand he held a coiled whip, but his right hand was hidden by a dirty, bloodstained bandage. His whole appearance was worsened by his wet, bedraggled state. Obviously he had been out in the rain and was dripping water where he stood.

He was grinning and showing his blackened teeth, but his grin hardened to a scowl when he realised that both Harry and Meg were a smidgen taller than him.

"And where do you think you are going?" The white-haired woman said as she entered the hallway from the door on the right. "And look at the mess you are making. Go and wait in the stable I will send for you when these young ones have eaten."

"But the master…."

"Don't you dare argue with me, now go."

The white-haired woman ushered Harry and Meg into the room on the right. There was a blazing fire in an open hearth at the far end of a lighter, larger room than the sinister place on the opposite side of the hallway. A long table almost filled the room and benches provided seating for the diners. Heavy shutters to the barred windows were secured in the open position to provide light additional to the torches on the back wall. There were two doors in the end wall, one at either side of the large hearth. Harry and Meg followed the white-haired woman through the door nearest to the front wall into a large kitchen. An old man sat by the open fire, turning a spit that held a small pig. Jennie was the only other person in the room. She was peeling vegetables and putting them in an iron pot. She paid no attention as Harry and Meg were taken to the far end of the kitchen and told to sit at the table where a bowl of very thin porridge awaited them. There was so little oatmeal in the porridge that it would have been easier to drink it than use the shallow wooden spoons they were given. There was also a slice of stale bread, thinly spread with pork dripping for each of them.

Moments later they saw the white-haired woman pull on a hooded cloak and hurry to a door at the end of the room. She turned and spoke to Jennie.

"I am going to speak to the High Priest, I shall not be long."

She went out into the rain, closing the door behind her. Jennie left her vegetables and almost ran to the window. She looked out for a short while and then hurried across to Harry and Meg. In little more than a whisper she told them, "Ruth has guessed that you are here. Last night the priest who teaches us how to be pagans gathered us all together and asked us if anyone knew two boys called Harry and Greg. Ruth looked at me and I shook my head and frowned. Later at bedtime she asked me if you were really Harry and Meg. I denied it at first but she said she didn't believe me and began to cry. I had to tell her, Meg, that you were pretending to be a boy who couldn't speak. I told her that we mustn't tell anyone. She agreed and I'm sure she meant it."

Before either Harry or Meg could speak, Jennie hurried across to the window and with only the briefest look she dashed back. "Sister Rona is coming back. I have to get back to my work."

Meg touched Jennie's arm and begged her to give Ruth their love. Jennie replied that she would and then ran back to her vegetables.

The white-haired woman, Sister Rona, came in and slammed the door behind her. She removed the cloak and shook the rain off it before taking it down to the fire to hang up to dry. She scolded the old man for not turning the spit evenly and accused him of going to sleep, which of course he vehemently denied and then chuckled wickedly as she came back up to Harry and Meg. She said that she was sorry that there was only water to drink and explained she was saving the goat's milk for the younger children.

The short, red haired man came into the kitchen and said that the master wanted the new boys down at the saw mill at once. The 'boys' followed the red haired man to where they saw two men talking heatedly beside a horse drawn cart half loaded with timber. The logs were about a hand's span thick and a man's stride long.

As they drew near they turned to see the approaching trio and Harry saw that the man on the right was Trisk. The other was a tall thin man whose clothes were very muddy. He spoke first.

"Get the lads up on the cart Red and be quick about it."

"Now you hold on Garvey, I was promised…." Trisk began.

"All promises are off. There may be some lads still alive behind that last fall and we need all the help and timber we can get. The High Priest has agreed that we shall have the two new captives."

The 'boys' were shoved up onto the logs. Garvey stood on a board across the shafts behind the horse and Red sat on the back of the cart. A sharp word from Garvey and they moved off, following a wide track that ran steeply down to merge with the deeply rutted track that came up from the quayside. The horse was young and lively and they were treated to a very bumpy ride, but they managed to keep their eyes open. They saw the smaller mine high up on the mountain side where there appeared to be very little activity. Crossing the bridge over the small river, they continued up alongside the main river for some distance. The rain had stopped but it was very cold up on the cart.

At the next bridge they saw that the wide road continued along the riverbank. They turned right before the bridge onto a track alongside a stream that tumbled noisily through a narrow gorge that eventually opened out into a wide valley.

Suddenly the horror of what had happened at the mine stood before them. The devastation was frightening. A huge slice of the mountain had slithered down into the valley, bringing rock, earth, trees and probably people with it. Two wooden huts had been pushed in front of the avalanche and crushed against the trees that bordered the stream. There the advance of the debris had halted just short of the water. The dwellings in the forest on the east bank of the stream appeared to be little more than hovels but they had escaped serious damage. They were untouched by the avalanche but not by the tragedy. Many of the huts bore the mourning wreaths that announced that the occupants had experienced a fatality. The bridge that crossed the stream was blocked by a wall of mud and rock as high as a house. Garvey continued upstream to where Harry could see a cluster of bell tents away to his left and crude temporary shelters just up ahead. Several men came out to meet them, all of them wearing mud stained clothes. All of them looked tired and near to exhaustion.

"Have you brought some food for us, Garvey?" one of the men called out.

"Only some stale bread and some goats milk for the youngsters, Cram," the waggoner replied.

"Those priests and merchants will sit down to better than stale bread and goat's milk tonight Garvey."

The man called Cram, grumbled and as he looked into the cart he said angrily, "Is this all the timber you could bring? That is useless. Did you tell them that we think some of the youngsters may still be alive behind that last fall?"

"I told them all that and I asked for more men to come and help and all I got was these two lads. All the High Priest could think about was how soon we could be sending more ore out."

"Did you tell him that we are starving out here?"

"I did Cram. All he said was that the Gods of the river and forest will provide all the food we need if we go and hunt for it. But when I said we are so busy trying to dig the young miners out and producing ore at the same time we have no time to go foraging and we are not skilled at hunting, he threatened to have me flogged for being insolent. He said we are to worship the gods and make a sacrifice to them. He said that the gods are angry and that is why they sent the earthquake. He said we are not producing enough ore and that has made them very angry."

"Make a sacrifice?" Cram roared angrily. "Make a sacrifice of what? We have got nothing left. The gods have taken everything."

Chapter Thirty Two

The man called Cram turned his attention to Harry and Meg and glared at them angrily. "What use are these two? Have you ever worked underground?" he growled.

"No sir. We are just hunters' sir. We could catch fish and bring you birds and animals for to cook sir. My brother is also skilled in medicine. He has been apprenticed to the healer in our village for some time. His name is Greg. He cannot speak but he hears you sir. I am Harry the Coracle Boy sir."

"Oh are you now," Cram said mockingly. "I suppose you want me to give you a hunting bow and some arrows and a nice sharp spear and send the pair of you off into the forest never to be seen again," he laughed ironically.

"Where would we go sir? We are orphans and have just come north to escape the Raiders who killed our father and burned our house down." As an afterthought Harry added, "You could send a man with us sir."

It was clear that Cram was taken aback by the boldness of this young lad and looked thoughtfully at Harry and then at Meg. He realised that this might be the answer to the food problem.

"Suppose I sent a man with you, how do I know that one of you won't put a spear in his back at the first opportunity?"

"He could stay an arrow's flight behind us," Harry offered.

"What do you think Garvey?" Cram asked as the Waggoner stepped down.

"We have lived on boiled cabbage and turnips since the flour and oatmeal ran out and the dried meat and fish is buried under all that mud. We have to have something more nourishing if we are to dig the youngsters out. I say let the two boys go and bring us some proper food. As the boy Harry said, "Where would they go?"

After a moment's thought Garvey continued, "You could send that tall, lanky soldier with them. He seems to have more common sense than any of the other useless lot."

Other men joined the discussion and it soon became obvious that the overwhelming majority favoured allowing Harry and Meg to go, with an escort, on a hunting trip and the tall, lanky soldier was sent for.

Ronal, proved to be accurately described. He had a smile that seemed to be glued in place and long black hair tied back with a leather thong. His clothes were good quality as befits a soldier. His weapons were a sword, a dagger at his waist and a throwing spear.

The plan was outlined to him, but he shook his head and explained that Sergeant Garth, the only man with rank left alive, would not allow it. Ronal had suggested a similar venture to him only two days ago, but he said that he wouldn't reduce their strength. How could he guard the mine with only himself and sixteen men left alive?

A delegation consisting of Cram, Garvey and Ronal strode across to speak to the sergeant. They were gone some considerable time, but they eventually returned with permission to use the services of Ronal for just one day. Any further arrangements would depend on the success of the morrow's hunt.

Harry proposed that as it was not yet midday they should try to catch some fish in the stream. Ronal agreed and said it would be a good way of getting to know Harry and Greg. The trio set off upstream. Harry selected three straight young hazel saplings and made a four pronged fish spear for Meg, Ronal and himself as they walked along. Ronal turned out to be a talkative young man, probably about twenty years of age, Harry thought. It transpired that Ronal and fifteen other soldiers and one sergeant were the only survivors from a total complement of six officers and forty men at the big mine. There was one officer, a sergeant and twelve men at the small mine. One man had been sent over the mountain pass to get help and reinforcements.

Ronal took them to a place where the stream meandered down from the boggy heathland and entered the forest. At the many twists and turns the stream had formed a series of small, deep pools.

"Greg, you take the first pool. I'll take the next and Harry will take the third so that we are all within easy hailing distance. If either of you even thinks of running off, I'll outrun you before you have run ten paces and give you a beating you'll not forget. Is that understood?"

"Perfectly," Harry replied, Meg nodded vigorously and smiled.

Standing motionless on the bank beside the stream they were all very cold, but they were catching fish, at least Harry and Meg were. Ronal was impatient and threw his fish spear much too soon. By moving to undisturbed pools further upstream they ended the afternoon with thirty-two good sized trout. Harry suggested that they should return to the camp. The afternoon sun was getting low in the sky and he knew that pagans are afraid of the dark unless they have a lighted torch to fend off the evil spirits. They were just about to enter the forest again when Ronal signalled for them to stop. He crouched down and dropped the fish spear before bringing his throwing spear into his right hand. He slowly stood up and hurled the javelin into the shadows of the trees. He ran forward into the woodland and moments later came back into view carrying a young roe deer.

Suddenly there was a loud crashing and a large dark shape came out of the forest. It was a brown bear and it was turning towards Ronal who had also seen the animal. He quickly turned and began running for the trees, dropping the deer as he ran. His nearest refuge was an oak tree and without thinking, he was soon up amongst the lower branches, but the bear was now climbing the tree after him. Harry and Meg watched, horrified as the slavering beast stretched and clawed Ronal's right leg. They heard the young man cry out and saw him pull the leg up out of reach. At the same time he turned, sword in hand and struck at the animal. Then the bear remembered the roe deer or it could have been the sharp sword that changed its mind, but the lumbering shape scrabbled down the tree and ambled across to where Ronal had dropped the deer. Picking up the deer in its huge jaws, the bear loped away noisily into the forest.

Harry and Meg ran to the tree where Ronal was trying to descend, but he was obviously in pain and blood was dripping from the gash in his leg.

Harry climbed up to help the young soldier down. Meanwhile Meg had run back to an area of marshy ground where she gathered some special moss she had seen growing there. Harry helped Ronal down the tree. He was lying comfortably when Meg opened her medicine pouch and was ready to do what she could for their injured friend. She cleaned the wounds made by the bear's claws, two deep gashes about a hand's width long in his right thigh just above the knee and two similar slashes on the calf, but not quite so deep.

Meg packed the deepest cuts with salve from her medicine pouch and then the healing moss she had collected was held in place with the linen bandage that Eliza Pegg had given her bound tightly around the leg. Ronal was in obvious pain. Harry cut an ash sapling that had a fork in its growth to make a crutch for Ronal, but he needed two crutches and Harry went in search of another similar young tree. But there was something else worrying the young soldier. It was getting dark and they had no torch. He needn't have worried though, Meg had seen his fear and had a fire started by the time Harry got back with a second support for Ronal. They cooked some fish on the fire and made torches from tightly bound bunches of heather, but they burned out too quickly. They knew they would need a greater amount to see them back to the mine. Harry remembered his training with Dan the tracker. He had made a long-lasting torch from the bark of a cedar tree. It smouldered for a very long time, but hardly gave any flame at all. However, by making small torches from whatever came to hand on their route, they could be ignited from the slow burning bark as they followed the stream back to the camp at the mine.

Meg was to be in charge of the torch making and keeping the glowing ember alight by either blowing on it or swinging it as she walked. Harry was to carry the day's catch and assist Ronal as necessary. The young soldier was adamant that he could manage perfectly well with the crutches that Harry had made, but it soon became apparent that Ronal was in real difficulty with the crutches. As they made their way back to the camp, the make-do crutches became caught in the undergrowth, there being no real path other than the tracks they had made earlier. Eventually he fell forward when his good leg tripped on an exposed root. Fortunately his fall was broken by the tangled undergrowth.

Harry dropped his burden and stooped to help him up and rescue one of his crutches from the intertwined jungle. Meg lit an extra torch and saw that Ronal's wound was bleeding through the bandage. She caught Harry's arm and made hectic signs to Harry.

"I can't see what you are saying in this light Greg," Harry said and then got the gist of what Meg was miming. He continued, "You think that we should stop?" Meg gave more signs as she pointed downstream.

She shook the Coracle Boy's arm and held a torch out to him, and then Harry got it. "You want me to go ahead and get help. You will make a big fire and stop here with Ronal. Good idea Greg." He turned to Ronal whose face was distorted with the pain and he was perspiring freely.

"Ronal, Greg is going to make a big fire and stay here with you while I return to the camp to get help to carry you on a litter." There was alarm on the young soldier's face, but Harry spoke before Ronal could object to the plan. He assured him that it was the only way.

Soon Meg had a good fire blazing. Harry told a worried Ronal that he was a Christian and the pagan evil spirits would not harm him, but he took the burning ember with him just to satisfy the injured man.

Harry set off as fast as he could, but it was so dark in the forest that he could only manage a brisk walk. It was fortunate that the route followed the stream and sometimes thickets of scrub made him move away and he had to rely on the sound of the water to keep on course. Eventually he saw the light of the campfire through the trees and soon he was in the clearing. He heard a voice shout something and he could see men gathering around the fire. The group waited at the fire. No one came forward to meet him.

Harry had managed to keep the glowing bark alight by swinging it as he walked. Now he swung it more vigorously as he hurried forward. It had been the circling light that had alerted the sentry, but still no one moved. Harry slowed to a steady walk and called out that he was Harry and that Ronal has been attacked by a bear and was lying injured, but Greg was with him and they had a good fire but they needed help. Two men with a litter was all that was required.

Harry saw a handful of men, perhaps more, some leaning forward, peering at the boy who now stopped several paces from the men but in the full light of the fire. Nobody moved. There were mutterings and the men shuffled about nervously.

"I have brought the fish we caught before the bear injured Ronal. He had killed a roe deer but the bear took it." Harry took a couple of paces forward but saw the men step back as if in great fear. He placed the willow loops that held the fish on the ground and then stepped back and waited. There was obvious consternation amongst the men gathered at the fire. Harry called out again that he had brought food and that Ronal needed help. At last one of the men stepped forward and shouted nervously,

"It could be a trap! The evil spirits of the forest are using you to lure us into the woods to kill us all."

"That is not so. Your evil spirits fear us Christians," Harry replied. Still no one offered help and it looked as if Harry would have to go back and wait for daylight before he would get help. And then the Coracle Boy heard a harsh voice demanding to know what was going on.

The big man heard Ronal mentioned as he stepped into the light of the fire. There was a noisy exchange and then the newcomer shouted above the din and told them all to be quiet. He turned and took a few paces toward Harry. "What's all this about my man Ronal? Where is he?"

Harry assumed that this was the sergeant and stood to attention, wondering if he should salute. He decided not to.

"Sir, he is some distance upstream. He was attacked by a bear. My brother, a healer, is with him and keeping a large fire alight."

"You say he's been attacked by a bear. How bad are his injuries?"

"He has deep claw marks here and here sir." Harry indicated on his own right leg. "My brother has bandaged the wound and I made crutches for him sir, but they are not a lot of help in the undergrowth and he fell down and opened the wound again. That is when we decided to come for help sir."

"Is this the fish you caught?"

"Yes sir."

"Come closer boy, let me get a good look at you. What are you called?"

"Harry sir and my brother is Greg." Harry stepped forward and picked up the fish and handed them to the sergeant.

The sergeant looked hard at the boy and then took the game and turned to the men gathered at the fire. "Who wants to eat tonight? Trout is a lot better than boiled cabbage."

"How'd yer know he ain't poisoned it sarge?"

"One way to find out. He will eat one of the fish and you with so much to say can choose which one he must eat."

The man stepped forward apprehensively and touched a fish and then stepped back. The sergeant roared with laughter as he turned to Harry and held out the fish and asked the boy if he would eat it.

"Certainly sir, but we have to hurry so I will eat it raw," Harry replied as he produced his knife. Harry gutted, scaled and filleted the fish and began slicing off strips of the meat, which he consumed with relish.

The sergeant laughed and clapped his huge hand on Harry's shoulder and guided him to the fire. "Warm yourself boy, while I organise a litter and some help," the sergeant said as he moved away.

Harry noticed that none of the men would meet his eye and gradually most of them shuffled away. He also saw women at the edge of the gathering. They had not seen women earlier in the day.

The sergeant returned with three men, one of whom carried a rolled up litter consisting of two long poles and two short ones with an animal skin to be stretched between them when needed. Another man carried several torches.

"You're not dead yet young man, so I reckon we can get started. You lead the way." Harry was given a blazing torch as he set off followed by the sergeant and the three men, all bearing torches.

The journey back to where he had left Meg and Ronal was both quicker and better illuminated than Harry's journey downstream. They saw the blaze of Meg's fire some distance away and hurried forward. As the group approached they saw Meg standing with her back to the fire and brandishing a fish spear.

"It's alright Greg, I'm back with some help for Ronal. How is he?"

Meg looked past her brother at the strangers he had brought. She smiled and indicated that Ronal was asleep. On hearing the voices Ronal awoke. The sergeant questioned him briefly and when Harry's story had been confirmed, he was lifted onto the litter. The fire was left to burn out and they set off on the return journey. It was slow and uneventful. There were fewer men around the fire as they came out of the forest, but the sergeant led them back to the group of tents on the other side of the stream. There were two soldiers sitting by the fire and they immediately stood up as the party arrived.

"Stand easy lads. Have you erected that other tent?"

"Yes, sarge, on the far end, like you said sarge," the soldier replied and led the way up the line of tents. There were five in all. They stopped at the fifth.

"Right lads, put him down and help him inside and you two," the sergeant turned to Harry and Meg, "You two will share his tent and look after him. There's some bread and cheese and plenty of bedding in the tent so get some rest and we will talk in the morning. Goodnight."

The only illumination in the tent was a rush candle on a flat stone beside Ronal's bed. The three of them shared the food and then Meg checked her patient's dressing and gave him some of Eliza Pegg's sleeping draught. They made their separate beds and lay down. The candle would stay alight in case Ronal was ill in the night. They agreed that it had been a very long day and said goodnight. Harry guessed that it must be midnight.

Chapter Thirty Three

Harry was awake at first light and knew that there had been a sharp frost in the night, but they were snug in their woollen blankets. The soldiers seemed to be very well provided for at this remote outpost, until the earthquake struck.

The Coracle Boy sat up and saw that Meg was still fast asleep and so was Ronal who was gently snoring. Harry undid the flap of the bell tent and took in the sharp, frosty air and looked out on a clear blue sky. In the distance he saw the snowline had receded further up the mountain. He guessed that the mountain he was looking at was the one from where he and Allen had seen the big mine. Harry turned back to see Meg watching him from her snug, warm blankets. She smiled and quietly joined her brother and mimed that she wanted to wash. They went down to the stream and, their ablutions completed, returned to the tent. No one else was about and they saw the fire that had been in front of the centre tent had burned down to a pile of glowing ash. Ronal was still asleep and so Harry said that he would try to revive the fire. Meg joined him. It was their intention to stick together even if they had to make a dash for the forest to keep their freedom.

"Can I trust you two not to run away if I sent you hunting without an escort?"

Harry and Meg turned to see the sergeant emerging from one of the tents and speaking to them sternly.

"Yes sir, where would we run to? We have no shelter or weapons sir. We would willingly hunt for you," Harry replied.

"Well, see if you can bring down a deer or a young wild pig with this." The sergeant handed Harry a small hunting bow and a quiver full of arrows.

"Greg is a better shot than I am," Harry said as he handed the bow and ammunition to his sister.

"I don't care who shoots the best, just be back here before nightfall with some food. I don't want to come looking for you," the sergeant said menacingly.

Harry and Meg returned to their tent. Ronal was still sleeping soundly. They ate the last of their share of the bread and cheese and said goodbye to the sergeant. The pair left the camp, armed with one hunting bow and two fish spears and Meg's medicine bag. At the first opportunity Harry cut an ash sapling and made a sturdy spear as their only defence against a bear. They followed the stream until they arrived at the place where the stream entered the forest. They fished the pools and at midday they built a fire, which they used to cook some fish and ate their fill.

While Harry fished, Meg gathered moss and waterside plants to replenish her diminishing stock of herbal remedies. When she returned she sat beside her brother. "We have not seen any signs of deer or wild pig, Harry. Do you think we dare risk going into the forest? Bears do hibernate, don't they?" Meg asked tentatively.

"I don't know much about bears. They were hunted until there were none in our forests a long time ago, father told me." The Coracle Boy looked out across the heath. "There is a copse of young oak and birch trees over there on the higher ground, we might find a few deer resting in those bushes."

With the wind in their faces, they approached the copse cautiously. Thankfully there were no deer or any signs of them and so they turned their attention to the ducks they saw on a pool. Harry shot two before the others caught sight of them and took to the air. Meg suggested that they had a good haul with two ducks and forty-one fishes and should start back to camp. As they left the birch trees and entered the copse of young oak, Harry held up his hand and lowered his end of the pole on which they carried their catch. He pointed to the ground where Meg could see the disturbance where an animal had been digging for acorns. She knew this to be the work of pigs. If it was a full grown wild boar, they were in danger and in just as much danger if it was a sow with piglets. Harry signalled Meg to put an arrow on the bowstring, He moved forward and parted the bushes very carefully. There in front of him, not five paces away, he saw three half grown pigs lying fast asleep. He crept back to Meg to decide on a plan.

He had watched Allen and the other hunters kill wild boar and deer only a few weeks ago, but they had proper throwing spears and heavier bows than the hunting bow that Meg held. It was more suited to the smaller animals and birds like ducks. Harry would have to use his sturdy spear. He would have to creep as close as he dared and then hope to drive the spear into the sleeping animal. There would be an awful commotion and the pigs' squeal could bring an angry sow charging out of the copse, or worse a vicious wild boar. Harry told Meg to be ready to climb into the leafless branches of an oak tree at the very first squeal. He would do the same once he had driven the spear home.

With all the stealth he could muster, Harry went forward to the thicket where the wild pigs had chosen to make their bed. He selected his target carefully. The animal nearest to him was lying awkwardly but the second one was just right. He would be able to pierce its throat. It would be a swift kill with the minimum of noise if his lunge forward was accurate.

Harry realised that this was not an easy task. He had no idea how the other two pigs would react. Would they run or attack? Were there other adult pigs nearby? He could think of a hundred reasons not to do this and only one to do it; survival. They had to make themselves useful to the soldiers, otherwise they would be sent to work in the mines.

Harry prepared himself and, gripping the spear with both hands, he channelled all his energy into one almighty thrust as he hurled himself forward and drove the pointed shaft into the animal's neck, just as it drew its front legs up to rise. The sharp point and the long taper allowed the spear to pass through the neck and pin the animal to the ground. The other two pigs ran off into the scrubland. Harry left the dying pig and climbed the nearest tree and called out to tell Meg that he was safe and she should remain in her refuge until he called her forward.

There was no sudden attack by an irate boar. The squeals soon died away and Harry descended to examine his prize. He quickly realised that this was going to be a heavy load to get back to camp. Harry gutted the pig while

Meg made a litter on which to carry the carcase. Four poles set a hand's span apart were woven together with birch branches to form a basketwork bed on which the pig, fish and ducks were loaded. They harnessed themselves, side by side, to the litter and dragged it away towards the forest. It was hard work, but they eventually reached the stream and continued on into the forest. Harry realised that it would be dark soon. They took a short rest and then made their final push and made the camp with very little daylight left.

On arriving back at the camp, they were greeted by the sergeant who said he was about to send a search party for them, but then he saw the spoils of their hunt and grinned. Orders were shouted and the big fire was refuelled. One man was told to prepare the pig for roasting and some miners and a few children were given fish to take back to their families. Harry and Meg went back to their tent where Ronal was waiting patiently to hear how they had managed without him. Harry told him of their hunting success while Meg cleansed and dressed his wound.

Ronal told them that four boys, who had run away when the earthquake struck, had returned just after Harry and Greg had gone hunting. They were tired, frightened and hungry. They had gone up the river hoping to find a safe place to cross, but the river got wilder and the gorge narrowed until they could go no further and they thought that the pass over the mountains had been destroyed by the earthquake. They had to turn back."

"Where are the boys now?" Harry asked.

"Up at the mine, but those lads are in for a thrashing when Trisk, the overseer, discovers that they are back. That man is evil. He delights in hurting people."

"Can we take some food up to them?"

"No Harry, you keep away from the mine. The miners will make slaves of you two and no mistake. You and Greg stay down here and hunt for us. We will make sure the lads get their share."

After they had eaten, the sergeant said that all the pork, fish and duck had been eaten by the soldiers and the miners and their families and that Harry and Greg would have to go hunting again in the morning.

Soon after first light, Harry and Meg set off on another hunting trip. This time Harry had been able to borrow a second hunting bow and a sword for each of them, primarily for self defence. They followed the stream further across the open heathland and found the fishing very productive. Six ducks and a goose fell to their arrows. By midday they had about as much as they could haul on their improvised sledge and, after Meg had gathered herbs, willow bark and moss for her medicine pouch, they ate a hearty meal and set off on their return journey.

The pair hadn't realised just how far they had travelled. They had quite a long trek before they arrived at the edge of the forest and the sun was low on the snowcapped mountains when they came within earshot of the camp. There seemed to be more noise than usual.

The two young hunters approached cautiously. There was a lot of shouting, but they could make no sense of what they heard. Harry signalled Meg to move back. "I think that we should turn into the forest, cross the stream and try to get behind the soldiers' tents, Meg."

Meg nodded her reply as she got back into her dumb boy character. It was difficult hauling their load through the undergrowth, but eventually they could see the backs of the soldiers' bell tents. When they parted the foliage, they saw the soldiers standing in a line in front of the tents, spears at the ready, shields in position and the sergeant in the centre.

Well outside the range of the spears, Harry and Meg saw a line of men moving down from the direction of the mine jeering at the soldiers and carrying bundles and torches. They made their way across the shambles of shattered trees, piled up rocks and destroyed buildings. Some men were trying to run with their burdens. Two men were fighting, it was a scene of utter chaos.

"What has happened Harry?" Meg whispered.

"Something drastic I should think Meg. The soldiers look as if they are expecting an attack. I think I should call out and let the sergeant know that we are back." Meg agreed.

"Sergeant, it's Harry and Greg. We're back. What shall we do?"

"Stay where you are lads, I'll call you forward when it's safe. You might have to wait for darkness."

It was quite dark when the sergeant called the two young hunters forward. He inspected their catch and was impressed. "We will have to wait until those renegades have gone. If they smell cooking, they could be upon us like ravening wolves."

"What has happened?" Harry asked.

"We heard this morning that the pass through the mountains was destroyed when the earthquake struck. Then everybody from the village and some from the other mine went up to the big mine and stormed the strong room. My three lads were lucky to escape with just a few bruises."

"But why? Surely it's their gold? Why steal it?"

"No, the gold belongs to our King. The miners have long complained that their share was not enough, but with twelve armed soldiers and an Officer guarding the strongroom at any one time, they dared not risk an attack. I expected trouble after the earthquake, but they knew that reinforcements had been sent for and held off. But when our messenger returned this morning and said that the pass through the mountains had been destroyed completely, they attacked the messenger and almost killed him. Then they went up to the strongroom inside the mine and would have killed the three guards, but they were too busy fighting amongst themselves and my lads got back here safely. We are cut off from our capital city except for a long and difficult journey through thieves and murderers in the forests to the northeast."

"What are we going to do sir?" Harry asked the sergeant.

The sergeant squinted at the row of lights bobbing about as the line of torches diminished and the looters moved back towards the village and now there was total darkness out there.

"Do, Harry?" The sergeant said as he rubbed his hands together. "We are going to cook some of that fish, and oh, is that a goose I see there? But a couple of my lads can do that. You and your brother look after Ronal and the messenger. His name is Trad. He's in with Ronal."

Harry and Meg found their patients both sitting up waiting expectantly. Ronal asked Meg to look after Trad first. Although he looked a terrible mess, it was mainly small cuts and bruises. Both his eyes were almost closed and would be really black before morning. Meg found that Ronal's wounds were healing nicely. The sergeant had been observing Meg at work from the open tent flap. He smiled and nodded approvingly.

After they had eaten, everyone was given their duties for the night. Four torches were set up some distance away from the tents to illuminate the approaches to the soldiers' compound. Harry and Meg were to be sentries with orders to watch the area illuminated by the first torch at the top end of the line so as to be near their patients. They would do the first watch together because they were not used to soldiers' duties. Three other soldiers were set to watch the areas lit by each of the other torches. When Harry asked why there was a need for guards if the pagans were afraid to go out in the dark the sergeant said that the overseer Trisk was the ring leader and it was known that he was in league with the evil spirits.

When they were alone, Harry and Meg discussed the change in their circumstances. They spoke in whispers even though they were well out of earshot of the other guards, Meg always with her back to the soldiers, but making all sorts of hand movements to give the impression of sign language.

"I've been thinking Harry, we have to get back to the village and try to rescue Ruth and Jennie, in all this confusion we might just get the chance."

"I have been thinking along those lines too Meg, but what about Ronal?"

"I have told him to start exercising his leg and the other young soldier will wake up in the morning with a sore head but nothing more serious than that."

"So what are you thinking?"

"Why don't we come clean with the sergeant? He seems to be a reasonable sort of man. Tell him we are here to rescue Ruth and Jennie. Knowing how these pagans fear the dark we could go tomorrow night."

"Why not go tonight? Why wait for tomorrow?"

Harry and Meg swung round, shock and fear on both their faces. They were speechless as they saw the sergeant emerge from the shadows.

Before either of them could speak, the sergeant went on, "I think you two owe me an explanation. I don't like being made a fool of."

Harry was totally confused as he looked from the sergeant to Meg who was close to tears. It was those tears that cleared his befuddled brain.

"Sergeant Garth, sir, we did not intend to make a fool of you and we are sorry if it looks like that, but we have to rescue our little sister before she is taken to the east into slavery."

"But why is your sister pretending to be a boy, and a dumb boy at that? I think you had better tell me your story. But first tell me this, are there soldiers following you?"

"I honestly don't know sir. We have sent messages back but we have no way of knowing if they got them." As soon as the words were out, Harry knew that he had made a mistake and the sergeant's next question confirmed his worst fears.

"How have you sent messages back?"

"We found two boys wandering on the other side of the river." Meg spoke first. "We took them downriver to our camp where Dan and Susan are waiting for us. It is our hope that a search party will come and bring some soldiers to rescue all our children."

"Dan and Susan. Who are they?"

"They are pagans sir. They live in our village," Harry explained, "But Dan has been very ill and is unable to travel."

"And where is this camp of yours?"

Harry and Meg looked at each other not sure how to answer this question, but they were saved by a commotion at the other end of their camp. A sentry had challenged someone coming from the direction of the stream and carrying a torch.

"You two stay here and keep a sharp lookout and stand back into those bushes, you make too good a target standing by the torch."

Chapter Thirty Four

Sergeant Garth hurried away to meet their late night visitor. Harry and Meg moved into the shadows and peered into the darkness. The challenge had awakened several soldiers and they were gathered around the newcomer. Ronal appeared outside the tent supporting himself on a pair of improvised crutches. He wanted to know the cause of the disturbance and was soon joined by an equally inquisitive Trad. Meg returned to being a mute boy. The sergeant came up towards the big fire holding the torch in one hand and gripping the visitor's upper arm with the other. He ordered all the men to parade in the shadows at the rear of the tents. He introduced the visitor. His name was Sol and he was a young novice sent by the High Priest who was ordering the sergeant to bring all his men to defend the Temple. They were being attacked by a mob led by Trisk, the senior overseer.

"Why are they bothering to attack the Temple? I thought they would want to get away to the east as quickly as possible," the sergeant asked the young acolyte who was clearly terrified.

"There is a lot of gold in the Temple," the timid young boy answered.

"Who are these people in the Temple?"

"The High Priest and three other priests, Captain Ragar and his servant, Gant, and Sister Rona. She is looking after the children. There are some women too."

"How many children?" Harry blurted out. Again he regretted his haste.

The young novice thought for a moment and then guessed there were more than twenty. He was not sure. The sergeant asked how many men were attacking the Temple.

"The High Priest told me to tell you that there are over one hundred men in the raiding party sir."

"I don't believe a word of it. Most of the men are more afraid of the priests and all the evil spirits they control than they are of Trisk. I doubt if that treacherous brute could raise more than twenty men," the sergeant said dismissively. He then asked the young boy how he had been able to get past such a large band of men.

"Mark, one of the priests, took me up a secret tunnel that had ladders and steep climbs and it led to a cave where a hermit lives. It's high above the village."

"I know where the hermit lives, but surely they would see your torch down in the village," the sergeant said.

"No sir," the young messenger replied. "It was daylight when I left."

The sergeant stroked his chin and considered all the boy had told him

"What are you going to do?" one of the men asked the sergeant.

"Everyone back to their duties or beds, I have to think. One of you take our young friend and give him food and a place to rest."

Harry and Meg returned to their sentry duties. Both were anxious to know what the sergeant would decide. The sergeant walked across to them and asked, almost in a whisper, if they were really Christians and would they travel at night without a torch? They both said that they were and had often travelled at night and had never been bothered by evil spirits.

"Would you be prepared to go to the village and report back on what is going on over there?"

"We will go willingly sir, but it is a half day's walk there and back, even longer in the dark sir."

"What I need to know is how many men does Trisk have outside the Temple and is the boat taking men out to the east? Can you ride, Harry?"

"We both ride and we don't need saddles sir," the Coracle Boy replied.

"We have the officers' horses in a meadow back there beyond the landslide, I'll send a man with you."

They found the horses in a makeshift stable, there were four of them. They were very nervous at first, but some quiet words from Harry and he soon had bridles on two sturdy young ponies. Harry and Meg quickly mounted and followed the man with the torch back to the camp and, after receiving a few final instructions and a torch that they would need in the caves, they set off into the night. Harry guessed that it was midnight. There was a waning moon that gave them enough light to follow the well worn track. As they passed by the miners' huts, they saw the torches but no men. They were able to hear several voices coming from one of the hovels. It sounded like a heated argument. Beyond, there was no one on the road and they were able to maintain a steady canter and they quickly came within sight of the village. Harry led the way up into the trees where they tethered the horses. Following the sergeant's instructions, they climbed high up into the forest until they found the path at the foot of an escarpment that would lead them up to the hermit's cave.

As they rounded a bend in the path, they saw ahead the dull glow of a fire or a torch spilling across the path several paces away. At the same time they heard a dog bark. No one had said that there would be a dog to greet them. As they approached, the bark became a long, low growl. A voice said something that neither of them understood, but they took it to be words of caution to the animal. The voice then raised and called out inquiringly in a strange language, "Who is there?"

"We are Harry and Greg. We have a message from the sergeant for the High Priest. Sol. The young boy the High Priest sent, told us that you would show us the way sir."

"Step forward. Let me see you. You need not fear my companion, he has a lot to say but he does not bite."

Harry and Meg pulled aside the animal skin that partially covered the entrance and stepped into the cave, which was no more than a vertical split in the rock. They saw a very old man sitting on a blanket covered bed platform hewn into the rock wall of the cave. A fire burned in an iron brazier. The smoke went up into a fissure the height of two men above the cave floor. A torch flickered in a sconce mounted above a table that had parchment and goose quills arranged neatly on it. The dog, a black and white sheep dog, sat on the bed beside his master and wagged his tail a little uncertainly, until Meg spoke softly to the old man's companion.

"So young Sol got through. He's a good lad and will make a fine priest one day. What are your names?" Suddenly the old man looked alarmed and exclaimed, "You carry no lighted torch. Are you Christians?"

The old hermit drew back and pulled a rough woollen blanket up to his chin and looked fearfully at them both.

Acting on the advice of the sergeant and something that Dan the pagan had told him, Harry told the old hermit that they were pagans, but of a different sect who had made peace with the evil spirits of the night and so were allowed to travel unhindered and without torches. The old man seemed to relax a little and asked Harry where they worshipped.

"At the great stone circle far to the east, sir." Harry hoped that there would be no more questions because he had exhausted his knowledge of pagans.

Gradually the old man smiled through his full, white beard and pointed further down the cave, which became lower as it went back into the darkness.

"Light your torch at the fire and follow the cave until you come to a ladder. At the bottom, go down to a second ladder. Below that you will see a heavy oak door. Knock three times on the door and you will be asked who you are. You will say that you are messengers from the soldiers. You will be taken to the High Priest and you must kneel in front of him and not get up until he tells you to, and do not speak until you are spoken to."

Harry lit the torch and thanked the old hermit before setting off into the darkness, closely followed by Meg who held onto the hem of Harry's doublet. She had not been this far into a cave before and was very frightened. They found the ladder and at this point Meg expressed her fears to the Coracle Boy.

"Would you feel better if you carried the torch?" Harry asked.

"No, I would be afraid of dropping it. Perhaps if I went in front of you Harry."

"That is going to be difficult down the ladder. You will be in almost total darkness."

"I'm sorry Harry. I will have to try and put my fears behind me."

"That's the spirit, Meg. Just think about meeting Ruth soon. I'll get on the ladder and go down a few rungs and try to light you as best I can."

Meg stepped onto the ladder and began her descent. Fortunately she was not afraid of heights, but she was having to feel for the rungs with her feet and hold onto the sides of the ladder. Her progress was very slow, but she was conquering her fear of confined spaces. She counted every step she took and said to herself that it was one step nearer to finding Ruth. There were twenty-four rungs down to where Harry waited in a much larger cave that twisted this way and that and went downhill steeply. A rope had been fixed to the left-hand wall at hand height and proved to be necessary on some of the steeper sections. They found the second ladder and Harry remarked that they must be near the end. He could feel a cold draught coming up from below. Meg counted twenty rungs this time. At the bottom they saw the door the hermit had described. Following instructions, Harry picked up a piece of rock and struck the door three times and waited. The Coracle Boy was about to knock a second time when a muffled voice behind the door asked who they were.

"We are messengers from the soldiers sir, sent by Sergeant Garth. He has spoken to Sol, the messenger you sent."

"Wait!" came the short reply and after a long pause they heard a scraping noise and then they saw a small square grille appear. It was no more a hand's span across and quite high up in the door.

"Stand back and hold the torch so that I can see your faces." Harry obeyed. "Now shine the torch behind you."

Harry did as he was asked and illuminated the cave behind them. There was quite a long pause and then the voice told Harry to go back up the ladder and untie the rope that held the ladder in position. Harry handed the torch to Meg and went up and untied the ladder. When he returned, he was told to take the ladder down and lay it on the floor of the tunnel. It was a difficult task because it was a very sturdy ladder and needed both of them to remove it.

The heavy door swung open quietly on well greased hinges and a tall man in a white hooded robe stepped into the cave, bringing with him just a hint of a warm, welcoming draught and the smell of food.

"Leave your torch in the sconce to the right of the door. Quickly now," the man ordered.

Harry and Meg went through the door into a well lit passage and waited as their escort dropped two heavy timbers into iron brackets to secure the door. The hooded man turned to them and asked their names.

"I am Harry and this is my brother Greg. He cannot talk but he hears and understands what you say. He speaks to me using sign language."

"Follow me and speak only when you are spoken to."

They followed the tall man down a flight of steps along a passage to another door. After a knock the door swung back. Another hooded, white robed man stepped back and gestured them to enter. They were facing a thick curtain just three paces in front of them. They waited while the door was closed and barred and then their escort stood between them, his hands on their shoulders. Their second escort walked past them and through the curtain and spoke quietly to another person.

They waited patiently until the curtain was drawn back and they were guided forward into a room furnished with a highly polished wood table and chairs and a desk with books and documents strewn about. It had a high ceiling and appeared to be hewn into the rock. The walls were covered with painted signs featuring the moon and five pointed stars, with snakes and grotesque faces, weird animals and black ravens. On his right Harry saw a huge ram's head with curled horns and evil eyes stared down from high on the wall. It was yellow and shone in the flickering light from the several torches. Harry wondered if it was made of gold. On a dais beneath the ram's head, sitting on a beautifully carved chair, he saw a white robed man with a bushy beard. He was not an old man, about the same age as Abe Tull, Harry guessed. Their escort pushed them both forward and told them to kneel.

"So Sergeant Garth has sent you and why has he not come himself?" the High Priest asked, looking hard at Harry.

"Sir, he told me to tell you that he only has ten men able to fight and all their weapons are buried under the avalanche except for the swords and spears they were carrying when the earthquake struck."

"Where are all the officers?" the High Priest demanded.

"Sergeant Garth said that they were all buried under the avalanche, but there is one officer with a sergeant and twelve soldiers at the small mine sir."

"We sent a messenger there first but have had no reply. What else did the sergeant tell you?"

"He said we were to find out what the rebels are doing, count them and see what weapons they have. Greg is to go back and report what we have seen and I am to go to the small mine and tell the officer there that the senior officer's last orders were for him to shut down the mine, seal the strongroom and return to barracks sir. Sergeant Garth said that I am to tell the officer that he will be at the river bridge at first light to receive orders sir."

"But how is your brother going to tell the sergeant anything if he is dumb?"

"A soldier called Ronal can read Greg's sign language sir."

"So who is guarding the big mine and the strongroom now?" The High Priest asked, his voice raised and angry.

"No one sir. The rebels overpowered the soldiers and have emptied the strongroom."

At this the High Priest flew into a rage and called on all sorts of gods to come down and destroy the rebels. He stood up and strode around the room shouting and banging things. He told the priest to take Harry and Greg out of the room as he returned to his chair.

Suddenly the door, to which Harry and Greg were being guided by the priest, burst open and the gentleman whom Harry had met when he first arrived at the village, barred their way as he stood in the doorway. He looked very angry. The priest stepped back, pulling Harry and Greg with him, obviously in awe of the gentleman.

"Captain Ragar." The High Priest stood up again and glared at the intruder. "What is the meaning of this? How dare you burst into my private chapel?"

"That priest you sent to negotiate with Trisk has changed sides and he will lead the rebels to the secret tunnel," the captain replied angrily.

"I sent no one to negotiate with that treacherous lout," the High Priest said as he looked across at the other two priests and asked them what they knew of this matter. They both denied any knowledge of it.

"Then who let him out?"

"Your priest, Nargor, browbeat my man Gant into letting him out."

"Then it is your entire fault Captain Ragar, you are to blame. I shall tell the Elders and the King's Councillors of your dereliction of duty."

"If Trisk gets in here you will be lucky to be alive to tell anybody anything."

Captain Ragar's last remark had a very sobering effect on the High Priest. He slumped into his chair, his pomposity dissolved and he became almost docile as he spoke to the captain using his first name.

"Kurt, dear boy, I was a little hasty with my remarks. It has been a trying time with the gods being so angry. Please accept my apology."

Captain Kurt Ragar ignored the High Priest and turned his attention to Harry and Greg and asked Harry what he was doing here.

"They are messengers from…." the High Priest began.

"I asked the boy, priest," the captain growled. "Now, Harry and Greg, isn't it? You see I remembered your names and you are both expert in the use of the coracle and you are looking for a valley where the sun always shines and the game is plentiful. Aren't we all?" The captain pulled the chair out from the desk and sat down.

"Now Harry, tell me your story. How is it that I find you here?"

Harry began when Sol had arrived at the soldiers' camp with the High Priest's demand for help and told the story truthfully, up to the point when the captain had entered the private chapel. The captain turned and spoke to the High Priest in a calm, even voice.

"Why was I not informed of your decision to send for help? You know that the soldiers cannot leave their posts. We can hold out here for weeks. Trisk has no more than twenty men and very little food, whereas we have plenty of food and water, thanks to your greed. But now that one of your so-called priests has defected, he will lead the rebels right down to our back door."

"Nargor would not tell them of the secret tunnel."

"Tell them?" the captain replied sarcastically. "Nargor will lead the way."

The two priest escorts standing either side of Harry and Greg had remained silent after telling the youngsters to kneel. Now the Captain addressed them.

"Mark, what part have you played in this charade?"

The taller of the two priests replied that he had agreed with the High Priest that they should have the protection of the soldiers, but he understood that the captain had agreed also. The smaller priest replied in the same vein.

"I have known of this secret tunnel but have not seen it," the captain said. Will someone show me where it is?" There was silence until the High Priest told Mark, reluctantly, to show the captain to the secret passage.

"Captain, sir." Harry spoke to the officer.

"Silence boy. I told you to speak only when you are…."

"It's alright Mark, let the boy speak. What is it Harry?"

"Sir, it will be getting light soon and the rebels will see our horses. What are we to tell the sergeant sir?"

"The boy has a good point there High Priest, what do we tell the sergeant to do? Now that the strongroom at the big mine is empty, I will order him to come here. I will not take the guard away from the small mine. The lieutenant and his men can protect that strongroom and the last report told us that the earthquake had not caused them any damage. We must try to salvage something from this disaster." The captain thought for a moment and then asked if there was another way out of the caves and mine workings other than through the hermit's cave. He was told that there was no other way out.

"Then I think that they should continue with their plan."

"Keep the dumb one here." the High Priest demanded.

"As a sort of hostage?" Captain Ragar asked. "No High Priest. We stick to the sergeant's plan."

The priest took Harry, Greg and the captain back to the tunnel where they erected the ladder and tied it securely. The captain, Harry and Greg then climbed the ladder, whilst Mark, the priest, returned to the Temple. The trio made their way back to the second ladder and the hermit's cave. The old man chuckled and said he had never seen so much activity in all his years of living alone.

The captain went out of the cave first, but soon returned to report that there were no torches visible. He would go part of the way with Harry and Greg and then return and deal with the rebels. He planned to go back into the cave, fetch his man, Gant, then as the rebels came down the first ladder, one at a time, they would be waiting at the bottom.

Harry and Greg found their horses tethered where they had left them. They walked their mounts down almost to the road, before mounting up and cantering into the increasing light of the dawn.

Chapter Thirty Five

The sergeant could not hide his delight, and relief at seeing the pair of them back safe and sound. He gathered all the soldiers round the fire as breakfast was cooked and they all listened to Harry's report.

"I have heard of Captain Kurt Ragar. He's part of the King's bodyguard and a highly decorated soldier, I believe. So that's it lads, we march as soon as you have gathered all the weapons and food you can find. Use one of the horses for the heavier stuff. Harry and Greg need their two horses. They have been up all night and Ronal needs the other one. So come on now, move yourselves."

The spirits of the men showed a distinct change for the better and then Harry had a thought and spoke to the sergeant.

"Sir, would it be a good idea if Greg and me went ahead and told the lieutenant at the small mine what was happening?"

"Good idea Harry, his name is Lieutenant Kester. Wait for us at the river bridge if you are there first. If not, then Ronal will wait for you."

Harry and Greg set off with the sergeant's blessing and soon came to the river bridge that crossed a tributary of the big river. A short distance upstream of the bridge they found the zigzag road that led up to the small mine. As they approached the bend at the bottom of the last slope up to the mine, they saw two soldiers at the top of the slope levelling spears at them. They also carried swords and shields. They were ordered to stop and state their business.

"We are messengers from Captain Kurt Ragar of the King's bodyguard. I have to speak to Lieutenant Kester."

Several other soldiers had arrived at and they carried bows and arrows. Suddenly the two soldiers carrying spears came to attention and a young man stepped past them.

"I am Lieutenant Kester. What is the message?"

"Sir, the rebels have closed the big mine and emptied the strongroom. There are no officers left alive sir. Sergeant Garth has been ordered to attack the rebels led by a man called Trisk. Captain Ragar said that you are to remain here and guard the strongroom and prevent the miners from leaving."

"My compliments to Captain Ragar. Tell him I shall do as he asks, but we only have two miners and the fifteen boys left and we are short of food."

"Sir, we will deliver your message. We are to meet a soldier called Ronal down at the river bridge…."

"Ronal you say? I know the man. Send him up."

Harry and Meg began to turn their horses when the lieutenant called out, "Not both of you, send the other boy back. You stay where you are."

"Go Meg, let's hope that Ronal understands. Go, I'll be alright."

Meg set off down the poorly surfaced track. She rode cautiously, not wanting to lose her mount, her speedy horse may be needed later.

To Meg's surprise, Sergeant Garth and his soldiers were coming across the bridge. The sergeant ordered the soldiers to halt and then ran to meet Meg when he saw that Harry was not with her. Meg turned her horse so that she had her back to the soldiers and made hand signs as she whispered to Sergeant Garth, telling him of what had transpired up at the mine.

"Let me have your horse Greg. Ronal, come with me," the sergeant called. The two rode back up to the mine where Harry was waiting patiently.

"Go back and join your brother Harry, I'll deal with this young man."

Harry found Meg looking a little worried. She was afraid that some of the soldiers were becoming curious about the mute boy called Greg.

Moments later the sergeant and Ronal came down from the mine and said that the lieutenant was happy to stay as ordered. "I don't think he wanted to get blood on his nice new sword," Ronal whispered.

The column set off at a brisk march. Harry, Greg and Ronal brought up the rear with Sol, the novice priest, Trad, the messenger and the three guards who had been injured by the miners.

It was midmorning when the village came in sight and Sergeant Garth ordered everyone up into the woods. He told Harry and Meg to get some sleep, he took a patrol forward. It was late afternoon when Ronal shook Harry's shoulder and said that the sergeant was back and wanted everyone on parade.

"There's hardly anyone in the village," the sergeant told them, "except for a couple of rough looking thugs outside the Temple which looks secure. The ferryman and a few of his helpers are still down by the river." The sergeant became much more serious. "It is a different story up at the hermit's cave. Trisk must have close on fifty men up there and they are well armed with at least ten fighting bows. We have a couple of lightweight hunting bows, but Captain Ragar and his manservant seem to be holding them."

The sergeant sighed wearily and said that he and the patrol must rest. He instructed Ronal to wake him when the sun was down to the top of the mountain opposite.

When the sergeant was asleep, Harry asked Sol if he was sure there was no way out of the cave system other than through the hermit's cave. Sol was a long time answering.

"What is it Sol?" Harry prompted.

"There is a dreadful serpent down there, the High Priest has seen it."

"Has anyone else seen it?"

"I don't know, but Joel was locked in there and he never came back."

"Who is Joel and when was this?" Harry asked. Sol seemed reluctant to answer, but Harry asked the question again forcefully.

"Joel was learning to be a priest. He was my friend and older than me, but he was always arguing with the High Priest. One day, four moons ago, he shouted at the priest and called him a bad name. He was taken to the cave and locked in. When everybody was asleep, I took him some food and when I opened the grille it was dark and Joel didn't answer when I called his name. I went to the door many nights, but he was never there."

"Perhaps he went up the ladder into the hermit's cave."

"No. The ladder was taken down and was laid in the passage that leads to the Temple. It was only put back when the gods shook the earth."

"So it is just possible that Joel took the torch and found a way out," Harry mused.

Ronal, who had been listening, suggested that the young man had got lost and perished when the torch went out. Harry had to agree that that was a possibility. Then Harry asked Sol how often anybody went up to the hermit's cave by the secret way.

"Mark said that we were the first for ages. I go up with one of the priests at least four times each moon and on feast days to take him food and make sure he has firewood, but we always travel up the path through the woods."

Harry was in deep thought as he wandered aimlessly up the wooded mountain to sit with his back against a tree trunk. Meg joined him. Covering her mouth, she asked him in a whisper what was troubling him.

"Something's not right Meg, I saw no serpents in any of the caves I have been in. What would they live on? And there's another thing, when I was untying the second ladder I noticed something change, but I can't think what was so different, and then in the struggle with the ladder I forgot all about it."

Meg shrugged her shoulders and made various hand gestures to suggest that they were talking. Harry leaned back and rested his head against the tree trunk and closed his eyes. He was still tired and both he and Meg were soon asleep, but not for long. Ronal was shaking Harry and saying that the sergeant was awake and wanted to talk to everyone.

Sergeant Garth told them that they would have a meal and then move off. They had to be at the hermit's cave just before dark. Ronal, Trad and the wounded men would stay behind with the horses.

"Sir," Harry said hesitantly.

"What is it Harry?" the sergeant asked.

"Sir, if Captain Ragar is able to keep Trisk's men from getting into the caves, well, the old hermit can't have enough food up there to feed that many men, or enough torches to keep the evil spirits at bay sir."

"So?"

"If Greg and me went forward now sir, Greg can do numbers. He could see how many men leave and when they go down for food and rest, perhaps we could overpower the ones they leave at the cave...."

"And we could defend the cave with very few men." The sergeant seized upon the Coracle Boy's suggestion as he grinned broadly at his young friend.

Harry and Meg left at once with a guide to take them to the vantage point the sergeant had found that overlooked the clearing in front of the hermit's cave.

It was getting dark when the sergeant arrived at their observation post and Greg held up both hands three times and then added one hand plus three fingers, indicating that he had counted thirty-eight men leave for the village.

"That suggests that Captain Ragar has had some success Harry."

"We saw Trisk and the traitor priest go down sir."

"There could be as few as ten men left in the hermit's cave, which makes the odds about even." Harry reminded him that the hermit had a dog.

"Not any more Harry, the rebels put an arrow into him. We found the body thrown down into the woods." The boy felt his anger rise. The old hermit loved his companion. He would be very upset.

Just at that moment a man holding a torch came into the clearing from the cave. He picked up a large log and went back into the cave.

"Shall we wait until they are asleep sir?" Harry inquired.

"No lad, my men are all pagans. They want to get down to that light."

Slowly the sergeant took them down the mountain until they were at the clearing. They could see the dull glow from the mouth of the cave. The men were eager to get away from the darkness of the woods and the sergeant had to hold them back and urge them to take it slow and quiet. He wanted surprise to be on their side. Harry, Meg and Sol had agreed that they would go straight to the old hermit and protect him as best they could. The cave was wide enough for three men to walk side by side all the way to the ladder down into the labyrinth and that was how they went in.

There were four men inside the cave entrance. One was adding a log to the iron brazier, two were sitting on the hermit's bed and the fourth was asleep on a pile of animal pelts. The hermit was nowhere to be seen. The column kept going right up to the first ladder shaft where two men were sitting near the top of the ladder, waiting. There was little resistance from any of the men. They were miners and no match for Sergeant Garth and his soldiers.

The sergeant called down into darkness asking for Captain Ragar.

"Who wants to know?" The captain's voice came firm and strong.

"This is Sergeant Garth of the mine guard sir."

"How do I know that you are who you say you are?" the captain asked.

"Your man Gant will know me sir, if it's the same Gant who gets drunk at the riverside alehouse by the garrison when he has money in his pocket sir."

"Come down the ladder slowly sergeant."

Gant was able to confirm that the sergeant was indeed Sergeant Garth, an old acquaintance with whom he had shared the occasional jug of ale.

It was getting rather crowded up in the cave when the captain and his manservant came up the ladder. The prisoners had been bound hand and foot and made to sit further down the cave. Harry and Meg had found the old hermit beyond the ladder sitting on a pile of kindling wood in near darkness. He was very upset that his dog had been killed and begged Sol to see that the animal got a proper pagan funeral.

The captain approved of the sergeant's plan to barricade the mouth of the cave with the wood from the firewood stack near the entrance. Six men would be detailed to defend that area. Harry, Meg and Sol would follow the captain, the sergeant and the remaining four soldiers down into the Temple. The soldiers were used to being underground. Only Sol showed signs of fear and was glad to see the second ladder a short distance away.

They waited at the top of the ladder while the captain reported to the High Priest. Suddenly Harry caught Meg's forearm instinctively and then realised that he didn't want the others to hear what he needed to tell Meg. He apologised to Meg and said that he had lost his balance on the uneven floor. Harry had realised what had struck him as being odd when he untied the ladder on their first journey down to the Temple, but it would have to wait until he and Meg were alone.

The captain returned and they were allowed to descend to the cave below. They were told that there would be very little light as they were to pass through the High Priest's chapel.

The priest, known as Mark, led the way down a few steps, his smaller companion closed and barred the door behind them. As they passed through the second door into the dimly lit chapel, Harry noticed that something was draped over the shiny ram's head above the High Priest's chair. The High Priest was sitting on his throne in his white robe, his head covered with the hood, his face barely visible.

They were ushered quickly across the room and through the door that had earlier brought Captain Ragar into the chapel. It led into a very large room that echoed to the sound of their movement. They were in the pagan temple. This large room too was dimly lit, but a door on the other side of this eerie shrine opened to let in more light and the sound of many voices, mostly children's voices!

Harry and Meg looked at each other with a mixture of joy and fear. Was Ruth in that room? Would she give the game away? What would happen if their intention to rescue their sister was discovered? Would the sergeant reveal their secret?

Chapter Thirty Six

Mark, the priest, stepped aside and told Sol to take Harry and Meg through the Temple to Sister Rona in the dining room and return quickly. The young trainee priest ran across to the door. It was held open by a boy of about twelve whose right arm was supported in a sling. Harry and Meg followed rather more cautiously. The boy holding the door open gave them a friendly grin as he closed the door. The dining room was warm and well lit. There were several long tables. Harry and Meg were looking at a host of young faces all turned towards them. They saw Sol talking to Sister Rona and then Sol was coming back. He told them to go to Sister Rona. He said he had work to do and left. Harry and Meg started towards the white-haired woman who was smiling and beckoning them forward.

Suddenly there was a scream from the direction of the group of children. They turned to see Ruth struggling to get away from Jennie and then, breaking free, she ran to Harry and Meg. Meg went down on one knee and held her arms out to her little sister. Ruth was crying as she ran into her sister's arms. Harry looked across at Sister Rona, fearful that she should discover the truth. The tall, white-haired woman smiled and repeated the summoning gesture. Harry saw that Meg and Ruth were both crying. They had been joined by Jennie. She too was crying all three locked in each other's arms. He saw the four boys together at the front of the group, they looked uncertain. Harry returned their gaze and shook his head slightly. He turned and walked across to Sister Rona, she reached out and put her hand on his shoulder.

"Harry, isn't it?" Harry heard warmth in her voice as she added, "You are safe now and reunited with your little sister. Yes, I know your story Harry, don't look so alarmed. No one else knows except the four boys from your village and we will try to keep it that way."

She told Harry to bring his family to her, including Jennie. She took them into a large storeroom. There were barrels and sacks stacked against the rear wall, which appeared to have been hewn into the solid rock and there was also a flitch of bacon and several hams hanging from hooks in the rock ceiling.

Sister Rona told them to sit on the benches at the end of a long table, Meg and Ruth on one side, Harry and Jennie on the other. Sister Rona sat at the end. "Where shall I begin?" Sister Rona said thoughtfully. "First, I think I must tell you that your little sister was very ill when she arrived here and that it was Jennie who gave her the strength to pull through."

Harry put his arm around Jennie and gave her a hug. Meg reached across the table and touched her hand while Ruth still clung to Meg.

"It was when Ruth was so poorly that I first heard you name Harry. She often called out asking for Harry and Meg and sometimes Simon. Jennie, loyal as ever, said she didn't know who it could be. It was not until you left for the mine that I realised that Greg was really Meg, and the old man turning the spit in the kitchen confirmed that Jennie had talked openly to you both."

"So what happens now?" Harry asked.

"I think that we should leave things as they are. Only we five know the truth and with all this fighting going on, I think that we must wait until the miners have come to their senses."

"What about the boys from the village?" Meg asked, "There are four of them."

"Yes, I saw them." Harry added, "In the other room. They looked as if they recognised me. Surely they will have told their friends."

"You could be right Harry. I'll go and speak to them, but first you must eat. There is fresh baked bread and cheese but only water to drink."

"I thought you were short of food Sister Rona," Harry said, looking around.

"The High Priest does very well for himself. That is his private pantry." She indicated the open door behind her.

Jennie and Ruth had just eaten so Harry and Meg sat down to the best meal they had had in days.

Suddenly there was a commotion coming from the next room. Sister Rona hurried out closing the door behind her. Harry went to the other side of the table and held his little sister in his arms.

"Jennie always said you would come and rescue us Harry," Ruth said. She had stopped crying by now and was smiling. Although she was pale and thin, there was a sparkle in her eyes.

Sister Rona came back into the room. She looked worried.

"Two boys were fighting. It appears your secret is out Harry. One of your village boys was singing your praises and an older boy disagreed with him. Why do boys have to fight?" Sister Rona said despondently. "Unfortunately," she continued, "Young Sol was there and he is bound to tell the High Priest at the first opportunity."

"What will happen to us now Sister Rona?"

"You and Harry will be separated almost certainly. They might even put Harry in gaol until the mines can be reopened and he can be put to work, but you will be able to stay with Ruth until the spring when all the girls will be sent to the city and put to work in the houses of the rich people."

Meg looked anxiously at Harry and asked what they were going to do. His answer stunned her. She was appalled.

"What can we do?" Harry said without meeting Meg's eyes. "We have to accept that we have done our best. You, Ruth and Jennie are together and Sister Rona will look after you until you leave here."

"Harry!" Meg almost screamed his name. She jumped to her feet, her pretty face contorted with anger. There were no tears. Her eyes were wide open and her fists clenched. "Harry!" Meg repeated his name, "What are you…."

"Meg listen to me," Harry said firmly as he raised his head and met Meg's horrified stare. "Look at Ruth, how could she face a journey downriver? She needs rest and the chance to get well again. Now that you are with her you can nurse her back to health. Think about what is best for Ruth Meg."

Sister Rona said that Harry was right. She must accept that Ruth was not well enough to travel. Besides, they would not be allowed to leave.

"No, no, Harry, you can't do this. Not after all we have been through."

Meg spoke calmly now, shaking her head slowly from side to side. It was as if she had not heard Sister Rona. She held Harry's gaze until he looked away. He looked down at the table and picked at the woodgrain with his fingernail. Meg sat down on the bench and drew Ruth to her. She looked across at Harry's bowed head and the tears started down her cheeks. She looked away and bent to kiss Ruth's golden hair.

"Harry, I want to go home. Why can't you take us away from here?" Jennie asked as she tugged Harry's sleeve. She too was crying.

"That's quite enough Jennie," Sister Rona said harshly. "Harry has explained why. Now I must go and send the boys to get the straw for the bedding and I'll find out what is to happen to you Harry."

Sister Rona left the room. There was a long, difficult silence and then Meg raised her head and said in a very even, controlled voice, "What has happened to you Harry. Why have you given up so easily?"

"I have led us both into a trap. I walked into it with my eyes wide open, but try walking out of here." Harry gave an ironic laugh. "Do you think the High Priest would open the front door for us and offer us a free passage home?"

"But Harry, surely…."

"But Harry, nothing. Meg, I have made a right mess of it this time. There is no way out of this place."

"But Harry, the sergeant is our friend…."

"That's rubbish Meg," Harry replied harshly. "He was our friend while we were hunting his next meal. He would laugh in your face if you asked him to let you go."

Harry stood up and turned and looked at the door. It was roughly made but very strong. He moved quietly towards it and listened at the door. He put his eye to a small space between the boards and then held up his hand to quieten Meg who was accusing him of letting them all down. She stopped her tirade and cuffed the tears from her cheeks. Harry beckoned Jennie across and told her to tell them when Sister Rona was coming back. He turned to Meg.

"You can stop now Meg, but start again when Jennie says that Sister Rona is coming. We have to make Sister Rona think that we have really fallen out."

"But Harry, what….?"

"Don't interrupt, Meg. I have to think of a way out of here and tonight if at all possible." Harry moved across to Jennie who kept her eye to the gap in the boards and called her name.

"Yes Harry? Sister Rona has gone into the High Priest's private chapel. I'll tell you when she comes back."

"That's fine Jennie. Keep looking and tell me where you will sleep tonight."

"Out there. We all sleep on straw. We can't get to our usual place, the rebels are in there and the school too. They have smashed all the cupboards and furniture looking for food."

"What do you know about the secret passage up to the hermit's cave?" Harry asked. At the same time he looked across at Meg. She was beginning to understand her brother's strategy and there was the hint of a smile on her tear stained face. The Coracle Boy turned back to listen to Jennie.

"Nothing really. Only that if you are really naughty you can be shut in the cave for a whole night and there is a serpent in there. But if you are really sorry and promise not to be wicked again, the serpent will not eat you."

"Stories put about by the priests to frighten you," Harry replied.

"No Harry. Sol had a friend who made the High Priest angry and he was put in the cave and was never seen again."

"Alright Jennie, keep your eyes open for Sister Rona. As soon as she comes back, run and join Meg on the other side of the table. You are all very angry with me and we are not speaking to each other."

"Harry you really scared me. Did you have to be so horrid?" Meg reached across the table and took Harry's hand in hers as he sat down opposite her.

"We have to convince Sister Rona that we have had a bitter argument and have fallen out. All three of you must pretend to hate me."

Suddenly Jennie ran from her post at the door, proclaiming that Sister was coming and the sergeant was with her. The girls all bunched together and began crying. Meg was saying that she would tell Abe Tull about his wicked behaviour when they got home. At the same time Harry was sitting with his back towards the girls, telling Meg to shut up and that he was fed up with dragging her around. As the door opened they all fell silent. Sister Rona came in followed by the sergeant. The sergeant was first to speak.

"Well, did you ever see the like of that?" he declared. "You're right Sister Rona. Greg is a girl and I never noticed. That's why he, I mean 'she,' never spoke. Reckoned her voice would give her away." The sergeant turned and grabbed the collar of Harry's shirt and hauled him to his feet.

"Come along Harry my lad, I've got a small job for you."

As they left the room, Meg shouted that she hated him, but as his little sister, Ruth, called after him, her voice held only sorrow and it almost made him turn and ruin the whole charade.

Harry was bustled out into the Temple, where he saw the four soldiers at the embrasures on either side of the main door into this gloomy hall. Harry was shoved across to the door into the altar room held open by a pale and frightened Sol. The priest, whose name the Coracle Boy had not heard, told the sergeant to bring Harry forward. Sol was ordered to close the door and stay there until he was sent for.

Harry was pushed forward and made to kneel before the High Priest and told not to speak until he was required to answer a question. For the first time since they arrived at the Temple Harry felt really afraid. He could not say why but there was something dreadful about the hooded figure sitting menacingly above him. The sergeant had moved back to stand with the two priests against the back wall and Harry felt utterly alone.

"You are a liar and a cheat," the High Priest shouted. "You come to spy on us," he screamed at Harry. "You accept our hospitality and then you send messages back to the soldiers of your King." The fearful figure leaned forward and went on in a hoarse whisper, "You will find out what we do with spies when the sun rises in the east. The gods are waiting for a sacrifice before they will placate the miners and show us where the new seams of gold are. You will be that sacrifice. Now take him away."

Harry was picked up bodily before he had time to stand up. The sergeant and one of the priests placed a hand under each arm and hurried him backwards, his feet hardly touching the ground as they entered the dimly lit passage that led to the door into the secret passage up to the hermit's cave. Harry saw the heavy ladder lying in the passage and knew that he was to spend the night with a very hungry serpent.

At the door the sergeant held Harry while the priest removed the two heavy timbers that secured the door. As the priest struggled, the sergeant whispered in the boy's ear and told him to stay by the door. He would be back later. The heavy door was pushed open silently and Harry was shoved roughly into the cave and the door was closed and the timbers dropped into their brackets. A single torch flickered in the sconce and was almost burnt out, it made the only sound in this near perfect silence. Harry had no wish to be left here in total darkness and looked about for a replacement. His search was fruitless.

The Coracle Boy sat on the floor of the cave and again he felt that awful fear creeping up on him as he remembered the High Priest's words. He was to be a sacrifice to their gods in the morning. He did the only thing that brought him a crumb of comfort. He prayed to his father and mother. He begged them to show him a way out and how he could rescue all the children held in captivity here. Harry went through his pockets and found that he had nothing of any real use in his present situation, except his knife. It was still in his belt. But everything else was in his shoulder bag on the table beside Meg's medicine bag, and the torch was getting dimmer all the time. He considered taking what was left of the torch and running as far as he could while it still burned, but he realised that just removing it from the sconce would be enough to douse it anyway. And then he remembered the sergeant's words, 'Stay by the door, I'll be back later'. Was it a genuine offer of help, or was it a cruel hoax? He had kept the secret of Greg not being a boy and not being dumb. Yes, he would trust the sergeant. Anyway, what else could he do? He was so tired. It had been a long and very eventful day. Harry lay on the hard floor, put his head on the crook of his arm and fell asleep.

A scraping noise wakened Harry. He was in total darkness and at once filled with fear. There it was again and then a narrow shaft of light appeared as the door opened slowly and silently and then Harry recognised the sergeant. He was carrying a large bundle under his right arm. The big man helped Harry to his feet with his left hand and then he whispered, "Harry lad, there is only one way out and that is through the caves. Captain Ragar is up with the hermit, you'd never get past him. I have enough torches here to last two days, perhaps a bit more. What do you want to do?"

"I will take my chances in the cave sir, but what will happen to my sisters and the other children?"

"Me and my lads will look after them. Now I have to light this torch and then I must seal the cave and get back to my post."

The sergeant came back with the lighted torch and handed it to Harry. "Your sister told me that you spent many days in some caves near where you live. She says you will find a way out." The sergeant clapped Harry on the shoulder and hurried away, closing the door and dropping the timbers into place. The silence was back.

Harry saw that the rope used to secure the top of the ladder had been left on the floor of the cave. He used it to tie the bundle of torches so that he could carry them on his back, leaving him with a free hand. But there was something that Harry had to confirm. He held the torch as high as he could in the shaft in which the ladder had been installed and he saw the effect on the flames. There was definitely a strong draught pulling air from somewhere and as the passage to the Temple was sealed by the door, it had to be coming from the outside. This lifted Harry's spirits. He took the burnt-out torch from the sconce to give the impression that he had gone into the cave system with only one torch. He set off on his quest for a way out of his prison. The cave turned sharply to his left and he quickly lost sight of the door to the Temple. Now he was on his own.

Chapter Thirty Seven

The tunnel that Harry followed was obviously man-made, there were chisel marks on the walls and timber frames where the rock was unstable. But then he noticed that the torch now had a steady flame and the draught on his face was hardly noticeable. Holding the torch as high as he could, he retraced his footsteps only a few paces and he saw his mistake. The draught from a natural fissure in the rock made the flame turn back on him, threatening to extinguish the torch. Harry quickly withdrew the flame, lit another torch and set them both in a cairn of loose rocks clear of the draught. The split in the strata started at about waist height and was wide enough to admit Harry and became wider as it went down and away to the right. The pull of the moving air was less severe the further in he travelled and Harry decided to try to get a torch into the fissure. His first attempt failed but the second effort, using a new torch that burned fiercely for the first few moments, got him forward into the wider, calmer section of the cave.

Gradually Harry brought all the torches forward into this natural cave. The keen breeze encouraged the boy considerably. As he went forward he discovered that his new route was becoming difficult over a moraine of smooth, loose rocks. It seemed that he was at the top of a steep slope that fell away to his right. Loosened rock clattered away to end in a splash of water some distance below him. He would have to be very careful. Harry was covering the ground twice as he moved the torches in a leapfrog fashion, but now that the air flow was more constant he wondered if he dare extinguish one torch. He decided against this idea. In this sort of terrain it would be easy to drop a torch and be left in the dark with no means of lighting another.

Suddenly Harry saw a wall of solid rock in front of him. The only way was down and as he went slowly from rock to rock he felt the air current grow more active and he could now hear the water. His torches revealed a small stream running from a long, narrow pool stretching away to his right. To follow the stream and the strong breeze, he turned left into a low cave where the current of air threatened to put out the flames of his leading torch. Harry fixed one burning brand amongst the loose stones clear of the turbulence and ventured into the cave, holding the light well in front of him. He had to crawl on his hands and knees for a considerable distance until he was able to stand up. He looked back and realised that the cave had curved to his left and he could no longer see the light he had left behind. With his torch wedged in a rock crevice, Harry returned to collect the lit and the unused torches.

The way ahead appeared to continue down a rock strewn incline and the cave widened out so that he was entering a lofty gallery. He saw his flame reflected in another pool of crystal clear water. Harry looked up and realised that there were stalactites hanging from the roof, the first he had seen in these caves. Moving cautiously and holding firmly to the torches, the Coracle Boy picked his way forward. He soon found that he would have to abandon one of the burning brands. He needed a free hand to get down the slope ahead. Wedging the oldest torch between two boulders, Harry continued on down the slope to where it levelled out. The stream flowed quietly here but there was the sound of a cascade not far away. He knew that he must rest soon. He collected the torch from between the boulders and settled down on the driest patch he could find and lit a new torch. He extinguished the one of the other two with the weakest flame so that, if he did fall asleep, he would be sure of light when he awoke.

Harry was tired and hungry, but he soon fell asleep and dreamed of his old home in the forest. In his dream, his father and mother were there, they were sitting on the bench under the window into the cottage. It was a bright, sunny day and Meg and the young 'uns were splashing about in the river, while Harry was making a new coracle. The sky clouded over and they all went into the house, but there was no roof on the house and now his father and mother were not there. The boy then looked for Ruth and she was being carried away in his new coracle towards the great river. He turned and saw Simon riding Star away into the forest, the foal trotting behind them. He called out but Simon rode on into the dark woods. Harry turned and reached for Meg's hand but it was like vapour and slid from his grasp as she too turned away from him. He looked across the river, only to see that the bridge had gone and only the small white cross that marked his mother's grave remained and then that was slowly lost in a cold mist that fell like a blanket around him and he was alone.

Harry woke with a start. It was almost totally dark. The newest torch had fallen over and the flame had gone out. All he could see were the last burning embers of the weakest torch with barely enough glowing to light a new torch. He reached for the smouldering brand very carefully, groping in the semidarkness and hoping that he wouldn't accidentally drop the burning spark into the water. He found the handle and cautiously closed his fingers round the wood and lifted it up to his face. He blew gently on the embers but there was little to burn. With his free hand, Harry fumbled in the darkness until he found one of the unused torches and put it beside the dying glow and exhaled until a spark ignited the resin in the new torch. Now he had light and, refreshed after his sleep, he decided that he must move on. Hunger was now becoming a problem and for a brief moment he wondered if he should turn back, but it was only for a moment. There was no point in going back to be sacrificed to some heathen god. He would go on until he died of hunger if he had to.

A very determined Harry entered the cave, leaving a burning torch at the entrance. He found that it became narrower and higher. He was unable to see a roof of any kind. The noise of the cascade was louder now and after a few paces Harry saw the water plunge down into the darkness. The noise of the water hitting the rocks below echoed and the Coracle Boy realised that he was now in some kind of chamber and was standing on the edge of a precipice. With the short rope that had secured the ladder, Harry lowered a lit torch down, clear of the falling water, as far as the rope could reach. It revealed that the precipice was about the height of three men. There were rocks strewn about at the bottom, getting down there was going to be a problem. The rope was not nearly strong enough, it was old and frayed.

Harry retrieved and doused the torch and sat down. This was a setback, but sitting down wasn't helping, he must find a way down. He stood up and searched the rocks to his right and stepped across the stream, but saw nothing to encourage him. To his left it looked just as hopeless. Nonetheless, he returned back over the stream and saw something sticking out of a crevice just above head height. It was a burnt out torch. Harry's heart leapt as he wrenched the dead brand from the rock face and stepped back to safer ground to examine his find. The wooden stick that had held the torch was not old and Harry realised that Joel, Sol's friend, might have got this far, or there were other people moving in this cave system. Harry would have to be careful, and he still had no idea how he would get down to the floor of what seemed to be a large cavern. There was something else puzzling him. How had Joel travelled so far with only one torch?

Assuming that it was Joel who had put the torch in the crevice, Harry decided to do the same and placed one of the lights in the fissure. He looked down into the darkness and was not encouraged. He relit the torch that was still fixed to the rope and suspended it down into the darkness again and saw a ledge not more than half his own height below the rim he was standing on. And then he had another idea. He laid out all the unused torches and knew that he had more than a handful. He would light one and throw it into the cavern. If there was water down there, it would be lost. If not he might be able to retrieve it later. It was worth a try.

Harry lit another torch and swung it through the air to get a good blaze going and then reached out an arm's length and dropped it. It landed amongst scattered boulders. It lit up the face down which Harry would have to descend and it was clear of the waterfall and dry down there. Harry hauled up the rope and unfastened the torch and used it to return to where he had left a light burning at the entrance. As he returned, Harry looked carefully for signs of a human presence in this cave, a footprint, scratch marks on the walls, but there was nothing. Perhaps it was too much to wish for. After all, it was more than four moons ago when Joel was locked in the caves.

Back at the precipice, Harry examined the route he would have to take. It was clear of the water and there appeared to be several good handholds, but it was not going to be easy. Realising that he would need both hands to scale down the cliff and he would have to rely on only two torches, Harry tied the remaining torches together and lowered them to about halfway before letting them fall. He had to hope they didn't roll down to the burning brand and ignite all of the torches. Luck was with him.

The burning torch at the bottom of the cliff illuminated the face very well. The problem was that Harry's body would cast a shadow and he would be working in his own light. He lay down and gradually eased his body over the edge and felt with his feet for the ledge. He found it and carefully transferred his weight to the foothold. Harry found a crevice to his left that proved to be a secure handhold. Now he was able to feel for a lower projection and found one just as he was about at the full extent of his reach.

The crevice in which he had jammed his left hand continued down and Harry was able to use it for another two steps. He was now almost halfway down. A second crevice appeared on his right. It was wider than the first and Harry put his hand into the slot and then clenched his fist so that it tightened in the gap. This took him down another three small steps. He looked down and wondered if he could drop that far. It was not worth the risk of a broken ankle. There was a projection away to his left. He searched for a handhold on that side and found a tiny ridge in the rock, but was it enough to hold his weight? There was nothing else. He would have to risk it. Harry relaxed his clenched fist, tightened his grip on the tiny ridge and stretched with his left leg until it touched a ledge. He was committed now and placed his right hand flat on the rock and pushed himself across until he was standing with one foot on the projection. His right hand replaced the left hand and Harry frantically searched for a handhold. Luckily he found a crack just wide enough to get his fingers in and give him the support he was hoping for. He pulled himself across until he had both feet on the shelf of rock. Another couple of difficult moves and the Coracle Boy was able to jump down onto what he discovered to be sand.

Harry rescued the torch he had thrown down and gathered the bundle and then sat down on the soft sand. He examined his grazed knuckles and chafed fingers. They would be sore, but there was no serious damage. Suddenly Harry realised that he was hungry. He had lost track of time and, as for direction, he had not the faintest idea of where he might be.

The climb down the rock face had exhausted a tired and hungry Harry and he decided to rest. The light was still burning at the top of the precipice and lit up the chamber he was in. It was much larger than any of the caverns under Westown. The stream reflected the glow of the flames as it meandered away, making small pools and tiny cascades that were soon lost in the darkness.

Suddenly the Coracle Boy sat up and listened and then realised that it was not his ears that had picked up a sound, but his nose that had detected a scent. Harry stood up and moved away from the resinous odour of the torches and went to the edge of the light and sniffed the air coming into his face. Yes, he was sure of it now. Wood smoke! That meant fire and fire usually signalled the presence of people, and hopefully food. In his excitement Harry almost shouted out, but managed to stop himself. Anyone could be making the smoke. The pagans could be waiting for him to emerge, or Joel could be somewhere out there. Perhaps there was a village near the mouth of the cave. Harry decided to follow the smell of the smoke, but he must be very careful and so he followed the leapfrog system he had developed earlier. It was time consuming but necessary, if he was to remain free.

Four times he had to move the torches before he came up against a vertical rock face. The stream turned sharply to the right into a narrow cleft in the wall of rock and the sound of yet another waterfall came up through the fissure together with the scent of wood smoke. It was stronger now and Harry was reminded of a forest fire, but quickly dismissed that terrifying idea because it was the wrong time of the year.

The fissure was just wide enough to allow the Coracle Boy to enter, but it meant walking in the cold water of the stream, a small discomfort, if it brought him to human companionship and food.

The cave widened and he was able to walk on the dry, sandy floor and now he could see the blue, curling smoke drifting past him. He must be very close to the fire he thought.

Harry put the bundle of unused torches down and built a cairn of small rocks to support one of the lit flames. He crept forward with a single torch held low and then he saw it, the red glow, faint at first and now flickering on the damp wall where the cave turned left. Harry wedged the torch in a split in the rock and crawled forward in semidarkness that was becoming less oppressive with every step. The play of the flame reflections on the cave side suggested a large fire.

At that point Harry heard voices, men's voices, two men, one laughing, sharing a joke perhaps. Crawling forward into the increasing light, he could now see the fire, it was indeed a large blaze and then he smelt food. Meat was being roasted and it was very tempting to reveal his presence. All he could see was the top of the licking flames and the smoke curling into the crevice high above him. Harry had emerged into another lofty cave somewhere near the bottom. The fire appeared to be burning on a ledge a short distance above him, but it was the possibility of food that occupied Harry's thoughts, he was so hungry.

Harry was startled by a loud shout from somewhere beyond the fire. He wriggled back into the darkness and listened. Had he been seen?

"Osbert," the voice called again. "Come and lend a hand."

The muffled reply was lost in the echoes that bounced off the walls of the cavern. Now there were several voices it suggested the arrival of a group of people. Discernible conversation was lost as the sound reverberated round the cavern, only the occasional word understood.

Satisfied that he had not been discovered, Harry stole forward, again keeping low and using every bit of shadow that was available. But the whiteness of his skin against the blackness of the rock would give him away and yet he had to be able to see these men. Harry retreated once more, he had to think of a way to be able to spy on his adversaries, if that is what they were. He had been so keen to see where the firelight was coming from that he had forgotten about the stream and where that went. The noise the men at the fire were making almost covered the sound of the small waterfall somewhere down to his left.

Harry followed the stream as it tumbled over smooth rocks or disappeared for a short while beneath larger boulders. It was quite a long descent until he arrived at a pool where the stream joined a small, fast flowing river. But what made Harry's heart beat faster was the glow of daylight he could see in the distance. He wanted to run towards it, but the route ahead was lost in black shadow. He would need a torch to make any progress.

To his right, Harry could see a boulder strewn slope and at the top the large camp fire and men, a handful of them, sitting or moving about, but there were more of them judging by the noise they made. Perhaps if he waited until they went away or slept, he could steal some food. No, they would never leave their food unattended.

The cave from which Harry and the stream emerged into this huge cavern was in total darkness and he had to feel his way back. Keeping tight against the wall, Harry ventured up the steep slope where some of the boulders were huge, great slabs of smooth rock that must have fallen from the roof, whilst beneath there were smaller rocks that were easily dislodged and rolled away noisily, but the men appeared not to notice. An overhanging feature near the top of the slope became the Coracle Boy's target.

Chapter Thirty Eight

Keeping as low as possible, Harry squeezed between boulders or picked his way over the smaller stones and reached the cover of the overhang. His line of sight was just below the crest of the slope. He could see the backs of several men as they sat facing the fire, talking and laughing as they ate.

Suddenly a dog barked. Harry squeezed down between the rocks and froze, his head held low so that his face was hidden, but the dog stopped barking and Harry slowly raised his head. The men continued to eat and talk. Harry moved cautiously further up the slope to where he could watch through a narrow slit between the rocks. Now he could see that there were more men on the other side of the fire and at that moment the dog barked again. This time it came into view and stood barking savagely at the edge of the slope. The dog was looking in Harry's direction. Someone told the dog to be quiet and tossed some of his food at the animal. The dog ignored both command and food and continued to bark, but less aggressively now. There was movement on the other side of the fire. A big man stood up and came towards the dog and spoke to the animal. The barking stopped and the dog sat. Harry kept his eye to the gap between the rocks, the slightest movement would be seen by the dog. The big man went down on one knee beside the dog, both were looking in Harry's direction. To the Coracle Boy they were just black silhouettes against the glow of the fire.

There was more movement on the far side of the fire and a second figure, shorter and leaner than the big man, came to stand by the dog. There appeared to be some conversation between the two men, but they were too far away for Harry to make out any words. The big man stood up and the other man turned as if to return to his place on the far side of the fire. That is when Harry saw the blue sash, the blue sash that signifies an officer, but now he was confused. Did the blue sash apply to all armies? Lieutenant

Kester, at the small mine, certainly wasn't wearing one. Harry noticed too that the dog had stopped barking and was now standing. He was looking in the boy's direction slowly wagging his tail. Suddenly Harry knew who was up at the fire, it was Brian and his dog, Scrap!

Slowly Harry stood up until his head and shoulders were above the surrounding rocks. Brian called to the officer and then others came to join the two men. Soon there was a large group of men staring in the direction of the Coracle Boy, some with drawn swords. The officer ordered the men to take up defensive positions. Men ran to the left and right.

"Who are you? How many of you are there?" the officer called.

"I am alone sir. My name is Harry sir."

"Harry?" Brian roared. "Harry, the Coracle Boy, be that you son?"

"Yes Brian sir," the boy replied hesitantly, "Can I come out sir?"

"It's a young boy," the officer said incredulously. "Do you know who this young person is Brian?"

"Sir, that be young Harry sir, the son of the forester what died on the bridge sir. He be Harry the Coracle Boy, him what saved all them Eastowners sir. We all thought him dead or captured."

The officer turned and looked across at the boy. He called out that he would be welcome and told the men to remain alert, it might be a trick.

A very tired Harry scrambled carefully from one large slab of rough rock to the next. These boulders had not been smoothed by the passage of water over them. The boy's footwear was almost worn out. He might have managed just as well barefoot. As Harry clambered up the last few paces Brian put out his hand to haul the boy up onto the flat area where the fire burned and men looked on from the shadows. No one was sitting down.

The big man shook Harry's hand and asked if the boy had seen Sami, his son.

"Yes Brian, he's with the others. They are all safe."

"Thank the good Lord," Brian said and a tear started down his cheek."

Brian turned and introduced Harry to the officer. "This be Harry sir. Harry, this be Captain Giles, he's in charge of us. Where be Meg your sister? What's happened, lad?"

"The boy looks exhausted Brian, let him sit down. Bring him some food and water, he can answer our questions later," Captain Giles ordered.

Brian brought a ram's horn filled with water and a wooden platter with bread and slices of meat cut from a pig that was roasting on the other side of the fire. Scrap, the dog, was nuzzling up beside Harry who stroked and patted the animal, giving him the occasional morsel from the well laden plate. The Coracle Boy finished his meal and thanked Brian and the officer. He was anxious to know what they were doing in the caves. Were they here to rescue Meg, Ruth and the other children? But the officer was eager to know all that Harry could tell him about effect of the earthquake. What was happening in the village? Who was fighting whom? How many soldiers were there? Harry answered every question as best he could. Captain Giles was glad to discover that there were so few soldiers left to defend the place. Harry also told him of Meg's plight and the need to free them as soon as possible.

Now it was Harry who wanted some questions answered, but the captain departed saying that he would be back later. The sergeant would be in charge. Harry turned to see the smiling face of Sergeant Rudd and beside him Osbert, the tall, rangy soldier who last summer had followed him into the underground river and the caves beyond.

"Hullo Harry, I'm Sergeant Rudd. You won't remember me, it was dark when we met, and you went off to find the underground river." Sergeant Rudd held out his hand. "Osbert here has told us about your adventures. I wouldn't have believed him but Major Redman said it was all true."

"Yes sir, sergeant. I do remember you, it was in the forest not far from the southern tower."

"Hullo Harry," Osbert said as he shook the boy's hand and then added, "Lieutenant DeGray's with us, I'll tell him you're here, he'll be pleased to see you. Often talks about you, he do. Fine gentleman the lieutenant. Got to go now Harry, I'm on picket duty. See you at sunset."

Osbert gathered his weapons and hurried away. The sergeant told Harry to get some rest. He could use Osbert's blanket and there was plenty of dried bracken to lie on. Sergeant Rudd deployed two men to watch in the direction that Harry had come from, in case the boy had been followed. Harry went to sleep to the drone of muted conversation between the men and the crackle of burning wood. Whilst Brian sat down beside the boy, Scrap, the dog, lay sprawled at the boy's feet.

Chapter Thirty Nine

Harry was roused from a deep sleep by Scrap barking, plus the sound of many voices. He sat up and rubbed his eyes. Men were standing around him, the flickering light of the bonfire throwing grotesque, shimmering patterns across their faces. He recognised Brian.

"It be alright Harry, sorry if we woke you. I brought a visitor to see you."

"Hullo Harry, remember me? Lieutenant Roland De Gray."

Harry took the proffered hand and felt the firm, warm handshake of the young officer, his befuddled brain struggling out of the deep sleep, trying to remember. At that moment Brian came and knelt beside the Coracle Boy and it all came rushing back.

"Brian!" The boy put his hand on Brian's forearm. "Meg and Ruth and the others. We must rescue them."

"Aye lad, that we must, but we need to know more about what we are up against. That be why Lieutenant DeGray needs to talk to you son."

"Harry, tell us how you came to be in these caves. Captain Giles said something about you being offered as a sacrifice to the pagan gods."

"That's right sir. The High Priest said that I was a spy and that I have been sending messages back to the soldiers of our King sir. I was to be sacrificed to please their gods sir."

"But how did you get into the caves?"

"They put me in the caves until they were ready to sacrifice me, I reckon sir. There is supposed to be a dreadful serpent in the caves, but I saw no serpent. What would he live on sir?"

"Quite so, Harry, but how did you find your way in the dark?"

"Sergeant Garth helped me sir. He gave me a bundle of torches. I still have some left, they are back down there." The Coracle Boy pointed down into the darkness. He also explained who Sergeant Garth was.

"Is it possible to get into the building where the children are held from these caves?"

"Yes sir. There is a passage from the High Priest's special room into the caves, but there is a very thick oak door with two heavy beams locking it from the other side sir."

"Could you lead us back there Harry?"

"I'm not sure sir. It was not like the Westown caves sir. There I had to remember the route in case we had to return." Harry went on to describe the hermit's cave and the ladder down into the caves. Also, six soldiers were defending that access to the Temple. He told of the four soldiers supporting Sergeant Garth who was actually in the Temple building.

"There are this many men waiting with the horses, but all are wounded sir," Harry explained, holding up one hand with his fingers spread.

"Where are they?" Lieutenant De-Gray asked.

"In the woods just west of the village sir."

Just at that moment a young soldier came running up the slope and gave the lieutenant a small rolled parchment. The young officer opened the message and tilted it towards the firelight and started reading. He rolled the document and put it inside his tunic before calling the men to order.

"Men, we are ordered to march within the hour. That means we will be marching through the night. We know that the pagans have a great fear of the darkness, so we must take advantage of that weakness. We rendezvous with Captain Giles at Wolf Rock at midnight so we have no time to lose. Leave nothing here, hopefully we won't be back. Sergeant, take charge here and muster out in the clearing as soon as you can. Harry, come with me."

Harry and Roland DeGray set off at a brisk pace down the slope and soon turned left into a cave where the daylight lifted the boy's spirits. They stepped out into a cold winter afternoon where men were pulling on warm clothing, buckling on swords and shields, loading two packhorses and taking one last warm at a blazing fire.

"Harry, I want you do something for me. We have taken several prisoners and I want you to look at them and see if you recognise any of them. Most of them say that they are miners. There are fifteen of them and I can't spare the men to guard them."

The lieutenant led the way down a path at the foot of an escarpment to another cave where a fire blazed in front of a much larger opening than the one they had just left. Three soldiers stood near the fire. A fourth was roasting a deer on a spit and adding fuel to the blaze. The flames illuminated the group of men huddled together on the other side of the fire. All four soldiers carried spears and had swords strapped to their waists.

Harry recognised two of the guards. They had been on the underground river adventure and both men grinned broadly when they saw Harry.

"Have they behaved themselves?" the lieutenant asked, nodding towards the prisoners.

"Quiet as lambs sir," one of the guards replied. The others nodded their agreement.

"I want them brought round one at a time. Harry will see if he can recognise any of them. Are you ready Harry?"

"Yes sir," a rather nervous Coracle Boy replied.

A soldier brought a tall lanky man whose clothes were in tatters.

"I saw this man at the miners' village sir," Harry said.

"You be the lad what fetched us some grub, fish as I recall, you and the other lad." He turned to the lieutenant, "Did us proud he did sir."

"Do you think he was a miner Harry?"

"He lived in one of the miners' huts sir."

"I suppose that makes him a miner. Stand over there away from the others and bring the next man."

It was a similar story for almost half of the prisoners and then the next man arrived and went towards Harry and was restrained by a soldier.

"It be young Harry. You remember me Harry."

"This is Garvey sir, he is a miner for sure."

Next came Cram, who also recognised Harry as did some of the remainder, until the last man was brought forward. He was weak and very thin and looked more like a hermit than a miner. His long robe was filthy and there was no cord at the waist. The cowl that covered his fair hair was pulled right back by the guard as he came to stand in front of Harry. The boy looked up at a young, haggard face. Intense blue eyes looked down at him for a moment and then the head dropped until the man's chin rested on his chest.

"I have never seen this man, but I believe his name is Joel sir."

The young man's head moved up quickly causing his guard to take a pace forward and grip his forearm.

"What makes you say that?" Lieutenant DeGray asked.

"Sir, he has a friend at the Temple called Sol. They are learning to be priests and Sol said Joel was put into the tunnels as a punishment by the High Priest."

"Is that correct?" the young officer asked. Slowly, like a tired old man, the novice priest nodded his head.

"Don't just nod your head, speak up. You have a tongue in your head! Are you called Joel and are you a priest in the pagan church?"

"Yes sir, I am Joel and I was hoping to become a priest in our church."

Lieutenant DeGray called Garvey back and asked if he knew this young man.

"Aye sir, but only in passin' as you might say. Seed 'im up at the Temple sir. 'Im and young Sol brought us goat's milk for the little 'uns when they was sick sir. He ain't a bad lad sir."

"Take your men back into the cave Garvey."

"What be goin' to 'appen to us sir?"

"I'll tell you that when I am good and ready, now go back into the cave."

The lieutenant turned his back on Garvey and stared into the forest. He was deep in thought. Sergeant Rudd came down the path and said that the troops would be ready to move off soon and what should he do with the prisoners?

"I can't kill men in cold blood sergeant, could you?" the lieutenant said.

"No sir, not unless you ordered it sir."

"And I will not order you to do something I can't do myself."

"Dare we turn them loose sir?" the sergeant asked.

"I can't see any alternative sergeant."

The sergeant grinned and asked the young officer to leave it to him.

"With young Harry to back me up, they will be so scared they won't dare follow us sir. The young priest may be a bit awkward but I think I can handle him. Anyway, he's too weak to be much trouble."

"Thank you sergeant, I'll go and get the men started."

Lieutenant DeGray hurried away up the path. As soon as the officer had gone the sergeant called one of the soldiers to him and, after a whispered conversation, they stood back and the sergeant pointed in the direction of the top of the escarpment. Moments later the soldier collected his personal belongings and cut a whole leg from the roasting deer and left at a run in the direction Sergeant Rudd had pointed.

"Come on young Harry, let's go and put the fear of the devil into those pagans. All you have to do is agree with me even if you don't agree, because I might tell a few untruths. Oh, one other thing you can do is cut fourteen notches in that willow stick by your foot."

"I can't do numbers sir." the Coracle Boy replied.

Sergeant Rudd held up both hands with the fingers spread. "It's that many and then this many." He held up one hand with four fingers spread.

"You are not going to kill those men are you sergeant?" Harry looked worried.

"No son, I'll not kill anyone if I can help it, that's a promise. But first I'll send the priest to the other side of the fire."

As they approached, some of the men were sitting on the ground, others leaning on the rock face. The young novice priest was lying on a pile of bracken. As Harry and the sergeant got nearer they all stood up, all except Joel. Sergeant Rudd told him to get up and go and stand by the guards on the other side of the fire.

"You ain't going to kill us are yuh' sir?" one man whined.

"I will if you don't shut up," the sergeant snarled. "Now listen to me, your gods are very angry with you because you steal children to do men's work. The gods have taken the gold out of the ground. They have sent earthquakes to bury your mines. They have closed your escape routes and killed all your soldiers. Every last one of them is dead. And if you venture out into the darkness, they will send wolves to kill you. Only the god of fire is your friend." Sergeant Rudd glared fiercely along the line of men and then continued, "We have only one God and he has sent us to take back our children. He protects us from the night prowling killers and the serpents your High Priest keeps in the mountain. This boy has walked right through those many tunnels, but the serpent is afraid to harm him. We have come with an invisible army to take back every child we can find. We don't want your gold mines because there is no gold left in them. Your gods have seen to that."

The sergeant paused and looked at each man and what he saw in every face was fear, and not one of them could look him in the eye. Even the usually vociferous Cram was silent. He looked down at his feet and shuffled like a naughty child.

"So what am I going to do with you? Young Harry says that I should spare your miserable lives, but I…."

"Please, don't kill us sir, I have a wife and child at home. Spare us and we will leave these cursed mountains for ever. Please…."

The young man who spoke had been silent up until now, but was cut off by another growl and sharp rebuke from the sergeant. "Just shut up and stop your snivelling. Here's what you will do." He paused and glared at the terrified men. "You will stay here tonight and then, in the morning at first light, you will go north to the end of the lake, cross the river and march down the other side to where the river falls down the cliff. You will turn east and follow the path along the top of the escarpment until it drops down to meet the road from the east. Keep going east until you come to our outpost, where you will hand a counting stick to the guard. If there are fourteen of you he will let you pass. Any more or less and you will die."

The sergeant took the stick from Harry and counted the fourteen notches that the boy had cut.

"Who can count?" the sergeant asked. No one offered a reply. "Then let us ask the priest." The priest was brought forward and confirmed that there were fourteen marks on the stick.

"Garvey, I'm putting you in charge of your party. You will carry the counting stick. You are responsible for getting fourteen men to that outpost. I suggest an early start if you are to reach your destination before dark. One other thing, I have sent a man to the top of the cliff to make sure you obey my orders. He will not be able to see you until you get down to the lakeside and he may lose you from time to time, but he will be able to see you when you reach the waterfall, at about noon, where you turn east. We will leave you the rest of the deer and a few crusts of bread."

The sergeant looked down the line and saw relief, even excitement on most of the faces. Two looked a little uncertain, but no one appeared hostile. "Well, do you approve or would some of you prefer the sword? I can soon cut another counting stick."

There was a shuffling of feet and then Garvey stepped forward and said that he and Cram would make sure that they all kept their word. They agreed to the terms entirely.

Without another word the sergeant turned away and walked back to where the priest was sitting on a log near the fire. He sat beside the young man and poked the fire with a stick as if he might find the right words in the embers, he threw the stick into the blaze. "What are we going to do with you young man?"

"I do not wish to meet the gods while they are so angry with us, but if you have to kill me then burn my body because, as you rightly said, only the god of fire seems to be our friend."

"Did you steal our children?" Sergeant Rudd asked.

"No! I did no such thing," the young priest answered hotly.

"Then why should I kill you? Come along, I am needed up at the other camp," the sergeant said as he helped Joel to his feet.

Two of the guards took an arm each and almost carried the young priest up the steep path. At the clearing the men were ready to move off. Harry saw the man who had been sent to the top of the escarpment sharing his leg of venison with his friends. He asked Sergeant Rudd why he was not at his post up on the cliff to see the prisoners depart and check their progress.

"The prisoners think they are being watched. They are frightened men and can't get away from this place quick enough. They don't need to be watched."

"Will the guards at the outpost let them pass?"

"There are no guards and there is no outpost Harry. They will be far away before they realize that." The sergeant laughed and turned his attention to the young priest who had sat down by the fire as soon as the guards had released him. He looked very dejected.

"Now young man, Joel, isn't it? You are in no state to travel with us so you will be left here with enough food, water and firewood to last for three or four days. We will send your own people back for you once we have gained possession of the Temple and got all the children back. Is there anyone you would prefer us to speak to?"

"Speak to Mark, he knows that the High Priest is corrupt. He brought me torches and food. He and young Sol will come for me."

"Here comes Lieutenant DeGray. We must leave you now Joel." Sergeant Rudd turned and saluted the young officer.

"Everything alright sergeant?" he enquired.

"Prisoners leave at first light. They think they will be watched sir. The priest will stay here until his own people come for him sir."

"And you, Joel the priest, are you satisfied with the treatment you and your countrymen have received?"

"I cannot put my gratitude into words sir. I listened to the arrangements your sergeant has made for the release of the miners and now the provisions you have made for my wellbeing. Such generosity is beyond me. All I can say sir is thank you and may all the gods protect you and your men."

"Thank you Joel, now you need to rest and we must leave you, it will be dark soon. Come along Sergeant, Harry."

The young priest reached and touched Harry's arm and smiled as he made a sign with his other hand and whispered, "Thank you Harry." Harry smiled and nodded and wondered why Joel should thank him.

Chapter Forty

"Harry, I want you to travel with Osbert in the middle of the column."

The lieutenant went to the front of the troop from where he sent two men forward as scouts and then they set off up the wooded mountainside. The going got harder as they climbed higher. The two packhorses seemed to cope with the steep slope better than some of the men. They soon left the dense pine woods and came into groves of ash and oak. The ground beneath their feet was strewn with moss covered rocks and was very difficult to walk over, but their discomfort was short-lived. They came to a track where one of the scouts was waiting. It was still some distance to the rendezvous point at Wolf Rock. The path was an animal track. Osbert examined the spoor and said that they were deer hoof marks, but he couldn't rule out the presence of wolves on this remote mountain. The scout came back to warn the lieutenant that the path travelled along the edge of a dangerous cliff. He suggested that he should lead one of the packhorses, with a rope attached, across first and tie the rope to a tree. Lieutenant DeGray agreed to the plan. Packhorses are more sure-footed than men.

Although it was a clear night, there was no moon, it would not be easy getting everyone and the horses across. Harry got the impression that Osbert was more nervous than him as they gripped the guide rope and trod carefully. However, they completed the task without mishap.

Captain Giles was not waiting for them when they arrived at Wolf Rock. The men were pleased to take advantage of his absence and get some rest. There were very few trees at this height and their only shelter was found behind the huge boulders that littered the crest. One of the scouts had climbed to the top of the rocky outcrop. Presently he called down to Lieutenant DeGray and informed him that there was a signal fire to the south.

"Tell me the moment you see the second fire. Sergeant Rudd get our reply torch lit." The sergeant had anticipated the young officer's order and the torch flared almost at once.

Everyone waited in silence until the scout shouted down that the second fire had been lit to the right of the first fire. The blazing torch was handed up to the scout, who waved it for a short while and then handed it back down before climbing down. The lieutenant took his place and called the sergeant up to take a look. When the lieutenant and sergeant came down, several men scrambled up, including Harry and Osbert. Harry saw the two fires. They appeared to be only a short distance apart. But before he could ask a question, everyone was ordered back down. The second scout had just come up from the east side of the mountain. The larger party was near.

To Harry's surprise, the men took up defensive positions amongst the boulders. The torch was doused and silence was ordered. It seemed an age to Harry before the approaching group could be heard as they stepped on the loose scree.

"Halt! Give the password and identify yourself," a voice called out.

"Westown castle. Major Redman. We are coming in."

Harry heard the name and his heart leapt. He wanted to run out and greet his old friend, but this was the military, protocol had to be observed. Harry also noticed that Captain Redman had been promoted to Major.

As soon as the party was recognised and the civilities dealt with, Major Redman told everyone to take a rest and some food. "I understand that you have an old friend of mine in your party, lieutenant."

"Indeed we have sir." The lieutenant turned and called Harry, who almost ran to take the outstretched hand of Major Redman.

"Hullo Harry, I have been hearing about your adventures from some of your friends, one of whom is with us."

He turned and pulled Peter forward. Harry stood dumbfounded. The tall, broad shouldered, blonde haired young man stepped forward and shook Harry's hand warmly. "Did you find your sister, Harry?"

"Yes, but she is a prisoner. She and all the children are being held in the pagan Temple. Did you …." Harry was cut off by Major Redman.

"Sorry Harry, you will have to save your questions for later. We have a busy night ahead and I need Peter to come with Captain Giles and me."

The Major, Captain Giles and Peter went up towards the crest from which the signal fires could be seen. The three men appeared as barely visible silhouettes against the night sky. And then they hurried away to their right. Harry was mystified and asked Sergeant Rudd what was going on.

"They are trying to line the two signal fires with a point on this ridge. When they are in line the Major will know that he is directly above the pagan Temple and the hermit's cave."

"But won't the pagans see the fires sir? Harry asked.

"No, son, the fires are set a long way back from the edge of the hill and we are much higher than the signal fires."

"But the lookout on the high point at the bend in the river will be able to see our signal torch, won't he?"

"No, Wolf Rock over there hides us from him. We have to thank your friend Peter for that bit of information."

Soon the Major was back and the officers and sergeants went into a huddle. It transpired that the party was to be split into four sections. Section number one would work with section number two and attack the village from the east and west simultaneously and then converge on the Temple. Section three, a smaller party, would strike at the hermit's cave, whilst section number four would capture the small mine and disarm Lieutenant Kester and his troop. Major Redman and Captain Giles would command sections one and two respectively. Lieutenant DeGray would attack the hermit's cave. Sergeant Rudd was to rendezvous with Sergeant Defoe at a point above the small mine. Peter was to go with the Major and Harry was to travel with Lieutenant DeGray.

Harry was pleased to be with the young lieutenant. They might be first into the Temple, that would be his greatest wish.

Orders were quickly relayed. Harry wondered how everyone seemed to know exactly what to do and where to go.

"Discipline!" Was all that Sergeant Rudd said in reply to the boy's query.

Sergeant Rudd had a small party of ten men. Lieutenant DeGray said that there were twenty in his squad, all specially chosen for this the most hazardous part of the assault. The hermit's cave entrance was in a sheer cliff face and the soldiers would have to abseil down the height of eight men. The terrain above the sheer rock face was very steep and covered with stunted trees and coarse clumps of heather. Harry knew this from his earlier scouting with Meg. The lieutenant was glad of this information, he had only been able to view his target from the other side of the river.

Sergeant Rudd's party left first, moving back down the slope. Lieutenant DeGray moved off next, going up the steep slope to the crest and then turned right. After a short distance they came upon a soldier who challenged them. The password was recognised and the soldier pointed to a marker. This was the position from which they would start their descent. They were just below the snowline and it was bitterly cold. Going down in a straight line was aided by keeping the two blazing beacons in line for as long as they could see them.

Harry, the lieutenant and two soldiers were roped together. The rest of the men were grouped and roped together in a similar way. They set off in single file. They were warned that a dislodged stone allowed to roll down the steep slope would give them away so extreme care must be taken. It seemed to be a long time before they found the scrubby trees giving way to clumps of heather. Here they stopped. Lieutenant DeGray detached himself from the short rope that held him to Harry and the two soldiers. He passed the end of a long, thick rope through a metal ring fixed to a leather belt at his waist and then tied it to a secure tree. The other end and the rest of the coil he passed over his left shoulder, across his back and reached for it with his right hand. He handed the remainder to a soldier who took up the slack. At this point they lost sight of the beacons.

The lieutenant stood up and began to step backwards whilst the soldier paid out the rope. The young officer soon became a ghostly shape as he descended into the gloom. The soldier had used almost half of the coil when there came three sharp tugs that told the soldier to stop. He took up the strain and the rope moved to the right and then the left. The second soldier reached forward and held the rope. With two men holding him, the boy was sure that the lieutenant was safe.

The wait for the officers' return felt like an age to Harry and then the dark shape of the lieutenant appeared, he was breathless. He rested for a few moments and then he gathered the men to him.

"They have no sentries posted," the lieutenant reported. "There appears to be something draped across the entrance. Harry?"

"Yes sir. It's a sheet of animal skins sir."

"And you are sure that there were only six soldiers in there."

"There were this many sir." Harry held up one hand and one finger.

The young lieutenant grinned as he peered into the gloom to count the boy's fingers.

"Yes, that's six Harry."

Next, the lieutenant described to his men the plan of attack. They would abseil down on two of the long ropes. Half of the squad would go down to the left of the entrance. The lieutenant would take the remainder and Harry down to the right of the mouth of the cave.

"We are right above the centre of the cave so you will need to traverse about ten paces east. I will do the same to the west. There is a stack of firewood near your landing place so be very careful. Wait there until you see me standing in the pool of light and then follow my signal. If I am challenged before I can give the sign, come as fast as you can. Any questions?" There was no reply. "Then let's do it. Good luck, men."

Lieutenant DeGray started down the steep slope. Harry and the two soldiers he was roped to were told to move aside and allow the eight soldiers to follow down the rope. Harry was disappointed not to be at the front with the lieutenant, but then he realised that this was soldiers' work.

Still attached to the two soldiers, Harry took hold of the thick rope, as did his companions, and began their descent, stepping cautiously backwards. At first it was mostly tussocks of heather. Next it was coarse grass and then bare rock.

Suddenly the boy was halted and told in a whisper to wait. Harry looked over his right shoulder and saw the pool of light that was at the entrance to the cave. He saw movement at the woodpile, this meant that the second team was in place. The excitement was almost too much to bear, Harry's heart was pounding in his chest and his palms were sweating. Would the rope slip through his hands? And then he remembered the two soldiers who had him held firmly. Still they waited. Gradually shadowy figures to his right, barely discernible, could be seen gathering just outside the circle of pale light. Looking directly below him, the boy could see the lieutenant's group preparing for the attack.

Lieutenant DeGray stepped cautiously into the illuminated patch of smooth rock. Still no challenge came. Would his next step bring a hail of arrows to cut him down? A second figure came from the opposite side. Hand signals were exchanged. More figures came into view and Harry saw that there was more than one handful gathered at the cave entrance. Suddenly with hardly a sound the boy saw men pour into the cave. Harry guessed that about half of the group had gone into the hermit's home. They could hear nothing. No shouts or screams. No sound of battle, nothing.

Harry was eager to get down there but his companions held him fast. Waiting for something to happen was becoming almost unbearable. The boy looked at the soldiers, they appeared to be content to wait for orders. A figure stepped out of the cave and silently signalled the rest of the men to go in. He made a sign to Harry's companions. He asked if they could go down now.

"Patience lad, we wait for orders," the nearest soldier whispered.

Harry looked about. The cloud was breaking up and moonbeams lit up the snow covered peaks in the distance. The snowline was well above them although they had seen patches of snow as they came over the crest.

Movement down in the pool of light caught the boy's attention. It was the lieutenant. At last they were beckoned down. The young officer sent a soldier to collect one of the ropes, the other rope would be left in case they needed to retreat. Harry was untied from his protectors and followed them into the cave.

The scene that met Harry was entirely unexpected. There was no bloodshed. There were no prisoners, only a frightened old man and a young boy. It was Sol.

"Is this the boy you spoke of Harry?" the lieutenant asked.

"Yes sir, can I speak to him? His name is Sol sir."

"Please do Harry. Ask him what happened to the ladder leading down into the caves you spoke of. Neither of them will speak to me. And tell them we mean them no harm.

"Hullo Sol, remember me? It's Harry."

"Are the soldiers going to kill us Harry?"

"No of course not, they are only here to get our children back. Where are the soldiers Sergeant Garth left here?"

"The sergeant sent me up with a message. He wants all the soldiers down at the Temple to guard the children. He fears that the High Priest will want to sacrifice some of them to please the god of fire."

"What happened to the ladders Sol?"

"The soldiers took them down to stop anyone following them."

"I think we know all we need to know for now Harry. Thank the boy and ask him to take care of the old hermit."

Harry passed on the lieutenant's message and joined the officer at the entrance to the cave. A bowman sent a flaming arrow into the sky.

"That is to tell Major Redman and Captain Giles that we have taken the hermit's lodgings and they can begin their attack," the lieutenant explained. "But now we have to figure out a way to get into those caves. Ah, the rope has arrived. Osbert, go and find a good sturdy beam from amongst firewood out there. It needs to be long enough to span that shaft over there."

Osbert hurried out into the night and soon came back dragging the trunk of a young birch tree. It spanned the shaft with plenty to spare.

"Can I go down first, sir?" the boy asked.

"Osbert and your two body guards go first. You follow next to show us the way. Tell your friend Sol, and the hermit that I am leaving two men to guard them from attack by those mutineers down in the village."

Harry passed on the message and then joined the soldiers at the shaft.

The shaft was much deeper than Harry realised. It had been easy when there was a ladder to use, but going hand over hand down a rope was much more difficult. Armed with a torch to every six men, they began their descent. They found the ladder laid at the side of the tunnel just around the first bend. Harry had warned the lieutenant of the steepness of the slope and the rope fixed to the wall of the cave. Even so, he could hear the soldiers grumbling as they slipped and skidded on the uneven surface. The timber they had brought with them to span the second shaft was proving to be longer than they really needed. It was difficult to get round some of the bends and it slowed them down.

They arrived at the second shaft to discover that the ladder had not been taken down. Lieutenant DeGray ordered complete silence. Using hand signals, he indicated that he and Osbert would go down first. Next the two bodyguards went down and then Harry followed. He noted that there was no torch in the sconce, only their own torches illuminated the heavy door The soldiers all had their swords drawn. The boy explained that the door opened into the cave. He also indicated the approximate position of the two baulks of timber that secured the door. There was no handle on the cave side of the door. A huge man, carrying a great axe, bigger than Harry's father's felling axe, came down the ladder. He approached the door and ran his hand down the centre plank. The axe man stepped back and swung the axe at the door, hitting the centre plank. As he pulled to free the axe, the door began to open.

"It's a trap," the lieutenant shouted and charged at the door with his shoulder. The axe man had the same idea. Together they pushed it back into its frame. The two men were joined by others, all intent on holding the door against an assault. Harry, pressed hard against the cave wall by his bodyguards, saw four archers, two kneeling and two standing, ready to loose a hail of arrows into the front ranks of their attackers.

Lieutenant DeGray stepped back. He had been expecting an attack but there was no hail of arrows. Nothing. He had the timber they had brought to span the shaft brought down and jammed it against the door. This released the men from their arduous and risky task.

With a mixture of signs and whispers, the lieutenant sent half his men back up the ladder. Of the others, he took three men and the axe man to be with him. The remainder, together with Harry and his bodyguards, were sent to where the cave turned to the left. One man would remain in view to receive orders.

The lieutenant and his four soldiers approached the target cautiously. The axe man removed the timber and placed it on the floor about a pace from the door. Still nothing happened. The men were ordered to stand behind the door and to the right.

The door and its frame were narrower than the tunnel opening at this point. It had been built in using large blocks of stone. The young officer studied the hinges, he saw that the door could not be lifted off its hinges because it was housed into a frame. The only way was to open it and hope that there was no one waiting for them.

Lieutenant DeGray signalled to the axe man to pull on the axe still embedded in the plank and open the door slowly. When the gap was about a hands span the young officer threw a burning torch into the passage beyond. The door was slammed shut. They waited, and then the lieutenant remembered that he had heard something in the brief period that the door was open. He signalled for the door to be opened even further this time and dared to take a quick glance into the passage as he listened. He saw only an empty corridor but he heard faint shouting. Or could it be crying? Was that a scream?

The young Lieutenant Roland DeGray pushed the door almost fully open. His four companions joined him as he stood, daring the enemy to attack. Yes, there was screaming. There was no time to lose

"Get the others," he snarled. "Everybody," he added.

In moments there were eighteen soldiers packed into the tunnel behind the lieutenant. He turned and told the bodyguards to look after Harry.

"We move fast and silent," the lieutenant said quietly. "Come on."

Chapter Forty One

The lieutenant hurried past the two baulks of timber leaning against the passage wall and wondered why they had not been used to secure the door. This could still be a trap. They continued down the short flight of steps and along the passageway to the second door. It was closed. The cacophony was louder now and very disturbing. Harry was brought forward and asked about the lock and whether there were any bars or other security device on the door. Harry recalled that there was only one bar across the middle of the door and that there was a curtain about three paces in front of it. He explained that the door opened into the High Priest's private chapel.

The lieutenant tried the iron ring that operated the latch on the other side of the door. The latch lifted but the door must be secured by a timber bar. It didn't move at all. Battering it to pieces would take time and they would lose the advantage of surprise, but they would have to sacrifice surprise for speed. There was nothing for it but to smash down the door.

The axe man was brought forward again. Once more he selected the centre plank and drove the axe in, but this was a much thinner plank. It split and the axe almost went right through. He retrieved the heavy weapon and stepped back. The curtain had been drawn back. The room beyond was well lit and appeared to be empty.

"Strike it again and then drop to the ground. They may have an archer waiting for a target," the lieutenant ordered.

The axe struck the board next to the split one, but this time the blow was aimed across the grain. The hole it made was almost large enough for a man to get through. The axe man had dropped to the floor, but he was first to rise and peer into the room.

"Nobody in there sir. The room be empty sir, shall I hit 'e again sir?"

"If you are sure there is no one in there."

The axe man made short work of the door and the lieutenant stepped into an empty room. He saw the dais and the ornately carved chair to his right. The ram's head that Harry had mentioned was not in place and the highly polished table, which was really an altar, was leaning against the door to his left and that was where the noise was coming from. It was obvious that someone was trying to break down the door. The shouts and screams coming from beyond the door were becoming intolerable, especially to Harry.

Suddenly the uproar coming from beyond the door began to subside. The battering ram ceased its pounding and soon there was only a murmur reaching into the High Priest's private chapel. The lieutenant hurried across to the door and listened at a split in one of the boards. Someone was speaking to a large gathering in the main temple.

Lieutenant DeGray pressed his ear tight against the boards and then he stepped back and signalled for the axe man to join him. The axe was aimed at one of the damaged boards. Again it made a good sized hole that allowed the lieutenant to look through at the startled faces on the other side. Suddenly the uproar started again and then a mighty roar told the crowd to be quiet. It took a second roar to restore a reasonable noise level.

"I know that voice," the lieutenant said.

"It's Sergeant Hathaway sir," Harry shouted as he struggled unsuccessfully with his bodyguards.

"The first four men come and remove this altar, if that is what it's supposed to be. Come on, put your back into it."

The lieutenant saw that a desk was also pushed tight against the bottom of the door. He moved forward and called out, "I am Lieutenant Roland DeGray. Who is out there?"

"Sergeant Hathaway here sir. Hold fast lieutenant. Do not open that door until I can get some men over there. Is the High Priest with you sir?"

"No sergeant, he must have gone into the caves."

"You all heard that," the lieutenant heard Major Redman tell the crowd. "Your High Priest has gone to meet the beast he has been frightening you with for these many years. Now, all of you move to the centre of the room and sit down with your hands on your head. Anyone who shows any sign of resistance will feel either blade or arrow."

There was a lot of shuffling and grumbling as the orders were obeyed. Soon soldiers were able to walk around the perimeter. Sergeant Hathaway was first to get to the door to the High Priest's private chapel.

"Good evening. Lieutenant DeGray. Sir, could you open up sir and bring your lads around to the left? We think that the children are being held in the rooms at the back sir." He went on, "Don't happen to have a certain young Coracle Boy with you, do you sir?"

The door was quickly cleared and Harry was reunited with his old friend, Sergeant Hathaway. Brian and scrap were there too.

The lieutenant led the way, followed by Sergeant Hathaway, Harry and his bodyguards and then Brian and the remainder of the troops. They were heading for the door to the room where Harry had last seen his sisters.

Coming round the temple from the opposite direction, the boy saw Major Redman. He was followed by what seemed like a never-ending stream of soldiers. Soon there were more soldiers than prisoners. At the door they waited a few moments for the Major to arrive. He strode up to the door and struck it with the pommel of his sword.

"You in there, I am Major Redman. I am here to take our children away from this dreadful place. Are they in there with you?"

"There are children and women in here sir, but how do I know that they are the children you seek sir?"

"That is Sergeant Garth sir," the Coracle Boy said anxiously. "Please sir, ask him if Meg is there and is she alright?"

"Who are you sir?" the Major asked.

"I am Sergeant Garth of the Mine Guard sir."

"Do you have a young lady by the name of Meg, sergeant?"

"Meg is here sir. She has a brother, Harry, they call him the Coracle Boy."

Harry could contain himself no longer and called out to Sergeant Garth. "Sergeant, it's me, Harry. Are Meg and Ruth alright? Can we come in?"

"Ask the Major what will happen to me and my men. We have defended these children against the priests and the renegades."

"Sergeant, this is Major Redman. The worst you can expect from us is that you become our prisoners of war. But from what Harry tells me you have been fighting our battles for us. Put down your weapons and let us in. I and one of my lieutenants and Harry will come in so that we can parley. You are a party of eleven. We are but three."

"I hear you Major Redman sir. I fear that some of the children could be hurt if we put up a fight. We will remove the barricade and trust to your goodwill."

The sound of furniture being dragged across the stone floor and the chatter of excited children came to the waiting group. At last the door was pulled open by Sergeant Garth and one of his men. The Major stepped into the room. He noted the pile of swords on the floor. Major Redman looked across at a group of children. The chattering had ceased, uncertainty etched into their faces. They were all kneeling behind upturned tables. Except Meg, who was standing beside a tall, white-haired woman who stared defiantly at the Major. Meg was the only one smiling.

Meg made to step over the barricade.

"Stay where you are young woman," the Major said loudly. "We have to observe the niceties of war. Sergeant Garth, is that what they call you?"

"Yes sir and these are my men sir, and good men they are sir."

"Do you and your men agree to unconditional surrender?"

"We do sir, but I can't speak for Lieutenant Kester at the small mine sir."

"I shall know shortly all about Lieutenant Kester, I'm sure he will surrender. Sergeant Hathaway, will you take the prisoners and find a secure building? See that they come to no harm."

The prisoners filed out, escorted by Sergeant Hathaway's troops. Major Redman turned his attention to the fidgeting children. He saw that Meg was holding a little blonde girl in her arms.

"Harry, help your sister before she falls over that barricade," he said, smiling.

Harry ran across the room and embraced his sisters. Brian came in next, closely followed by Scrap. He scooped up his son and hugged him. He then knelt down as the sons of Mal, Bram and Bernard asked tearfully after their fathers.

"They will be here shortly, except for Bernard. Sorry Joe, your father got hurt at the village in the marshes, but I will look after you son. They are with Captain Giles' group." He then saw Jennie crying openly as she stared at the door. "Sorry Jennie, your father could not come either. His leg is not mended enough yet. He asked me to look after you. Perhaps the four of us can travel together?"

Jennie turned away and hid her face with her right arm and wept bitterly. Meg saw this and handed Ruth to Harry and put her arms around the younger girl's shoulder and wept with her.

"I want to stay with you and Harry, Meg," Jennie sobbed.

"Then that is what you will do Jennie. I will explain to Brian, he will agree."

There were a lot more children than Harry had seen earlier. All the recent arrivals were there. Finding their parents was not going to be easy.

Suddenly Harry felt exhausted and had to sit down on a bench at one of the righted tables. Ruth clung to her big brother as if she would never let go of him. They were joined by Meg and Jennie. Soon all four of them were asleep in one uncomfortable huddle.

Chapter Forty Two

Harry woke with a start. He saw Ruth. She was laughing as she shook his shoulder. "Wake up lazybones. Meg is making breakfast and the head soldier wants to see you."

"That's right Harry, Major Redman will be back shortly, come along." Sister Rona took Ruth's hand and led her into the storeroom, telling her what they would need to collect to feed so many people. It all sounded so ordinary and yet it was far from normal.

The Coracle Boy found that he had slept on the floor on a thick bed of straw. The last he remembered was sleeping at the table across on the other side of the room. He stood up and stretched. He felt refreshed, but he needed a pee and had to visit the latrine. He could hear voices coming from the Temple. He found Mal and Bram loading weapons onto a handcart. Their boys were helping them. Mal and Bram explained how they had started back with Luke to get reinforcements when they met Major Redman and had joined up with the soldiers.

"We met the Major on the second day of our boat trip Harry, but it took four days march through forest to get back to Dan and Brian." Mal laughed.

The Temple was empty apart from the salvage operation. Harry wondered where all the prisoners were. Outside it was a glorious morning, cold, but the sun was shining. There were soldiers everywhere, a group of officers with their blue sashes prominent, sergeants' narrower, red sashes scattered amongst the soldiers. Orders were being shouted, men were forming up in ranks and others were being marched off to perform their various military duties. It all looked so busy to the boy.

Back in the Temple the men from Abe Tull's village had almost finished their harvesting of abandoned swords, shields, spears, axes and knives. The handcart was full, it made a grim picture.

Meg was sitting at the table waiting for her brother. She ran to Harry and threw her arms around him and kissed his cheek. She released him and led him to the table and sat opposite him.

"You have done it Harry. You have…."

"No Meg, 'WE' have done it. Together we did what we set out to do."

"I think that mother and father were helping us too Harry."

"I am sure they were Meg, especially when the earthquake struck."

Sister Rona entered the room carrying two baskets of food. Ruth was trying to help but not really succeeding. Meg got up and took one of the baskets from the white-haired woman. She told Harry to hurry up and finish his breakfast; Major Redman would be here soon.

Harry began to wonder where everyone had gone. Where were Sergeant Hathaway and Brian? He had heard that Sergeant Defoe was here too? He had seen Peter briefly and also Osbert and Sergeant Rudd. Harry decided that he would go and talk to the men from Abe Tull's village, they might have news of Dan and Susan. Were they still at Friar Godwin's cave?

The Temple was empty and the door was closed and the two windows were shuttered. The only light came from two torches, one on either side of the room. Their flickering light only increased the eeriness of this sinister hall. Harry felt the chill of the place and was about to make for the door that opened to sunshine and a blue sky when he heard the scraping of the damaged door to the High Priest's chapel. Sergeant Hathaway stood in the well lit doorway.

"Harry lad, I was about to wake you. Have you eaten yet?"

"Good morning sergeant. Yes, I have had my breakfast, thank you."

"Then you'd best come with me. The Major sent me to find you."

Harry hurried across the room to the big sergeant and followed him through the shattered doors and along the passageway, up the steps and into the cave system. He saw Major Redman and Captain Giles standing where the cave began to turn to the left.

"Hullo Harry, you've met Captain Giles. We need to know how you found a way though the caves, this one only leads to a dead end." The Major sounded rather impatient.

"This way sir, hold your torch up higher sir." Harry saw the dark shadow of the fissure and pointed it out to the Major.

"But that is barely wide enough for a full grown man to get through, let alone several men carrying a large chest." The Major was obviously angry and started back to the temple. At the High Priest's chapel, he sat on the highly polished table and told Sergeant Hathaway to fetch Lieutenant DeGray and his squad of men. He would have a thorough search made of the whole cave system.

Harry was almost at bursting point with questions he wanted answers to. But he dared not interrupt the Major, he must wait until he was in a more amiable mood. It was almost as if the Major had read Harry's thoughts.

"I had better put you in the picture Harry. It seems that the High Priest and Captain Ragar with about five others have disappeared with a chest of gold."

"Can you have some soldiers at the other end to meet them sir?"

"They are on their way Harry. But who is to say there aren't several ways out of the caves? They could come out above or below us."

"Are you sure they went into the caves sir? Did someone see them go in sir?"

"Of course no one saw them go into the caves. The door to the Temple was closed and the heavy table was leaned against it. The man they call Red helped them prepare for their escape. That is why you found the door to the caves open and the ladder to the hermit's cave in place. He said there were seven of them and he was supposed to go with them, but Trisk sent him to collect extra torches and when he got back they wouldn't let him in."

"But sir, why is Trisk with the High Priest?"

"Not now son, Roland is here with his men." The Major went to meet the young lieutenant at the door into the Temple. He saw that his troops were carrying several bundles of torches. Immediately the three officers went into a huddle, planning the strategy for the hunt, the boy guessed.

There was something not quite right here, but Harry could not see what it was that was bothering him. He walked across to the door into the passage that led to the caves. He walked a short distance, then turned and walked back to the door. 'What is it that I can't see?' he asked himself.

"Harry, can you tell us about the main danger points that you encountered on your journey through the caves?" Major Redman called Harry across.

At the same moment the Coracle Boy realised what it was that was not quite right here.

"Sir, Major Redman sir," Harry said excitedly. "They can't have gone into the caves sir."

"Of course they have gone into the caves. Where else could they go?"

"Sir, we had to break the door down to get into the chapel because it was barred on this side sir. And there was nobody in the room when we got in. If they have gone into the caves sir, who bolted the door behind them sir?"

"Captain Giles, get Lieutenant DeGray, tell him to stand his men down."

With the three officers back in the chapel, Harry was asked to repeat his observations and the question.

"Well gentlemen, who did bolt the door?" the Major asked.

"Harry's right sir, there was no one in the chapel when we broke in and no way out that I could see."

"Is the High Priest some sort of wizard?" Captain Giles asked. "If he is, why did he take so many with him? Why didn't he just whisk himself and the gold over the mountains and far away? No, gentlemen. There must be a secret passage out of here. Start by tapping the walls for a hollow sound. You too Harry."

"Sir, I have been looking at the High Priest's chair sir. It's fixed to this slab of stone a hand's span above the floor. Perhaps it covers another cave sir. It might slide across the floor or tilt to the side sir."

"Roland, bring your two strongest men and see what they can do."

The axe man and an archer, both huge men, came into the chapel and examined the carved chair and the slab to which it was fixed. They pulled and pushed the throne but nothing moved. They got down on their knees and tried their combined strength against the plinth but to no avail.

"Break the chair off its fixings, we need to see how it is held there," Major Redman ordered.

The two strong men soon wrenched the throne from its anchorage. Harry was sorry to see such a beautiful piece of carving so roughly treated. They discovered that bolts through the stone slab had secured the throne to the dais.

"Break that stone slab out," the Major ordered.

A heavy hammer and a crowbar were brought. The axe man swung the hammer in a wide arc and brought it down near the centre of the stone. His second blow in the same place cracked the stone. The archer drove the crowbar into the crack and levered at the same time as the third blow struck. Now the split in the stone was widening. Soon it was open enough to allow the men to get their hands down far enough to discover that there was a void beneath, but something was still holding the stone. There was nothing for it but to smash all of the stone to small pieces.

Chapter Forty Three

As soon as there was a hole big enough, a lighted torch was dropped into the void to reveal stone steps leading down into yet another cave. "This was their escape route," the Major commented. "But how did they shift this large slab of stone and not leave any scratch marks on the floor?"

The question was answered when the hole was large enough to allow the slim Lieutenant DeGray to squeeze through and down onto the stone steps below. He discovered that the slab was hinged on one side of the throne and had two bolts on the opposite side. Two heavy stones hung on short chains to counter balance the weight of the slab at the hinge side. When the bolts were not in place, the chair would act as a lever to open the access to the stairs. But where would the stairs lead to?

"It depends on how far away the High Priest's party is, whether they have heard the discovery of their escape route or not," the Major said as the debris was cleared away.

Harry saw a rectangular hole in the floor and some very steep steps with extremely narrow treads cut into the rock leading down into the darkness. A man would have to go down sideways and hold onto the steps to steady him. There was no handrail.

"Right gentlemen," the Major addressed the captain and lieutenant, "We need to formulate a plan. I propose to lead a party of handpicked men and see where this passage leads."

"Sir, with respect sir," Captain Giles spoke firmly. "Sir you should not put yourself in such danger. As commander of the whole operation, you cannot justify taking such a risk."

"Are you telling me how to do my duty captain?" Major Redman said sharply.

"No sir, I am asking you to reconsider, we need you to lead us. There are almost one hundred men under your command sir. Leave this small skirmish to us junior officers. I beg you to revise your plan sir."

Before the Major could reply, there was a bellow from the big Sergeant Hathaway as he made a way for a lieutenant through the curious soldiers crowding the doorway. The young officer saluted the Major and reported that both mines had been made secure. He also reported that many children were coming out of the forest. Most of them had escaped from the big mine when the earthquake struck. The problem was that there was not enough food to feed them all.

"They really are in a bad way sir." the lieutenant concluded.

Major Redman turned to Captain Giles and said in his usual authoritative way, "Take charge here Captain Giles and round up those scoundrels, if you will."

The Major addressed the messenger. "Lead on lieutenant, let me see these young scallywags. Harry, come along, I might need your help."

The Coracle Boy was desperately disappointed. He would much rather have gone into the caves with Lieutenant DeGray. Reluctantly he followed the Major into the Temple and on out into the sunshine.

It was several moments before Harry realised what he was seeing. Two horse drawn carts were hauled up in front of the Temple. Each cart seemed to be overflowing with its load of children. They were dirty, their clothes were ragged and mud stained. They were obviously malnourished and very frail. Most of them appeared to be between ten and twelve years old, but a few were in their early teens.

The Major ordered a sergeant to get his men to help the children down from the carts and get them into the Temple. "Make sure there is straw for them to sit on," the Major ordered. "Harry, tell your sister to be prepared to deal with casualties. Several children appear to be injured and warn Sister Rona that they are hungry."

Harry hurried away and found Meg, Ruth and Jennie in the room he had slept in earlier. They were sitting at the table with several other children who looked terrified, but their faces lit up when they saw Harry and the questions came thick and fast. They all wanted to know what was going on.

"Brian and the other village men have taken their children," Meg explained. "Jennie asked to stay with me and Brian agreed. But what will happen to all these other children?"

"I don't know," Harry replied. "There are a lot more youngsters coming into the Temple. A lot of them have injuries, Meg. Major Redman wants you to dress their wounds. Where is Sister Rona? The Major wants her to prepare some food for them."

"She said she was going to the bakehouse to make bread. She didn't say where it is."

"Can you keep Ruth and Jennie with you as your assistants?"

"Yes of course. They will be by my side until we get back to Abe Tull's village."

Harry found the bakehouse. Sister Rona was supervising two other women who were bread making. The boy passed on the Major's request.

"Can you help me Harry? Can you fetch a bag of oats from the High Priest's pantry? I will make porridge for them, they do look a sorry lot. No child should have to suffer like that."

Harry's task was to carry the heavy bag of oatmeal from the store to the kitchen and collect water and firewood. Two of the boys who had worked in the sawmill helped him. They were there because their stepfather had sold them to the slavers when their mother died. They had nowhere to go.

Harry was feeling restless, he wanted to get back to Abe Tull's village. He and Meg had achieved what they had set out to do and yet there was so much to do here. He couldn't just walk away from the chaos that ruled. No, he would send Meg, Ruth and Jennie back to the village with the first group to leave. He would ask Major Redman when that was likely to be.

It was getting dark when Harry saw the Major enter the Temple with Harry's old friend Sergeant Defoe. Following them he saw Brother Michael and Ned. The Temple had become the headquarters of the operation. All of the children had been moved into the schoolroom. As Harry entered the Temple, he saw that a table had been set up and was strewn with rolls of parchment.

Sergeant Defoe strode across to the Coracle Boy, his hand outstretched in greeting. Harry shook the hard, calloused hand of this tough, amiable soldier. "Harry. Good to see you again son. Major Redman has been singing your praises. In fact everyone I speak to, even that fancy lieutenant at the small mine, mentioned you and your brother. Was that Meg he saw with you?"

"Yes sir. Meg, my sister, came with me dressed as a boy. She has been wonderful, as good as any boy. She's training to be a medicine woman. She delivered a baby at the smoke house, downriver. Oh, there is so much to tell you sergeant and so much I need to know from you."

"Ah, now that's what Major Redman said and that's why I'm here. The Major will be busy for some time yet and he sent me to answer your questions. So fire away young Harry."

"First of all, has Lieutenant DeGray caught the High Priest?"

"That part of the operation is not going too well. The lieutenant found the tunnel collapsed not very far in. They started to move some of the rocks and found two dead priests buried under the fall. They have not yet reported that they are through the blockage." The sergeant saw the look on the boy's face and told him not to worry, the High Priest would be caught.

"Who sent for the soldiers?" Harry asked.

"Why, Abe Tull, of course. He sent a messenger the day the children were taken. He arrived at Westown Castle just before the blizzard struck. We were snowbound for a week and then he sent a second messenger to say that you and your sister had gone up the great river to search for little Ruth. We all thought that the messenger had made a mistake, but when we got to his cave, the hermit said he guessed it was a boy and a girl. He hadn't said anything, he was sure that you must have good reason for the disguise."

The sergeant paused for a moment and then continued, "I have got ahead of myself, let me go back to the arrival of the second messenger. I told Martha and Mother Bowdler about you and Meg that evening. They were very upset, what with the weather and you two youngsters on the great river. Martha said I should go after you and find the little girl. Well, what could I do? I am a soldier and can only leave my post on the orders of an officer. I went to see Major Redman and he had already sent word to Colonel Richmond, who was at a meeting with Lord John of the High Plains."

At that moment there was another disturbance at the door into the Temple. Sister Rona was demanding entrance. The Major and Brother Michael had been joined by three other officers. They all turned to see what all the fuss was about. It transpired that Sister Rona needed to get to her storeroom. The only access was through the Temple because it was the High Priest's private pantry. It was the only place where there was food in the whole village.

The Major summoned Sergeant Defoe who detailed two men to assist Sister Rona for as long as she needed them. Harry saw that Meg, Ruth and Jennie were with Sister Rona. He asked the lady if his sisters and Jennie could stay for a while.

"Bless you son, with two fine soldiers to help me, of course they can stay."

They followed Sister Rona into the dining room and on into the storeroom.

"My word, the High Priest certainly lived well," Sergeant Defoe commented.

With the soldiers carrying all that Sister Rona required, she sent them up to the kitchen at the schoolhouse. She filled a tankard from a barrel of beer and gave it to a grateful Sergeant Defoe. She escorted them all back into the dining room and then locked the door to the storeroom.

"I'll come back for the girls at bedtime Harry." Sister Rona said as she closed the door that led into the Temple.

"Sergeant Defoe, this is my sister, Meg….

"I know Meg and Ruth and I remember Jed telling me about his daughter Jennie. I'm right pleased to meet you all at last. I have been hearing all about your adventures together Meg. I was about to tell Harry about our journey here to rescue you all, only to find that you two have done all the hard work for us."

They all sat down at one of the long tables, Sergeant Defoe and Harry on one side, and the three girls opposite them. The sergeant took a draught of beer and nodded approvingly.

"Now where was I? Ah, yes. Well, as I said to Harry, Abe Tull sent two messengers, but the blizzard was so bad it was not possible to travel up the west bank and marching almost one hundred soldiers through the forest of the east bank was almost as difficult. I reckon we arrived at your starting point, opposite the abbey, a week behind you. Brother Michael joined us there and that young novice with him. We were snowed in for two days, but we pressed on and met Luke the evening of the earth tremors. He told us of your scouting trips. The Major got very anxious at that point and had us on the march at first light. We arrived at the Friar's cave, it had taken us thirteen days hard marching to do what you and Meg had done in five using the coracle, and some of the lads were close to exhaustion. We rested a couple of days. Your friend Peter arrived with his wife, Lisa and their baby."

The sergeant drank a little from the tankard and continued. "Well, Peter turned out to be a real treasure and his wife was good company for Susan, Dan's wife. With Peter's knowledge of the area, he knew a way to get into the miners' village from above and we were able to form a plan. Young Lieutenant DeGray and a dozen men went off with Peter to test the plan. Lisa and the baby stayed with Dan and Susan. The lieutenant found a large rowing boat at the pagans' village and sent it back down to us at the friar's cave, it proved to be a great help. We moved everything up to the deserted pagan village." Sergeant Defoe paused and tasted the ale.

"That's where we found proof that we were on the right track. I found a little wooden cross that belongs to Ruth," Meg explained.

The sergeant examined the small crucifix and then handed it back to Ruth. "The next day a messenger arrived from the lieutenant." The sergeant continued, "We were to move upriver to where Peter left you on the night you set off to find Meg. The Major sent a lieutenant and six men to arrange the signal fires above the old abandoned mine south of the river. The rest of us set off to meet Lieutenant DeGray."

The sergeant took another drink of beer. "Peter was waiting for us when we got to his landing place and it was getting light. We spent the day hiding in the reed beds. As soon as it was dark, we set off and arrived at the waterfall. We moved east along the foot of the escarpment to where the lieutenant was waiting. He had fixed several ropes to hang down the cliff face for us to climb up. At the top of the escarpment we saw the lake. The lieutenant and two of his men went off at a run around the lake to be at the cave, where he met you, before if got light. The rest of us had to spend the day hiding in the forest to the east of the lake until darkness fell. And then we skirted the lake and split up. The two main parties headed for Wolf Rock. I took a few men to check out the new mine and was joined by Sergeant Rudd later. That young lieutenant couldn't surrender fast enough."

"What will happen to all the prisoners?" Harry asked.

"The miners and the children are free to go east whenever they like. The children who have no home to go to are welcome to return to Westown with us. The soldiers? They will be left here to do as they please."

"Did you find some wounded soldiers with four horses sir?" Meg enquired anxiously. "They were in the woods to the north of the village."

"Indeed we did. Their leader spoke highly of you and Harry, he reckons you saved his life, something about being attacked by a bear."

"That's right."

Harry went on to tell of their hunting adventure and then followed their experience of the earthquake and the meeting with Peter and Lisa. The stories flowed excitedly like a mountain stream, until Sister Rona called to collect the girls. Sergeant Defoe escorted the ladies back to their quarters and returned to his duties. Harry bedded down in the dining room.

The next morning Harry was up early to discover that the High Priest had not been captured. Work on unblocking the tunnel was proving to be very difficult and dangerous. Some speculated that there was a secret way out of that tunnel and the High Priest, his accomplices and the gold were long gone.

Brother Michael came looking for Harry soon after breakfast to ask him what his plans were. The Coracle Boy explained that he wanted to return to Abe Tull's Village and see Meg, Ruth and Jennie settled. He would then have to start to earn a living.

"You should think about learning to read and write Harry."

"Sister Mary will teach me in the evenings sir."

"Would you consider coming into the church my son? We would support your family and give you an excellent education. You would be expected to work in the orchard and help me with the ferry, but you would be well fed and clothed and always have a warm bed."

"Thank you sir, but I want to get back to the river sir. I have been thinking of setting up a shed by the river to make coracles to sell them."

"That sounds very enterprising Harry, but who would buy your coracles?"

"I would take them down to Westown and sell them on the wharfage sir."

"Do you think you would earn enough to keep a family of four?"

"I would do my best sir."

"Of that I have no doubt Harry, but think about it my son. At the monastery you would spend half of the day working, the other half learning."

Harry looked down at the floor. This was so difficult. He liked Brother Michael and hated to let him down, but he had never liked the large, dark building that seemed to glower at him menacingly.

"Sir, can I think about it? I need to talk to Meg."

"Of course you can. Ah, I think Sergeant Defoe is looking for you. We will talk again Harry. Sergeant Defoe, you look as if you need to speak to Harry."

"That I do sir. Major Redman would like a word with Harry sir."

The Coracle Boy followed the sergeant out into the morning sun. There was a strong breeze blowing down the valley, but not a cloud in the sky. Children were playing noisily in front of the schoolhouse. Washing was flapping on makeshift lines. Men were hauling bundles of firewood up to the woodshed. Everyone appeared to be very busy.

The sergeant led the boy down the zigzagging steps to the wharfage. The Major was talking to the ferry master. They finished their conversation and Major Redman turned and walked to meet the new arrivals.

"Good morning Harry, did you sleep well?"

"Yes thank you sir,"

"I have had to stop work on the escape tunnel, it has become much too dangerous. They have found a small incoming cave cascading water into the escape tunnel."

"Perhaps the men who dug the tunnel came upon this watercourse and enlarged it to suit their purpose sir."

"Lieutenant DeGray had the same idea Harry."

"We could trace it sir, by adding lime to the underground stream and see where the colouring comes out," Harry suggested.

"There is a tub of lime in a shed up by the sawmill sir." Sergeant Defoe said excitedly.

"Mix up a bucket of lime wash sergeant and pour it in on my signal. Harry, you stop here with me. We need to talk."

Major Redman sat on the framework that supported a single pole derrick used to offload heavy objects from the ferry. The landing stage had been cleared of everything. There were no stacks of barrels and boxes, even the fishing nets hung to dry on the cliff face had been removed. There were two lean-to sheds at the other end of the quay. Even they had been emptied and searched for the outlet to the escape tunnel.

"Sit down Harry," the officer said cheerfully, "What are your plans for the future?"

"Brother Michael asked me the same question earlier sir. He asked if I would like to go to work for the church in the orchard and on the ferry sir. He said that they would look after my family and give me a good education sir."

"Brother Michael is a good man and I believe you would get the very best education at the monastery. However, the Church is a vocation. A vocation, Harry, is an occupation that demands dedication. You have to really want to be a priest. It can be a very hard life if you are not devoted to the Church."

A shout from the top of the escarpment told Major Redman and Harry that the bucket of lime wash was ready. The Major gave the signal. The ferryman and three helpers lined the wharfage looking for the telltale sign. The ferry was moored upstream of the derrick. Harry and the Major strained to see the sudden discolouration of the water. There was a shout from the ferryman. The Major and Harry ran to the man's side. There, coming up from beneath the boat, faint cloudlike swirls that quickly dispersed in the fast flowing current.

They were hailed again from the top of the steps, another bucket of the white colourant was ready. The Major sent a man up to tell them to await his signal, he needed to have the ferry moved. This done, the second bucket was added to the stream and now they could see the white liquid clearly. About the height of a man below the surface of the crystal clear water they saw an opening in the rock that was about a hands span across. They probed deep below the surface of the water with a boathook, but no larger opening was found.

Harry became aware of the rising wind and dark clouds overhead. Spots of rain soon became a downpour just as they entered the Temple. The Major led the way into the High Priest's private chapel where the ornately carved chair still lay on its side. The head and shoulders of Lieutenant DeGray emerged from the shaft that was discovered beneath the chair. He looked grubby and very tired. The Major told him of the results of the lime wash test.

"There must be a tunnel going upstream or downstream sir," the young officer said despondently. "It can't be a submerged exit like the one Harry escaped through. I can't see the High Priest getting his feet wet, let alone his fancy vestments."

Chapter Forty Four

By mid afternoon the rain had turned to sleet and a full blown storm raged up the valley and it was almost dark. But everyone had a shelter and food and the mood of both victor and vanquished was optimistic. Most of the miners were glad to be getting out of that awful place.

The lieutenant and his men were ordered to get some rest. The Major, Harry and Sergeant Defoe went to the dining room and sat at a table. The sergeant spoke first and asked the Major what he knew of this place. He had heard of this region called the Golden Mountains. The officer laughed, but it was a cynical, humourless laugh.

"My grandfather was the last man to work these mines, sergeant. His father, my great-grandfather, discovered the gold and became a rich man, but the gold ran out and my grandfather nearly lost everything. Several people have tried since but they all failed. There is nothing here. This is a dreadful place. These miners were sold mining rights by the pagan Elders and the same men sold them children to burrow after specks of the metal. The Elders even persuaded their King to finance the venture, but when the gold didn't arrive, he sent Captain Ragar to investigate. His orders were to mobilise the guards and arrest the priests and their henchmen. Captain Ragar and his man, Gant, arrived the day before you Harry."

"How do you know all this sir?" the sergeant asked.

"The man called Gant, I spoke with him this morning. He was sent as a servant to accompany Captain Kurt Ragar. They discovered that there was not the great fortune the Elders had promised. Gant is loyal to his King. He heard the Captain and the High Priest negotiating with Nargor, the traitor priest, and Trisk, to steal what little gold there was. Split four ways it would give each man enough to live comfortably for many years and then Gant made the mistake of enlisting the help of the man they call Red, who betrayed him. Trisk and his two henchmen attacked Gant and left him for dead. Sister Rona found him and stopped the bleeding, but the High Priest made the mistake of not taking Red with them and he can't do enough to help us capture the High Priest and Trisk."

"Will the man Gant be alright sir?" Harry enquired.

"Thanks to Sister Rona he will make a full recovery, but he will not be able to lie down comfortably for some time to come. Trisk used a vicious whip on the man, it was a savage attack." The Major stood up and said he must leave.

"Sergeant Defoe, I think you and I should do a tour of inspection."

"I agree sir. Keep the sentries on their toes sir." Sergeant Defoe laughed.

Harry realised that he had not seen Meg or Ruth all day and was about to go in search of them when Ned walked into the dining room, that huge beaming smile firmly in place.

"I thought your companions would never leave, Harry," Ned said laughing.

"Hullo Ned, it's good to see you. I heard you were out with Peter looking for lost children."

"We found six and one of them was Peter's brother, Cal. I have never seen two happier people."

"I can believe it Ned, they told Peter that his brother was killed in the earthquake. I spoke to Brother Michael this morning," Harry said, hoping that the remark would start a discussion on Brother Michael's proposal.

"And he wants you to go into the church."

"Yes, how did you know?"

"I know Brother Michael. He is a good man Harry. A fine priest, a true man of God. I know of no one who can equal him. I know that I can never reach his level of piety and dedication to the Church. I also know that he has high regard for you Harry. If you want, really want, to go into the Church Harry, then you could have no better mentor."

"What is a mentor Ned?" Harry asked.

"An experienced advisor. Someone whose counsel you can always rely on. In short Harry, a true friend."

Before Harry could continue the discussion, the door opened and Meg came into the room. She was wet and dishevelled. She was wearing a fine woollen cloak that the boy had not seen before. Meg removed the rain-soaked garment and draped it across the back of a chair.

"Hullo Meg. I was about to come and find you but Ned arrived. Oh, you've not met Ned. He is...."

"I met your sister earlier;" Ned interrupted. "I saw the likeness immediately and introduced myself. Your sister is doing excellent work up at the schoolhouse."

"I'm sure I'm doing what any girl would do in these circumstances."

"Well sit down Meg, tell us what's happening." Harry dragged a bench across so that Meg could sit facing the two boys across the table.

"I can't stay long," Meg replied. "I came to ask you to come and say goodnight to Ruth. She's not seen you all day. She gets upset so easily."

"Why don't we escort Meg back to the schoolhouse now? The men will be coming in for a meal soon," Ned suggested. At that moment, as if to reinforce his remark, the army cook and his two assistants arrived.

Harry helped Meg to pull on the wet cloak. She drew the hood up over her raven black hair. In the Temple soldiers were sitting on the reed covered floor, they looked tired and bedraggled.

The door leading out of the Temple was opened by a sentry. Outside the storm had not abated. The trio raced up to the schoolhouse and into the schoolroom, the door was slammed shut and bolted. Ruth saw her brother and immediately ran to him and jumped into his arms regardless of the wetness of his clothes. The other children made room for them near the open fire. All too soon it was time for the smaller children to go to bed. Harry and Ned said goodnight and went out into the storm. They stood in the porch for a while, hoping for a lull in the force of the blizzard. The sleet had given way to rain and so improved the visibility.

"What's that?" Harry whispered, "Over there by the cliff edge."

"Somebody with a covered lantern Harry. It must be the ferryman."

"What's he doing wandering about on a night like this? It must have something to do with the High Priest's escape. Will you alert Major

Redman? I'll follow the man with the lantern. Hold on, he's going down the steps, it must be the ferryman."

"I think that we should follow him and see what he's up to before we raise the alarm Harry."

"Yes. The soldiers wouldn't thank us for dragging them out on a night like this, especially if there is a good reason for the man to be about," Harry replied as they left their shelter and ran towards the cliff edge.

The start of the steps down to the river was clearly marked by a cairn as tall as a man. The boys crouched down on the lee side when they reached the pile of rocks. They leaned forward and saw the dull glow of the lantern much closer to them than they expected.

"It will take him ages to get to the bottom, this cairn keeps the wind off us but we're still getting wet," Harry grumbled.

Eventually they considered the man to be far enough away from them for it to be safe to start down the steps. Because this side of the escarpment faced south, it gave better protection from the storm than the cairn did. But the difference had little effect on the already drenched boys and progress was slow and painful. With no light to guide them they had to feel for every foothold. At the turning point of one of the zigzags, the step was much wider and Harry waited for Ned to join him. They crouched down and waited

"I think we are about halfway down, Ned," Harry said quietly. Then, suddenly, Ned gripped the Coracle Boy's shoulder and pointed down towards the river.

"Look Harry, another light. There's someone down there."

"It could be the ferryman, but he came up with us and the two men with him. Yes, Sergeant Defoe was the last man up."

Harry realised that their whispers were getting louder, he cautioned Ned. They crouched in silence and eventually saw the two lights meet at the bottom of the steps. Immediately the two men turned downstream past the two lean-to sheds and on towards the derrick. Harry and Ned continued to the bottom of the steps, where it was so dark they couldn't see the ferry or the edge of the wharf. They could hear the water lapping the sides of the boat still moored where Major Redman ordered.

"Keep tight against the shed and the cliff face Ned. The river runs fast and deep here," Harry warned. They passed the two sheds and could see both lights. They appeared to be placed on the floor and the men were busy doing something at the foot of the derrick. As they got nearer they heard shovelling and brushing noises, scraping, swearing and hammering, as the men laboured at their task.

The boys crept closer. Now more mumbled conversation could be heard. "Red, get over here and take hold of this rope. Now pull until you can get the hook through the mooring ring. That's it, keep pulling."

"The hook is through the ring," Red replied. Further instructions were issued to Red but were lost to the howling wind.

"Good man, Red, now come and help me swing this pole a bit to the right. You pull on this rope as I slacken that one. Good man, keep your rope tight."

The boys listened, mystified. "It must be Red and the ferryman," Harry whispered.

They were unable to see what was happening to the derrick, but then they heard the ferryman call, 'Stop!' There was more moving about and then the lanterns were moved. One lantern was hung on the derrick and illuminated the winding gear. The other shone on the hook and ring in the floor of the wharf. The boys crept a little closer. A figure moved to the handle on the big wheel of the winding gear and began to turn. There was a loud clattering noise and the man operating the mechanism stopped.

"Red, get over here and hold this lever. The pawl is rattling on the sprocket." They saw the second figure arrive and there was more inaudible talk and the lantern was moved.

Now the boys could see the drum around which the rope was wound. The winding operation was resumed and the slack in the rope attached to the ring was taken up. There seemed to be some sort of hold up with both men scurrying between the derrick and the ring in the pavement. Scraping noises could be heard. Both lanterns were relocated at the ring. Suddenly Harry tugged on Ned's sleeve and whispered that they should move further back. The Coracle Boy moved right back to the first lean-to shed. There was no door on the building. They moved into the shadows.

"What is it Harry?" Ned asked. "What are they doing?"

"That ring in the floor must be fixed to a slab that covers the way out of the escape tunnel."

"Are you sure Harry? What do we do now?"

"Will you go back up to the Temple and find Major Redman or Lieutenant DeGray and tell them what we have seen."

"Yes, but had I better wait until we are sure it is the way out of the escape tunnel Harry?"

"Look, they are starting to lift again." Harry let Ned's question pass. He would be better able to answer it in a few moments perhaps.

With bated breath, they watched the two men struggle with the winding gear. They could hear no conversation at such a distance and in the howling wind, but they could see, though dimly, that the slab of rock was rising. "There's your answer, Ned. Will you go and find the Major? I will need to move back beyond the boat. They will probably want to use it in their escape."

"Look Harry, they are moving the slab sideways," Ned exclaimed.

"Shhh…, not so loud, the wind will carry our voices down to them."

"Sorry Harry."

"Come on, let's find the steps and get you on your way."

"I'm soaking wet and getting cold Harry," Ned whispered as they left the shelter of the lean-to shed and ventured out into the driving wind and rain.

"You'll soon warm up running up those steps, here we are. Remember the Major or Lieutenant DeGray, if you can't find either, then Sergeant Hathaway or Sergeant Defoe. They will know what to do. Hurry Ned."

Harry watched until his friend was lost in the storm. Cautiously he crept back to the lean-to from where he watched as the two men struggled to push the slab clear of the opening. A man's head appeared and then his torso and finally he stepped onto the wharf helped by either Red or the ferryman. Next a heavy box was handed up. As more men emerged from the cave, Harry counted six on his fingers, he could hear raised voices, whether in joy or anger he could not tell. He also saw that they had another two lanterns. The heavy box was carried by two men. He left the cover of the lean-to just as the party started to move in his direction. The Coracle Boy had decided to go up the steps, from where he would have a better view. He found no shelter at all at the first bend, but at the second a protruding rock gave him better protection.

The party below arrived at the boat just as Harry had got settled. Now that there were four lanterns he could see that the boat had a crude shelter erected. The box was handed to two men who had climbed on board. The rest of the men tumbled aboard in a great hurry. No one was going to be left behind, but one man, carrying a lantern, was still on the wharf. Harry saw the figure walk up to the huge horizontal wheel and remove a large timber and drop it to the ground. He ran back to the boat and clambered aboard. The moorings were cast off but the boat remained stationary. It took four men, pulling on a rope fixed to a bollard on the wharf downstream near the derrick, to get the boat moving, but it was painfully slow. Regardless of the slow progress, Harry was beginning to worry that they would get away. He looked up into the gloom and saw nothing to raise his hopes.

With all the lanterns on the boat, Harry realised that he could move back down the steps and perhaps hear something useful. He discovered that he could hardly move. He was bitterly cold and the cold intensified as he stepped clear of the shielding rock and felt the full blast of the cruel storm. Gradually Harry got his limbs to cooperate and reached the first bend. The occupants of the boat were so preoccupied with hauling on the rope, the boy risked a dash to the bottom. No one noticed and now he was looking straight at the crew and passengers. Harry recognised the High Priest and the ferryman. Nagor, the traitor priest, was standing behind them. Captain Ragar was urging the men on the rope to put their backs into it. Trisk, his two henchmen and Red were hauling on the rope.

Suddenly Nagor shouted and pointed up to the top of the cliff. "Look, look, they're coming. Hurry, they're coming," he screamed.

Captain Ragar sprang forward to help on the rope. The ferryman lifted the pole from the bottom of the boat and tried to push the ferry further from the river bank. He shouted to Nagor to come and help him, but Nagor and the High Priest had disappeared under the makeshift awning.

Harry looked about frenziedly. From his position at the foot of the steps he couldn't see what had caused the traitor priest's outburst. He needed to stop the boat and then he remembered the ferryman removing a baulk of timber near the big, horizontal wheel. Harry broke cover and, in a running crouch, made it to the baulk of timber, but it was too heavy for the boy to lift. He looked back at the cliff and saw a procession of torches. He willed them to make all haste, but they were barely halfway down and the ferry would be too far from the wharf for them to stop it.

Major Redman was the first to arrive, closely followed by Lieutenant DeGray and Sergeant Defoe and several soldiers. For a moment they stood looking angrily and hurling blazing torches at the receding craft. And then they heard, 'Over here', and saw Harry bent over the baulk of timber.

"I think it's some sort of brake, but I don't know where it fits sir," Harry informed them as they lifted him bodily out of their way. They made several attempts to wedge the timber and stop the wheel but without success.

"Let me cut the rope sir." It was the big man who had smashed the doors at the Temple.

"No! That would be murder," the Major replied angrily.

"Look sir, the ferryboat is on fire sir," a voice shouted. One of the torches must have found a dry place to land and ignited the oiled sailcloth of the awning.

"Cut the rope," The Major ordered. "They will stand a better chance of survival if they get through the gorge."

The huge axe severed the rope at one stroke. The tension was such that the thick hawser snaked rapidly away through the air before it fell into the water. The group stood and watched as the boat careered towards the narrow gorge.

The fire illuminated the fate of the boat as it struck the north side of the gorge, turning broadside on to the current before it finally capsized. The flames were extinguished and all was in darkness.

The Pagan Gold, what little there was, had gone forever. There was shocked silence.

Chapter Forty Five

Sergeant Hathaway seemed to appear from nowhere as he charged through the officers and men to kneel by the recumbent Coracle Boy. "Harry!" the big man roared. "What's up with the lad? The lad's sick," were the big man's only words as he lifted Harry and ran to the steps followed by Sergeant Defoe and the lieutenant.

At the top of the steps the exhausted sergeant handed Harry to Sergeant Defoe. The lieutenant ran ahead to the schoolhouse where he knew Meg and Sister Rona would be. Harry was taken to Sister Rona's private room beyond the kitchen. His wet clothes were removed and he was wrapped in a woollen blanket.

"Your brother is a very sick boy, Meg. He'll not be able to travel tomorrow or for many days after that I fear," Sister Rona said gravely.

Meg and Sister Rona took it in turns to sit with Harry through the night. The Coracle Boy's temperature rose alarmingly. He was very restless and rambled on incoherently, sometimes shouting out loudly. Meg was becoming upset by her brother's illness.

Sister Rona calmed her and assured her that Harry was a strong, healthy lad and would survive the fever. She expressed greater concern to Major Redman when he called to enquire after the boy's progress at first light. "That young man needs greater skills than I have sir," she explained. "There is no one else but you and his sister. Please, do your very best."

"That we will sir. That girl has greater skills than I possess sir, but she is so grief-stricken because she has used the last of her supply of potions and is afraid to leave her brother to go in search of fresh herbs."

The Major asked to speak to Meg. Sister Rona took him to Harry's bedside where he saw her kneeling beside her brother as if in prayer.

"Meg, Sister Rona tells me that you need herbs to make Harry better. Tell me what you need and I will try and find it for you."

Meg looked up at the officer and said that she did not know the name of the plant; she would have to see the herb.

"Does the plant grow hereabouts Meg?"

"Yes sir, it grows by the stream near where the road goes up to the new mine sir."

"Can you ride, Meg?"

"Yes sir."

"Then let us go and find a horse for you and we will go together to find what you need to make your brother well."

The storm had now cleared and they rode in the morning sun at a brisk canter to where Meg has seen the plant growing in the margin between the stream and the track up to the mine. She saw their destination up ahead. "Turn right before the bridge sir," she called.

The Major saw the track and they both turned and brought their horses to a halt. Meg leapt to the ground and began pulling at the leaves she needed. The Major saw the vegetation that Meg was collecting and he too soon had an armful. They stuffed what they had gathered into an empty oatmeal sack, brought for the purpose, and returned to the schoolhouse. Meg went straight to the kitchen to prepare her elixir while Sister Rona sat with Harry.

Outside, Major Redman met up with Sergeant Defoe. They discussed Harry's illness as they returned to the Temple. Lieutenant DeGray had finished his investigation into the lower end of the escape tunnel and was waiting to make his report He explained how a fissure in the rock had been enlarged. When the wharf had been constructed, a small room had been built at the end of the tunnel, barely large enough to accommodate six men. It must have been very uncomfortable.

"They must be feeling even more uncomfortable now as they make their excuses to Saint Peter at the Pearly Gates," the Major said wryly, "There couldn't have been any survivors, could there?"

"I doubt it very much sir," the lieutenant replied. "But to be sure, I took a few lads downstream at first light sir. Plenty of wreckage but no survivors sir."

"How did you get downstream without the ferry?" the Major asked.

"We went up behind the schoolhouse to the top of the escarpment and abseiled down sir."

"Without my orders lieutenant?"

"Came to look for you, but you were busy with young Harry sir. How is the boy sir. He looked in a bad way the last time I saw him sir."

"He is very ill lieutenant. But changing the subject will not work with me. Act without orders on a risky escapade like that again and you will be up before Colonel Richmond. Clear?"

"Yes sir, sorry sir. What are my orders now sir?"

"If you are so keen to expend your energy, take your motley crew down to the wharf and demolish the derrick and the ferry winding device. Collapse the tunnel as well if you can."

"Yes sir, right away sir." The lieutenant hurried away.

"And you can wipe that stupid grin off your face, Sergeant Defoe. Young DeGray is an undisciplined officer and needs a tight rein."

"I agree sir, but before you put him in irons sir, perhaps you should read the rest of his report sir."

Major Redman picked up the report and read how the lieutenant had found various pieces of wreckage from the ferry and the body of Trisk caught in an overhanging willow. The counterbalance barge had run aground on a mud bank close to where the fishermen hauled up their boats. On the last page he went on to describe how they had entered a derelict shed and found four good horses, fed, groomed and saddled and waiting for riders. They also discovered two boys of about fourteen, with orders to look after the animals. Lieutenant DeGray gave the boys what food he and his men had with them and told them to continue their care of the animals and more food would be sent to them.

"That's interesting sergeant. Why only four horses? We need to talk to those boys. Send a man to tell Lieutenant DeGray to get up here at once."

Major Redman and Sergeant Defoe studied the implications of the lieutenant's report until the young officer arrived, breathless, from the wharf.

"Lieutenant, I have read your report. You say there are four horses stabled in the fishermen's village. Did you see evidence of other horses having been stabled there?"

"No sir, there is only room for four sir, and there were no horses in any of the other huts sir."

"What! You searched the fishermen's dwellings?" the Major exclaimed.

"The villagers were very cooperative sir, especially when they saw that Trisk was dead."

"Ah yes, about Trisk, tell me about him. You say his body was caught up in a willow tree?"

"Yes sir. He was laying face up sir. It's Trisk alright sir. The headman identified him."

"What did you do with the body?"

"I drafted in a couple of fishermen sir. They hauled the body onto the shore feet first, just clear of the water sir."

"Right lieutenant, here's what you do. Set up your abseil lines as quickly as you can. The sergeant and I need to take a look at what you have found. What are you grinning at lieutenant?"

"Nothing sir, I'll attend to it at once sir." The young officer saluted and went out of the temple at the double. Sergeant Defoe looked away to hide the smile as he remembered a young Lieutenant Redman who had been equally resourceful.

It was late afternoon when Lieutenant DeGray reported that the abseil lines were fixed and ready for use. Major Redman and Sergeant Defoe found torches burning at the launch area and at the landing place at the foot of the escarpment, all in preparation for the approaching night.

The Major and the sergeant descended first, followed by the lieutenant and Osbert. Two other soldiers followed. The lieutenant and Osbert led the way to the stable where two rather frightened boys stood outside the rickety building. Osbert spoke to the boys and gave them a bag containing bread and oatmeal. Osbert was able to understand the boy's dialect and translated both questions and answers.

It transpired that there were only two horses, brought in from the east several days ago, just before the lieutenant and his reconnaissance party arrived. The other two belonged to Captain Ragar and his man. Trisk had organised the stabling and threatened the boys with work in the mines if they failed to comply with his orders. There was little else that the boys could offer and so the Major asked to speak to the senior man in the village. A wizened old man told them that there were two families living downstream of the gorge. They supplied fish to the village and they were worried about their future if the village was closing down. The Major advised them to wait for summer and then move downstream and ply their trade in Westown.

Major Redman asked to see Trisk's body and was taken to the riverside. He looked down at Trisk and then told Sergeant Defoe to take the whip from the slave masters belt and burn it so that it could never be used again

"Turn him over onto his face," he ordered. He saw that the back of Trisk's head had been stove in. It was a terrible sight.

"That was no accident," Sergeant Defoe said.

"A falling-out amongst thieves?" The lieutenant questioned.

Major Redman nodded his agreement and asked the village elder to bury the body. The old man said they could leave it to him. The Major then asked him to report the finding of any other bodies. The old man's reply surprised the Major.

"What do I do if they be alive sir?"

"I think that is very unlikely my good man," Major Redman retorted.

"That ferryman be a powerful strong swimmer sir. Seen him swim down through the gorge many-a-time sir. He do it for a bet sir."

It was getting dark now and torches were being lit. It was agreed that there was nothing else they could do until the morrow. They all returned to the Temple with orders to meet after the evening meal in the High Priest's chapel.

After his meal Sergeant Defoe first went to enquire after Harry's condition. Meg told him that Harry was sleeping and had taken some soup a short while before. But best news of all was that Harry had not developed the fever Meg had expected. She said she must thank Sergeant Hathaway and went on, "I think Harry became so cold and wet, if Sergeant Hathaway hadn't noticed him, he would have become very ill. A few days' rest, some good food and warmth and he will be up and about and raring to get back to his coracle."

"Tell the lad we are all rooting for him Meg. I'll try and visit him in the morning," Sergeant Defoe said as he hurried away to the meeting.

In the High Priest's chapel the sergeant found that the meeting had started. There were eight other people seated around the large table that had been an altar until it was used to block the door to the Temple. Major Redman and Captain Giles sat at one end. Father Michael and Lieutenant Quail, Captain Giles' second-in-command, and Sergeant Rudd down one side. Lieutenant DeGray was alone on the other side of the table. Major Redman indicated that Sergeant Defoe should join him there. Much to his surprise, Sergeant Defoe saw that Lieutenant Kester and Sergeant Garth were seated at the other end of the table. As he took his seat, he received an admonishing glare from the Major.

"Just making sure Harry is alright sir."

"And is he alright sergeant?"

"Yes sir. He's on the mend thank God, sir."

The Major returned to the meeting, explaining that the loss of the ferry would multiply their difficulties. It would add at least three days to the journey back to their various destinations.

"We will have to march around the mountain behind us and the lake beyond. And with women and children we will have to follow the escarpment until we can descend easily to the road going east. We who are going south will have to travel back along the foot of the escarpment to the waterfall."

The Major turned and asked Captain Giles if he had completed his head count.

"Yes sir, but it has been difficult with some of the miners and their families just wandering off without a word to anyone. They all seem to be heading east sir."

"So how many refugees will return to Westown with us captain?"

"Twenty-seven children sir. Seven women sir, Sister Rona and her two helpers, two miners' wives and two widowed ladies. There are twelve men sir, of whom two are miners. Three worked at the sawmill and four worked with the horses to pull the ferry and do general carting work sir. The remaining three are general labourers. A total of forty-six persons sir," the captain concluded.

"So how many children can we return to their homes?"

"Fifteen sir. There are our own six children and nine from the village in the marshes. The other twelve children, we hope, will be adopted. Peter and his family have already been adopted by Brian and will be returning to Abe Tull's Village sir.

"I thought there were more children than that," Major Redman exclaimed.

"Most of them have gone with the miners' families, hoping that conditions in the east will be an improvement on this place sir."

"I suppose it's a case of 'better the devil you know than the one you don't'," the Major said. "We will need to transport the women and children downriver as far as the old transit camp by boat. What river transport is available?"

"We have secured the ballast barge that went aground on the mud bank sir," Lieutenant DeGray announced. "All we need to do is throw the ballast overboard sir."

"Thank you lieutenant. Are there any other boats we could use?"

"I'm sure the fishermen would help if only to earn a few rations sir."

"We have a party of forty-six to escort to safety," Major Redman said. "Far fewer than I expected. Speak to the fishermen tomorrow Lieutenant DeGray and enlist their help if you can." The Major then turned to Lieutenant Kester. "Lieutenant Kester, what am I to do with you?"

The lieutenant jumped to his feet, his face was a deathly white.

"Major Redman sir, we are prisoners of war and must be treated as such." The lieutenant remained standing to attention staring at a point way above the Major's head.

"I was not aware that war had been declared. Have you heard anything about us being at war Captain Giles?" the Major asked with much irony.

"I would have brought it to your attention at once sir."

The captain smiled. So too did Sergeant Garth. Lieutenant Kester was now red-faced but remained standing to attention.

"Sit down, lieutenant. You are not about to be executed. How many troops does the lieutenant have, Captain Giles?"

"Hard to say sir, they disappear along with the miners. There is only Sergeant Garth and about six men left. I think that Sergeant Garth may have a request to make sir."

"What is this request sergeant?"

The sergeant stood up and looked nervously at the seated lieutenant.

"Sir, with respect sir, me and six of my lads, well sir, we ain't got nobody waiting for us back east sir. We would like to come south with you sir. We could join your army if you are recruiting sir."

"Is there another reason why you do not wish to return to your garrison? If you come with us, whether it be as a soldier or civilian, you will be considered a deserter and that can mean the death penalty if you return to your home."

"We will be blamed for the loss of the gold and the slaves' sir. That carries the death penalty too. It's alright for the lieutenant sir, his father is a very rich merchant. They never get punished."

"I will consider your request sergeant, and my decision will be given to you in the morning. Sergeant Defoe, see them back to their quarters and then return here."

As soon as Sergeant Defoe left, the Major asked Brother Michael what success he had had in converting some of the pagans to Christianity. The priest had to report that not one pagan had converted yet. However, he had high hopes for several of the refugees they were taking back.

Sergeant Defoe returned and the business of planning the evacuation of the area scheduled to begin at sunrise. Everyone going east would be given enough food to last four or five days. Beyond that, they were expected to fend for themselves. It was a ten day march to the first town and another week to the coast and the garrison. The news of what had happened at the gold mines might not have reached the pagan city yet, but the tremor of the earthquake must have been felt even that far away and triggered off some kind of investigation.

It was almost midnight when the meeting broke up.

Chapter Forty Six

The next morning Harry awoke early and got out of bed. Sister Rona agreed to let him get up providing that he take all his exercise inside the building. The Coracle Boy could see the sun shining outside and people getting ready to move off to their various destinations.

At noon Harry had an unexpected visitor. Major Redman called to see him. Meg brought a chair so that he could sit by Harry's bed. The Major asked Meg to stay as he wanted to talk to them both.

"I thought I had better come and say a proper thank-you to both of you. We owe the recovery of the children to you. The courage and determination you have both shown is an example to us all. I shall be sending a full report to Sir John as soon as I get back. I am sure the King will hear of it in due course."

"No, please sir, we don't want any fuss sir. We only did what we had to sir. We got Ruth and the other young 'uns back sir."

"Sorry Harry, I have to make a full report and I am bound to tell the truth. Now to bring you up-to-date on what is happening." It was obvious that the Major was not going to allow Harry to argue. "You will remember the man Gant, Captain Ragar's man, well he is not just a servant as Captain Ragar thought, he is a trusted and personal friend of their King. He is taking responsibility for the safe return of all those who wish to return to the east. As we have no use for the horses, once we are on the river, Gant will use them and all the carts he can find to get his people back to their homes. He will be assisted by Lieutenant Kester and those soldiers who wish to return to the east. Sergeant Garth and six of his men have asked to be allowed to come to Westown with us. I have agreed. They include a tall lanky soldier called Ronal, he says that he owes you two his life. I think a great many people can say that to you both."

"Now, as to your return journey," Major Redman said, "I am sending Lieutenant DeGray ahead with a small party. I would like you to travel with him. He will see you both back to Abe Tull's village and then continue on to Westown to arrange accommodation for the refugees."

"When will that be sir?" Harry asked.

"Lieutenant DeGray is organising the transport. I expect he will be along shortly to discuss the journey with you and Meg. Now I am afraid that you will have to excuse me, I have much to do.

It was beginning to get dark when Lieutenant Roland DeGray arrived. Peter and his brother, Cal, were with him. Harry and Meg were introduced to Cal who was the living image of his big brother. After the introductions and solicitous enquiries had been completed, Lieutenant DeGray said that they were there to discuss the return journey to Abe Tull's village.

"I suggest that we use your boat Harry. Peter has brought it up to the fishermen's village," the lieutenant explained. "I and the four soldiers travelling with me will use two canoes. We have also managed to get Luke's boat up here and the three pagan boats too. Dan remembered that Susan had heard the two traitors mention a path alongside the river. When the snow melted, he found the path. It was well above the high water line and almost invisible from the river. Jennie told us that they had to walk along the path roped together."

"So they hauled the empty boat through the gorge?" Harry mused "So that's what happened."

"Yes Harry, it means that we can take the women and children all the way down to Westown by boat with only the three portages to walk. The soldiers and able-bodied men will march back."

"When do we start back?" Meg asked eagerly.

"As soon as we can get you round the mountain and the lake and back to the fishermen's village, which could take a couple of days," Roland DeGray replied.

"Why can't we abseil down like you did sir?" the Coracle Boy asked.

"That might be alright for you and Meg but what about Jennie and Ruth?"

"We could lower them down in a basket," Meg suggested.

"I will speak to Major Redman in the morning Meg, but I know what he will say and give me a telling-off for even bothering him with such an idea."

"What is this idea I will be telling you off for?" Major Redman stood in the doorway into the small room.

Lieutenant DeGray sprang to his feet, saluting smartly as he explained the situation and Harry and Meg's solution. Major Redman stroked his chin thoughtfully. It seemed an age before he spoke.

"I don't like the basket idea. Suppose you harnessed the two girls to yourself lieutenant. That might be a better plan," The Major suggested.

The lieutenant could hardly believe his ears and before he could think of a reply, Harry spoke.

"Sir, I think that Ruth would be happier with me sir. She hardly knows Lieutenant DeGray." At that point Meg suggested that Ruth would be better travelling down with her and Jennie would feel safer with Harry taking her down.

"If the two girls agree to travel that way, then you have my blessing. But they must not be forced in any way. Is that understood Lieutenant DeGray?"

"Yes sir. If either child refuses then the operation will be called off sir."

"When do you intend to make the descent?"

"Tomorrow morning if the children agree and Harry is fit enough sir."

"I'll be fit sir," Harry said, confidently. "You could lower me down on the pulley wheel like you do with your boxes of equipment sir."

"Sir, I intend to lower all non-military personnel by that method sir."

"Good idea lieutenant. If you are able to get down the escarpment tomorrow it will give you a two day start on the main party, which would be a great advantage. Inform me at once if you are successful. You will be carrying a full report to Sir John, to be delivered to him by you and no one else. Now, I think all of you should get a good night's sleep. You have an arduous journey ahead of you over the next few days. I wish you good night."

Ned arrived just as the Major left. He had been running and was red-faced and out of breath. "I just wanted to let you know that we are ready to escort you round the mountain tomorrow if you are fit Harry."

"Sorry Ned, we are going down the cliff in the morning. That way we get back home a couple of days earlier," Harry said.

"What? Are you sure you're strong enough to abseil down that precipice? What about little Ruth and Jennie?"

"We will only do it if Ruth and Jennie agree and we are being lowered down on a pulley wheel," Meg announced, in a manner that suggested she did this sort of thing quite often,

"You two never cease to amaze me," Ned said. "I was hoping to have a long chat with you both on the journey, but it can wait. I leave the abbey after Easter, but before I travel to my home in the north, I will come to see you at Abe Tull's village, if that's alright."

"We will look forward to that Ned," Harry and Meg replied together.

"There is one other snippet of news. Joel and Sol were very upset to hear that the two priests had died and so they are staying here to look after the hermit. They will also attend to the fishermen's spiritual needs."

"I wondered what would happen to the old man. Tell them both we wish them well and the hermit too."

"I will. I can't keep Brother Michael waiting. I'll see you both at Easter. Goodbye." Ned hurried away out into a cold, clear night.

Chapter Forty Seven

Lieutenant DeGray and Sergeant Defoe had been up well before dawn to be at the abseil site at first light. The quartermaster sergeant and his assistant had worked through the night to make harnesses to strap the two girls to Harry and Meg. Peter and his brother, Cal, arrived and said that Meg was talking to the two young girls. They would be along shortly.

Meg and Ruth arrived first, Harry and Jennie moments later. Harry had experienced abseiling once before, but on this occasion he and Meg would be lowered down on a pulley wheel by Sergeant Defoe and Osbert.

Suddenly there was a shout from someone coming up to the abseil point and then Brother Michael appeared breathless.

"God be praised. I thought I would be too late." The good monk leaned forward and placed his hands on his knees and regained his breath. "Let us kneel and say the Lord's Prayer. That includes you Peter and Cal. God knows that it's not your fault that you are not Christians."

Everyone knelt on the short, dew laden grass. The prayers were said and then Brother Michael blessed each one of them. He stepped back and made the sign of the cross. He turned and hurried away.

Harry would be the first to go down, with Jennie harnessed to his back. If Jennie was afraid, she didn't show it. The lieutenant was sure she would panic as soon as Harry walked to the edge of the escarpment, but she could have been going for a walk along the riverbank for all the concern she showed. Harry and Jennie descended without giving any concern. But would Ruth be as calm?

Meg suggested that Ruth should face her and be able to put her arms around Meg's neck. This required a minor adjustment to the harness. To everyone's surprise Ruth found this amusing and giggled as she hid her face in Meg's clothing. They made the journey without mishap, much to the lieutenant's relief. The rest of the party quickly followed.

A message was sent to Major Redman. The lieutenant decided to explain some of the details of their journey while they waited. He would lead in one canoe with one soldier, whilst Osbert would bring up the rear with the other two soldiers in the second canoe. Harry's boat would be piloted by Peter.

As they were travelling downstream with the current, they would only need one oarsman who would stand facing downstream and use the oars to steer with and use as brakes. The first day they would travel down to the pagans' transit camp where they would be met by Sergeant Rudd whose men would guide their boats through the gorge from the path above the water. They would then continue down to Friar Godwin's cave and meet up with Dan, Susan, Lisa and the baby who had been moved down to the friar's cave for safety. They would spend the night there. The next day all except Friar Godwin would travel with them for the rest of the journey, whilst Friar Godwin would travel down to the abbey with Brother Michael, Ned and the main party. The breaks in their voyage for the remainder of the trip would be dictated by progress and weather.

Major Redman arrived with the documents, which Lieutenant DeGray would deliver to Sir John at Westown. Sergeant Defoe was with him and after they had completed their business with the lieutenant and his men they turned to Harry and Meg. The Major addressed them both. "I think that everything that needs to be said has been said and repeated many times to you both. I will only add that you have the undying gratitude of us all. Thank you both."

The Major shook their hands and then spoke to Jennie and Ruth. He told them that he was proud of them and wished them a safe journey home. Peter and Cal also received the same sincere handshake and good wishes. Major Redman turned and spoke to Lieutenant DeGray, while the Sergeant said goodbye to his young friends. With one last wave the Major and the sergeant disappeared into one of the abandoned huts that had become their office on this section of the river.

Lieutenant DeGray called everyone together and led the way down to the water's edge. Harry saw the stolen boat that had belonged to Trisk and had mixed feelings about using it. But then he remembered what an evil man Trisk had been and perhaps this will be a way for him to make amends for his cruelty. Anyway, the boat needed a good home. Perhaps Brother Michael could make better use of it, he thought.

Harry the Coracle Boy and his sister, Meg the Healer had almost nothing left of the things they brought with them, apart from the clothes they stood up in. They still had their shoulder bags but these were much depleted. Everything had been used up, lost or given away. They were returning with nothing, except that which they came for, their little sister and the other kidnapped children.

The Coracle Boy's thoughts went back to the start of the adventure. He realised that he could not have done it without Meg. It was her stoicism and cheerfulness that had inspired him. She had never complained, she just got on with what had to be done. Harry was very proud of Meg.

Harry saw that the lieutenant and his soldier crewman were paddling their canoe away from the riverbank. He was last to climb into the sturdy rowing boat and took his seat in the rear of the boat, beside Meg,. Ruth and Jennie were sitting in the bows of the dinghy. Peter cast off and pushed the boat clear of the jetty and moved downstream to follow the lieutenant. Osbert and his two companions took up their position at the rear.

Harry looked back at the canoe and waved. He let his eye travel back to the Devil's Gorge and the black precipice through which the river spilled with such force. Turning his back on the dreadful place he looked downstream and saw the ferry ballast boat moored on the north bank, whilst opposite he could see the steps in the escarpment that led to the landing stage that he had destroyed.

Further down, the crude fishermen's boats were drawn up on the north bank. Soon they were at the confluence of the Great River and the small tributary that spilled down from the lake. Here the river swung south and they were on their way home.

THE END

The Coracle Boy Trilogy

Book One

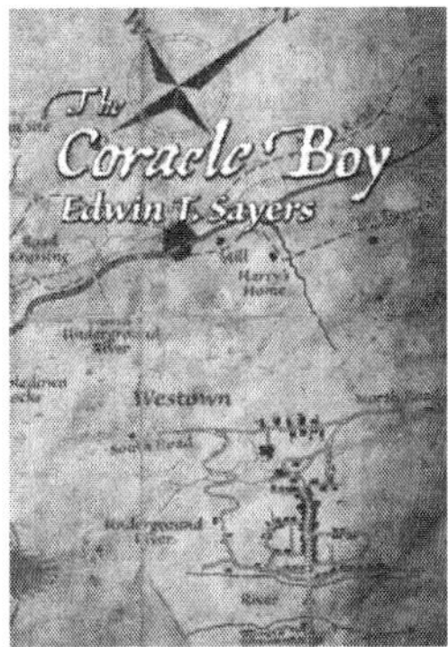

A long time ago, in a land not too far away, there was a fabled and mysterious place known as 'Farland - the land of the great swamp'. At its heart lay the town of Westown, the home of Harry, the 'Coracle Boy'.

Time and time again pirates and robbers from all over this land came to plunder the good folk of Westown, rampaging and taking anything they could. The people of Westown dare not venture into the forests and even the river that had supplied food and goods from far away were now deemed unsafe to travel.

But Harry knew the river like the back of his hand and no-one knew how to use a coracle more than he. And now, more than ever, Harry's skill and determination were desperately needed. For it was only Harry who could navigate this dangerous, swollen river and get a message to General Smith that the notorious King Axel was about to mount his most vicious assault…

Will Harry be able to save the day? The future of Westown depends upon the 'Coracle Boy'.

ISBN 978-1904166-38-2

Available from www.dreamstarbooks.co.uk. Tel 0800 020 9348
or direct from the author: etsayers@btinternet.com

Book Three

Coming Soon!

Pre-order direct from the publisher www.dreamstarbooks.co.uk.
Tel 0800 020 9348